The Tree with No Name

Drago Jančar

The Tree with No Name

Translated from the Slovene by Michael Biggins

DALKEY ARCHIVE PRESS
Champaign / London / Dublin

Originally published in Slovene as *Drevo brez imena* by Modrijan, 2008
Copyright ©2008 by Drago Jančar
Translation copyright ©2013 by Michael Biggins
First edition, 2014.

Library of Congress Cataloging-in-Publication Data

Jancar, Drago, author.
[Drevo brez imena. English]
The tree with no name / Drago Jancar ;
translated from the Slovene by Michael Biggins.
-- First edition.
pages cm
ISBN 978-1-62897-054-8 (pbk. : alk. paper)
I. Biggins, Michael, translator. II. Title.
PG1919.2.A54D7413 2014
891.8'435--dc23
                                        2014006599

Partially funded by the Illinois Arts Council, a state agency and
by the University of Illinois at Urbana-Champaign \ This translation has been financially supported
by the Slovenian Book Agency (JAK) \ This book was published with the support of
Trubar Foundation at the Slovene Writers' Association, Ljubljana, Slovenia \
Ta knjiga je bila objavljena s pomočjo Trubarjevega sklada pri Društvu slovenskih
pisateljev, Ljubljana, Slovenija

www.dalkeyarchive.com

Printed on permanent/durable acid-free paper
Cover: design and composition Mikhail Iliatov

The Tree with No Name
/ 7

Translator's Afterword
A Madness That Heals
/ 269

The Tree with No Name

The eye is not satisfied with seeing,
nor the ear filled with hearing.
The thing that hath been, it is that which shall be;
and that which is done is that which shall be done:
and there is no new thing under the sun.
Is there any thing whereof it may be said,
See, this is new?
It hath been already of old time,
which was before us.
There is no remembrance of former things;
neither shall there be any remembrance
of things that are to come
with those that shall come after.

Ecclesiastes 1:8-11

87.

Sunrise, morning, the mowers—he had already left all of these far behind. Also the cellar he had crawled out of, and the pit he had fallen into—all of this was far away, long ago, somewhere else. Most recently—and this he remembered distinctly—he had been sitting under some tree. There were mowers approaching, three of them, and so he retreated into the forest. Through the tall ferns he could see them unshoulder their scythes and he could hear their voices, but he couldn't make out any words. He could also hear the whetstones as they drew them in regular strokes along the sharp, ringing metal. Then they assumed their positions at the edge of the meadow and simultaneously began mowing in broad, regular strokes. It had been raining steadily for three weeks, and the heavy, green stalks had barely begun to dry, had barely lifted themselves back up in the June morning sun, when they started to fall in thick swaths. In those powerful peasant hands the scythes began to whistle through the morning grass glistening in the sun.

Then, for a long time, he walked through the forest, through the shafts of sunlight angling down past the tree trunks, through wisps of fog in the ravines, and his bare feet felt the soft leaves, the moss, the earth exuding dampness. This was another world. The ancient Slovenes believed that if you dropped on a rope into a deep cave, and went down far enough, you would come out in the other world. They also believed—these Pohorje Mountain Slovenes, who lived in vast forests—that you could reach the other world by climbing a tree. Either way, up or down, another world was waiting for you. Even as a small boy he had known this. Back then he would pull the covers over his head and listen to the men's voices from the kitchen as they grew fainter and fainter, because he was retreating, climbing with great ease up the tree, at the top of which, somewhere way up high, he would be able to step off into some other place, some other landscape. And even when he was big, grown up, verging on old, in fact, he knew this. One night around four o'clock he woke up and noticed that the room was bathed in silvery moonlight.

His wife Marijana, who should have been sleeping beside him, was nowhere to be seen, but this didn't strike him as at all unusual as she had left him several days before—in fact nothing had surprised him for quite a long time now, so on that night this unusual light drew all his attention. He got up and went to the window. Strange, he thought, how did this garden suddenly get here? Because this was the garden that had always been outside his office window at the Regional Archive, and now it was suddenly here, bathed in the moonlight that was also flooding his room in a silvery torrent. But what of the old cherry tree that should have been growing in it, if only so that, after long hours at the computer screen, reading, he could rest his weary eyes on its gnarled limbs and its white blossoms in spring? Because this wasn't a cherry tree growing outside his window, but some kind of tree he had never seen before. It wasn't a pine, or a beech, and it wasn't a cypress or a eucalyptus, either. He knew immediately that this was the tree his mother had read to him about when he was a boy, the wondrously tall tree, the likes of which the world had never seen and never would see.

It rose up into the sky like the smoke of a land on fire.

But that tree, the one he had always wanted to climb, grew somewhere in the uplands of Pohorje. And before he had a chance to think why it was suddenly here, with its broad trunk and its top somewhere under the stars, he was suddenly in it. Everything had been so effortless, and he himself was all at once so light, and he quickly started to climb up the tree. It wasn't just effortless, it was also a little silly: 'Ants climb the tree,' he said—that was the name of a dish in the Chinese restaurant, he thought, or his name right now as he climbed up the tree, at least that's how God would see it. Like an ant on a gigantic tree that might be a pine, or maybe a spruce—a pine because pines are bigger. But it wasn't a pine or a spruce, either one. This tree wasn't just bigger, it was a gigantic tree, with its top nestled someplace just under the rocky cliffs over which the clouds hung. And once you're this far up on the tree, amid its branches at one moment and clinging to its bare trunk the next, it really doesn't matter whether God sees you as an ant or whether you're just a meatball, a soy dumpling atop noodles in the dish called ants climb the tree. You probably are just a meatball or soy dumpling if you let go of the branch, if you slide down the coarse bark of the tree to the place where he had just caught sight of Marijana jumping and waving her arms, her voice inaudible, even her face there getting smaller and smaller, a face with no mouth and no eyes, just a white surface turned upwards—at first there had been startled eyes getting smaller and smaller, and now just this white surface getting smaller and smaller. There was also the mouth inaudibly asking, 'Where are you climbing, Janez? Where are you off to?' 'Up,' he said. 'I don't know where, just up. I'm climbing this tree, I'm scaling it with incredible ease, and I don't even know if it's a fir or a spruce or a maple or oak. Actually it's none of those, it's something completely different.' I could also climb down, he thought once again, it doesn't really matter. The ancient Slovenes believed that if you dropped on a rope into a deep cave and went down far enough, you'd reach the other world, because the other world is up there and down there, just not in between, which is where the world was that he wanted to leave. And finally, after you've climbed or dropped down far enough, you'd discover the radiant land, with beautiful green meadows and willows growing alongside water flowing in placid, meandering streams, and it was like being in a little paradise. Handsome young mowers did the mowing there, and you could help them and cut down a few swaths, yourself, if you liked—or not, if you didn't. This tale about the tree, he thought, comes from Pohorje. The ancient Slovenes told it to each other on autumn nights when the wind blew and they were just a little afraid, but had also drunk just a little brandy so they wouldn't be. The forests there are vast, he thought. Maybe at the top I'll come out in some forest hollow or on some broad, spruce-covered hillside.

But that's not what happened. As soon as he stepped off the tree, as he slid down a fat branch onto the ground, he saw that he was standing in the middle of a country road lined on both sides with chestnut trees. Somewhere in the distance there were some large houses where the lights were still on, but he thought that this was not the place for him to stop.

He set out down that long tree-lined road in Lower Carniolian Springs that he had once dreamed about. Of course he had dreamed about it—he and Marijana had once gone there. People dream about things they've already experienced but which then get transformed in their dreams. He thought that Lower Carniolian Springs was in a completely different part of the country than Pohorje. He had expected to be deposited on some green Pohorje hillside, but here he was on some tree-lined road in some quaint green valley whose paths all led into the dark forests of the hills near Kočevje or even farther south, into Croatia. The path that led through the two rows of chestnuts had not been graveled. It, too, was covered in soft grass, possibly moss, that gently gave way underfoot as he made his way in the moonlit night.

There were vast flatlands around him. Even though the silvery moonlight had vanished by now, the night still wasn't pitch black. The stars shone sufficiently for him to see the flatlands all around, and now, once again, he had the impression of being in some totally unfamiliar terrain, even though he was walking down a tree-lined road in Lower Carniolan Springs. When the road ended, he wandered for a long time through meadows and fields, and suddenly there wasn't a house to be seen. They had all vanished. He stopped at the foot of some hills, looked around to figure out which way to go next, and finally headed into a gorge that had a river roaring through it. He felt the chill coming from the cold water and he realized he was cold and hungry. He hadn't once felt hungry while climbing the tree, not even after he ran out of food. And he hadn't felt cold, even when he was very high up and should have. But since stepping out onto the flatlands and especially now, heading through the gorge upstream, he felt everything: fatigue, hunger, the shivers on his skin. Janez Lipnik didn't know what he wanted. He felt a slight tightening in his chest—perhaps he'd struck out a bit too far. At that point a light flickered in the distance. It was at the far end, where the gorge opened up into a broad, welcoming valley. He walked in the direction of the flickering light, watching it grow.

Soon he arrived at a house that had just one window lit. He knew what he was going to see there—there would be a beautiful woman lost in thought, sitting at a table, her head propped on one hand. So he approached cautiously. The window was just a bit too high and for a while he looked around, until his eyes lit on a block that was used for chopping wood. This he dragged under the window, which turned out to be really high. He stepped up on it and looked through the lace curtains into the room. Everything was the way it was supposed to be, except that the beautiful woman lost in thought was not propping her head on one hand. She was grading school notebooks. For a while he looked at her face, which seemed familiar to him from somewhere. It occurred to him that this was the face of his schoolteacher, illuminated by a table lamp. This woman bore a powerful resemblance to her, even wearing the same pretty white blouse, although she was certainly somewhat younger. He summoned his courage and tapped on the window.

88.

He saw her start and then suddenly put out the light. He heard her footsteps approaching. Then she was standing by the window and he thought he could hear her breathing. 'Aleksij?' she said. 'I'm not Aleksij,' he said. 'Don't be afraid, ma'am.' He thought she would be afraid because he wasn't Aleksij at the window—but why should he be Aleksij? Why would Aleksij, a man the woman knew by name, be tapping on the window? Aleksij would probably knock at the door. 'Who is it?' she whispered in the dark. He told the truth: Janez Lipnik. I don't know you, she said. Of course you don't, he answered, I seem to have gotten lost. Of course he didn't know if he'd gotten lost, but he had to say something. Cautiously she drew the curtain back. I'll turn on the light, she said. Can you step into the light so I can see you? Go ahead, turn it on, he said, I'm not trying to hide. She turned on the light and opened the window. I don't know you, she said once again. There's no way you could know me, he said, I come from far away. From Kočevje? she asked. So Kočevje is close to here? he thought. Then why did I have to knock myself out like that just to get near Kočevje? Kočevje is only three hours by foot from Ljubljana. From Ljubljana, he said. There aren't any foresters in Ljubljana, and you're a forester, I can see. Or are you a woodsman? He said that he'd climbed up a tree, then walked for a long time through a forest and a gorge until he saw her light. Oh, go on, she said, what would you be climbing trees for, you're a forester and you mark trees. You're from Kočevje, that's where foresters live. Whichever you prefer, he said, woodsman or forester, if you could give me a glass of water, I'd be profoundly grateful. She brought him a glass of water. He drank it down quickly, unaware that he'd been so thirsty. If I'd known, he thought, I would have drunk from that river that runs through the gorge, it seemed to be pure, unspoiled water. I'm kind of cold, too, he said. She looked at him mistrustfully. I can't let you in, she said. Who are you? I told you, I'm Janez Lipnik. I used to be an archivist. So why are you cutting down trees now? she asked. Who said I was cutting down trees? If you're not a forester, then you can only be a woodsman, she almost laughed. I know, she said, you're a refugee. There are lots of people on the run and in hiding. The church rectory is across the road, why didn't you knock there? Rectory? He had thought that the house stood off by itself. I don't know, he said. This is where I saw the light shining. Anyway, I doubt they would have let you in, she said, these are such evil times. Just then, in the light shining through the window, she caught sight of his bare feet. Poor thing, she said, you're barefoot. Where did you leave your shoes? Under some tree, he said. On a forest hillside, he added to make it more convincing, even if it was true to begin with. She turned things over in her mind for a while. Listen, she said at last, I'll let you in the house and give you some food. But then you're going to have to leave right away. She closed the window and then, a moment later, opened it again. But just so we understand each other, she said, Aleksij will be here in ten or fifteen minutes. You heard me say I was expecting him. Just so you know, Aleksij is an officer. Then he heard her go to the door and unlock it, and he went in.

The warmth of a well-tended household and the smell of a woman, of her scents and her skin, enveloped him as he entered. Here the world was real.

89.

"Good evening. So where do you come from?"

"Good evening. I come from out of a tree."

"You were hiding in a tree, poor thing."

"No, not hiding, I climbed up it."

"You climbed up in a tree to hide. People are hiding everywhere these days."

He sat down at the table and watched her stoke the fire and put milk on to warm. She had taut thighs under her skirt, just like his teacher. His teacher had taut thighs—whenever she leaned over his bench, its wooden edge cut into those thighs through her skirt. She smelled like the ink his hands got spattered with every evening, and at the same time she smelled like feminine skin under her blue skirt and white blouse. She resembled her so much, except that she seemed to be just a bit younger. She could sense him looking at her.

"Aleksij won't like it," she said, "that I've let you in the house. There are all kinds of people roaming around these days."

He looked away and fixed his attention on an old-fashioned radio receiver sitting on a shelf. Then he picked up a notebook and opened it. She came up to the table and—"Pardon me," she said—took the notebook away from him. She picked up a whole stack of them and put them on a shelf, then she cut off a big slice of bread and some bacon and brought out some warm milk. Now Janez Lipnik could feel how very hungry he'd become, having not eaten for so long. He took hold of the bread, but stopped when he noticed her looking at him sternly. His hands were filthy black, as black as they used to get from the ink. Maybe that's why she took the notebook away from him. So that her students wouldn't think that she'd got it dirty. She probably gives them talks about hygiene, maybe she even checks every morning to see if they've scrubbed their necks. He asked if there was somewhere he could wash up. She opened the door to the bathroom. He didn't know why it surprised him to see real plumbing inside, even a bathtub you could let water into and sit in. But the thought of just taking his clothes off and bathing when he'd barely entered this house embarrassed him. He decided he would wash just his torso and face. She held out a clean shirt for him through the half-open doorway. He noticed its collar was slightly frayed. Probably Aleksij's—an officer's shirt. He thanked her and put it on. When he went back out, she gave him some thick woolen socks, grayish, probably also officer's socks. It was June and he thought, these socks will get hot during the day, it's cool at night, but the days will be hot. Even so, he was glad to have them and thanked her. I'll need shoes, too, he thought, but everything was moving along so nicely now that he thought he would be handed shoes presently, too. She turned a dial on the radio and her white blouse hiked up over her skirt in back, revealing a patch of skin. She even had the same kind of blouse as his teacher—how old had he been then? Twelve? All schoolteachers used to wear the same white blouses and blue skirts. All of them were pretty. She found some old-fashioned music, an orchestra crackling its way through some old tune. She turned around and adjusted her blouse.

"Aleksij will be here any minute," she said.

And what if he's not, he wanted to say. Despite his hunger he felt a sudden urge to tease this nice teacher a little, the way he had that other one, who looked so uncannily like this one here. But he didn't say it. It could have frightened her, she could have gone across the road to wake up the people in the rectory. Just what I need, he thought, having the priest ask me where I'm from. He tackled the bread and the bacon and warm milk, and the world came to seem quite real to him. When you're wearing a fresh shirt and woolen socks and swallowing big bites of bread with bacon and pickles, and you're sitting across from a young schoolteacher with plump, ruddy cheeks, wearing a white blouse, the fragrance of her skin wafting up through her open collar, no less, that's not just some stupid dream, this is a warm, living world that gets that chilly blood of yours circulating, this is the real world, where a person can get downright hot.

"I feel downright hot," Janez Lipnik said.

"Where will you go now?" she asked cautiously. She didn't want to chase him off right away, but it was also clear she wasn't about to offer a stranger a place to stay the night.

"I don't know," he said. "Someplace."

For the moment he didn't feel the need to go anywhere. The night outside was silent, so silent that several shots could be heard in the distance, followed by a long, crackling burst.

"What's that?" he asked. "What's that popping sound off in the distance?"

"Gunshots," she explained as only schoolteachers know how. "When it crackles as if someone were breaking dry branches, those are rifle shots. Mortars whistle, like this—wheeeeyuuuuu—before they explode. And then they explode."

"Gunshots?"

90.

The fact was that he hadn't slept in a long time, and despite the crackling in the distance his eyes began to close. It occurred to him to cross the road and ask if those really were gunshots. Maybe I really will go across the road, he thought, and knock on the rectory door, but they won't let me in, he thought and felt how heavy his eyelids were getting, how warm it was in this tidy place, where there was a fire in the stove, a tub in the bathroom and a radio on the shelf, and as his head started to nod, he thought out on the edge of his consciousness about how one afternoon one of his colleagues at the archive, who generally did nothing, nodded off after lunch, just slumped over the table, and Janez Lipnik dropped off to sleep. In the distance he heard the clatter of a sewing machine, that's how his mother used to sew, way back in his childhood, brrrrr, brrrrr, and he lifted his head and saw the schoolteacher in her white blouse, not sitting at a sewing machine, but washing the dishes.

"What was that rattling?" he asked.

"Nothing was rattling," she said. "Those were gunshots."

"Who's shooting?" he asked just before his head dropped back onto his arms, which continued to sleep on the table and hadn't woken up at all the way his head just had for an instant. It thought that the shooting was coming from over the mountains, that between those mountains and this house there was some big body of water, that the house was on an island, in fact, and that the sound of gun shots was drifting here to the island from just over those tall mountains on the mainland. The stitching of the sewing machine turned into muffled drumming, or maybe that's just thunder, he thought, there's going to be a storm, good thing I'm here. Also good I'm not dreaming about that tree. That tree and the man in it that my mother used to read to me about. Each time she finished reading, she'd go sit at her sewing machine. While it clattered, he would cover his head so as not to hear the men's voices from the kitchen. They were there every night, his father and his father's friends. And if, when I covered my head, I dreamed I was climbing the tree, it would be cold and there would be thunderclaps all around my head until I climbed up to the uppermost branch. And whenever I finally did reach that branch, I would arrive at a house that had just one window lit, I would approach it and look in through the window, and a beautiful woman would be sitting at a table, lost in thought, her head propped up on one hand, and I would muster my courage and tap on the window, and the woman would open it and say, Young man, where do you come from and what are you looking for here? I'm looking for work and a place to stay the night. I've climbed up that tree for seven years and I've finally arrived in this land, and now I don't know where to go. The woman would put him up for the night and the next morning offer him work as a hired hand. It won't be much work, she would say. You'll have three horses to tend: the bronze, the silver and the gold. If you look after them well, you'll stay with me a long time. You'll do well, the table will always be set, and you'll have whatever you want. If I were there now, I'd feed and groom the bronze, the silver and the golden horses. Ah, that's what his mother used to read to him. He would lie in bed before going to sleep and she would read. He thought that this is what he was dreaming about just now. Perhaps he was dreaming that he was dreaming. His mother would then take off her reading glasses and put out the light. Every night, half asleep he would listen to the clatter of her sewing machine.

91.

The muted drumming faded away, the storm got lost amid the mountains, and he heard the roar of a motorcycle coming to a stop outside. He started awake. Good thing I'm not really dreaming, he thought. He could hear someone tapping on a pane of glass. Janez Lipnik opened his eyes and saw the teacher in the white blouse standing at the window.

"Aleksij, is that you?" she asked quietly.

He could hear a man's voice from the other side. She ran to the door and opened it. He could hear her explain something to him at the door. Then they both came into the room. Aleksij unshouldered his submachine gun. He made no response at all when Lipnik got up from the table and wished him good evening—why should he acknowledge a stranger who had suddenly turned up at his young teacher friend's, and indeed, why should this swarthy man with the piercing eyes—clearly an officer after all—bother to acknowledge anybody who wasn't from his unit? He wasn't an officer just on the strength of those piercing eyes with which he riddled the unwelcome guest, but because he had a heavy pistol holstered to his belt and some sort of gold epaulettes on his shoulders.

"So where's he from?" he asked, as though the question had nothing to do with the person who had stood up from the table in his stocking feet and then awkwardly sat back down.

"He says he's from Ljubljana."

"He could be from Kočevje, too," Aleksij said.

"The young lady is right," Janez Lipnik said. "I'm from Ljubljana."

"We'll see about that," Aleksij said, adjusting his officer's harness. "Do you have any papers?"

Lipnik felt through his pockets, then shrugged.

"What about there?" Aleksij asked, pointing to his shirt.

Lipnik felt through the pockets of the army shirt.

"It isn't mine," he explained.

Aleksij the officer came up close to him, examined the shirt and cast an admonishing look at the schoolteacher.

"You gave him my shirt."

He wasn't happy that she'd given him his officer's shirt. Lipnik thought, good thing he hasn't noticed the socks. Those are his, too. And socks may well be an even more intimate item of clothing than a shirt.

"You should have seen how in tatters he was," the young schoolteacher said. "I felt sorry for him."

Like all true officers, Aleksij wasn't one to waste words. That's why he didn't say, 'But you feel sorry for everyone,' nor did he say, 'Why would you let a stranger in the house?' They had already settled these issues at the front door. All that remained to be settled here was, 'Who is this person and where did he come from?' This would already have been settled, too, if the stranger only had papers. But he had none. Tight-lipped as he was, Aleksij just set his submachine gun down on the table and sat down on the bench, with one hand still on the weapon. He waited for his girlfriend to bring out a bottle of brandy. He even poured a glass for Janez Lipnik and shoved the shot glass in front of him. He downed his glass in one draft and wiped his mouth with a napkin. He didn't wipe it the way peasants do, with the back of their hands—he used a napkin. Aleksij was an officer, and probably a fairly senior one.

"So you say you're from Ljubljana?"

"That's right."

"And you worked in an archive?"

"Yes."

Officer Aleksij didn't like it when someone was more tight-lipped than he was.

"Can't you think of anything else to tell me?"

Oh, but I could, he thought. But who would believe me? He downed his brandy, too, and it was even better than the yellow whisky he'd been drinking lately, before he'd come up here. Or down here to Kočevje. Or wherever this was.

"I lost my papers when I was climbing the tree," he said. "Most likely," he added.

He didn't want to lie outright. There was still a chance for him to tell everything the way it really was. So far he hadn't told a single lie.

"So they're under that tree," Aleksij said, piercing him with his sharp officer's eyes. Janez felt as though he were being riddled with holes. The way a burst from that black metal thing on the table might riddle a person with holes.

"Pardon me, but is that thing loaded?" he asked.

"This thing is always loaded," the officer said. "I keep it next to my bed at night," he added.

Janez Lipnik fidgeted in his seat. Why did he say that? Does this officer think that somebody, perhaps even me, Janez Lipnik, might pick that thing up in the middle of the night and threaten somebody with it, for instance this young schoolteacher living alone in an empty schoolhouse in the midst of a war? Or even Officer Aleksij himself? Or maybe both of them? He didn't dare contemplate the prospect that Officer Aleksij might grab the machine gun himself and shoot both of them dead, Janez and the schoolteacher, one after the other. This Aleksij probably didn't have a very good impression of him.

"Fine," Aleksij said. "Tomorrow we'll go out, have a look under the tree and find those papers. What's your name?"

"Janez Lipnik."

"So we'll check to make sure your travel pass says Janez Lipnik. You do remember what tree your papers are under?" he said, piercing him again with those sharp eyes.

He nodded. What else could he do? Tomorrow would be another day and maybe, after a good night's sleep with his schoolteacher and his machine gun, this officer Aleksij would wake up in a better mood. It was obvious now that he was ill-disposed toward him. He wasn't going to throw him out, or do something even worse, only because he was protected by the young woman's pity. Officers don't like for women to see them as roughnecks. They prefer to be seen as noble, even gracious people. The reason he's ill-disposed toward him is undoubtedly because he found him with his sweetheart, scrubbed and fed and, worst of all, wearing his army shirt. And his socks, which fortunately he hasn't noticed yet. Even the young schoolteacher sensed, with the unerring instinct of a young woman who lives with an officer, that it was precisely these things that were the source of the misunderstanding and of her Aleksij's considerable harshness toward this poor, lost, barefoot fellow who'd been hiding up a tree, and so she said:

"If he was climbing the tree at night, maybe he won't be able to find where he lost his papers."

Janez Lipnik looked at her gratefully. That was precisely what he had wanted to say, but hadn't, to avoid getting even more tangled up. But with this well-intentioned support for the stranger the young schoolteacher didn't improve the situation, rather she inflamed it. Perhaps she was just a bit too supportive for Aleksij's taste, in spite of all his nobility.

"Don't you start on me with that," Aleksij said. "Don't you start."

He didn't say what—he was a tight-lipped man—and now he decided he'd been too talkative for too long. He pointed to the bench where he was sitting, that's where the nighttime visitor could sleep, they weren't going to wake the people in the rectory across the way. Even though they could put him up, having enough space. But tomorrow morning they were going to see just what was up. He picked up the machine gun and he and the young lady in the white blouse went into the next room, apparently the bedroom. Janez could hear him taking his boots off, then something metal dropped on the floor, probably his harness and the pistol. A while later he came back out in his shirt and trousers, with his suspenders down and a towel over his shoulder.

"Is Ljubljana still full of Communists?" he asked on his way to the bathroom.

"Yeah. It is," Janez Lipnik said, and he wasn't lying.

92.

Janez Lipnik was one of those people who remembers every single thing they read. He was an archivist, after all, and that counts for something. If there is a rifle hanging on the wall in the first act, he'd read somewhere, then it has to go off in the second. Perhaps what he'd read was that it goes off in the last act, or maybe the second, exactly which one didn't matter just now.

What mattered was that it went off.

The reason he recalled this truth buried deep in his memory was because somewhere immediately close by a gun was going off fiercely—or rattling, more precisely. He sat up and tried to jump off the bench that had been designated as his bunk, and slammed his head into the edge of the table. That's not a rifle, he decided just after his head collided with the wood, it's a machine gun, and those aren't volleys, they're bursts. The machine gun that just a short time before had been lying on the table and was now supposed to be on the floor in the next room, or maybe slung over a bedpost, was going off in short bursts, punctuated by the officer's abrupt, unintelligible shouts—orders, apparently—with the young woman in her night-shirt right there, it suddenly occurred to him. For a split second he thought about hiding under the bench, but before he had time to figure out what to do, the room next door fell silent. Then he heard sobs coming from it. Had somebody been killed? That's probably what they were thinking in the rectory across the way, where he noticed the lights had come on.

He moved carefully toward the bedroom, toward the strip of light that escaped from under its ill-fitting door. He stopped and listened, not daring to open it. He heard her sob and then speak—she was saying something in a monotone. He heaved a sigh of relief: the young schoolteacher was alive. He tapped lightly on the door, and when no one answered, he opened it. Officer Aleksij was lying on the bed in his skivvies and undershirt, his machine gun lying on the floor. His head was resting in her lap, and she was stroking his hair and saying comforting, reassuring words to him, as if to a child. One of his legs was convulsing, as though he were having terrible cramps. Whatever those convulsions were, at least they meant that officer Aleksij was alive too. All the more so when he raised one hand to remove some bits of plaster from his mouth and from around his eyes. Both the schoolteacher and Aleksij were white with dust from the plaster that had fallen from the ceiling, where the machine gun had been aimed, its bullets leaving huge holes. The bed was covered in dust too, and chunks of ceiling plaster were strewn over the floor, along with red chunks of brick, because once Janez Lipnik had a good look around, he realized that the walls had been strafed as well.

The girl looked at him with tears in her eyes.

"Sometimes he dreams he's surrounded," she said. "Usually he jumps out the window and shoots from there."

Janez Lipnik nodded in sympathy and understanding.

"But tonight he just started shooting here," she sobbed, brushing the sweat-soaked hair away from his forehead. "My poor, sweet Aleksij."

Lipnik asked if he could help somehow. She pointed to Aleksij's leg, which was still convulsing. Could he get a grip on the leg and try to calm it down? He approached cautiously. Perplexed, he stared at the leg as it continued to twitch spasmodically.

"Go ahead, take hold of it," she said. "Don't be afraid, he's not dangerous now."

She looked at him through her teary eyes as she might look at a friend, or even a brother. This gave him strength, so with both hands he firmly took hold of the shaggy beast that apparently led some life of its own, since its convulsions and shudders didn't abate in the slightest.

"Grab on tight," she said. "It always works, it just takes a while."

He grabbed on tight, and when that didn't work either, he leaned onto the leg with the weight of his whole body and tried to tame it, becoming downright angry when he felt it still convulsing against his belly. At that point he bore down with all his might until the leg gave way and bent beneath him after something in the officer's knee snapped, and finally, just as Aleksij's young lady had predicted, the leg became still. It twitched a few times, but the shaggy beast was clearly now at peace.

It lay there motionlessly beneath Janez Lipnik's body, as though it really did belong to the man whose head was resting in the school-teacher's lap, instead of rampaging of its own accord and tangling the sheets. The sheets were warm from their bodies, and only now did he notice that the young lady's nightshirt was hiked high up over her bare thighs. Aleksij reached a hand towards his mouth, spat out a piece of plaster then, rubbing dust from his eyes, opened them. His pupils roamed about aimlessly, before coming to rest. He stared at the ceiling, probably trying to figure out who had shot it up like that. Undoubtedly he was thinking about something, be-cause it took a long time before he looked around the rest of the room. Finally his eyes settled on Lipnik's face.

He sat up, propping himself up on his elbows.

"What is he doing on the bed?" he asked.

"It's all right, it's all right, it's all right," she sang to him, the way a mother sings a child to sleep, and this helped, her singing miracu-lously helped.

Janez Lipnik hurriedly got up. He could see that officer Aleksij was drenched in sweat and that the movement of his arm as he re-moved bits of plaster was feeble. Still, he wasn't going to wait for it to reach for the machine gun lying on the floor; it was probably empty now—but how long did a trained soldier need to change a clip? A few seconds.

Someone tapped on the kitchen window.

"That will be someone from the rectory," the teacher said. "Go open it and tell them everything is all right."

Without knowing why, Janez Lipnik was happy to obey her in-structions. Maybe it had to do with the fact that he didn't feel comfortable around the officer, whose eyes had been darting around their sockets and then the whole room just a moment before, and whose hand could just as easily reach for his pistol as the machine gun. If the circumstances had been different and less unusual, he might have been afraid to go, but now there was no time for fear, something had to be done. He went to the kitchen as the tapping grew louder and louder. Why is it everyone around here taps on windows? he thought irritably, forgetting that he had been one of them just hours before. He opened the window and said, as though he lived there:

"Why are you tapping on the window? We do have a door, you know."

An ample-bodied woman was standing under the window. She was wearing a nightshirt, too, with a shawl draped around her shoulders and wooden clogs on her feet. When she saw him, she put her hand over her mouth, probably to keep from shrieking. What's so frightening about me? Janez Lipnik thought. She stepped back a pace from the window, regaining her composure, but she still seemed fearful, and also a little surprised.

"Who are you?" she said. "What are you doing here?"

"Nothing to be afraid of," he said. "Everything is all right."

93.

It didn't seem to the woman that everything was all right. She kept stepping back, then turned and ran off, back to the rectory. Janez Lipnik called out after her that the schoolteacher, the young schoolteacher, said that everything was all right, but it was no use. The woman looked back in fright one more time, then vanished into the entryway of the building across from the school. Then lights came on inside, and shadows approached the windows and leaned out.

He went back into the bedroom to report what had happened. It struck him that there seemed to be an awful lot of commotion over there.

"They're afraid," the young schoolteacher explained. "First they heard the shooting, then they saw a stranger at the window. How else should they react?"

She took hold of Aleksij under his arms.

"Now help me with him."

He helped her get the officer on his feet. He wasn't drunk, only shaken, but as soon as they got his trousers on him, he apparently wanted to get drunk to manage the shock he'd just experienced.

"A glass of brandy would be good," he said in a feeble voice.

Janez Lipnik felt embarrassed for the brave officer who had once escaped from a house under siege. Poor man, he thought. Such a brave officer and such a poor man.

They held him up on both sides. Janez Lipnik could feel that the officer's arms were no longer so frail—he felt the iron grip of one arm around his neck and he thought that the young lady could not be faring so well if her officer had her in a similar hold. He also thought it might be possible that Captain Aleksij was gripping him so tight in order to strangle him. Minutes before he had discovered him lying in bed, in her bed, in his sweetheart's bed, and it wouldn't be strange at all if a man who shot at ceilings decided to strangle someone like that. But he was mistaken. He wasn't preparing to strangle him. This was a soldierly embrace, the embrace of a buddy. As soon as Aleksij emptied his glass of brandy with the other hand, his grip slackened, he looked at him with gratitude and said:

"You didn't get scared."

Lipnik extracted himself from the embrace, and now the officer put his hand on Lipnik's shoulder, like a soldier, a buddy.

"Once I escaped from a house under siege by jumping out of a window," he said. "You have no idea what being in a house under siege is like. There's nowhere to go. I landed on some fellow's head— he was just then arming a hand grenade to throw it inside. I landed on his head and to this day I don't know how I made it into the woods."

Of course Janez Lipnik had been scared—how could he not have been? When he heard the gunfire in the next room, he had banged his head into the edge of the table and he could feel the stinging bump growing just above his hairline, but he didn't say anything about it. Nor did he say that, clearly, Officer Aleksij had also been scared as he dreamed of being trapped in a house under siege. He knew it was not a good idea to tell an officer that he'd been scared. Officers don't get scared. So why had he not jumped out the window the way he usually did, as his sweetheart said when explaining why he had shot up the ceiling and walls? But Lipnik said nothing and asked nothing, preferring instead to down a glass of brandy himself.

"Every soldier understands that," Aleksij said, as though to a friend.

Janez Lipnik was not a soldier. He had never wanted to be anything like a soldier, but that would change. The times were such that he would soon be a soldier, too.

Perhaps he'd already been one, because he leapt to his feet when he heard a noise from the road. Both of them started, except that the captain remained quietly seated at the sound of excited voices out on the road. Someone knocked loudly on the door—on the door, for once. He heard the voice of the young schoolteacher in the entryway, explaining something. But clearly that didn't help, because the excited people demanded more. The priest entered, wearing a raincoat draped over his pajamas, followed by the woman who had tapped on the window a while before, and then a sturdy young man with big pimples all over his face. In his hands, which rippled with the strength of the knotty muscles under his skin, he held some sort of truncheon, a cart axle, a pole—this is what he held in one hand, while the other hand held a length of wire.

"Captain," the priest said, "this must come to an end. That goes for you, too, miss. Your visits are upsetting folks around here more and more."

"What visits?" the schoolteacher asked, upset. "Aleksij just comes to be with me. Those aren't any visits."

"So who is this?" the priest said, pointing a trembling finger at Janez Lipnik.

The teacher looked down, embarrassed. Even if she'd wanted,

she couldn't have explained who he was.

"So who is this?" the young man carrying the truncheon and wire in his hands repeated.

"Quiet, Franz," the priest said. "You keep quiet."

"I am quiet," Franz said. "I was just asking."

"I asked him that, too," the woman standing behind them said. "Who is this, I was so afraid he'd killed somebody."

Captain Aleksij tried to settle the matter by inviting the priest to have a seat and talk things over with him. There's nothing to talk over, the priest said. "The visits she gets have been upsetting the people around here for too long. Then there's the shooting, first in front of the house, then out behind the barn—it's got everyone upset."

"There's a war on," Aleksij said calmly. "Where there's war, there's shooting."

A war? Janez Lipnik thought. So there's a war?

Captain Aleksij had been perfectly calm in saying there was a war on, but the calm in his voice was so cool that nothing good could come of it.

The priest said that in war one shot at the enemy, at the front, and not just at random, in the middle of the night, and indoors on top of that.

"We're protecting you, Father," Aleksij said in a very quiet voice.

"If there's a war on," the priest persisted, "and if you're protecting us, Captain, there's no need for you to ..." The priest's voice broke.

Lipnik, who only now learned that the officer was a captain, perceived that this business was coming to a head.

"That doesn't mean," the priest continued in his quavering voice, apparently intent on bringing this matter to a head, "that does not mean that you have a right to pimp, carouse, and debauche."

"There's no call to be carousing every night and all the rest," the woman seconded from the rear.

Franz, apparently feeling awkward, shifted his weight from one foot to the other. Perhaps he felt embarrassed at his mother's mention of "all the rest." Franz knew what all the rest was, and, in front of the pretty schoolteacher, who was always wearing a white blouse—which, as it was, was more than he could bear—and was now standing here in a nightshirt, no less, he couldn't do much else but awkwardly shift his weight from one foot to the other. He shook the cart axle in one hand and the wire in the other.

Alexij did not react to this well.

Janez Lipnik was amazed to find that what he had just heard— that there was a war on, and that he was suddenly stuck in the midst of it, or maybe at least on its periphery—didn't surprise him at all. What did surprise him was the priest's apparent inability to understand. It was fine if he refused to understand why two men should turn up in the middle of the night in the local schoolteacher's apartment. What was strange was that he didn't get that officer Aleksij was talking in a very low voice. If someone who's just been shooting a machine gun starts talking to you in such a low voice, then you should understand that this is a dangerous sign. If a war's on and if the captain is talking in a very low, very dangerous voice, then if he were the priest, Janez Lipnik would not keep carrying on, he'd say goodnight, sorry to bother you, and leave. And even if he understood and said that, it might still be too late.

Aleksij was not pleased to see Franz the handyman shaking that item of hardware and that wire like that. His officer's hand, the hand of a captain, started to circle around the tabletop where the machine gun had lain earlier that evening. Janez Lipnik knew where the machine gun was now: on the floor of the room next door, covered with plaster bits.

"May I ask why your fellow Franz has that wire?" Captain Aleksij said straight into the priest's face, so quietly he could barely be heard.

The priest didn't reply, even though the question had been directed at him. At this moment he thought it would be best just to leave.

"To tie you up," Franz said.

Oh, if only he hadn't said that.

"Tie me up?" Aleksij whispered. "Really? You papist flunky. You think you could tie me up?"

Franz gave the priest a plaintive, offended look.

"How can you talk like that, Captain?" the priest said.

"How can you talk like that about Franz?" said the woman, who turned out to be his mother. "Franz is my son and he helps us out in the rectory."

Then she explained in more detail.

"All the commotion gave us a fright. So Franz got up and got that thing from the cart that he's holding here so he could defend us. As for the wire, I don't know why he brought that along."

"To tie them up," Franz said.

What Aleksij then picked up off the bench was not the machine gun—that was lying on the bedroom floor—instead, from a leather holster he extracted a heavy pistol, a small cannon, a Browning. Then he rose to his full officer's height so they could get a good view of him—even if he was only in his undershirt with suspenders let down over his trousers in back, and even if there were no epaulettes on his shoulders, he still cut a fine figure—at least the young schoolteacher looked at him admiringly—he stood up, cocked the pistol and spoke.

"If you don't get out of my sight this instant, I'm going to take this lackey out behind the barn and blow his head off."

For a few moments there was complete silence.

Then, in a heartrending voice, the woman cried out, "He's going to shoot my boy! My Franz!"

And she placed herself in the way, like a true, courageous mother determined to protect her child, albeit a child that was as strong as an ox, and pimply-faced to boot.

Franz was not to be cowed. He flexed his muscles and tried to protest with the axle and wire in hand. He pushed his own mother away so he could take on the officer. But by now the priest had finally realized that this was a real war and that the sort of fellow who jumps through windows and shoots up bedrooms so the plaster goes flying everywhere was indeed capable of taking someone out behind the barn and blowing his head off—or even doing it right here, in the kitchen.

"Fine," he said. "We'll take this matter to a higher authority."

And with that they left.

The only thing Lipnik was sure of was that, like the rifle that fires, even if it is a machine gun, the wire for binding that young Franz was holding was not there by chance. Nothing that people make such a fuss about, and for so long, simply appears at random.

94.

Aleksij put the pistol away and poured himself another glass of brandy, this time a bigger one.

"These papists," he said. "We protect them from those red bandits, and they come threaten me with barbed wire and some higher authority. I'll show them barbed wire. I'll show them a higher authority."

The lights stayed on in the rectory for a long time after that. The lights also stayed on in the schoolteacher's apartment. By the time the last stars began to fade in the sky and the roosters chimed in, the bottle was empty, and the officer and his soldier got fried eggs and bacon—good, yellow food—served up on the table for them by the captain's young lady friend. For by the time she brought the food to the table and sat down on the bench, Janez Lipnik had become a soldier, without that causing him the least surprise or provoking any objection from him at all. It was certainly far preferable, he thought, to having to point out which tree he'd lost his papers under. He wouldn't want to be out in the forest with this officer and have him realize there were no papers. Toward morning, with the last stars fading, the first roosters crowing, and the glimmer intensifying just over the mountains—at the point when the fried eggs and bacon arrived on the table, Aleksij made a solemn announcement.

"We're not going to look for those papers of yours. That's what I've decided."

He put one arm firmly around the young lady in the nightshirt, while he slapped Janez Lipnik on the back with the other.

"When you were helping to get me into my trousers, I realized you'd help a wounded man, too. That's important, Janez, it's the most important thing in a war, that you don't hightail it when you see somebody's hurt."

It made Janez Lipnik feel good to have the officer, a man who was capable of blowing somebody's head off out behind the barn, call him by his first name. It also made him feel good and warm to have the last of the brandy splashing its way through his innards and into his bloodstream. Aleksij also felt good, which was apparent in the way he had softened.

"You two are the dearest people in the world to me," he said. "If anything happens to me, promise you'll look after her."

At this friendly, almost brotherly gesture, Janez Lipnik gathered the courage to look the young lady straight in the eye, and what he saw was indeed the sort of woman—fundamentally kind and ever so slightly vulnerable—that he would be glad to look after.

"What are you saying, Aleksij?" she said with an embarrassed smile. "What are you saying?"

"To hell with the papers." That is what Captain Aleksij of the Yugoslav Home Army said. "To blazing hell with the papers. Am I going to go crawling all through the forest looking for them? If a man's all right, he's all right. And you are all right, I saw that just as soon as you helped me on with my trousers. And you've got such a nice Slovene name. Even if you did hide up a tree. We'll find you a nice uniform and tomorrow you and I will go join up with my unit."

After this, Janez Lipnik finally went to sleep on the bench, and as he dozed off he could hear whispered exchanges and laughter from the bedroom and, yes, even the squeaking of bedsprings.

And so the night passed, extending into morning.

95.

In the morning Janez Lipnik knew that it was high time to be sober, high time to soberly consider and weigh what in fact was going on here. He thought how amazing it was for so much to have transpired in a single night. That evening a dangerous person, an armed person in uniform, had been so ill-disposed toward him that he had been downright afraid of him, especially as circumstances had put him in the man's shirt. Not to mention in his woolen socks, which had so far remained undetected. Wouldn't he, Janez, be ill-disposed toward some stranger he found in his apartment, with one of his favorite shirts on his bare skin? He might even be inclined to hate someone like that. But this fellow had practically made him his brother. And if anything were to happen to officer Aleksij—for instance, were he to fall in battle—then he, Janez Lipnik, would have to look after his pretty young schoolteacher. He had to admit that the thought of it wasn't unpleasant. It's incredible, he thought soberly, yet in amazement, how human nature can change, especially in wartime. In the light of day, when a person weighs things soberly, he found he had to sincerely admire both human nature and Officer Aleksij's character as a prime example of it. Not to mention the young schoolteacher. She was not only pretty, with nicely rounded cheeks and everything else, but it was apparent she had a good heart and, more importantly still, the upbringing to match it. And that meant she had compassion. Twice she had shown this—first when she let him, a stranger, into her home, and then when she compassionately stroked the head of her unfortunate officer, paying no heed to the fact that both of them were practically covered in plaster. She even sang to him, 'It's all right, it's all right, it's all right.' How else was one to characterize this scene, if not as a pietà? She wasn't even bothered by the fact that Aleksij had not jumped out the window as usual and shot up the yard, the road and the area behind the rectory's barn, but had done it right in her bedroom. Just imagine how many days it would take her to remove the last bit of plaster dust from the bed covers and collect the last bit of lead that had flown out of the gun barrel. The young schoolteacher and human nature in general had truly amazed him. But he didn't consider that it's also part of human nature not to ask where a stranger comes from and where he's going—this he didn't consider, because he already knew the answer: the reason we don't ask those questions is because we're afraid of the future. The future is unknown, no man knoweth of that hour and day. But we're also a bit afraid of the past. People don't like to have the past follow them around, because if they did, they wouldn't go anywhere—not to work, not in to town, not to the library, not even to market. They wouldn't move through time and space, the way the life of all living creatures moves. They'd sit at home paralyzed, ignorant and stupid. Like an insect, a book-worm, a woodworm. But even those don't sit around forever, even-tually they grow wings and take flight. That's how it is: whichever path we choose into the future, the past is still there, dogging our heels. That can't be good. There are so many things in the past that are best off staying right where they are. When a person starts asking questions about the past, he puts his future in jeopardy. It's no won-der, then, that on the morning after that dramatic night Janez Lipnik was unable to ask what it was all about, and why it was hap-pening. That morning he didn't try to puzzle out where he had come from and where he was going. He wanted to know why, after every-thing the young schoolteacher had gone through—not just the business with Aleksij, which was more a matter of survival than go-ing through it—but also at the priest's hand—the hurtful words, the threats from Franz, the shrieks of that woman—how was it that she was able to go back to bed with the initiator of all this disorder? Why? Wasn't she afraid he'd start shooting again? That still more plaster would rain down on the bed and furniture? That his leg would start convulsing so hideously and unbearably again?

It's human nature to ask a lot of questions, and so it was with Janez Lipnik. In fact, this trait often led him into all sorts of un-pleasant life situations. But it was mostly because he didn't know how to ask the right questions that this morning he spent time thinking about the young schoolteacher who was waking up next door, probably not even wearing a nightshirt, and who probably thought it was already late, maybe even getting on toward noon, and that she was late for school. He thought about how she didn't have anyplace to be late to, since she lived right here in the school-house. This puzzled him and he wondered, 'Where are the children, why don't I hear any kids shouting, given that the young school-teacher lives in the Dobrava school and that her apartment is in the same building as the classrooms?'

This is what he wondered, instead of wondering, 'Where to now?'

He was a soldier now, after all, albeit without a uniform or a weapon. Aleksij had told him he was a soldier, that they weren't going to look for his papers, that he'd get new ones. The soldier was wondering, 'Where to now?' And this is what Captain Aleksij also wondered and immediately answered, "On to Kočevje." He came out of the bathroom with a towel draped around his neck, washed, shaven, smelling of soap and shaving cream, looking and acting like a true officer, an officer who constantly has to know the answer to the question, 'Where to now?' And point out the way, so that his men don't sense any uncertainty.

"First to Kočevje," he said, "that's where our forces are gathering, then after that we'll see. Maybe even on to Ljubljana."

Outside in the warm September morning Janez Lipnik climbed into the sidecar of Aleksij's motorcycle. The warm June days when he was still walking along the embankments of the Ljubljanica were long gone, and now here were warm September days, with the birds waking up and chirping cheerily in the early morning hours. He was grateful to this September morning for being warm, because he still didn't have any shoes. Aleksij hitched the machine gun over his back and used the foot pedal ignition to start the engine. The curtains on the rectory windows drew apart. The engine roared and the machine bounced down the road full of potholes toward the forested hillside. There Aleksij stopped and looked back toward the house where the young, now once again lonely schoolteacher lived, the dearest person in the world to him. It wasn't a wistful look, because Aleksij was a soldier and, more importantly than that, an officer, and it's a well known fact that officers don't show their feelings.

Even so, he leaned toward Janez in a sign of friendship.

"Can I confide in you, Janez?" he said.

"As long as it's nothing military," Janez replied. "I don't want to know anything that has to do with military secrets or secret offensives or secret police."

"Last night there was none of what you think there was."

At that moment Janez Lipnik was not thinking about what Aleksij thought he was. He was trying to figure out where to hold on to survive this trip.

"I absolutely did not fuck her," he said, casting another dreamy glance toward the window at which she, the dearest person in the world to him, was quite possibly standing. "Even if you think I did."

But this confession made no impression on Janez. What was more vivid in his mind was the shooting. That was unforgettable. What were some squeaking bed springs in comparison with a mighty fusillade like that? Although it was true, the bed did squeak after all the gunfire. But apparently he was mistaken about the squeaking.

"I'm telling you, the old prick didn't stick. She had warm blood trickling down her thighs."

He said he was going to come back and finish what needed to be done, or he was no officer of His Majesty's Army. "No, whatever a man's station in life requires him to do, if he can do it, it's his duty."

But he didn't come back, ever. He adjusted the machine gun on his back, tucked his officer's cap under his tunic, gave Janez Lipnik, down there in the sidecar, a pat on the shoulder, and said:

"Now watch us fly."

And as they zipped down the forest road, Janez Lipnik got bounced around so nastily that he had to hold onto the edges of the sidecar with both hands. The forest's morning freshness soothed the freshly shaven skin of both men, does darted through the brush, and the tires splashed water out of puddles left by the rain. And when the forest road turned up a long, grassy hillside, the wind tousled their hair and Janez stared admiringly at the driver hunched over the bars of the motorcycle slicing through the morning mist.

They raced up the hillside to where they could see over the valley, and it was beautiful.

He felt as though he could even take flight.

Barely had that thought occurred to him when it actually happened. On a curve that cut across a broad hillside, where the road wrapped around a mountain, he said, Look, down there, that's Soteska Castle. At the very instant he caught sight of Soteska Castle far below, both of them went flying, as though they were taking off from the road overlooking the green hillside. Not that they flew all that far. Only as far as a lone oak that was waiting for them in all its bushiness and solidity. They crashed into the trunk of the oak, and they fell like two oaks from Prešeren's poem—'the oak that winter winds have hurled to the ground'—first into the trunk, along with the motorcycle and sidecar, and then onto the ground, the soft, green, autumnal Slovenian ground. Before they even landed, Aleksij swore as only an officer of His Majesty's Home Army knows how. Slovenia is thick with forests and pastures and that was their great fortune. Well I'll be fucked, at least we landed on a heap of manure. They really had been lucky. First of all, because, as soon as they took off from the curve in the road, they flew over the crowns of some modest pines—that's probably where they'd been reforesting. But then also because farther on, below the pines they flew over, stretched the soft surface of a grassy hillside that was totally pliable, probably from being heavily manured. It wasn't actual dung, more like barnyard compost—a thoroughly natural, practically vegetarian filth.

And thirdly, of course, because there's an old Slovene proverb to the effect that fools and drunkards get all the luck. The luck the two of them had just experienced may well have been thanks to their drinking a bottle or two of homemade brandy the night before, shooting in the air, adoring the young schoolteacher (one of them more, the other less), driving off the priest and his flunky Franz with the barbed wire and axle in his hands, driving off their cook, Franz's mother, eating eggs, emptying another bottle of brandy and then with every bit of speed that their Puch motorcycle with sidecar was capable of, trying to fly. They hadn't actually managed it—well, maybe they had, just a bit, but not very far.

"Some day I'll fly for real," Aleksij said. "Some day I'll fly like a

Stuka, like a Messerschmitt."

I'll make a note of that, Janez Lipnik thought. Who knows what ideas are jostling around in the head of someone like him. Maybe some day he really will fly farther than the first oak jutting up out of a hillside.

For now they'd been only slightly battered. One cracked forehead and one lacerated and possibly fractured cheekbone. Some blood.

There was warm blood trickling down the skin of the oak. As it had down the young lady's thighs the night before.

Blood.

Janez Lipnik felt his face with his hands. It was warm with blood, warm blood from his forehead, which had smacked into the oak bark. Through a warm, filmy coating he could see some people running toward them. They were carrying dangerous-looking blades.

Mowers.

"We're in luck," Aleksij said.

Janez Lipnik didn't understand what he meant by that. What luck?

Perhaps this: three mowers were running across a green hillside.

When the dew glints on the blade, that's when mowers' luck is made. That's when a mower speeds across a field like a star shooting through the sky.

And he lost consciousness.

96.

When he awoke, Captain Aleksij was sitting on the edge of a bed next to him. The first thing Lipnik saw were the gold epaulettes glinting on the shoulders of his jacket, then a white bandage partially covered by his officer's cap with the royal insignia. Janez Lipnik raised a hand to feel his own head and face. He was bandaged too, leaving just one eye blinking at the dark room.

"Where are the mowers?" he asked.

Aleksij laughed out loud.

"It's not mowing season here yet."

He heard laughter coming from the other beds, too.

When the dew glints on the blade, that's when mowers' luck is made.

Janez Lipnik looked around and realized he was lying among wounded men in a makeshift field hospital. The place smelled of iodine and damp. They were in some sort of cellar with thick walls. Near the ceiling there were apertures that let in commotion, the squeaking of carts, orders, shouts, metallic clatter.

"They're unloading ammunition," Aleksij explained.

Ammunition?

Surely they weren't planning to start shooting with him still here. At whom? What for? Who brought us here? Where are we, anyway?

"Turjak Castle."

"Turjak?"

A shudder went down Janez Lipnik's spine, sending a vague premonition up through his neck and into his confused brain. Could I be dreaming this? Turjak Castle is going to be surrounded by the partisans. With the help of Italian artillery they're going to blow these thick castle walls to bits.

He propped himself up on his elbows and called out, "They're going to surround us."

"Aleksij," said a uniformed doctor. "Did you bring this hysteric here?"

The doctor had a red cross affixed to his cap, as distinct from the royal insignia on Aleksij's.

"They're not going to surround us. Our forces are in Zapotok and Lašče and all across the area."

"They're going to surround us," Janez Lipnik repeated more quietly. "I know it. I know the history of these events."

"He banged his head into a tree," Aleksij said, as if apologizing for him. "If by some accident they did manage to surround us, we'd be dead."

An argument started up among the wounded as to whether it would be best to stay at the castle or strike out toward Ljubljana.

"And who's going to drag you all there?" the doctor with the red cross said. "This is the only place you'll be safe."

Aleksij and the doctor left the room.

But the wounded men were agitated now, and each of them wanted to talk. These walls are so high and so thick that the Turks never managed to breach them. All those ages the castle was never taken—one meter thick, they pointed out to each other. There's no shell gonna get through that. We're safe here. And anyway, who's going to surround us? The reds? They call those shock brigades? In fact, said one soldier with a bandaged chest, as he got up and stood on his bed, in fact they ought to call them rapid hightail brigades. Laughter spread all through the cellar. The Fourteenth Rapid Hightail Brigade. Where all the wounded have to lie on their stomachs, because they've been shot in the butt. We've even got a few of those here. This guy got it in the head. Somebody pointed to Janez Lipnik. But not from a bullet or shrapnel. But because he was flying. Into a tree.

The cellar of Turjak Castle shook with laughter. But Aleksij, his head's harder than any oak. This is when he found out who Aleksij was. Captain of His Majesty's Home Army, Aleksij Grgurevič. A hero. His father had been a Ukrainian Cossack. A hetman who had chased the Bolsheviks over the steppes. Just as Aleksij was chasing the Communists now. Their partisan shock brigades, so-called, were turning into hightail brigades, as these heroes of the Royal Army and the Village Guards called them. Aleksij broke into the head-quarters of one hightail brigade and they all jumped out the windows. He seduced one of their political commissars, a woman. He'd been the national champion at the parallel bars. A member of the Sokol, the patriotic athletic society. A hero, a Prince Marko of our time. A Bogdan the Brave. It was an honor for me, Janez Lipnik thought, to go speeding through the forest with a man like that. To go flying with him into that solid oak.

Spirits were high at Turjak Castle all that afternoon and into the evening.

That evening, despite the roar of the trucks that kept bringing more and more soldiers into the castle, despite the laughter and con-

versations going on in the cellar all around him, Janez Lipnik fell
fast asleep.

Around four in the morning a metallic sound woke him up and
his first thought was that someone was sharpening a scythe. A mower hones his scythe and the harvest girl reaps. He stood up on his
bed and peered through the cellar aperture. Out in the courtyard
the moonlight revealed the motorcycle and sidecar they had arrived—or rather flown—in on. Somebody was bent over the bike,
gently tapping the slender ignition pedal with a hammer. When he
stood up, the moon outlined the face of Captain Aleksij Grgurevič.
How had this motorcycle found its way into the courtyard of Turjak Castle? The last time he'd seen it, he was lying at the base of an
oak, on a heap of compost, in a thoroughly sorry state. He thought
the people who'd brought them here must have brought the vehicle, too. Maybe someone had thrown it into the back of some truck
with them. He tried to attract Aleksij's attention without waking
the others, Pssst! Aleksij turned toward the window and then came
closer.

"If you're going to leave, take me with you," Janez Lipnik said
quietly.

"Who said anything about leaving? We're surrounded."

He could feel his grip on the latticework of the cellar windows
slacken and he slipped back down onto the bed, his face sliding
down the cold stone wall, as if he were sliding down the tree he had
climbed. Surrounded. Trapped in the cellar of Turjak Castle, which
was now surrounded by every partisan brigade: the Prešeren, the
Gubec, the Shock, the Hightail—what were their names? The castle was defended by Village Guards and a few officers of His Majesty's Yugoslav Army. The Communists shoot any wounded they cap-
ture, Janez Lipnik thought, this is historical fact, they shoot every
last prisoner, including the wounded. He could feel his panicked
blood pounding at his cracked forehead under the bandage, while
the thumping of his heart echoed off the vaulted ceilings of the huge
cellar, which had once been used to store barrels but was now full
of wounded soldiers moaning in their sleep. This is for real now.

This is for real and much worse than in any bad dream, he thought. Now what he really needs to do is wake up just one more time. When he was a boy, before falling asleep he would often imagine he was with Robinson Crusoe on the deserted island, or that he himself was Robinson Crusoe and that he was on Treasure Island with a parrot perched on his shoulder, and that he had a hiding place up in a tree with guns and machetes that would protect him from the natives and pirates. Then he would build a raft and sail back home to England. Or some Dutch merchant ship freighting coffee from South America would sail by and rescue him. He would also dream he was climbing a tall tree, but then he always wound up in a green valley where mowers were slicing through grass still aglint with the morning dew. He had never wanted to dream of being trapped with the wounded in the cellar of Turjak Castle; in September of 1943, right after Italy had capitulated, when the anti-Communist forces retreated to Turjak Castle to regroup before striking out again at the Communists, at the retreating Italians and at the approaching Germans. He thought this had to be the worst dream of his entire life and that any moment now he would have to wake up. And call out to Marijana: Hey, Marijana, you won't believe what I was dreaming just now. That we were on Dugi Otok, Marijana would say. No, not Dugi Otok, in a cellar, Janez would say. Well, you may have been on Dugi Otok, but I was with the wounded in the cellar of Turjak Castle. The Communists had surrounded the castle. And the Communists shot all the wounded captives. Go on, Janez, nobody shoots wounded people. And if there's no way I can wake up, Janez Lipnik thought, then at least I have to get out of here fast. He stood back up on the bed and craned his neck up to the window. Captain Aleksij Grgurevič was gone. What am I going to do without him? he wondered, aghast. How am I going to get out of here? If I'm going to have to run, how am I going to run in my stocking feet? And what will happen to the young schoolteacher? Then he noticed the motorcycle and sidecar still standing there in the moonlit September night as it slowly turned into dawn. He calmed down: there was no way Captain Aleksij was leaving here without his motorcycle.

97.

Sunlight was not yet showing over the nearby hilltops when a sustained crackling started up around them, coming from all sides. The wounded in the cellar, or at least those who were able, started to get up and exchange anxious glances. There was a long screech and then somewhere close by a shell exploded. Mortars. Machine guns. Through the one aperture that faced away from the castle they heard the battle cry of the attackers. Give up, white bastards, there's no way out. Then through the other apertures they heard the surrounded soldiers shouting back. Come and get it, red fuckers. Where are you hiding, cowards? Gunfire poured out of the castle's embrasures, machine guns rattled and hand grenades exploded. He heard an officer shout, 'Hold your fire! Resume firing when they get close.' The castle's first wounded defenders were brought into the cellar from the medics' station. A theology student from Ljubljana whose shoulder had been shattered by a round from a machine gun. He was bandaged up like a mummy, his head bobbing in every direction as two sweaty soldiers brought him in and set him down on some straw. His eyes searched the ceiling and his lips were moving. Janez Lipnik thought he was praying. He went over to him and put a hand on his forehead. Now he realized that he wasn't praying. Medic, he was saying, medic. That's right, Lipnik said, they brought you in here from the medics, who swaddled you up like a newborn. The fellow's blank look betrayed complete incomprehension: Medic, medic. A blond peasant boy had a bloody neck, with blood still seeping through the dressing wrapped around his head and neck. His ear got blown off, a medic said. He can't hear. What ear? Janez Lipnik thought. It's my eye that's bandaged. I hope I'll see with that eye again. But I hope even more that all I have is a cracked forehead, like they've told me. What do you mean I can't hear? the blond peasant boy protested noisily. I can hear and I can see. They're dropping like flies, he said. They're charging on the castle and dropping like flies, the red bastards. The doctor with the red cross on his cap came in and examined the most recently wounded. He turned to a medic and said, we ought to air this place out. Of course we ought to: The cellar didn't just smell of iodine and blood now, but urine and excrement, too. The medic looked at the doctor perplexed. The place had no windows, just narrow slits that let in dust with each exploding mortar round. He shrugged and went upstairs. Doc! a boyish voice called out. What's going to happen to us? The doctor stopped as though thinking of something, then turned around and spoke into the silence that had just engulfed the cellar, broken only by occasional shots from the upper stories: Everything will be fine, he said. Then came a hail of questions and pleas: When, how, where are the reinforcements? You can't leave us here, they'll kill us all. He waited for all of the voices to subside.

Here's what he said: We're not going to leave you, because no one is leaving. The commanders have decided we're going to defend the castle until help comes from Ljubljana. We've got clear assurances from the high command. They've been slowed down because the Italians surrendered their arms to the Communists and some of their units switched sides. The English have landed in Istria and will reach Ljubljana before the Germans do.

Then he was silent for some moments.

"That's the situation," he said past the silent crowd of wounded men, in the direction of the apertures, as waves of battle noise rolled through them unabated.

"Do you hear that?" he said. The sound of the castle defenders singing came in through the slits. "That's our guys singing. These walls are impregnable."

The instant the singing began, attacking gunfire rained down from all sides and the battle intensified once again. But, clearly, the walls were impregnable.

Toward evening the shooting and shouting died down. Two soldiers brought in a kettle of hot soup. They were accompanied by a tall, seasoned soldier, a leader. Anyone here who can hold a rifle goes out on guard duty, he said. The fellows upstairs are tired. He reached out his arm and with a finger as long as a fishing pole pointed at Janez Lipnik.

"You."

"He's not a soldier," somebody said.

"Can't you see, he's just in his stocking feet," said another and all of the wounded men grinned.

"He had a tree trunk run into him," said a third, and once again the whole cellar shook with buoyant laughter. "The oak that's out in the Turjak courtyard."

"He'll do for guard duty," said the leader, who hadn't been able to resist the urge to laugh.

Janez Lipnik was given a rifle, an Italian carbine. But there were no shoes to be found for him. He and the leader then made their way through the courtyard, which was full of scattered military equipment, supporting beams and shattered bricks. The motorcycle was still there. They climbed up a staircase past sleeping soldiers. Even the one he was supposed to replace at a passageway window was leaning on his rifle as he nodded off. Finally, he said, and Janez Lipnik, the Village Guard, defender of Turjak, looked out at the nighttime landscape. The burning landscape. Not far from the castle one of its outbuildings was on fire. It was so quiet he could hear the flames crackle. The kid at the next window was looking entranced at the tall flames as they consumed the castle outbuilding. Then, in the glow, he came over to him and exclaimed, 'Alcazar! Alcazar!'

"Is that the password?" Janez asked.

The other said nothing and turned to look at the fire again. He was a poet.

Then somebody slapped him on the shoulder. He spun around and sighed in relief. Aleksij was standing beside him. Grgurevič. The hero. The hetman. Where have you brought me, Aleksij? How are we getting out of here?

The gunfire subsided, and both sides waited to see if the sparks that were shooting up in fat streams from the belly of the burning building were going to dive toward the castle. The previous afternoon partisan mortars and fusillades from their heavy machine guns had nicked its tile roof, and in the warm September night it was to all appearances just a matter of time before the fire from the outbuilding ignited the wooden framework of the castle roof. This was the end. Aleksij knew they had to get out, out of the cage they were trapped in. He had been insisting on it all these days, but now it would be the fire that forced them out into the open.

If the wind starts blowing in our direction, said Janez, who sat leaning against the wall beside him, we'll sizzle just as sure as we would in hell.

"We have to make a break for it," Aleksij said.

"And get mown down like rabbits," Janez said.

"Make up your mind now," Aleksij laughed, "whether you want to sizzle in hell or get mown down like a rabbit in the clear."

Even though he didn't feel like laughing, he did.

"I can't believe you can crack jokes at a time like this," Janez said.

"For three days I've been saying we need to organize a breakout. Soften them up with machine gun fire from the towers, then charge on out with grenades in hand. We'll have losses, lots of them, but whoever makes it to the edge of the forest has a chance of surviving."

For a long time they watched the fire as it consumed the outbuilding and its walls collapsed. A light breeze blew over the castle rooftop down toward the outbuilding, drawing the flames and the sheaves of sparks in the other direction, away from the castle. They don't get to broil us, Janez Lipnik said before he dozed off. Perhaps he had some vague thought about how they would make a break for it tomorrow morning. As his eyelids became heavy, he saw himself running toward the forested hillside, he could see the forest within reach, he could smell its green dampness as it suddenly went up in flames before him, the whole forested hillside on fire, with the flames racing up the slope of Goli and down the other side, through the marshlands and on toward Ljubljana.

98.

When he opened his eyes his first thought was that he was still dreaming. But he wasn't dreaming anymore. It was six o'clock, the outbuilding had burned down and was still smoldering, but the fire had not jumped to the castle roof. Aleksij was nowhere to be found. My God, he thought, I've fallen asleep on guard duty. At that instant he caught sight of some vehicles moving in the morning light and he heard the rumble of trucks. Dreams always dissolve just as soon as we begin to understand them. Only now did the scene before him come into full focus: artillery. The news passed like lightning around the castle, from one embrasure to the next: artillery. The trucks that were towing the big guns were followed on the road from Kočevje by several smaller tanks. Tanks!? The Italians had surrendered their armaments to the Communists. Cowardly, treacherous wops! The guards stood up and carelessly approached the castle's windows and fire slits, yet not a single round was fired from the surrounding lines. There was no need to fire. The Italian gunnery crews, interspersed with the partisans, had dug their field pieces' firing bases into the ground and trained their barrels on the castle walls.

"I could take him out, the motherfucker," said Aleksij, who suddenly appeared beside him again. "I've got him in my sights."

Aleksij's fidgeting hands switched back and forth between his binoculars and his trusty machine gun.

"Who? Who could you take out, Aleksij?"

"That pig. The 'tenente. Where did he come from, the motherfucking pig?"

Aleksij was more agitated than if he were trapped in a building under siege. Now he was in a castle under siege, which was far worse. Here he couldn't even jump out a window, as he might do if he were in a house that was surrounded—it was at least thirty or forty feet from any window to the ground. He got more and more worked up as he watched the Italian lieutenant leaping around one of the field pieces, adjusting its settings and aiming a finger at some point on the castle.

"His name is Guido," Aleksij said. "He's been after my woman."

But a machine gun wouldn't shoot that far, and neither would a rifle. But an artillery shell could reach here, no question. The Italian officer dropped his arm, the gunner yanked on a long cord tied to the trigger, and an instant later there was a terrible explosion on the castle roof and bits of tiles sprayed all over the courtyard. Ceiling plaster sprayed all over the defenders. No, they're not going to roast us, Aleksij said, they're going to blow us to bits. Or maybe both together. I told them we had to get out, I told them. Now we're trapped. He went up to the aperture and fired a short burst toward the artillery lieutenant who had made him so furious, but it was pointless and he knew it was. The bullets went flying off into the void, but still he fired. Up your ass, he shouted, having learned to swear in officer's school—he was a Yugoslav officer, after all, a regular Prince Marko, Bogdan the Brave, a Cossack hetman who got his courage from cursing. What are you firing for, he shouted as the poet at the next aperture started to shoot. What the bloody fuck are you firing for, wait until they come close. They're not going to come close, Janez said. Doesn't matter, we still can't waste ammunition, Aleksij said. If we're careful, we've got enough ammunition, explosives and rations to hold out for three months—all the officers think so. They're not going to come close because they don't have to, said Janez. A grenade exploded in the neighboring chamber. Janez heard shouts and then the wailing moans of the wounded. They're not going to come close until they've killed all of us. In the courtyard outside some men were removing a dead soldier, half of whose head had been carried off by a grenade. Wistfully Janez Lipnik watched the dead soldier's shoes as they bobbed into the room where the bodies of the dead were being kept. He lifted his head up to the window: the Italian officers were taking their time recalibrating. They kept recalculating the azimuth and trajectory, with explosions on the roof resulting each time, until finally one of the salvos flew square through the window of one of the castle's chambers—clearly, the 'tenente knew how to calibrate. Janez could see a tank digging in on one of the surrounding forested hillsides: now they're going to bombard us with tank fire. The walls won't take it. He glanced at the poet standing at the next fire slit, all white, covered in plaster, spitting the dust out of his mouth. Let's get out of here, Aleksij said. What are you saying, Janez said soberly. They'll pick us off like rabbits.

The poet standing at the next fire slit had a long rifle in hand. He was looking into the distance and saying things that made no sense to Janez Lipnik. This is our Alcazar, he said. They defended it from evil. The forces besieging it brought evil into the world. They conjured Satan. But in the end evil is always doomed to defeat. God exists because evil does. In order to defeat it. I don't understand him. Why has he forsaken us? We're his warriors, not them. Maybe God has other things to worry about, Janez Lipnik said. If you believe he governs every last detail, you still have to admit it's them he's given the cannons, not us.

The Italian cannons, the occupier's. At least we have their small arms. If God governed every last detail, he wouldn't permit Stalin to exist, or Mussolini, for that matter. The instant murder appears on earth, it turns out it's fratricide. Cain killed Abel. What we see happening now is Cain's legacy. I have come, he said, to cast fire upon the earth, and oh, how I wish to see it flare up and spread! Do you think I came to bring peace to the earth? No, I tell you, I bring division. Brother against brother, father against son, son against father, mother against daughter, and sister, and on and on. At the end of times evil will vanish. Now the spirit is torn, beaten, crucified in space. That is because man wants to become God. He's taken everything into his own hands. Bakunin says, even the instinct to destroy is a creative instinct. Bakunin? We contain everything: reptilian brains, tribal hatreds, the will to murder. All of me burned for the Lord, the God of all armies, because the Children of Israel abandoned your covenant, tore down your altars, and smote your prophets with their swords. I alone remain, but they are about to take my life, too. But when a thousand years have expired, then Satan shall be loosed from his prison. And he shall go out to deceive the nations which are in the four corners of the earth, Gog and Magog, to gather them together to battle. Their number is as the sand of the sea. They shall compass the land of the saints about and the beloved city. And fire came down out of heaven and devoured them. And the devil that deceived them was cast into the lake of fire and brimstone, where the beast and the false prophet are. And there they shall be tormented day and night, forever and ever. And the fire shall chasten us, too.

That is what the poet said, and then he added, Perhaps we are in hell. Perhaps, Janez Lipnik said, but I'd prefer to wake up and not be here.

And anyway, hell is a mystery, and I'd rather go to sleep.

99.

The castle was on fire. Grenades had shattered the roof, while down below only splinters remained of the huge wooden doors. The partisans were climbing up the walls on ropes. The munitions dump in the tower had exploded, leaving a huge gap in the wall, toward which a partisan assault force was running. The roofing structure had caught fire and its beams began falling into the courtyard.

"Shine your light over here."

"On me, so you can see me."

Now you know who I am. The bringer of light. Lucifer. The master lampmaker. Life is the light that brightens the kingdom. This aperture here, this is the aperture that the beyond shines through.

For the last foe to be destroyed is death.

Janez Lipnik saw a mower coming who was as big as a mountain. *When the dew glints on the blade, that's when mowers' luck is made.* He strode over the Church of St. Ajax, who defended the wretched Slovenes from the Turks. But that had been an easy task, for the Turks were a small people and even their horses were smaller than ours— no match for our Styrian horses. But how was St. Ajax supposed to defend them from this scythe-wielding giant striding over the mountains, his other foot already planted in the valley near Zelimlje? My scythe, your scythe. A mower speeds across a field with it like a star shooting through the sky. I'm either going to wake up now or I'm going to die.

The one who gives witness to these things says, "Behold, I shall come soon."

"Amen," Janez Lipnik said. "Come, Lord Jesus!"

Then something happened that was far stranger than the mower that Janez Lipnik had seen coming. At the instant when the roof structure collapsed and its beams began to fall into the courtyard and onto the cobblestones in front of the great arched entryway, the castle gate opened. Some thought that the besieged army was launching its breakout, while others thought there must be a traitor who had opened the gates to the besiegers, who would now swarm into the castle with overwhelming force. In fact, these thoughts came later. It's doubtful that anyone thought anything at the time, because it all happened so precipitously. The gate opened and something fast and black came rushing out of the fiery courtyard. A black motorcycle with a side car, and a driver in the saddle. His officer's cap was tucked into his jacket and he had driving goggles perched on his forehead and a machine gun slung crosswise over his back. In an instant Janez Lipnik forgot about the mower striding over St. Ajax toward Turjak. He knew: That's him, that's Aleksij. The Slovene hetman. Our Peter Klepec. This is why he'd spent the moonlit night repairing its engine—so he could go careening through the gate on it. He turned onto the road and almost ran over Dule, the commander of the partisans, who, with the 'tenente, had just been recalibrating the cannon's trajectory, so they could wrap up their nearly accomplished mission with a few last shells. Dule managed to jump back in time, but the 'tenente froze in place, spellbound by the ferocious look of the dark rider.

They say that's when Aleksij the hero stopped the motorcycle and sidecar and said—actually, he asked: "What's the problem, Guido? Didn't the three of us meet somewhere before?"

Guido, as we've already indicated, was spellbound and frozen.

Aleksij nonchalantly drew the heavy pistol out of its leather holster—reportedly there was even some hitch when he first tried to draw it—and shot the Italian right in the forehead. Exactly in the spot where he now had a red star on his cap instead of the coat of arms of his defeatist, turn-tail army.

This was their second encounter, crystallized in the long parting glance, the kind with which people pass away into eternity, of two men who had been in love with the same young schoolteacher. Their first encounter had been in a hotel in Lower Carniolan Springs: Frozen 'tenente Guido Gambini from Friuli, who in the spring of 1942 was having dinner at a hotel in Lower Carniolan Springs, the young teacher hailing from Maribor, a female friend of hers, also from Maribor but currently an employee at the Auersperg estate, another Italian—a high-ranking officer, a major—and an individual who could well have been Aleksij Grgurevič. This is why he said 'the three of us' instead of 'you and I.' This is worth noting, Lipnik thought as he observed these events, because sooner or later it has to come out why this love story involving the death of Lieutenant Guido Gambini had to end outside Turjak Castle, far from the lieutenant's home.

But now this business needed to proceed, and quickly. It all took place in the space of an instant—precipitously, as we've indicated. It was witnessed by the entire Prešeren Brigade, including the soldiers already dangling from ropes, trying to scale the castle walls, just as it was witnessed by the desperate legionnaires, the castle defenders at the embrasures. In short, Commandant Dule jumps back, 'tenente Guido freezes, Captain Aleksij Grgurevič shoots him in the head and then goes speeding off down the road toward the forest like a bat out of hell. All of the eyewitness accounts are in agreement up to that point. The partisans standing near the cannon saw Dule jump back, the 'tenente freeze, grab his head and fall, and Aleksij speed off. It's the same thing that the defenders, having ceased fire, saw through the castle's embrasures. Actually, they'd all ceased firing and they were all waiting to see how this would end.

But from that point on the eyewitness accounts begin to diverge.

Some claim that a landmine blew the motorcycle to bits some fifty meters down the road, and that Aleksij, machine gun still slung over his back, went flying heavenward amid bits of metal, screws and engine parts, and that angels took hold of him in mid-air and carried him off to the heavenly Jerusalem. Along the way he probably had to dispose of the machine gun, because there's no way he could have gained admittance up there with it.

Others—and this group includes Janez Lipnik—claim to have seen the motorcycle slowly begin to rise up. There was no explosion, just the hum of the engine lifting the vehicle up in the air and carrying it over the tall pines and beeches around Turjak, high up over the dark, deep hollows toward Zapotok and on toward Goli and Krim. It's even reported to have circled over Goli, with some claiming it did so because that's where his lady friend lived, yet another of many.

Then the rider, the Slovene hetman, the daring hero and champion of the innocent, was carried farther on toward the Slovene peaks gleaming freely in the distance.

The notion that he flew as far away as Melbourne surpassed the imagination of the desperate castle defenders and even of the castle's ever more victorious besiegers. In any event, one way or the other, Melbourne is where he eventually landed. Legend has it that Captain Aleksij Grgurevič successfully flew over the mountains, then emigrated to Australia and opened a delicatessen. Featuring Italian specialty foods. But it's also entirely possible that he was blown up by a land mine or mowed down by machine gunfire from an ambush.

He told me to look after his lady friend if anything happened to him, Lipnik thought. She's so lonely and vulnerable out there in Dobrava, he thought, maybe I really should go be with her. But then again, he didn't even know if anything bad had happened to Captain Aleksij. He felt drawn back to Ljubljana, but at the same time he wanted to head out to Dobrava first. Suddenly everything was affecting him so strangely.

Clouds were gathering in the distance over Ljubljana and soon they would shroud the rocky peaks to its north. Lipnik saw fiery bolts of lightning jab at the city. He inhaled the chill air and felt the cold in his feet, which had only tattered stockings on them. He noticed how quickly the dark clouds were moving this way, toward the besieged castle, and soon the autumn rain began to clatter on the roof, or at least on what was left of it.

1.

He would have liked to be able to hear the sound of the rain. If it weren't for the loud music filling the space of the long promenade with its stores and flashing signs, he might have been able to hear the sound of the rain falling on the vast roof. He might also have looked up at the heavy cumulus clouds pressing down on the city. On his way here it had been thundering and bolts of lightning shot out of them as the long June rain went on and on, occasionally slowing down to a trickle or shifting from one storm cell to another. He can't see the clouds now, just the glass roof and the noiseless rainwater sliding across it. Then his eyes wander vacantly back to the bright surfaces of the display windows and the dressed mannequins behind them and finally settle on the legs of the custom done, looking reddish this time, with a tinge of red against a blonde base, she'd come and say, "You didn't even buy yourself any shoelaces?"

A pair of feet wearing tennis shoes stops in front of him and the voice attached to them asks if he minds if it has a seat. When he looks up, under the bright lights shining down from the transparent ceiling he sees the face of a young man, unshaven and blowing a huge bubble between its white teeth, could you ... a little room ... please. Lipnik moves the bags off the bench down to around his feet and a bottle of wine clanks on the floor. That was lucky, he thinks, it could have broken. He thinks how this would be the perfect time for him to get up and look for Marijana. But he doesn't move. He lacks the strength to get up. A vast fatigue has suffused his legs, and his faintly bulging eyes are wedged into the flicker of the digital clock as it flashes the seconds and minutes, the time fleeting by on this June afternoon of the year of our Lord 2000 on the edge of the city known as Ljubljana. For a moment he thinks that, despite all the flashing, time has stood still, then he realizes that his tired eyes, unable to pry themselves away from the pulsating clock, may have turned doltish. This is because it isn't time that's come to a stop, but more properly him, Janez Lipnik, archivist of the Regional Archives, amid the timelessness of some Monday—or maybe Tuesday—after the holiday that has just passed, at the end of June and at the start of the new millennium, on the edge of town, at the end of history.

He thinks that these mannequins are from a dream, that he's just dreaming their smiles, that it's only in dreams that things don't move and an instant lasts for such a long time. The mannequins in their big display windows smile, music throbs in the background, he refuses to hear it, but its rhythmic beats are impossible to ignore, they shove their way through his skin to his internal organs and through his skull into the soft tissue of his brain. The rain gushes down the glass roof—it's been raining a long time, the last time the sun shone was three weeks ago. Just this morning he had been at work. The office was empty and the window casements banged in the wind as it drove the rain inside at a slant. He had picked a rain-soaked sheet of paper up off the floor. It had been blown off the top of a stack of papers that somebody had removed from his desk, probably Mehmet the watchman or his colleague Beno. It was a note they had discovered in a poet's papers: *Outside it's raining. Cold and muddy. Ljubljana is shrouded in gray layers of clouds. From my window I watch the people go by. Walking listlessly, lifelessly. They're treacherous. Conniving. Bent on revenge.* That had been that morning, before he wound up in this bright shopping center promenade, where he now felt absent—absent from these lights, from this music, from these passers-by who weren't even sure if this was Monday or Tuesday. Of course they're not sure, time stands still in a place like this, even though everyone's in a hurry. He'd been in a hurry the past few weeks, too, always racing off somewhere, until he suddenly felt he had to stop and be absent, even if that meant here, on a bench in the middle of this promenade amongst a crowd of shoppers.

He thinks that time probably has to come to a halt precisely because he's been racing so much these past days and weeks. Three weeks ago the sun had shone for the last time and since then more had changed in his life than in all the preceding years. In fact, in the preceding years nothing at all had happened. He went to work, shuffled through old documents and classified them, organized collections and dealt with the issue of whether subject wasn't after all a more efficient organizing principle than provenance. Then suddenly events began to pile up and history began to inundate him, collecting like some huge body of water, ready at any instant to penetrate, burst and demolish the great dam of his peaceful life. Their, or more precisely her, Marijana's, history had suddenly welled up out of nowhere, out of some unknown subterranean springs. And some archival documents containing the notes and diaries of some long-vanished people had brought distant lives flooding down some mountainside and into their peaceful, always identical days. The story of a young schoolteacher and her young civil servant boyfriend. The diary of an attendant at the psychiatric hospital in Studenec. Suddenly there was more life in the archives than he was capable of understanding.

Just three weeks. And just a few days since the dam had broken, and the huge flood had drawn him with it and washed him up on the shopping center promenade. Under the cupola of noiseless rain that was pouring down the sides of the glass roof. In among the smiling mannequins in their displays, the rhythmic beats of the music thrumming sharply into his head, penetrating his cerebral cortex, into the soft tissue where memory is stored, the memory of other lives, his own life, the memory of everything. Three weeks before, when all of this began, the sun was shining.

2.

He remembers it shining. Three weeks ago the sun was still shining. They were leaning over the Ljubljanica embankment, watching the divers drag sunken objects up out of the water. The spring cleaning of the poor river whose bad luck it was to run through the center of the city, surrounded by cafes, restaurants and stores, always attracted lots of curious passers-by. It was a Saturday morning, the sun was shining, and Marijana said, "Just think how the sun must be shining on Dugi Otok." Janez thought about the surface of the sea, its barely perceptible waves glinting in the sunlight, a million tiny mirrors illuminating Marijana's body in a yellow swimsuit, lying on a rocky ledge near the water. Now she'll move right up to the water's edge and let the sea gently splash on her feet, she always does that. It will be quiet. As long as no jet skis come screaming by. He thought about the fact that soon it would be summer and they could take the ferry to Dugi Otok, the coast would recede farther and farther, the chilly silence of the Regional Archive would be replaced by the scorching stillness of the rocky island, they would see the lone lighthouse called Veli Rat, and there would be the smell of the pines in the island's forested oases.

"Look," Marijana suddenly exclaimed. "It's a bicycle stand." Laughter spread like a gentle breeze through the crowd of afternoon bystanders. What wonders had they not already hoisted out of the riverbed's silt? Steel trash cans, restaurant tables and chairs that late-night revelers had pitched into the river, car bumpers and lights, a traffic sign shrouded in algae. It smelled, or rather it stank of silt, not exactly of sewage, but still it stank. Now they had dragged a heavy bicycle stand up onto the river bank—and not just the stand, but a woman's bicycle that was locked to it.

"Can you imagine," Marijana chattered happily. "You lock your bike to a stand, you lock it, you go do your errands, and when you come back, not only is the bike gone, but the stand is, too. Now there's a mess. You'd have to think you were dreaming." She pushed her way through to the stone parapet, where both the bicycle and stand were dangling from a crane. It was an old bicycle, very old. The handlebars were high and curved, and the rear mudguard had holes in it for attaching a net that kept your skirt from getting caught in the spokes. At one time this had been an elegant bicycle, painted light blue—you could see patches of paint that had survived, though mostly it had rusted and what remained of the paint was riddled with cracks. It was close, but even so he put his glasses on to read the big red letters printed on what remained of the blue paint. PRES. He felt a jolt. He knew right away that the last two letters were missing. PRESTA, or maybe PRESTO. For a moment, despite the festive crowd all around him, he felt a sudden emptiness in his head, as though he were getting dizzy. As though he were back at the archives and had just discovered a priceless document long presumed to have perished. It was the same kind of dizziness he had felt when, while going through some material sent from Australia, he had chanced upon the name of a young schoolteacher who could have been her, a woman he knew. She had also ridden a Presto or Presta bicycle, and her lover, a young, lowly civil servant, had ridden a sturdy Puch. They would ride their Presto and Puch back and forth to visit each other, or sometimes they rode them together, and they laughed and made love while people all around them were trying to shoot, stab, throttle and bludgeon each other to death.

What was that Marijana had said? What's wrong, she said, what's caught your attention? What are you gawking at? He was fixated on that bike, that's what he was gawking at. At that chunk of metalwork that had once been a bike but that was now, with its twisted wheels and jutting spokes, dangling from the crane's steel cable like the remains of something, of some life that had vanished. Hello in there, Marijana said, are you dreaming? He wasn't dreaming at all. This was the kind of bicycle ridden by a woman who figured in a manuscript memoir, a stack of papers sitting on his desk in the Regional Archive.

She probably did assume he was dreaming. That's what she had said. What is it like when a person dreams, my dearest Marijana? It's as though you don't know what's real and what isn't. Like this bicycle—it can't be hers, the young schoolteacher's. But then how are you supposed to understand this freak coincidence, now of all times? It's like you're dreaming on the bank of the Ljubljanica on a perfectly fine Saturday afternoon.

3.

He wasn't dreaming. One spring long ago, in wartime, he had seen the young woman riding this bicycle, her skirt fluttering. One autumn long ago he saw Italian soldiers help her put the bike on a truck going from Lower Carniola to Ljubljana, a truck that was lost amid the madness of the times. It was exactly this kind of bike, said the trained eye of the researcher of old documents, maybe it was this very bike, said some inkling that was already pecking at the edge of his skull.

He said he was headed into the archives. There was something he wanted to check.

She just shook her head. Not again? Yes, again. He was going to the archives and he was going to get to the bottom of this. There were a lot of things he'd gotten to the bottom of in the course of his career, and this would be no exception. Marijana was used to having him rush off to his documents and manuscripts at the archive on Saturdays or Sundays, and sometimes even late afternoons or evenings after work. After all these years of married life she probably still viewed him as eccentric. The way she did at the beginning. At first it had appealed to her, then it began to bother her, and now she'd grown used to it. She would just shake her head, 'Not again.' She didn't even bother to ask, 'What about dinner?' She knew she would have dinner alone. Or with some friend or other. Maybe it would be best if she just headed out for lunch with that male friend of hers, the one he'd never met but that she enjoyed talking to so much. Whenever Janez Lipnik went rushing off to the archive there was no dinner. She would shrug and, after a few paces when he looked back, she would be smiling broadly, and he had to assume she was already talking with that fellow he'd never met about the bicycle that had been hauled up onto the riverbank together with its bicycle stand. Ah, Marijana. Why does she never think the same thoughts as him, for instance that one day a thousand years from now some archaeologist is going to rack his brain over these bicycles. In the course of these annual cleanings of the riverbed the divers have recovered more bicycles than anything else—and one of them was even still attached to a bike stand. But surely they haven't found all of them, surely a lot are still buried deep in the silt and the algae for some future archaeologist to find. He'll wonder why people threw them in the water. The way they wonder about the Roman swords that have been recovered from the river. In the case of Celtic swords, the archaeologists believe that some sacrifice was involved. They sacrificed the swords to their river god. *National Geographic* had written about it. But they didn't know why they kept turning up Roman swords. This had once been Emona. At some point or other some drunk Roman soldier had thrown his sword in the water and said, 'No more war for me,' and he swore in Latin and threw his sword into the river. Marijana would say, 'Don't you think you have an over-productive imagination?' That's what she always said in response to the hypotheses he'd formulate. You have an over-productive imagination and you're dreaming. What would she have to say about the hypothesis that this elegant, blue, woman's bicycle wasn't dangling before his eyes this Saturday afternoon just by chance? There are no coincidences, at least none like that. I'm not saying that it's her bicycle, the schoolteacher's, the one that figures in some émigré's memoirs—but can anybody prove that it isn't? And even if it isn't, why did they have to haul precisely that kind of bicycle out of the river right before his eyes?

He went straight to the archive, just nodding to the doorman, who was used to his unusual comings and goings at unusual times of the day. Even though he was no longer young, he skipped a few of the steps on his way up to his office.

"One of these days you're going to fall," the doorman called out after him.

His name was Mehmet. He was a nice enough man, but he had no particular fondness for Lipnik. He would come at the most unusual times of the day and he would leave at times when doormen like to turn on the television or leaf through a magazine. But he couldn't do that, because he never knew when archivist Lipnik was going to come bounding either up or down the stairs, even though he wasn't young enough to be taking the stairs two or three at a time that way. He could have a heart attack, or he might slip and suffer a nasty break.

He locked the door behind him, not because he was afraid of

anything, but simply because he didn't want anyone to bother him, least of all Mehmet the doorman, who also served as their watchman and would wander through the corridors and offices in the evenings and at night, turning off lights and checking the locks. He sat down at his desk and took a folder out of the drawer, which had several titles crossed out on its cover sheet, leaving just one written in his vertical script: The Great Lover. He eagerly began to leaf through the sheets. He was sure he would come across the brand names of the bicycles they had ridden: Puch and Presto, or maybe Presta. In any case, these were names he distinctly remembered from the sex addict's memoirs.

4.

The unusual text had come into archivist Janez Lipnik's hands in the spring of 2000, when he was organizing the contents of an accession sent by the elderly president of a Slovene cultural society in Australia. The society, which consisted mainly of political émigrés, had withered away, because its members had all either grown old or died. Anyone who had gone to Australia in 1945 now had to be almost eighty years old, if they were still alive at all. The distant land between the Alps and the Adriatic in far-off Europe didn't matter much anymore to their children. At least not enough for them to take the trouble to recite poetry, play the accordion and listen to speeches about some 'homeland' that they hardly knew. Consequently the package was sizable and contained various publications, typewritten transcripts of meetings of the Melbourne Slovene cultural society, photo portraits of choirs and girls wearing folk costumes as they recited verse from a stage with paintings of Triglav on the backdrop behind them, political speeches by émigré leaders about how the homeland has been enslaved, filled with dreams of a Slovenia that will one day free itself from the communist yoke, and clumsy manuscripts containing recollections of life in refugee camps and first experiences in Australian society—days spent slaving away in factories, the successes of small businesses, Christmas celebrations in the summer heat with artificial Christmas trees in the front yards. The Australian president of the society that was no more was obviously a person getting on in years who was now plagued by the question, 'What will be left of us?' He wanted there at least to be papers and photographs left that would attest to their journey to a distant land, their rise up from the depths, their suffering and joy, their faithfulness to their Slovene roots, their dreams of their homeland and the great, free continent that had enfolded these refugees from the misery and violence of communism in its safe, free wings. Nobody wants his life to evaporate on the way to the hereafter like water in the Australian outback. Better to let the homeland preserve the memory of everything they had experienced, even if only in some dusty archive.

If this Australian émigré material had come into archivist Lipnik's hands some years before, it most certainly would have been anything but boring. If that had happened before the big bang, when the old regime collapsed, and before the long years that it took for the great unified state that was called Yugoslavia, Tito's Yugoslavia, to disintegrate through the agony of the Balkan wars, his hands would have shaken. At least when he picked up the sheets containing the speeches of the political émigrés. In its day this had been explosive stuff. People had been interrogated and imprisoned on account of typescripts, pamphlets and books like it. The criminal code had an ominous paragraph referring to 'enemy propaganda'. But by the spring of 2000 the folders that came into his hands were merely boring. After just a few years all of it had become as humdrum as medieval urbariums. There had been a time when he would have been excited, but now he was bored. Nobody cared anymore what the political émigrés in Australia or Argentina had said, much less how people who had once listened to Christmas bells amid snow-covered mountains and meadows came to spend their Christmases under the white-hot Australian sun. Ah, the sun, he thought, the summer sun. Summer was coming, and he and Marijana would soon be taking off for Dugi Otok again. Every year they spent their vacation on that rocky Adriatic island. Spring was at its height now, and outside his window, in the courtyard of the archive, there was a cherry tree in bloom, its white blossoms fluttering in the breeze. He thought about Marijana, about her white breasts that would turn bronze at the seaside, and his spirit—that of an archivist and a man—flickered alive at the thought, like the cherry blossoms outside his window. How can it be, he thought, that I've suddenly become so sentimental? They had been living together for so many years, and he still came to life at the thought of Marijana, of Dugi Otok, and of the gentle spring breeze rustling through the cherry tree's branches. He looked for a long time at the white tree and the petals that drifted onto the courtyard at each gentle gust.

5.

He spent a while longer sorting through the papers sent from Australia, and just as he was getting ready to add all of them to the 'Australian collection,' assigning numbers and source data to them according to the principle of archival provenance, his eye was caught by a folder bearing the title 'The Women in My Life.' He leafed through it, looking at the multitude of photographs that had been carefully glued to the sheets of paper, each followed at least by brief notes, and sometimes by whole pages or even chapters of typescript in English. He quickly scanned the beginning and end of the folder, but couldn't find the author's name anywhere. Next to the women's photographs first names had been written, but no surnames, only at most the first initial of a surname: *Anna M.* Along with the photos and names there was also a year, and sometimes a season: *Summer 1942, Marika 1947, Lily 1964 (spring).* Or a place name, obviously the place where they'd met: *Gianna, Trieste 1942.*

His first thought as an archivist was that this text was something that didn't really belong with the rest of the material he had set out on his desk.

It was written in English, even though it had arrived with the shipment from the Slovene society in Australia. But by the look of the contents it didn't have anything at all to do with the Australian collection. After a quick technical scan he solved both problems. The author was clearly a Slovene. The first girls he'd photographed or who had given him their photos had Slovene names: *Dora, Zofi, Vanda, Slavica.* And the settings of the photos were all either familiar views of Ljubljana in the 1930s—a promenade in Tivoli, the Illyria swimming pool—or of Upper Carniola with rugged mountain peaks in the background. This meant the author was Slovene, probably a member of this society in Australia, most likely an émigré, and perhaps a political one, even though the contents clearly didn't have much to do with politics. Apparently, after years of living in emigration the author felt more at home in English than in Slovene, and what's more, he was passing his memoirs along to his two grandsons 'so they'll know what their grandfather did,' as the introduction said. However, this dedication had later been crossed out with a ballpoint pen.

He began to read. More with the thought of possibly identifying the author at some point than out of curiosity about all the women he was describing. Even though he had to admit to himself that it was an interesting case. He had been an archivist for a long time and he was used to seeing all kinds of things, but what he was reading now had nothing to do with political speeches or impassioned declamations about the homeland.

Then he came across a passage that made him pause. Among all the descriptions of women he came across a name that caused his hands to shake just a bit, and the page he was holding fluttered: Zala. Schoolteacher Zala D. And for the barest instant he didn't know if he was a child or an old man, if he was in some other town or in this one. The walls of the room shifted, the cherry tree outside his window turned into a white cloud, and time and space collapsed like letters on a computer screen that a virus has infected. He felt dizzy and had to hold onto the desk. Once the sensation had passed, he knew that what had excited him wasn't the practically pornographic content, but this woman's name appearing amid the descriptions of the young man's erotic adventures. Some intuition told him that this could be her, Zala the young schoolteacher, not just any Zala, but the one he had known and admired and secretly been in love with as a child, with all the might of a young child's soul—and not just soul, but body. Here's what he read:

"Oh, that's nice," Zala cried out in her Maribor accent. Her lack of inhibition charmed me. Almost too much. I moved beneath her body's fleshy embrace and could tell I wouldn't be able to hold out much longer. She noticed what was happening and stopped riding me, although she didn't pull off of my prick, which remained deep inside her. She just stopped and started caressing my face in an almost motherly way. Then, still on top of me, she unbuttoned her blouse and took off her bra. Her breasts grazed against my face. This didn't do much to slow me down at all, especially when she started to ride me again—slowly at first, then faster and faster, as though she were on a white Lipizzaner instead of me, a young and inexperienced civil servant. By this point I couldn't restrain myself. "I'm coming," I whispered. At that instant she dismounted, seized me by my throbbing prick and then gently and at length massaged my whole body. I was embarrassed, but at the same time it felt heavenly. She smiled. "Oh, you impatient boy," she said. "You didn't wait for me." For a while she lay next to me, then she got up, fetched a towel and wiped down my sweaty body, gave me a thorough, vigorous rubbing with it, so that I began to feel even warmer. She tossed the towel on a chair and took off her skirt, which previously, while we were making love, she had pulled up around her hips. Now she lay down next to me entirely naked, and as our bodies touched, I could feel my strength start to return.

Lipnik took off his misty glasses. As he wiped them, through his foggy vision he saw that the branches on the cherry tree continued to move, the leaves to flutter, and the petals to fall onto the pavement of the courtyard. Everything had turned white down there. Normally, as recently as yesterday morning, he would have thought, 'what a shame, because now all that will be swept up, after all those delicate blossoms get trampled on.' Now nothing of the sort occurred to him—the whiteness danced before his eyes and he thought, 'What's this now? Where did this come from?' But before he began to answer his own expert question, it occurred to him that he had in fact been placed in the role of observer. He didn't know who wrote this, or when or where, or who she had been—it was a situation that left him at a bit of a loss, as though he, too, had been drained of his strength by all the unrestrained physicality, by the lust of this woman who was unable to stop, and he confessed to himself that he couldn't stop reading: Why be hypocritical to myself about it? I can't stop reading. And at this realization his strength started to return. It went on:

As our bodies touched, I could feel my strength start to return. She began to caress me and to touch herself, her breasts and her crotch. Until then I had never seen a woman masturbate. She kept touching both me and herself, and then just herself more and more, and then she started calling out things that I don't fully remember. They were things like "Ah, that's nice... That's good... See what's happening... How big you're getting... Now we're going to do something for me... Bring that thing over here ..." She spread her legs and once again I slipped inside this frisky woman who seemed to be all play and no seriousness... This time she moved more slowly until she began moaning, "Yes... Yes... Now I'm getting close, too ..." She was breathing heavily and her arms and legs kept squeezing me tighter and tighter. Then she reached heaven, noisily and happily, and her juices ran down my thighs. I couldn't hold back and I came once again, this time inside her. Afterwards we rested and ate apples. I thought about how I had had some women before, but had never experienced anything like this. And in wartime, at that.

In wartime? Archivist Janez Lipnik needed a long time before he could hear the question 'in wartime?' inside his head. That was the professional archivist drilling away in his head. For the longest time the observer refused to let him get close: Leave me alone, he said, can't you see they're eating apples—does it really matter if it was in wartime or not? Then he read on—that the author of this mighty coital account couldn't go home in the middle of the night, so he stayed, and on it went. It was the curfew that kept him from going home. If he had tried riding his bicycle down the road, he could have been stopped by an Italian patrol, or they might not even have bothered to stop him and just shot him, instead. They often shot people without warning. The Italians might well have popped him off. They were so afraid of the partisans that they shot at anything that moved. Or he could have been riddled with holes by some partisan ambush. The partisans tended to shoot at anything that moved down the road. They themselves never moved down roads, since that was the domain of the forces of occupation and their local facilitators. Only now did Janez Lipnik understand the question that the professional archivist kept repeating in his head, 'in war-time?' As well as the question laden with dark foreboding that the child inside him kept repeating, the boy that Lipnik had nearly forgotten after all these years, that little Janez: 'Is this her? Is this Zala?'

If he wanted to get to the truth about Zala, he needed to iden-tify the unknown author of this erotic memoir. He composed him-self and began to read over various parts of the text again. But in spite of his great persistence and precision he met with no particular success. At first he had labeled the anonymous author, who so scru-pulously recorded all of his experiences with all of the women who passed through his life, or rather his bed, 'The Pervert'; and he wrote it on the file's cover sheet where he made his notes. But when he reread the text in greater detail, he realized that the author of these descriptions of erotic adventures had deeply human qualities, too, and that what interested him about all of his women was in fact something far more than just their bodies, and this is why he changed the file's code name to 'Casanova,' a label he kept for a long time. But the unknown sex maniac had neither the literary nor the political talent of his famous namesake. Politics, in fact, didn't inter-est him at all. He dealt with it because he had to, like everyone sucked into the vortex of the Second World and Civil War in Slove-nia. He just had a slightly more unusual human and male heart, which fluttered whenever a female entered his orbit, and also some demon that gave him no peace until he had unsettled the heart of that female sufficiently for him to conquer it, as they say. He could also have called him 'The Conqueror,' but that had too many associations with conquistadors, leveled cities and the landscapes of women's souls laid waste. But he kept on falling in love, not with the female of the species per se, but with each successive woman in particular, and each time afresh. What's more, whenever possible he left behind him not tears and emotional devastation, but amicable separations, understanding letters, photographs and fond memories. And this is why on the folder's cover sheet he had crossed out the words 'The Pervert' to the point of illegibility, had then crossed out 'Casanova,' and simply written 'The Lover.' And after some further consideration added the word 'Great.'

6.

The author of this extensive memoir had definitely earned that title, if only through the impressive number of his conquests. By Lipnik's quick, preliminary count there were about four hundred of them. Certainly by Slovene standards this is an extraordinary number, especially if we consider that in the course of his rather long lifetime his longest period of activity took place in one of Europe's smaller nations, one which not only has fewer soldiers, fewer mathematicians and fewer shoemakers than the larger nations, but also fewer women. Admittedly, later on his scrupulously documented list, furnished as it is with numerous facts and photographs, also begins to include some Italians, Germans, Australians, and Frenchwomen, as well as seven Thais, two Vietnamese and even a Serb. But the fact that of all the women described the majority are Slovenes does not in the least diminish his achievement. In the history of the Slovene nation there have not been that many exceptional people who have broken European records. There have been some famous grammarians, apiculturists and mountain climbers, a very few statesmen and generals, here and there an architect or an inventor of logarithms, a couple of cardinals and one near-saint. Even the inventor of the screw propeller, whom the Slovenes like to claim as their own, was really a Czech. Historians tell us that the history of the Slovene nation has been above all a struggle for cultural and social survival. Survival has been goal number one, with little time or leisure left for great achievements. Least of all in the domain to which this in some way assuredly exceptional person had devoted his life. For Slovenes, woman is first and foremost a figure to be revered and honored, not just a mother, but someone of saint-like proportions to whom the most affecting passages of our past literature are devoted. Not just a mother and not just a wife tending to husband and home, but also a lass, as the folk song goes, *As long as you'll have Slovenes living here, you'll have Slovene lasses to bring you good cheer.* And this is why the unknown author earned the epithet Great. The word Lover belonged next to it, because, quite simply, it described his area of endeavor. Lipnik would have preferred to be able to label him The Great Inventor or The Great Statesman, but that just wasn't going to be possible in this case.

Who have I written all this for? Myself, perhaps? I've reconsidered regarding my two grandsons. Perhaps it really wouldn't be the best thing for them to get to know that side of their sweet old grandpa. In any case, I've written it. After all, not many lives are this rich.

And that was the truth. But that wasn't the only explanation. Surely he wanted somebody to read what he had written. No one writes a memoir with the intention of having nobody read it. Lipnik, with his many years of archival experience, knew this all too well. But now it had come into the hands of a person who wasn't the least interested in the number of thighs, wet crotches, overheated bellies, hairy nether-regions, fevers and coolings down, thrusts and licks, or even in all these photographs; someone who, even with all this abundance, would have no problem turning away any of these women of various callings and proclivities—aristocrats and working women, churchgoers, nymphomaniacs and lesbians, married or widowed, childishly innocent or given to lascivious abandon.

Most likely the author of this memoir would have been none too happy if he had known that his reader in the Regional Archive was interested in just a single woman, and not on account of any particular sexual skills or appetites, but because she had opened some abyss in his soul, some memory that he wanted to get to the bottom of. Lipnik was drawn to that memory, he longed to enter it and get way down to the very bottom.

The vast majority of the women who had passed through the life of The Great Lover had given him photos of themselves, which he carefully pasted into his typescript. The first of them was Zala, as it said under her picture: *Zala, a schoolteacher from Dobrava, my first real woman.*

7.

And so when this document came into Lipnik's hands, not only did his hands shake, but on seeing the name Zala he was overcome with a sort of dizziness, as though the floor had been pulled out from under his feet and the space of his office, together with his desk and the blossoming cherry tree outside the window were no longer here, but somewhere else. As though he were looking into an abyss. Not, however, because of the impressive number of women who appeared there, but because of a single one whom he thought he recognized. Maybe it just seemed to him later that he had an attack of vertigo the instant that folder came into his hands. Maybe it was later, when he sensed—recognized?—the features of a familiar face in the photo of one of the women from the long list. A face with distinct, dark eyebrows and white teeth in this photo of a younger face with shorter hair, but still a face that caused the thought to course through him: I know you. Even though the woman in the photo was younger, even though she was dressed in a bathing suit that covered her body from crotch to breasts, even though the photo was shot in some foreign setting, on some rocks that could have been by the seaside or alongside some Alpine lake, and even though all these circumstances drew the viewer's attention to her body and the landscape, all he could look at were her eyes. He knew these eyes, the eyes of a gentle face from his childhood, a face that never smiled, a preoccupied face, a face turned in profile to the class, standing at the window and looking out at the suburban street in Maribor, the red lips saying, 'Very good, Janez, very good.' That face had often been preoccupied, the eyes would often stare straight ahead as though they were elsewhere, as though they were seeing something else, but this face was smiling broadly, the body's posture was carefree, the girl in the photograph was smiling at whoever was taking her picture. This couldn't be her. But, on the other hand, it could be, some intimation in him said. Maybe it's a coincidence, the same way that bicycle, that Presto or Presta encrusted with algae and silt that he'd seen being hauled up out of the river was probably a coincidence. But many years had passed since the days when he knew the woman who might be the one in the photo. He'd seen many faces. There was no real evidence anywhere. This was all just some hunch, a sudden dizziness, the abyss of the unknown that he'd glimpsed when the sex addict's memoirs had come into his hands. He'd written that Zala the schoolteacher had been his first real woman, a major chapter of his life.

Lipnik looked into an abyss that drew him down.

"Zala," he whispered. "Schoolteacher from Dobrava. This is her, my first real woman."

8.

When he looks down from the pulsating digital clock and tries once again to scan the huge, gleaming promenade where Marijana is likely to appear any instant, his attention is drawn to a woman wobbling strangely. Then he notices that her shoulders are suddenly bare, and that somebody is pulling the dress off her—at first pulling, then tugging, even yanking the delicate floral fabric off her. Her dress is strewn with flowers, sweet springtime flowers, daisies. It will be summer soon, these fabrics are light, they slide so gently over bare skin. Someone is standing behind her. All he can see is a man's hands. The head is concealed behind her back, but the hands keep relentlessly pulling the dress off her so that she wobbles dangerously and Lipnik starts to think she might fall. But the petite woman with the petite body that is becoming more and more naked stays upright after all, she doesn't fall, she just seems to lean slightly against the pane of glass. A few seconds more and she's completely naked and completely motionless. The man undressing her steps up onto a platform and pulls the hat from her head—first the hat, then her hair. He throws them straight on the floor, on some spread-out newspaper, but still on the floor—her light spring dress, and now her blond hair, making a little heap.

The chill of some memory causes Lipnik to shudder. Her hair lying on the floor, a heap of shorn hair.

The man removes the remaining pins stuck into her pink skull along the perimeter of where the wig had been. He holds them between his lips. If he falls now, Lipnik thinks, if that platform slips out from under him, he'll swallow those pins. If he doesn't spit them out first. He probably wouldn't be able to spit all of them out, so he'd probably wind up swallowing some. That naked woman, dressless, hairless, missing the pins from her head, with nothing but the shoes on her feet—Italian ones, for sure—remains leaning up against the display window. Lipnik has the feeling that her empty eyes are watching him.

For a while he watches the passers-by and tries to see their eyes, which are empty, too, like the eyes of the mannequin in the display window, just not as much. Some of them try to sparkle at the sight of the glittering clothes on display, the appliances, the handsomely designed metal objects, the style, the light, the spangles that ignite the spark in young women's eyes. They try for a moment to sparkle, but then they suddenly go out, because there's simply too much and it's impossible to be joyful and generate that glint in one's eyes when there's too much of everything and all of it is a jumble. His eyes refocus on the legs that walk past him or stop in front of the display windows. For a while he tries to figure out which of them are walking to the beat of the music coming out of the speakers, and soon he determines that some of the women's legs are in fact walking precisely in time with the music, and that, even after they come to a stop a few paces away from him, they keep moving in time with it, the legs bending at the knee, the right foot even turning out a bit to the rhythm, causing the pink skirt to shift over the knee slightly. It occurs to him that the nameless author of that typescript document would just walk right up to that woman and talk to her. But him? Had he ever just gone up to a woman and talked to her? Before Marijana, sure, he had then. But not after, not one time since. Back before there was Marijana, the sight of a woman's legs concealed under a floral skirt down to the knee, moving in time to some thumping music—oh, here it is again, there's that music again—would have caused him to wonder what it would be like if they were standing next to his bed. Or lying alongside him. That pair of legs in jeans over there that just joined the pair in the skirt—they would have been compatible with that train of thought back then, too. But nowadays he wouldn't even think of it, or even dare to remember the words he once heard a jazz musician say, late at night, back in the days before Marijana, when he went to a jazz club, 'Now that one deserves a good fucking. And that other one, too, just for dessert.' After he finished playing his set, the musician, he went and leaned up against the bar, leaned over toward the two girls, who first look at each other, then laugh. 'You I'd take first,' the drummer says. 'Then you for dessert.' What on earth is making me think about all this today, Lipnik says to himself. Where are these memories coming from all of a sudden? His tired eyes follow the legs as they disappear into the crowd, you I'd ... and you for dessert. Just like that memoirist with his sexual exploits, that's the kind of thing he'd say, that chronicler of erotica, erotic chronicler, the lawyer, the civil servant. He looks back at the naked mannequin leaning up against the display window. Its eyes are vacant, mine probably are, too. Marijana says that my eyes bulge when I'm thinking my private thoughts. His eyes don't just bulge from fatigue, and the vaguely imbecilic look on his face isn't just from the terrible, imbecilic din of the shopping center. There's also a tiny kernel of pain lurking in his breast that's dull and exhausted now, but could easily become acute and searing again in short order.

9.

On that Saturday three weeks before, on that sunny Saturday when a Presto bicycle covered with algae was dredged up out of the Ljubljanica, he buried himself in the archives. When he came home that evening, he jokingly asked Marijana who she'd been talking to on the embankment. Some former lover? She looked at him and he knew what she was going to say, that he had an over-productive imagination and that he was always dreaming something. She didn't say it, but he knew that's what she thought when she shrugged. She didn't quite take him seriously. That's why she chose not to joke back when he asked her, and just shrugged her shoulders, instead. With him, what started out as a joke could easily turn into a full-blown, pedantic investigation. She'd long been aware that his thoughts were easily drawn to some point, whether imaginary or real, which they would then drill into relentlessly. Sometimes the drilling verged on obsession. He didn't know how to stop and he didn't know how to back off. Years before, just a few days after he had moved into her apartment, where they were going to 'live happily to the end of their days,' as he'd said, he became fixated on a picture postcard from Budapest. She was just back from some strenuous afternoon lectures, she was tired and fed up with students in jeans that were too tight and even tighter blouses, who cared about nothing in the world except tight clothes. There was a postcard of Budapest's bridges on the table. She knew immediately who it was from. A friend from her student years had left days before for Hungary. She brightened up. She felt they both belonged to a generation that cared about something else besides too-tight pants and blouses—Byron and Keats, for example, or Lawrence at the very least. I know who that's from, she said, and went to the bathroom. When she came back, Janez was sitting at the table impassively. Aren't you going to read it, he asked. Which meant that he had already read the postcard, and that fact came close to putting her back in the bad mood she'd brought home from the university. The postcard was addressed to her and at the very least she had the right to read it first. She overlooked this detail, picked up the card, read it and burst out laughing. It said:

The age-old wish that every woman dreams of has come true for me. I know you'll be envious. I rode on a bus that was full of drunken Hungarian soldiers. Best wishes, Jana.

"I don't know what's funny about it," Janez said.

"It's a joke," she said. "Don't you see? A joke."

"If I understand it," he raised his voice slightly in indignation, "it's a joke about a possible rape."

"That's right," Marijana said. "Every woman dreams of being raped by drunken Hungarian soldiers."

"Don't take that sarcastic tone with me," he said. "The context of the message is insinuating, it's ambiguous, and it's unclear, and at the very least I would call it cynical."

"Cynical? About who? About what?"

"About a woman's dignity and physical inviolability."

Marijana grew serious. She tried to explain to him that the message was just the opposite, that Jana had probably felt awkward on that bus and that she probably couldn't wait for the trip to be over. It's peculiar, don't you think, why she had to take a regular intercity bus? Maybe, Lipnik said, she was making an excursion to Szentendre from Budapest. You can get there by bus or boat. But why would she take a bus to that little town with its old Serbian Orthodox church and ancient icons, and a regular intercity bus, at that? Why did she have to rough it like that, when she could have taken the boat? And if she'd taken a tourist bus, she wouldn't have had to travel with a platoon of drunken Hungarian soldiers. Maybe it was when she was going back to Budapest from Szentendre and the soldiers had gotten drunk in Szentendre—it's a wine-growing region and the bistros in town serve excellent wine, he remembers it well, he'd visited once. Marijana said the fact was her friend had taken the bus and not gone by boat, because there was no indication anywhere that she'd gone to Szentendre. When she was writing the postcard she remembered the journey and jotted down those few lines, and what was the problem with that?

Oh, but there was a problem. Though she may have known him for many years now, she didn't know him well enough. There was a problem the size of a mountain. A problem wedged deep in the subconscious of this Jana, her friend from college days whom he didn't know. If only he knew her better, he might be able to suggest why she should have the thought bubble up out of her subconscious about what might have happened to her on that bus. But he wasn't going to pretend to deal with Jana. She was the problem, his Marijana, whom he clearly didn't know well enough, and certainly not as well as she knew him. He couldn't imagine how anybody could write her something like that. Because if she could get a postcard like this from a friend who knew her well, knew her perhaps to the very core of her soul, then you might say that the two of them were on the same wavelength, that they were sending and receiving signals from each other that—she would have to forgive him—verged on the obscene.

And so on. Right through until evening when she finally invented some errand that would take her to her mother's, if only to put an end to this. But then it went on for a second day, and a third. A third! She had already run out of debating points on the first day—possibly in the first instant, in the single sentence which she should, perhaps, never have said: 'It's a joke.' Hadn't somebody written a book with that title, where the whole story is set in motion by some joke on a picture postcard? There's no comparison, he said, that joke was a jab at the whole totalitarian system. Something very different was at issue here, namely what, precisely, the sender and the receiver were thinking, what points do they share in common? And on it would go until other stories occupied his attention, usually from the archive. This spring it was the stories of some Australian Slovene, an émigré and apparently some kind of pervert, who had described his erotic adventures. This claimed his complete attention. Marijana was able to relax a bit, if only because they were no longer going at it over that miserable postcard. In its place, he began talking about some diary. A diary from a mental hospital. He could talk about nothing else. If he asked whether she'd been talking to some old lover there on the embankment, it was really only meant as a sign that, despite the fact that he was spending all his days at the archive and even at night would perch on the edge of the bed and talk about his hypotheses regarding those memoirs, he still loved her. Marijana would rather have had him deal with archival material than with her, maybe even with some postcard sent by a friend of hers from Budapest.

10.

On Monday afternoon—yes, the sun was still shining as late as that Monday, albeit for the last time before the great deluge to follow—he continued to deal with the memoirs of The Great Lover. He would have been a bad archivist if he didn't try to identify the manuscript's author. At first he thought the problem would be easily solved. He would need to look through the membership lists of some Slovene societies in Australia, make a few phone calls and ask some surviving members if they had known ... who? He realized that he wouldn't be able to describe him at all. Not just because there was no name, but there were no other details either, except for the names of some women and the towns where he had lain with them. There were lots of photographs of them, but none of him. Apparently he had taken some of the girls' photos, but none of them included him, The Great Lover. So who was he actually looking for? The only things he'd written about himself were his professions and the work that he did. He'd studied law, then he'd become a lieutenant in the royal army, like all recruits who'd finished college. During the war, at the point when Zala appeared, one of his life's great chapters—during the war he'd been a low-ranking civil servant on the old Auersperg forest estate. Zala had been a schoolteacher in Dobrava. Lipnik looked at the map: the author of the memoirs must have covered a huge part of that territory either on foot or by bicycle before encountering Zala. When he first emigrated he worked as an interpreter. Then he had worked in a bank, and finally in Melbourne he opened a delicatessen featuring Italian specialties. But Lipnik still didn't know who he was looking for. Who was this man who had gone into emigration via Trieste, judging from the lovers he had there, both Slovene and Italian. His eyes stopped on the photograph of a long-haired, tanned and smiling girl sitting at the seaside and probably photographed by the author.

That was the city for me. Even though the war was still on, Trieste was elegant and peaceful. We had coffee in the cafés and would go swimming at Miramar. Maria wore a very thin, tight swimsuit, and not only could you see that very appealing shape down below, but you could also make out the fine, black hairs through the yellow fabric. She was my age and from Sicily, where she'd taught high school gym classes. In Trieste she lived alone with her mother. She was tall and slim, with brown eyes, her nose slightly arched, her smile full of dangerously flashing white teeth. Whenever I looked at her I thought that making love with a woman like this would fulfill all my erotic ambitions.

There followed a long description of a Sunday afternoon at her apartment with her mother away. He tried to kiss her, but she bit his lip with those dangerously beautiful teeth. Even so, they took the tram up to St. Ivan. They found an inn where they drank a couple of glasses of wine. She told him she felt bad for biting him.

We got off at the last tram stop. Maria wanted to see the sunset. We sat down on some roadside stones and looked down at the radiant city. She had carelessly let her summer skirt hike way up her legs, exposing her bronzed thighs. I looked into her eyes. Suddenly she began to unbutton her blouse. She kissed me. Non ti mordo! she said, I promise not to bite you. My bloody lip was forgotten. My hand slipped down between her thighs. I was careful. I waited for her to give a sign to stop. But in-

stead she began to caress and embrace me and to unbutton my shirt. She reached her hand down into my trousers. We didn't look around to find some concealed spot, we just lay down by the side of the road. Soon I was inside her and she began to moan.

There were quite a few who passed through his hands in Trieste. There were also quite a few in Rome, where he immediately found an attractive chamber maid. And her sister. It became clear to Lipnik that identifying the author was not going to be an easy task. But it did become somewhat monotonous. Maria was barely number 27—a long way from number 100 and all the following hundreds. Number 69 was an eighteen-year-old Hungarian refugee girl whom he seduced with chocolate. She didn't care for spaghetti, but she did love chocolate.

She was timid and only knew a few words of Italian. When she came to see me, I gave her some more chocolate and we drank a sweet liqueur. It took me a long time to persuade her, but finally she lay down on the bed. After a few kisses she took off her panties and put them under the pillow. I stroked her whole body carefully, then between her legs—she wasn't a virgin anymore, but the passage was very small. I wanted to quit, but with the few Italian words she knew, she said, 'As long as we've gotten this far ...' She grimaced with pain. She didn't climax. She came to see me several times more for chocolate, but my desire for her was gone. I'm rather ashamed of that conquest.

But not enough to keep him from carrying right on with others. The names and the photographs came one after the other. Each photo supplied with a brief characterization:

Lea G., my landlady's frisky daughter ... Liana W., beautiful and animalistic ... Olga M., a Slavic soul ... Gerta E., crocodile hunter and my first group sex ('boys, you've torn me completely to bits') ... Billy B., a red-haired mountain of pleasures ... Anna Z., a volcano of orgasms ... Kyo San, insatiable Japanese vampire ... Gloria V., one night's disap-

*pointment in a hotel... Nevenka A., morning sex (when I arrived, she was cleaning the apartment and said in Serbian, 'Like I give a fuck')
... Genevieve H., schizophrenic French aristocrat... Nadia E., experience with a lesbian and her lover... Lily and G., a quickie in three (we ended up in her bedroom, where her girlfriend's moaning aroused me to penetrate her fragrant hothouse, too).*

It really became rather monotonous. These long series of dancers, hitchhikers, saleswomen, widows and wives or lovers of friends punctuated three marriages and the births of several children, but such details did not curb the constant activity. There were some crises, valium and alcohol, separations, divorces and hysterical fits, stalkings and jealousies, but the business went on, with new buttons and new thighs, new tits, some wonderful new blossom down there, afternoon stays in hotels, the back seats of cars, the shores of lakes and thrusts while standing up against walls in desolate streets. Somehow this business became a goal in its own right. And whenever that happens, it gets boring.

But most importantly, Zala the schoolteacher was nowhere to be found.

She had quite simply vanished from the entries of The Great Lover.

11.

He could have consigned the file to the vault, marked it as author unknown, described how the text had come to the Regional Archive, and that would have been that. For somebody else, perhaps, but not for Janez Lipnik. Senior Archivist Janez Lipnik was known for pursuing every issue to the end. On account of this trait he was rather disliked by his colleagues. For the sake of a footnote he was ready to sit in the archive, the library, or at his computer for days on end, even Saturdays and Sundays, much to the aggravation of Mehmet, the doorman and security guard. For a footnote he was even ready to drive his coworkers to reopen and pore through long-closed files. All for a footnote, said Beno, his colleague, for the love of Pete.

He noticed that in the course of his first eager reading he had overlooked a footnote. It explained that the description of the encounter and lovemaking with each new woman had been designated either as C, A, or M. C meant a Chapter, or in other words, that all the women marked as C had been chapters in his life. There were not many of these—there was an Ivica, a fellow student at college, the star student of their class, whom he was sure he could never have, but of course eventually did; there was Dora, who looked after him when he arrived in Trieste in 1944—and after these two some seven or eight others, all Slovenes or Italians. Then there was Ema, whom he married and soon after divorced, and a crazy Serbian scientist whom he married in Australia and who drove him to the brink of madness before he divorced her, too—this was the point where valium and alcohol entered his life, both at the same time. There were about a dozen more C's (i.e., chapters) in his life. But the majority had been marked A. These were the fleeting encounters, the afternoon coitions that might be repeated two or three times, the acquaintances from evening social events, coworkers from the bank where he worked when he first arrived in Australia, as well as Thais and Filipinas from his trips to sexual tourist destinations. The ones marked M were either instances of failed sex, which can happen occasionally even to a lover as great as The Great Lover or where external circumstances prevented sex—there were only a few instances of that—or of women who had fallen unhappily in love with him and then went on a rampage, while he tried his best to disentangle himself with a minimum of suffering (both theirs and his), and a minimum of tears, letters, and excessive phone calls. But the unknown author would not have been a Great Lover if he hadn't solemnly declared that he loved them as much as the others—yes, even the ones he'd marked M:

I remember them all, and I wonder how many of them remember me. For you see, my dear, whether you're a Chapter or an Adventure or a

Mistake, it doesn't matter, I still remember you. I loved you all. Admittedly, some more, others less. Some for an hour, others for months, years, decades, eternity. My emotions and physical sensations may have changed, but the memories never will.

But there was something Lipnik found that suggested the memoir's author may have been a soldier during the Second World War. One of the descriptions pointed directly to that:

Mileva sat down on the bed, still dressed, and after a few kisses took off her sweater. I'll never forget that fresh, uninhibited smile of hers. Nor her fine, small breasts, which I began to kiss. Suddenly she pushed me away, and I thought that maybe she'd reconsidered. She looked me in the eyes and said, "Ti amo signor tenente." I love you, too, Mileva, what fine linens slid down your body when you undressed, and then both of us slid into your moist, little body.

Signor tenente? Now this was a possible lead. Before the war The Great Lover had been in a school for reserve officers and had earned the rank of lieutenant. Someone like that couldn't have sat out the war as a junior civil servant on some estate, that wasn't possible. Someone like that had to put on a uniform. Which side did he join? The partisans? That would have been a stretch. The Communists had taken them over and Yugoslav Army officers didn't like them. The anti-communist forces, the Village Guards, and later the Home Guards? Or the Chetniks, who styled themselves His Majesty's Home Army? This was a riddle he would have to solve.

That Monday he wanted to research the etymology of the word *skebe*, which some Japanese actress had offered to The Great Lover—did it just mean 'womanizer' or also 'lover?' But he noticed it was time for lunch. He didn't actually notice—he didn't look at his watch, because when Lipnik immersed himself in his documents, he sensed no passage of time and he felt no hunger. Nor did he notice the applications from citizens stacked high on his desk, waiting for him to resolve them. To issue statements of ownership and inheritance. Reports for denationalization proceedings and issuance of restitution for damages inflicted on people by the communist regime, or confirmation of damages in wartime. He shoved all these applications and papers to the edge of his desk as his investigation of the sex maniac's memoirs took up more and more of his time. Finally the petitions and applications of all those people migrated from his desk onto a shelf. When Lipnik immersed himself in an archival investigation, he noticed nothing else. Not even Beno, his coworker, who had just perched his rear on the edge of his desk and said the sun was out. A couple of them were heading out for lunch and he could join them, if he wanted. He didn't feel like lunch with Beno, he didn't feel like hearing about everybody's plans for the upcoming vacation. But he did look out the window and see that the sun was out and that the white cherry blossoms were shining brightly in the afternoon light. Maybe so, he said, maybe I will join you. He thought about how he'd prefer at least to take care of this one thing, to find out what the word *skebe* meant, but the afternoon sun enticed him to go. If only it hadn't.

12.

In the spring of 2000 the memoir of some sex maniac came into his hands, and one sunny Saturday in June he watched from the banks of the Ljubljanica as divers pulled a bicycle covered in algae and silt out of the water. All afternoon he'd been looking through that accession, because he was convinced that Zala the schoolteacher had ridden the same make of bicycle, a Presto or a Presta. But he found nothing to confirm it. That Sunday he wanted to head back to the archives, but a reproachful look from Marijana had stopped him. Hadn't he promised they would go for a hike in the mountains? He had promised, but he'd forgotten. He'd immersed himself in his research too deeply, in some drama long passed. Why shouldn't the bicycle that Zala had ridden during the war turn up now in the Ljubljanica? It was an intriguing prospect, but he didn't exactly know what he meant to prove with it. He hadn't even been able to prove that the bicycle was mentioned in The Great Lover's memoirs. Even though he distinctly remembered a Presto or a Presta bicycle being mentioned somewhere. Had he read about the bicycle somewhere else? Did he dream it? Had a Puch bicycle also been mentioned, ridden by the young civil servant of the old Auersperg estate all over Lower Carniola during the war years of 1942 and '43, toward the end most frequently for long visits to the place where Zala the schoolteacher was living? Both bicycles would have to wait until Monday. He had promised Marijana they would go for a hike in the mountains today. So they went to the mountains. But on Monday, at lunch with his coworkers from the archive, he learned about a detail from Marijana's life that threw him off balance and for a while interrupted his research.

Precisely at that point in June when he was most deeply buried in his research, in the coincidences and intimations that stretched from wartime to the present day and back, from Presto and Puch bicycles to some memories from his youth, when he was nearly obsessed with the material into which he pushed deeper and deeper– it was precisely then that he again came back to Marijana, with whom he'd been living in peace and quiet for so many years that she'd become practically invisible. Actually, he almost crashed back into her when he learned a fact about her life that she'd never before whispered a word of.

Like everything else, it was easier for him to view her in the past tense than the present. Suppers of obligatory salads, hikes in the mountains—those are things that over time you can come not even to notice. Even the person keeping you company on those occasions can become invisible. But in the past the vacations on Dugi Otok, not to mention Zaglav, on the same island, turned out to be the most exciting events of their life together. Their first trip to Dugi Otok took place just after they had fallen in love, at the time when a deadly serious war was raging in Croatia. Almost as deadly serious as the one preserved in the documents from his archive. At Zaglav on Dugi Otok, at the bottom of some sheer cliff face, he had lifted her skirt. He saw her thighs in the moonlight and lifted her skirt, she turned around, and . . . this is where the great chronicler of erotic adventures would know how to go on, but not him, not Lipnik. He knows. The excitement is preserved in the depths of his memory: her heartbeat in the moonlit night, her moans, the laughter that followed.

The thought of Dugi Otok and of places with names like Božava, Brbinj, Telašćica, Sali or Zaglav was forever associated with that event. Even all these years later his heart would start beating faster whenever he remembered it. But it wasn't just the excitement associated with that night's passion—it was the scent of the pines, the sound of the waves splashing against the rocks, her tender skin drenched in moonlight. It was everything, everything. Maybe it was the most that had ever happened in his life.

After that spring when it all began, and after that tempestuous summer, nothing exciting ever happened in his life again, except maybe that episode with the peculiar postcard from Budapest, which to that day continued to puzzle him. Except for Zaglav on Dugi Otok, all the excitement and all the interest in Janez Lipnik's life was contained in the archive, in the documents that produced images of faces, landscapes, castles, military units, whole lives. Lives that he sometimes felt as intensely as though the people were still roaming around in his vicinity, at some vague remove, on the city outskirts, perhaps.

On that Monday, the last day of sunshine, he came crashing out of the past and out of his intimations into the present. On Saturday he'd seen the bicycle being pulled out of the Ljubljanica, and on Monday, an early summer day with the sun still shining as it had the lazy Saturday before, Janez Lipnik learned that his Marijana had lied to him. Maybe she hadn't actually lied, but just kept quiet about a certain detail from her past—but as far as he was concerned, that was the same thing as lying. And not just any detail, but one that affected him, because it had to do with their life together. It wasn't a joke, he didn't have an overproductive imagination, and he hadn't dreamed it.

13.

In the course of lunch with his fellow archivist, Beno, and the secretary, he learned of a detail from his wife's past that caused his eyes to glaze over for an instant. It was a sunny spring day that was almost as lazy as a day in summer, almost hot—indeed, it was a hot, humid day, because a storm was building and there was a pervasive stench coming from the garbage bins. On their plates, next to dirty heaps of wadded paper napkins were the remains of food, the remains of something that just a short while before had still looked quite appetizing, but now looked rather disgusting. The waiter refused to show up with their coffees, the men had taken off their jackets, and the secretary was putting lipstick on her plump, half-open mouth, in the process poking the nail of her little finger between two teeth to pry loose a bit of food.

"When I think about the sun shining on the surface of the sea, the gentle gusts of wind, maybe I wouldn't have to use the motor at all," his colleague Beno said.

"Nothing will come of it, Benjamin," the secretary said. "You'll drink your coffee so you don't fall asleep back at work and you'll sit at your desk until evening."

"Maybe I wouldn't have to use the motor at all," Benjamin said. "I'd row for a while, then I'd raise the mainsail and, ah, I can hear it catching the breeze, the sail fluttering, the boat shuddering ever so slightly, like a woman, and then it takes and we're off, sailing over the gently billowing sea."

"Like a woman?" the secretary puzzled and then took a silver powder case with a little mirror out of her bag.

An unpleasant odor came drifting over from the garbage can of the building next door. It stank of disintegrating food waste, bones, maybe even fish.

"Hey, Benjamin," she said. She always calls him Benjamin when she wants to tease him, otherwise she calls him Beno, which is his actual name. Hers is Nedeljka. "Hey, Benjamin," Nedeljka said as she began to powder her forehead, her other hand holding the tiny mirror out in front of her eyes, "I can tell spring is getting to you."

Janez Lipnik looked at his watch and signaled to the waiter, who was at the bar chatting with the barman. He doesn't see me, he thought. There's too much glare from the sun shining in through the window. Would he just bring that coffee already, he thought, and clear this mess off the table. I want to get back to my nice, cool office, or rather workroom—he hated the word office—where the cherry tree is still blossoming and there are folders of recently discovered documents from wartime lying on my nice, neat desk. He hadn't yet managed to identify the authors, nor even how those papers had found their way into the Australian collection. He wanted badly to be back up there. The different types of sails that Beno started talking about now didn't interest him, and that noxious smell of disintegrating organisms was wafting their way again.

"Back in the old days we'd head down there as early as spring," Beno was saying, "and sail as far as Kornati ... This job is killing me," he said. "I'm a man of the sea, not of the archives."

"We're going to Dugi Otok this year. Like we do every year."

Janez Lipnik said this because he had to say something. He didn't feel like hearing every last detail about sailing. Talk about sailing struck him as boring, the way women found men's conversations about where they'd spent their year of mandatory military service boring: What all they'd had to put up with, who had mistreated them, how adept they'd become at goofing off and drinking, who'd been the best shot and which of their buddies wound up with the woman they'd all been whistling at.

"Dugi Otok?" Beno said. "I was on Dugi Otok with Pepo. Let's see, what year was that? Definitely before the war in Croatia. So that would make it ..."

He couldn't remember what year it had been. You know Pepo. He's a policeman now, a detective. One night Pepo and I were having a beer after basketball. It was a spring day—or evening, a warm one—and Pepo just said, 'the boat is waiting.' That's all he said. Beno said nothing back, he just nodded and poured the rest of his beer into his glass—what was there to say, he knew what it meant if the boat was waiting, namely that there was nothing that could hold them back. Pepo said that they could invite someone else along, you sail by day and at night you drink a glass or two of wine with friends, you can't be such a fanatic about sailing that you don't take time to eat some nice fish and drink a glass of wine with friends. Beno was no such fanatic, and back then even less so, and he agreed, so they called up a couple of girls, one of them a fellow university student whose name he couldn't even remember, and the other was Marijana.

"Marijana who?" Janez Lipnik asked reflexively.

"Marijana. Not Marija Ana or Annamarija," Beno said. "There's only one Marijana. You know."

At the top of his stomach Janez Lipnik sensed a dull pain, as if somebody had punched him there with his fist, and a second later his eyes filmed over. Actually it was just a light veil, because he could see Nedeljka the secretary through it as she held out her compact, pressed her thick, thickly glossed lips together and examined herself in it.

"She never told you?" Nedeljka said.

Through the light veil he could see the waiter approaching with a tray. He's bringing coffee, he thought, and he's going to take this mess off the table. There was nothing else he could think.

"She probably told me," he said as insouciantly as he could, "I just forgot."

"He forgot," Nedeljka said. "All he thinks about is the archive."

He didn't forget. He would never have forgotten if she had told him that she had ever been on Dugi Otok before. Dugi Otok was their island, their story, rocky and sunny, beginning and end, alpha and omega.

"We had good winds but before we got to Dugi Otok a bonazza set in and the sea was like oil. We didn't drop anchor until eleven at night."

"At Dugi Otok?"

"Yeah. At Zaglav. There's a filling station there. That's where we usually fill up."

Lipnik wanted to say that he knew, he knew there was a filling station there that sailboaters used to fill up their tanks. Just in case the wind gave out. It was the year when there wasn't a single boat at Zaglav. Croatia was at war and Zaglav lay in silence. Near Zaglav there's a sheer cliff facing the water, he could point straight to the place.

"That's where Marijana jumped ashore in the dark," Beno said. "She slipped and twisted her ankle."

Beno made way for the waiter, who was reaching over his shoulder to set the cups of coffee down amid the dirty plates.

"That's right," Janez Lipnik said calmly. "How come I didn't remember that?"

"You didn't archive it," Nedeljka said, laughing loudly and almost unpleasantly. She had lipstick on her teeth.

"That's right," he said, also smiling. "I didn't archive it. That's all stuff from prehistory. We weren't yet married then," he added reflexively, as though he were trying to make an excuse for himself or possibly her, his one and only who twisted her ankle on the dock at Zaglav on Dugi Otok. But to get to that point two bored sailing enthusiasts had first had to give her a call after their evening basketball game. When—the night before? How long did it take to sail to Kornati?

He watched the waiter walking away from them and suddenly called out angrily, "Aren't you going to clean this up?"

The waiter nodded and vanished inside. Through the glass he could see him lean on the bar and resume his conversation with the barman. This made him furious. He got up and went inside.

"I asked you to clear that table off," he shouted. "And here you are lighting up a cigarette."

Both of them looked at him dumbfounded.

"And what's more, those garbage cans stink," he said, already calming down. No wonder garbage cans get thrown into the Ljubljanica. I'd throw them there, too. This thought reassured him somehow. You throw the garbage can in the river and so long, sucker.

He paid and left.

14.

When he sat back down at his desk in his quiet workroom, he pulled toward him the folder that had the words 'Conqueror' and 'Pervert' crossed out on it and replaced with the phrase 'The Great Lover.' He remembered that he'd been getting ready to find out what the Japanese word *skebe* means. The author of the memoir had visited Japan from Australia and several Japanese women had called him a *skebe*.

He shoved the folder back toward the edge of the desk. These pages with their meticulous writing suddenly didn't interest him anymore. Something else had entered his life. He turned the computer on to distract himself by browsing the web, finding some news, playing a game, anything at all. He noticed that his hands were shaking. Now what's this about, he wondered. Don't tell me it got to me. So what if she went sailing with them? Pepo's no *skebe*, Pepo's a policeman who works out night and day to build up those muscles, he doesn't have a thought in his head. Beno's the thinker, though not much of one, not at all after lunch, in fact, after lunch he puts his head down on his desk and takes a snooze. Maybe he's the *skebe*—he's such a lazy, useless archivist that he might as well be. What nonsense all this is. Marijana and one other girl whose name Beno can't even remember—maybe she was Pepo's, says something eating away inside him somewhere deep in his chest, causing a stinging sensation, maybe Pepo remembers her name, he's a detective, he remembers lots of names—Marijana and one other girl had gone sailing with the two of them, they stopped at Dugi Otok, and what of it? That was back before the two of them had even met. That was in the age they both referred to as prehistory. Their meeting in the university's main lecture hall had been Day One, and their history together commenced from then; everything that went before, all their previous relationships, all the men and all the women who had passed through their lives before Day One were just prehistory. The men she had been with—and there weren't many of them. The women he had met at the jazz club and taken home—there hadn't been many of them, either. Of course on occasion they talked about what had gone before—it's good to know about those things, lovers want to know everything about each other so that later they can magnanimously forgive each other and say, that was before, it doesn't matter, what's important is now, since you and I have been together, that's the only real history, ours. What he had learned at lunch wasn't their history, it was from before—but still, it ate at him. A brief, dull pain at the top of his stomach, as though he'd been punched there. And now this thing was gnawing away at him, nibbling somewhere inside his chest. We don't investigate prehistory, we don't ask questions about it, we don't have a right and there's no point, prehistory is the period for which we have no written record, no diaries, letters; it is the dark ages, farther, even farther back, the murk of the Pleistocene, no more than a postcard here and there reaching us from out of the Pleistocene murk. Day One is the advent of light, faithfulness, integrity. Beginning with Day One every event gets documented and photographed, dates are put on the backs of the photos, a note as to what town or village, all the vacations taken together, the one on Dugi Otok the most important of all, that night at Zaglav. And then the monotonous hikes in the mountains, the suppers of salads, reading in bed. Beginning on Day One all of it gets written onto your memory, from the first kiss and the first (hotel) bed to your life together, all the smiles, all the touches, all the little kindnesses, and the tears, and the illnesses, all the misunderstandings and the infrequent fights. Things that happened before Day One did not get documented, somehow the photographs had vanished, the keepsakes and letters, too, then even the memories slowly vanished, and if they did suddenly turn up, they got shoved back into the fog of obscurity, or at least insignificance. They had never talked about prehistory and it was good that way. Janez Lipnik knew it was good that way, you have to treat archival materials reasonably, scientifically, from a distance. It can be dangerous if they get touched, living people crawl out of them, injured souls, mortal sins, illness and death in obscure locations. He knew it was good this way, because he dealt with it every day. I can't, he would often say, I can't let these things affect me.

That Monday afternoon the sex addict's memoirs remained untouched. His experiences were displaced into some unidentified, less interesting past. While other people merely lived through the war, he fucked his way through it. That's what Beno had said when he confided in him about his discovery, 'That guy just fucked his way through the war.' And what of it? He did the same thing after the war. Why should that concern archivist Lipnik at the beginning of the new century and millennium? There were other questions suddenly starting to concern him a lot more: Who is Marijana? Who is the woman he's been living with all these years? What does he really know about her, compared to all he knows about the fates of others, stored in the collections of the Regional Archive?

He took a long walk through the park. He glanced at the bronze statue of a lithe, naked woman that he'd never noticed before. Somebody had taken red paint to her metal breasts, her dainty tits and her crotch. Why? Why had they done that? What sort of message was this? It occurred to him that he asked too many questions. What if, contrary to his convictions until now, it was impossible to answer them all? What if there was no need to answer all the questions that plague a person? Questions take a person back somehow, they lead you back in a circle, ultimately back to yourself. But as long as you're still traveling along the circumference of the circle you don't realize it yet. Why should that bicycle from the Ljubljanica be the same as the one some schoolteacher had ridden during the war? Or at least have any connection to him, who just happened to be walking by on the embankment as it was being lifted up out of the water, covered with algae? Why did it have to mean anything at all—the bicycle dangling from a crane, the aquatic plant growth entangling the bike, like history submerged in water, the water of forgetfulness, that slime, that shroud of algae. He sat down on a bench and buried his head in his hands. He wasn't going to ask her, he wasn't going to ask Marijana. He wasn't going to rack his brain over that bike, he wasn't going to rack his brain.

He wouldn't let this racket eat his brain, he would not let his heartbeats rock his skull, the muddle of the world was not going to overwhelm him. The world is governed by order, just like an archive. It can all be explained, it all has its place.

He tried to lose himself in some other reading, a real, live bit of the world's muddle that had been waiting a long time for his attention. In a folder labeled 'Studenec' there were assembled the papers of some woman who had been a nurse's aide in the mental hospital commonly known as Studenec, simply because that was the name of the town where it was located. But everyone in this country knew what it meant if someone said 'They took him to Studenec.' It meant that he was insane and that he'd been locked up in an insane asylum. The papers were painful to read. They would have been painful for anyone except Janez Lipnik. Apparently they had been written just after the war, when memory was still fresh and vulnerable, these papers from an insane asylum in wartime—as though the war itself hadn't been insane asylum enough, as if the whole world hadn't been turning into an insane asylum—written by a woman just widowed, her husband murdered. Who was the murderer of her husband, what was his name, she asked in her entries, and even Janez Lipnik would have liked to know. But better not. If you know the name of a murderer, it just hurts, it affects you, and he did not, decidedly did not, want to have anything affect him— people killed each other during the war, who doesn't know that? His job was to identify the person who had left these papers behind, and if in the process he discovered who killed her husband, then fine. If you're going to deal with these things, you have to maintain a cool distance from them, a scholarly distance, a rational distance, if you didn't want the whole business to suck you in.

15.

It was the same sort of distance that he tried to take toward that information from Marijana's prehistory—which was the only reasonable and honest thing to do. So on to find some peaceful music, but everywhere the wild sounds of throbbing rhythms and pushy ads boomed out of the speakers. He felt like he was looking at soiled, wadded-up paper napkins on dirty plates with food scraps, and his nostrils picked up the disgusting smell of that garbage bin standing on the hot spring asphalt. He saw Beno chatting with the waiter at the bar, where he'd stopped on his way to the men's room. The two of them were looking through the glass at him, but why? He heard his voice, 'Didn't she tell you?' She hadn't told him, but why? Because it was from prehistory. He got up again and went to the window and that flowering tree was outside—what sort of tree flowers at this time of year? At the seaside the trees flower earlier than this, at the seaside, at the seaside, on Dugi Otok, the thing eating away at him repeated, it was on Dugi Otok, at Zaglav that she twisted her ankle. When she jumped onto the dock she twisted her ankle. Was she carried into the house, and who carried her? Pepo, the muscular policeman, or that lazy archivist Beno? Now he felt another punch to that area over his stomach and he felt a sort of emptiness down in his guts, even with today's lunch still gurgling through them. He had the impression that the parquet floor was slipping just slightly out from under his feet. She'd been on Dugi Otok, but it was precisely on Dugi Otok that she told him she'd never been there before. It's a fine island, she said, like some stone boat, she said, I've never been on an island like this. He gripped onto the windowsill. Why had she kept that from him? What happened on that sailing trip that she kept it from him? They may not have talked about prehistory, but that didn't mean that they lied to each other about it. One was aware, in very general terms, of people and events that had passed through each of their lives before Day One. But that event was nowhere. Even in general terms, the event didn't exist. And neither did Beno or Pepo—and who was this Pepo, anyway? Beno works a floor down from him, next to the office of the director of the Regional Archive, but who was Pepo, except a policeman, a detective, maybe even Pepi, for all he knew—what did he know about Beno's friend, whom he'd only seen twice in his life? If we've heard right, neither one appears in a single document or a single memoir—there simply is no trace in any nook or corner of the archive of Beno and Pepo—fine names, admittedly, just the right ones for a couple of sailing fanatics. There was no sailing in his and Marijana's history, or in the history of the rocky island, there was no twisted ankle, or island, or even the trace of an island anywhere. He thought about how this Benjamin sitting a floor down from him was, despite the coffee, nodding off at his desk, because he was not a man of the archives. He was maybe a man of the sea, but he was no archival worm, even though he did work in one. Now Lipnik, there was an archival worm, and everybody knew that he was, even he had at one time referred to himself as *Blatta germanica, Periplanetta Americana*—he, Lipnik, was an *Anobium*, in common parlance a beetle, a borer, a bookworm. Bookworms ate books and archival material. Beno was no Lipnik and he wasn't an archival insect, he was a sea wolf, *Carcharodon carcharias*, he used the archive for sleeping, not for endless research delving through long past events, people and destinies. For research he had the sea, what else could a sea wolf want? This Benjamin, who thinks only of sailing and never the archive, who has no sense of discipline, perhaps this Benjamin had mixed some things up or even lied. He was supposed to believe that she, Marijana, just got up and went? In response to a phone call from Pepo or Beno? He couldn't make that fit with his image of her. And even if it was prehistory, it didn't work, it wasn't possible that she packed up her things and went sailing with two guys. And even if she did, if it was neither a mistake nor a lie, what did they do there, on that little sailboat, at a time when everybody had some little boat or other—where did they wash up, where did they go to the toilet, did each of them sleep in a separate cabin, or what? And if they did double up, then who went with whom? Had Marijana bunked with Beno's (unidentified—we don't even know her name) friend from the university, or had Beno's friend slept in the same cabin as Beno, because in that case Pepo (likewise an unidentified stranger), a detective by profession, would have slept where Marijana did. As a matter of fact, he thought to himself, 'How come we don't know the friend's name?' Marijana's friend's name was Jana. Only Jana could have agreed to go on the spur of the moment, the way Marijana had. Because their signals passed on the same wavelength. At least this question was solved. It had been Jana. The sender of signals and their receiver got along well, and it didn't matter in this case which of them was the receiver and which the sender. Only two people who are close, who have some shared secret in their past history, some base secret, can joke like that: *I know you'll be envious. I rode on a bus that was full of drunken Hungarian soldiers.* At least that was clear, but what wasn't clear was who slept with whom. For them to have all slept separately was out of the question. Unless they had four separate rooms, which was unlikely. And even if they did, they still had to go out on the island for meals, to drink wine, to laugh, to look at the moonlight reflected on the sea—and all of that, all of that and most likely everything else, too, was supposed to just vanish into prehistory?

Janez Lipnik knew that it would be best if he could just close the book on all of this—years ago (how many years, what month was it?) four young people had gone sailing. Period. No period, at least we could know when, what year, what month, who the other woman was, the friend from the university, we could at least clarify all of these things, even though we're reasonably certain it was Jana, the author of the postcard from Budapest, who had taken an intercity bus from Szentendre with a bunch of Hungarian soldiers and endured their oily, insinuating remarks, even if she didn't understand them, since Hungarian soldiers would be speaking Hungarian. But we have to clear up whether the other woman was Jana or not before we say period. Off Dugi Otok they lost the wind, a young woman twisted her ankle while jumping ashore from a boat in a harbor called Zaglav, and she just happened to be the woman who later became his wife. Period. It would be good, but he knew that it wasn't possible. When the two of them had first traveled to Dugi Otok, during their nicest vacation of all, she said she had never been there before.

You couldn't just close the book on that. That wasn't prehistory. Things began mounting up dangerously in his head.

16.

That evening he watched her making the salad for dinner, a steady, predictable woman, healthy food. Next she'll go to her workroom to get her notes ready for tomorrow's lecture, he thought, and again he thought that maybe he should try to hold back, pass over, forget this thing just as soon as possible, this perhaps insignificant discovery from prehistory. But the thing was stronger than he was, and he asked if she remembered when they were on Dugi Otok. She said it was when the war was still on in Croatia, why was he asking? He was just trying to figure out if it was 1995 or '94. I think it was '94, she said, setting a bowl of salad down on the table. Get the plates, she said. Why do you ask? How do people ever write their memoirs, he began thinking out loud, if he can't even remember the year when the war was still raging in Croatia—while on his desk at the archive lay the memoirs of people who remember every detail, every woman?

"Don't you remember every woman?" Marijana said.

He heard her question clearly as he was taking the plates out of the kitchen cabinet. We used to call these credenzas, he thought, it wasn't a cabinet, it was a credenza. In his childhood there had been a clock ticking away on the credenza. On the credenza? Does anybody know that word anymore? It doesn't exist anymore, just as that kitchen cabinet with the plates and soup bowls and various other long-lost things showing through the stained glass no longer exist, the same way that credenza and its name were gone, things kept disappearing and words disappeared. And the word 'credenza' contained an entire childhood. Occasionally words and things held on longer. 'Hope chest' or 'devotional nook' held on for whole centuries.

"Did you ever hear the word credenza?" he asked when he entered the living room.

"You didn't answer my question," she said.

He said he remembered how sometimes they heard sequences of dull thuds coming from over the mountains, from the mainland all the way to the island, and he often thought, 'Listen, that's people killing each other.' Because what would be the point of the thudding if they weren't killing each other. Surely they weren't loading heavy howitzers and firing them off just at random, while the two of them sunbathed, swam, took walks around the island, drank wine on warm evenings, and looked for fresh fish which was nowhere to be found, most likely because nobody went out fishing in wartime. There were also no motorboats or sailboats. Why do you suppose they kept pushing toward the sea during the war in Croatia? Because they wanted to break through to the sea and nowhere else. It's a question of ethics, she said sometime later, how did it not occur to us that just to the north, not far from the island, there were murders and rapes being committed? They were in love, what did they care about the war, they didn't want to hear about it, love is its own highest ethic.

He remembered that, but he didn't remember the year, '95 or '94, he did remember it was early August but the island was quiet— there had never been such quiet on the island at that time of year. He remembered their black humor about it, we'll always have to come here while there's a war on, but what if they run out of them soon? At any rate the war was far away, even though they sometimes heard it rumbling in the distance, maybe they're blowing something up, even if Croatian MPs were guarding every bridge in the country.

She said it was '94.

"You've got a good memory."

She sat down at the table and bowed over her plate as though she were about to pray. She never prayed and now was no different.

"I remember," she said, "because that was the last time I was pregnant."

He remained silent. He thought there was probably no need to go on now, maybe some other time. They didn't have children, even though they had wanted to have them. That hurt.

He got a beer out of the refrigerator, and she raised her head and looked at him. He never drank in the evenings, for that matter he didn't drink much at all, maybe a glass now and then with lunch. He used to drink a lot, too much. That's why she watched as he poured the beer into his glass and drank it greedily.

"Is anything wrong?" she said.

17.

Once they were in bed she read for a time, while he lay on his side and looked out the window, toward the sound of the nighttime rain, toward the beads of water creeping down the panes.

She set her book aside.

"What's come of that pornographer of yours?" she asked.

"He's not a pornographer."

"All right, the pervert. Have you figured out who he was?"

"It's looking like he was a soldier. He might have survived the siege of Turjak."

"I can't believe he was a soldier. When would he have had time to get all those women into bed if he had to shoot and retreat and do all the other things soldiers do?"

He explained to her that the soldiering came later, that he hadn't gotten all those women into bed in wartime, that during the war there was just the one. A few came before, but mostly after the war, in Trieste, in Rome, in Australia, Japan.

She said that all of a sudden here he was dealing with the war and some man's perversions. War is violence and perversion borders on violence. It's not good for him to be dealing with that.

Ah, Marijana. She always understood everything. And she knew how to explain things. Except for one thing. One day she'll explain it. She'll have to. His head won't be able to take it otherwise.

He said that people are said to experience exceptionally strong sexual desire in wartime. Who knows why that is. The sense that you may have to die? The survival instinct? Wanton abandon? I don't know. I read the account of a Jew who was being transported in a cattle car to Auschwitz. The car was packed full. A young woman was standing in front of him—he couldn't even see her face, because she had her back turned toward him. Somewhere out amid the plains of Poland, at four in the morning while half of the people dozed on their feet and the other half dozed crouching down, she started to move in front of him. He could feel her rubbing her rear against him. He was overcome with desire. She lifted her skirt and tried to bend forward, so he could approach her from behind. They fucked their way towards death—both assumed for the last time. He survived. It's not known if that turned out to be her last time or if some SS man assigned her to the camp brothel. In any case, she didn't survive.

"Does that make sense?"

"Of course ... I can't talk about it, it's too horrible. I can talk about Dugi Otok. We were on Dugi Otok during a war."

"Yeah?"

"Mhm. It was a real war, too, with artillery thundering on the other side of Velebit."

"That was our first time on Dugi Otok ... That was the first time for both of us, wasn't it?"

He had the impression she didn't hear this, something that she absolutely needed to hear.

"You and I didn't ... like you just said ... toward death. It was nice. There was the sound of the sea and at night the moon shining down onto the rocks and the water. And the seagulls each morning."

"He—my erotic chronicler—started in Lower Carniolan Springs. Do you remember the tree-lined road there? You and I hiked around there once. That's exactly where he would take walks with some schoolteacher. There were Italian officers staying at the hotel."

"Believe me, he was no soldier. A woman knows these things."

"How do they know them?"

"We sense them."

"How do you sense them?"

She didn't answer.

"He was a *skebe*. Do you know what that is? A womanizer, a la-dy's man. Explain to me, Marijana, how is it that women give in to these *skebe*s so quickly? What was it about him, what did he have that so many women wanted to jump into bed with him?"

"Maybe some special essence."

"What's that supposed to mean?"

"I don't know. Some invisible essence that binds a woman to a man."

"The kind that we had on Dugi Otok, that kind of essence? That kind of invisible essence?"

"That's right."

"Dugi Otok was our discovery, wasn't it?"

"Yes. I think I want to read just a little bit more now."

"Go ahead," he said gruffly. "Who's stopping you?"

She ran her fingers through his hair.

"What's wrong with you?" she said. "Don't tell me something's the matter?"

"Nothing's the matter," he said.

There are certain things she doesn't understand, that's what's the matter. On his desk at work he has the memoirs of some people from wartime. One set is from a mental hospital, left behind by some woman, which he'd come across entirely by accident. Love in wartime. Eros. Insanity in wartime. The Studenec psychiatric hospital ... He's unable to identify her, the file he found it in is some kind of financial affair that has no relation to her. The second is a notebook that some man used to record his erotic experiences. During the war and afterward he records which women he's laid and how—what was a person supposed to make of that? A lust for life? Or fear of death? The author of that memoir is unfindable, too, it's unlikely he'll ever be able to find him—he was an officer who might have been at Turjak during the siege. Purportedly he broke through the partisan encirclement on his motorcycle, one with a sidecar. Just before that he shot an Italian officer to death. Was that officer Guido Gambini, the same person involved in the shootings of innocent villagers? They would drop to their knees and beg for their lives. His soldiers were bad shots, so Lieutenant Gambini had to walk from one to the other and shoot them in the back of the neck. Outside Turjak he got his own gunshot straight in the forehead. A single shot fired by a motorcyclist on the rampage.

Is the officer Aleksij Grgurevič, whose name we find on a list of some unit of the His Majesty's Army, also the author of the erotic chronicle spanning nearly half a century? By now he's probably dead, or at best barely alive somewhere abroad.

"What does that have to do with Dugi Otok?"

Nothing. Some people lived full lives and left nothing, but nothing behind. Except for these memoirs. And even there it's impossible to establish whose they are. This scares him, this sense that things completely disappear, that things submerge in time and even the memory of them vanishes, leaving just sheets of paper with handwriting on them. How was he supposed to fit these into reality?

She said that it was all just archival material and he shouldn't take it so personally.

Archival material. Fine, we'll let it just be archival material. But what kind of archival material is stored there, behind her forehead, framed in the dark curls of her soft hair.

He said he was going out for a walk.

"Come back soon," she said. "I'll read for a while longer."

18.

Everything was so ordinary—a typical evening: Marijana would continue to read for a while, tomorrow she had lectures to give, while he would go out for a walk. When he got back, she'd already be asleep, the light would be on and the book would be sprawled over her belly, as it gently rose with her regular breathing. Tomorrow they would have breakfast and it would be a new day. Tomorrow he would return to his archival material and dig into it, perhaps he would get lucky and identify one or both of the authors. This research was becoming just a shade obsessive. He sensed that coincidence, also known as fate, had pressed something into his hands that he had to get to the bottom of—if not the actual people and faces, then their names at least. There was no way he could push them aside onto the dead letter shelf, these people had lived, they'd had faces and names, even if they had disappeared in the veil of time, in the nameless past of some distant war. Except for archivists, nobody cared about that war anymore, or the people whose lives it had changed or, quite simply, brutally ended. And not every archivist, at that, his colleague Beno didn't care, all he could think about was getting away to the seaside and sailing. To Dugi Otok. With his, Lipnik's wife. With Marijana. He'd been there with her when she hadn't yet become his wife. When she said that this was her first time on Dugi Otok. He, Janez Lipnik, had also been with her on Dugi Otok at a time when she wasn't his wife yet. When she said that this was her first time on Dugi Otok. There was a war on then, too, but the two of them hardly noticed. Why, when he had practically not noticed that war, was he becoming so obsessed with memoirs from some other, far more distant war? Maybe because he had been in love and incapable of noticing anything at all—how could he have noticed there was a war on down there? It was soon after their Day One. The island was almost deserted and only a handful of clueless or amorous tourists—like them—were sunning themselves on the beaches of the island's deserted inlets. It was as quiet and peaceful as at the Creation.

Janez Lipnik stopped on the sidewalk. His attention was absorbed by a gigantic billboard set up along the side wall of a big building: some nearly naked girls in swimsuits were advertising sunscreen as well as their own smooth, bronzed skin. There was a war on, he thought, yet we would sit up late over wine, gazing into each other's eyes. We prowled through every church and chapel and we had roast lamb in a village in the middle of the island. Then, in a totally quiet inlet, this jet ski came roaring by and the man driving it started describing big circles over the waves, and it made them so angry because it destroyed the quiet of the warm afternoon. They didn't notice the war. Whenever guns started to rumble over the mountains on the mainland, they would look at each other, and he would say that something was probably getting blown up. What else was he supposed to say—seriously, what? That people were getting killed over there? Even though he knew, of course, that people get killed in wars, with cannons, explosives, rifle shots and machine gun fire, most of which were inaudible from that great a distance. They refused to hear the war, but then were enraged by the incursion of some noisy jet skier. The newspapers featured reports from the battlefields, radio announcers would start with news of bombardments and raids on cities in the interior, and all of it had been going on for some years now, becoming monotonous and remote. The only thing that really reminded him of the war were the 'Serbian houses.' A 'Serbian house' was a building that had collapsed. Over wine some local had explained to Lipnik the difference between Croatian and Serbian houses. Until then Janez Lipnik had assumed that the people around here fought over linguistic or cultural differences or the devil knows what age-old hatred and that evil kept visiting itself on them. Evil. He imagined it as some invisible cloud circling over the earth, seeking out places with hatred steaming up out of the landscape, there to alight.

The cloud of evil. Now he started to think they were fighting over different architectural traditions, as well. But he was wrong. There was no difference in the way their houses were built, or at least not nearly as much as there was in their speech, their faiths, their historical traditions. In the twentieth century Serbs and Croats built the same sort of houses and, in Dalmatia's most recent period of prosperity, fueled by tourism, both groups built houses that were needlessly huge, with various towers and turrets and fanciful columns. The difference wasn't in how they were built, but how they were destroyed. A 'Serbian house' was one that had the roof still nearly intact, while everything else was practically demolished. That, explained his guide in the bar over a pitcher of the local red, is because our guys dynamited the foundations, the house would collapse, and if the workmanship was good, the roof was left whole. A 'Croatian house,' on the other hand, was destroyed from the air, its roof blown to bits. That's the renowned artillery of the famous Yugoslav People's Army at work for you, advancing toward Zadar. Their shells landed on the roofs of Croatian houses, but left the Serbian ones intact. The Yugoslav army had good gunners who didn't just fire at random. Still, they had to retreat as the Croatian army advanced with its excellent sappers.

Whenever they saw the locals engaged in their morning gossip and noisy, boisterous greetings, everything really did seem far away, even if it sometimes sounded close by. Nobody takes this war seriously, Marijana had said.

In Ljubljana people are living as though nothing were happening, and it's even like that in Zagreb.

19.

Even so, it was the war that caused them to leave. One strange morning both of them woke up around five and decided on the spot to go watch the sunrise. The rocky island shone in the red morning sunlight, a gentle breeze wafted through Marijana's hair, and it was lovely. Then they drove into town for coffee, noticing an unusually large number of military vehicles on the way and finding the town crawling with uniformed men. He turned on the radio. The offensive of the Croatian army and police forces is proceeding according to plan, the radio reported, the enemy's defensive lines have been broken along all major lines of attack, seven hundred and sixty enemy combatants have been taken prisoner, and large amounts of explosives and military equipment have been seized. They advised people not to go out on the roads and to listen to their radios, which would give them all the information they needed. That was too much. Now the war was approaching the island, so they left. Suddenly it turned out there were more tourists on the island than it had seemed. All of the roads were backed up, and then it looked like the ferry wasn't going to run because of the risk of mortar fire and the fact that the Serbs outside Zadar were already targeting ferries. Then the ferry started running even so, and when they reached the mainland, they saw their first 'Croatian houses.'

After long traffic jams they arrived home on a peaceful Ljubljana morning. The end result seemed more like arriving home from vacation than from a war.

He would forget about Dugi Otok. Dugi Otok is the past enshrouded in fog, in the kind of veil that dropped over his eyes after lunch. On the sidewalk he dodged a group of noisy young men and women equipped with bottles, and on a pedestrian crosswalk he had to jump back when a car ran the red light—but are we supposed to forget all that? Whatever we don't like about the past, whatever is inconvenient, whatever might even hurt and cause pain in your chest—are we just supposed to forget? Those manuscript memoirs lie on his desk there, he's been taking pains to figure out who might have written them, to become familiar with the material, to reconstruct the outlines of the people and events, and here he was supposed to force something that was his life—some life that had entered his life—into oblivion? The problem was that she was apparently able to do that. A person who lies about the past can lie about the present. What did he know about how Marijana led her life? Days would go by when they didn't see each other. It occurred to him to go through her drawers, yes, even her shoulder bag and notebook, maybe he would come across some significant phone number—Beno's? Or Pepo's, and who is that guy, anyway? Beno had said he worked for the police, so did this mean Marijana was fraternizing with policemen? To his left flashed the headlights of cars, and to his right illuminated store windows. Janez Lipnik walked through the nighttime city faster and faster as his determination grew to clear up this business tonight. He couldn't leave the question unasked, it kept coming back, and he knew in advance how the conversation would go. He'd enter her workroom—no, he'd sit down next to her on the bed and say, 'At supper I asked you something about Dugi Otok and when the war was in Croatia—do you remember me asking you?' She'll set her book aside and look at him with her dark eyes, he'll ask her why she never wears the pajamas she wore on Dugi Otok. No, he thought, we'll never get anywhere that way. There's just one way. He'll ask, 'When we were on Dugi Otok, you said that you'd never been on Dugi Otok before.' She'll be silent. Since she won't answer, he'll ask again, 'Were you ever on Dugi Otok before, Marijana, without me?' She'll be silent, as though she doesn't understand the question. So he'll ask straight out, 'Let me ask this straight out. Were you ever, at any time before our vacation on Dugi Otok in 1994 or '95—whichever was the last year of the war in Croatia—were you ever on Dugi Otok before then?'

She'll nod. He won't ask any more questions, as no details will be needed. Thank you, he'll say. That's all, and the thing will be done. Although it's precisely the details that would put this business to rest once and for all. If only she would just start talking. If only she would say who she was with on Dugi Otok, perhaps she'd remember the name of the friend that Beno can't seem to dredge up—there'd been so many of them on his boat that he couldn't remember any of their names—doesn't this woman understand how humiliating all this is for her—for her, not just for him? So it would only be right if she would admit to everything straight out, the whole story, how all it took was a phone call for her to pack herself and her luggage into some car and head off for a sailing vacation with two guys, how they had suppers, drank wine, looked at the moonlight, how they swam—no, there was no swimming, this was in spring—how the lot of them had—but how was Janez Lipnik supposed to know what goes on on a boat, he'd never been sailing. But he did know—and this he had heard about many times—that there were hygienic issues on boats—bathing, going to the toilet, and so on, and that there were nighttime noises—snoring and so on—that when it came to lovemaking, not to mention copulating, it got awkward for the others who had to listen to it—the male grunting, the female moaning—indeed, screaming sometimes, which was impossible to suppress even if the woman put her hand over her mouth, the way Marijana had in that hotel on Pohorje where the walls were so thin—Marijana! This is her we're talking about, Marijana, not just any woman that they scooped off the street with some phone call and drove to the sea.

Janez Lipnik stopped barreling down the street and paused. He wouldn't ask her for any details. No thanks, he'd say, he wouldn't even ask who she was there with. Even though each new day at work would remind him who she'd been with. And if he didn't recall on his own, he'd be reminded by that bored fellow at lunch, or over coffee as Nedeljka the secretary applies a fat layer of lipstick to her fat lips, when her lips, turned up derisively at the corner where they meet, where too much lipstick has gathered, say, 'I guess you didn't archive that, did you?' He won't ask her why she went, he won't ask who she was there with, the only thing he'll ask will be, 'Why didn't you tell me?' You were watching that sailboat, the only one out there, as it sailed past, now I remember, you were watching that sailboat with a dreamy look in your eye.

I wasn't thinking about any sailboat then, she'll say. There was a war on. If I was thinking anything at all, it was what did we think we were doing taking a vacation there, with the war on, and we were out sunbathing? Not only that, we got angry at that jet skier who came roaring into our inlet. The artillery barrages over the mountains didn't bother us, but that jet skier did, that's what I was thinking about, he thought. I have no idea what she was thinking about. Maybe she was thinking that her ankle still hurt. The one she twisted when she jumped from the sailboat onto shore. There are no oil spills or twisted ankles in dreams or fictional stories. She probably slipped because some oil had been spilled on those smooth rocks that they have in harbors. The first time she was on that island, the one she'd supposedly never been on before. Somebody helped her that time—strong masculine arms carried her back onto the boat and bandaged her ankle. Lucky thing that she twisted her ankle, because otherwise she might think she had dreamed it, or I had dreamed it, but an ankle is unforgiving, it hurts for real and reminds you of reality. If only it weren't for that ankle, he might have been able to put it behind him. As it is, here he is wandering through the city by night, with fewer and fewer people out and fewer and fewer cars. A train rumbled by on a railroad overpass and he could see a handful of lone travelers sitting at its windows. It occurred to him it would be nice to get away somewhere.

20.

When he got home Marijana was asleep. He sat down on the bed next to her and looked at her in the faint light cast over her from the living room. Her eyelids twitched now and then—she was probably dreaming. He didn't want to think she was dreaming about sailing, instead he thought about how his life with Marijana was the only life he had. After all these years he still loved her just as much as on Day One and he couldn't imagine a life without her. It was nice on Dugi Otok. One evening when the island was bathed in moonlight, she said, 'It's like being on the moon, there are no trees, only these silvery rocks.' She knew how to speak beautifully, my sweet professor—it wasn't for nothing she read all those English novels, she's probably saying something beautiful now, even as she sleeps. She said, 'This island is like some stone ship and it's like we're sailing on it—I've never been on an island like this before.' Never? On one like this? Maybe what she meant by that was ... But Janez Lipnik was too tired to follow the trail of yet another one of these speculations. Instead, he noticed some strange music, like a brass band playing beneath their window, and he thought that maybe he'd left the radio on in the living room, but he hadn't, he knew that he hadn't. It was as though this music with its metallic overtones was coming from some huge room—yes, back on the island, in that little town, on a quiet evening they hear the sound of a brass band and they head in the direction of the music, of the horns, the drums and cymbals. The sounds of a march being practiced by the local orchestra come out of an old building, some sort of community center, out through its windows. And the pauses, the voice of the bandleader giving instructions, or rapping his conductor's baton on the lectern, his voice so alone in the evening air, and the beats of the drum so alone when the conductor tells him to do something special, just the drum, just the drum and any second now: the cymbals, Bang, he says, and in come the trumpets, No, not like that, and he makes all of them stop, then talks for a long time in the huge empty space. The bandleader's voice in the big auditorium talking into the silence, with the bleachers pushed back to the walls, the players sitting in chairs, listening, their instruments in their laps. Now from the top, he says, and again the trumpets and horns boom mightily. They're playing an old march, they're playing 'We Builders,' he says. Isn't their repertory a little dated, she says, isn't that some old communist march? It is strange, he says, for them to play that now. And suddenly he takes her hand — 'What's wrong?' Marijana asks. I feel so anxious, he says. I just remembered something. Freedom's key, freedom's key.

The past is anxiety. As children we sang it in school, he says. '… and bright sparks from our hammers will shape our freedom's glee, our freedom's glee.' My God, how long ago was that?

Her name was also Zala. Zala D. She would make a sign in his notebook, a checkmark that looked like a big V that they called the 'seenit.' It meant that she'd seen it.

21.

He's still sitting on that bench between the Benetton display window on one side and a Philips window on the other. He sits there with the shoppers walking past him, immersed in his story that reaches backward and forward, upward and down, in the unforgiving present where time is just an illusion.

The seconds on the gigantic digital clock hanging over the intersection of the huge shopping center's two promenades speed toward seven o'clock. But despite the fact that the numbers marking seconds are flashing red and speeding through the minutes to the point that will mark two hours since Marijana left, time here stands still. The flashing numbers are just surface appearance—this is clear to Lipnik at last—just an illusion of time, which does not in fact move. Wherever it does move, an anxious evening casts long shadows over the landscape. Here there are no shadows and no landscape, here it's eternally noon. With sounds from the loudspeakers, with the rhythmic sounds of something they call music, the quiet passage of people walking, the naked, bloodless, hairless mannequin with the artificial blush on her face leaning up against the display window, looking at him with empty eyes. The people walking past him also have empty eyes that wander over the bright surfaces without knowing where they're actually going or where they've come from. Somewhere out there is home, and we have to drag food and clothing, cosmetic and fragrant substances back into it, but that sort of home is no different from what cavemen had—the troglodytes guarded their fresh chunks of meat and useful found objects, dragging them into their lairs and giving no heed to the morrow or the day before. Because there are no shadows there, it's always noon, with no before or after, just now, a motionless, shiny, grunting, crunching now. Janez Lipnik gets up several times and walked past the display windows—there's nothing here to excite him, there's no anxious or even interesting past here. What does he keep clinging to this big, noisy, ever unchanging present for? Nothing that happens here will find its way into any archive, none of it will excite any archivist fifty years from now, there's no past here and no future, either, because tomorrow will be exactly the same as today, history has come to a stop here for good, the Earth has stopped rotating. If it did rotate, it couldn't be flat. And this place was flat as far as the eye could see—bright, flat, motionless, with a multitude of lost people, people who've lost track of their yesterday and their tomorrow. They've lost the sky, because that up there is just a glass roof with the rain sliding down it, that up there is a cupola of clouds motionlessly covering this vast flat expanse. Even the jet ski is gone from his head, leaving something hollow and empty, something a lot like nothing.

Out of the corner of his eye he notices an elderly couple who have stopped next to his bags. They say something to each other, point to the bags, look around. Lipnik goes over, sits down and opens one of the bags so the couple will understand this is his bag. And indeed they understand. Wordlessly they begin to look around at various store entrances and try to figure out where to go next.

He too should figure out where to go next. To all appearances Marijana will not be returning. A misunderstanding? Has she gone home? There's nothing left for him here. And there's nothing left for him at the archive, either.

22.

A few days before the director had called him into his office.

"We've received some serious complaints," he said without any preliminaries. "Because you've failed to produce any evidence, people can't claim their property. Then there are the inheritance claims. These are serious issues, Mr. Lipnik."

He said that he'd been busy with the Australian collection lately. He was making an inventory of the documents. He'd discovered some records that needed to be examined.

The director said that the Australian collection could wait.

"It can't wait," Lipnik said.

"You don't make the decisions about what can and can't wait," the director said.

He said that he, Lipnik, had always done outstanding work and that all these years there had been no serious complaints. He, the director, was happy that Lipnik came in evenings and sometimes even weekends. But what he was actually doing no one knew. Customers were waiting for their evidence. There are serious issues at stake, issues of denationalization and inheritance.

"You already said that," Lipnik said. "The part about the serious issues."

The director tapped a pencil on his desk and was silent for a while. Then he said that he had no intention of interfering with his private life, but perhaps he was having some difficulties in his private life? It was of no concern to him, all he wanted was for the work to get done. And although it was of no concern to him, he still had to ask, "What's going on with you, Lipnik?"

Lipnik was silent. Should something be going on with him?

"I don't know," he said. "Should something be going on?"

How should he know if something should be going on with him when he didn't even know if Marijana had been to Dugi Otok before him, without him, and with some other people, or if that dolt Beno had just invented the whole thing? He couldn't get to the bottom of it. He couldn't even determine if Aleksij the officer and the young civil servant were one and the same person. They could be, but then again they might not be. He didn't even know if Zala the schoolteacher had ridden a Presto bicycle and if that algae-caked bicycle with the broken spokes that had been hauled up out of the Ljubljanica before his very eyes, that bicycle that was like some crippled memory, like history lost under water and river silt, had anything to do with events of fifty years ago or at least with the strange coincidence that he, Archivist Lipnik, precisely then, at that moment when they were hauling it out of the water, was standing on the river's embankment on a sunny Saturday morning. And he didn't even know why he was asking himself these questions when he didn't have any real answers to them. All he knows is that answers exist, that certain past lives are buried in those archival documents and that they are infinitely more interesting—indeed, more exciting—than the documents that some people are going to use to prove that their houses, fields or even factories used to be theirs. Those are just things—what did they have to do with life?—do you understand, sir, life.

He said, "I don't know why they're in such a hurry with these denationalizations. If they've gotten by without the property for fifty years they can wait a little longer."

The director took a deep breath. He didn't want to get angry. People are calm and speak quietly in archives. He just tapped his pencil.

"That's precisely why," he said in a calm, quiet voice. "That's precisely why they're in a hurry. They've been waiting for fifty years."

Lipnik thought that, in fact, they weren't the ones who had acquired that property. It was acquired through the hard work of their fathers and grandfathers. After the war it had been confiscated, but the fathers, grandfathers, mothers and grandmas were pretty much all, practically all, dead—why were their sons and grandsons in such a big hurry with that property now? He thought better of saying this, it wasn't his business.

"It isn't my business," he said, "but still, they didn't acquire it. It was the work of their fathers and grandfathers."

At this point the director forgot that one speaks calmly and quietly in an archive. He shouted loudly and agitatedly that these were strange things Lipnik was saying.

"Or perhaps they're meant as excuses, Mr. Lipnik, but they're strange excuses for unfinished work. To begin with, the Australian collection lay on your desk for months on end, and now you've been rummaging through it for three weeks instead of sending it on for processing and storage long ago, as you should have done. What is going on with you, Lipnik, what is the problem?"

Lipnik thought they had already covered this question and that they'd found no answer to it. He didn't find it necessary to answer this time, either.

The director got up and walked over to the window. He looked out at the blossoming cherry tree for a long time, the same tree that Janez Lipnik often looked at from one floor up—and not just looked at, but had so deeply imprinted in his memory that he even dreamed about it, the white petals of the blossoming cherry tree, bathed in bluish moonlight.

"Archival work," the director patiently explained, "is not as easy as people tend to think. Many an archivist has suffered a nervous breakdown over the sheer vastness of the job and the infinite precision it requires. Even if we're sometimes tempted to think of the fates concealed in the documents all around us, even though many of us sometimes think about how this building is stuffed from cellar to ceiling with human lives, with people from past times, past centuries, we mustn't think like that, Lipnik. We have to think in terms of collections—do you hear? Collections and documents. In terms of classifications. And organizing by subject or provenance. If we lingered over every document that passes through our hands and started wondering about the people connected with them, it wouldn't be good. We once had a fellow who went out one evening and sat naked in Tivoli Park, you probably remember."

Lipnik did remember. It occurred to him that maybe the fellow who had sat in the park naked was the same one who had painted the crotch and breasts of the bronze girl red. Wow, he thought at the same time, my thoughts really do go flying at frightening speed in the oddest directions.

"He drank too much," the director continued, "our colleague drank too much, which unfortunately is also something that happens to people in our profession. But his work was progressing the way yours is now, which is to say not at all. Everything had come to a standstill. What was going through the man's head to cause him to strip naked in the park with the temperature near freezing? I ask you. I don't even want to think about what was going on in the man's head, perhaps he was dreaming he was somewhere else, just not in the park naked in broad daylight—maybe he was trying to protest against something, maybe he was protesting against me, because I kept pushing him to work, but I don't want to even think about it, because it's beyond my ability to comprehend, I'm just wondering what goes on in the head of a man to make him do things like that."

"But you are thinking about it all the time," Lipnik said.

"Who is?"

"You are. You said you don't want to think about it, but all you've been doing is thinking and wondering what was going through his head."

The director seemed confused for a moment.

"Perhaps you're right," he said. "Perhaps I'm also thinking about you and what's going on with you, since in three weeks you haven't issued a single finding, no evidence from the property files, nothing."

"I've been reconstructing a story from the Australian archive," Lipnik said.

The director was silent for while. Then he said calmly that he, Lipnik, was not here to reconstruct stories. If he planned to continue reconstructing stories and not issue the findings and documents that were required for denationalization proceedings, then it would be wise for him to seek other employment.

"Other employment?"

The director sighed the way a person does when he can't seem to get through to someone.

"That's not what I said. I said *if.*"

He hadn't said he needed to seek other employment, he'd said that he needed to find it if he planned to continue reconstructing stories.

Lipnik said it was an interesting story.

The director said that may well be, but he didn't care. If it interested him, Lipnik, then he should devote himself to writing. But archival work was something else.

But it's interesting, Lipnik stubbornly thought.

It's interesting because the young civil servant met the young woman who appears in the memoir as Zala in the summer of '42, when he was working in the forestry office for the old Auersperg estate. If I were a writer, I would describe it. A lonely schoolteacher from Maribor who finds herself besieged in Lower Carniola in wartime. The young civil servant and his passion, driving him to evade partisan ambushes to get to her. You do risk an awful lot for a fuck, she said to him laughing. She hadn't said it exactly like that—we don't know exactly what she did say. All that's recorded in the civil servant's chronicles of his erotic adventures is: You really do risk an awful lot for a ... since the author didn't use indecent words. They ate apples. Lieutenant Guido Gambini from Friuli also came knocking at her door, right when she was in bed with her civil servant. A year later the civil servant was wearing the uniform of His Majesty's army, and at last he and Guido met outside of Turjak. It really is an interesting story, it really is. Actually, he had met her in the company of two Italian officers and her friend Antonia, a fellow servant from the manor house at Soteska.

23.

At least that was what he'd been able to reconstruct from the memoirs of the unknown author that archivist Janez Lipnik had first labeled with the words 'The Pervert,' then thought to change to 'The Conqueror,' but when that somehow seemed inappropriate for the sensitive nature of the text, had finally changed to 'The Lover,' adding 'Great' a short time later. But The Great Lover had not praised his own greatness right from the start. In the mid-nineteenth century the poet Jovan Vesel Koseski wrote that 'nature's law is such that great from little grows.' Likewise, in the beginning The Great Lover wasn't yet great. He had been a minor office worker on the Auersperg estate, at the Soteska Castle outside of Lower Carniolan Springs, a civil servant. He had his year of mandatory military service behind him, in Serbia, where as a law student he'd been called up to attend reserve officer training. He had returned as a lieutenant, was mobilized in '41, but never actually joined up with his unit, because the undefeatable Yugoslav Army, as it was referred to at officers' school, collapsed before he could. The nation had capitulated, and Ljubljana, where he was living at the time, was occupied by the Italians. There was evidence for all of this at various places throughout the typescript. But nowhere was the author's name given, not a one of his women called him by name. Of course they had, but the scribe had adroitly glossed that over, replacing their references to him with various epithets, such as we've already seen, 'Oh, you impatient *boy*.' Or elsewhere, 'Come here, my sweetheart.' Because at the beginning he wasn't yet The Great Lover, and because Janez Lipnik couldn't bring himself to refer to him as 'boy' or 'sweetheart,' he decided to call him by what he did when he wasn't in bed with some woman or describing what had transpired between them. He worked as a civil servant, he was a junior civil servant on the estate of Count Auersperg. Hence, the civil servant. But the women had names. Some had surnames in addition to given names, or at least an initial that stood for a surname, and details regarding their occupations, measurements and preferences.

The forestry office was in the small town of Soteska, in a pleasant valley that narrows at that point, alongside a river, with forests all around. He was twenty-two years old, he missed Ljubljana, and he felt—as he wrote—restless and lonely. He spent whole days working in the office where he also had his dinner, then toward evening he would go home to his comfortable room in a nearby peasant house. In his loneliness he wrote restless, homesick letters to some girl in Ljubljana—the mail was still getting delivered in late 1941. The only woman in his vicinity was Antonia P., secretary to the Countess, a woman with a horselike face, as he harshly described her, and even she had a lover, an Italian major who amused himself with her during his tour of duty in occupied territory. She'd go visit him in Lower Carniolan Springs, where the major's unit was stationed. In order to entertain her young, homesick coworker and dispel at least some of the gloom of his longing for Ljubljana, one sunny afternoon she invited him to go with her to one of the spa town's posh restaurants—she, of course, would be meeting her major there. One other Italian officer showed up for lunch, and Zala, a schoolteacher from Dobrava, which was not far from Soteska. The main purpose of the meal, which they rode to on their bikes, as did Zala from Dobrava, was for the equally young and lonely Italian officer to get to know the schoolteacher. The maggiore was a generous commander: He wanted to share his good luck in finding female companionship to ease his military service abroad with his subordinate, Lieutenant Guido from Udine in Friuli. The likelihood of forming a bond was all the greater, in that neither of the girls was from around here, either—they knew each other from their hometown of Maribor near the border with Austria. After the first introductory jokes and laughter accompanied by bits of broken Italian and Slovene, the civil servant realized that his presence wasn't needed. This was not the first time this company had met—today's goal was to bring Zala and the dark-haired 'tenente together, the way Antonia and the major had come together. He also felt superfluous because, with his head shorn like a monk's, he looked younger than he in fact was. As he describes it, he had shaven his head as a sign of obedience and penance for having to leave the city, with its promenades and cafes, to go work in this godforsaken place. And truly, soon nobody was paying the least attention to him, even though he apparently knew a few more words of Italian than either of the young women. Both couples—the first already deeply involved, the second just now in the making, in the earliest stages of their involvement—had quite a bit of fun trying to overcome their language barriers. The civil servant observed that while the Italians behaved like gentlemen, the girls permitted themselves a few bawdy remarks in Slovene at their expense, each followed by riotous laughter, with the officers laughing simply because Antonia and Zala were.

24.

When the meal came to an end and their bottle of wine was empty, it became clear that the women from Maribor were going to part, or at least Antonia took her major by the arm. The 'tenente offered to drive Miss Zala back to her school in Dobrava, but to everyone's surprise she turned the offer down. The young 'tenente, who already saw himself in the role of her lover, was offended. In an attempt to comfort him, Zala explained that it would be pushing things too far to have people see her in the company of a uniformed Italian officer. The major was of the same opinion—en route the car could run into a partisan ambush and at this point they already had orders not to venture away from larger towns. The 'tenente, who was utterly blinded by Zala's smile, by her white teeth, honey-blond hair and ample breasts beneath her white blouse, was clearly ready to brave even partisan gunfire. Out in the hallway he stopped her and in the civil servant's presence began trying to persuade her to go back to the hotel with him. Zala smiled and shook her head. She didn't seem to be annoyed, it just appeared that, owing to circumstances, she wasn't prepared to risk anything like that. The despairing 'tenente, who had clearly had something promised to him but was now watching the promised object become ever more unattainable, turned to the major for help. The major began negotiating with Antonia, who went over to Zala and tried to persuade her. Zala said, 'No, I didn't make any promises. If you did, that's your business.' The major said something to Antonia, which she then translated. Guido is young and despondent, he thinks he's going to die young in a foreign country. Those are some weighty arguments, Zala said. Guido realized that he could participate without the major's help.

He spoke to Antonia and she translated for him. He liked Zala a lot, and if he had to die, then it would be a great comfort to him if he could first see her home. Zala laughed out loud at this and Guido blushed as he headed for the door, hurt. Then Antonia whispered something to Zala. The civil servant caught part of it: Are you crazy? All of the hotel staff are Slovenes. You can play at this if you like, she said. But not me.

The church bells sounded the Ave Maria as curfew approached. Mr. Civil Servant, she said to the civil servant, you and I should be going. It was at this point, he explains, that he first thought he might have replaced the 'tenente. Part of the way home was the same for both of them. He offered to ride with her to Dobrava, these days it wasn't safe for a woman to ride on forest roads alone. Zala consented. He thought he might take the place of the unlucky young lieutenant whom they'd left back in Lower Carniolan Springs with his thoughts of an unjust fate, of death and his lost opportunity before dying. The civil servant was younger than schoolteacher Zala, his head was shaved and in his forester's uniform he looked, he reports, like some sort of Alpine yokel. There wasn't much chance of him replacing a dark-haired, dashing officer, but he thought about it anyway.

Mr. Civil Servant, she said laughing, you can see me home.

Antonia stayed with the major, but the 'tenente was left all alone. Zala D. and the civil servant pedaled their bicycles over deserted roads, through forests and empty villages. At this hour people no longer came out of their houses, they encountered only a few elderly women hurrying home from 'mass. When they arrived in Dobrava, the civil servant noticed curtains being drawn back from behind tiny windows: Our schoolteacher with some man, somebody from the Auersperg office?

Zala could also feel the stares, but she still invited him in.

Mockingly she pushed me away. "But Mr. Civil Servant, what will people say?" Then she left the room saying, "I'll go get some apples" … She looked so lustful, inviting, so natural, uninhibited … I was excited and confused. Is she teasing me? She was older, more experienced, would she laugh at me if I just jumped into her bed? Then I heard her open the front door downstairs and drag my bicycle into the entryway, then lock the door again. The last hint! With my heart throbbing I undressed in a hurry, jumped into her bed in my underpants and covered myself, thinking, 'How will she react? Che sarà, sarà.'

25.

She lived on the upper floor of the school at the end of the village. She unlocked the door with a big key and put her bicycle in the entryway. She showed him all three classrooms, each of which still had a portrait of the young King Petar in officer's uniform hanging on the wall.

It's summer vacation now, she said. This fall I'll only have enough students for just one classroom. People are leaving for safer places. And I suppose I'll have to take that king down.

Their footsteps echoed through the empty rooms.

Wasn't she afraid of being in this empty building? There was a war on.

What was she going to live on? Air?

She was twenty-eight years old and there were armed people everywhere. And those that weren't armed were terrified to death. They locked themselves in their houses and carefully drew the window curtains aside. She couldn't go to Maribor, where her home was, because the Germans had occupied it and there were no Slovene schools anymore. So she was left alone in this empty school.

Her quarters were nice. The windows faced out onto a dusty road, with green slopes rising up in the distance. They were gradually darkening now, absorbing the last rays of the August sun.

They drank apple cider.

She showed him photographs of her family. Her father had been an officer in the old Yugoslav army, here in a photo from Sarajevo, with epaulettes on his shoulders and a saber fastened around his waist. She had an older brother named Zoran, wearing a well-pressed suit in a picture taken on some street in Maribor. They had moved around a lot, until finally father was assigned back to his hometown. That's why it's not hard for her here, she's used to moving a lot. And what would she do there, anyway? Her father was a prisoner of war but supposed to be coming home soon. Her sister worked in a hospital. She got by. Somehow she got by.

He asked her if she liked the 'tenente.

"He's a nice looking little fellow, that Guido," she said.

So why didn't she go with him?

Because she knows these young officers all too well. They used to come visit them at home and drink slivovitz. Those were Serbs, the whole house stank of slivovitz. Most of them had mustaches, she said.

And she laughed.

"I hear they're growing beards now. They say they're not going to shave them until the king returns."

The civil servant thought of the young, beardless king. In his officer's uniform, with a saber. Officers everywhere, and here he was in his forester's garb, looking like some yokel. Although he was a lieutenant, too, in fact. A lieutenant in His Majesty's Yugoslav Army Reserves.

"Do you even have any whiskers yet?" she laughed.

When she leaned toward him to pour more cider, he kissed her on the neck.

"Oh, Mr. Civil Servant," she said, "what would people say if they saw that?"

He pulled her toward him and kissed her on the mouth.

She looked at him curiously.

"But you do know how to kiss."

A moment later she laughed again.

"Who taught you that?"

She said she was going to get some apples. They had a whole cellar full of them. He heard her open a door on the ground floor. Then he heard water running for a long time, she's washing the apples now. But why so long? Maybe she's taking a bath. As the lieutenant candidly reports, this thought aroused him. Then he heard her open the outside door and put his bike in the entryway. There could be no mistaking this now.

His heart began to pound wildly. He stripped down to his underpants and crawled into her bed.

She arrived carrying a plate full of apples.

"How dare you?" she said. But there was no anger in her voice. She was smiling.

"It will be dark soon," she said. "People saw you when you arrived."

She went to the window and drew the curtains. She turned to face him in her white blouse and gray skirt.

"What do you want from me? You didn't even ask for permission to get into my bed."

She sat down on a chair and bit into an apple.

"I have a boyfriend," she said. "What if he shows up?"

This was not something the civil servant wanted to talk about now.

"Aren't you going to offer me an apple?" he said.

She tossed him an apple, which he adroitly caught and set down on a stack of her books on the nightstand.

"I don't want an apple," he said. "I want you."

Zala laughed aloud.

He doesn't want an apple. Ah, so it's me he wants, the lonely little official.

"What do you plan to do with me, young Mr. Civil Servant?"

She went over to the bed and pulled the blanket off him.

"And what have we here?"

She cast a glance at the proud flagpole that was stretching his underpants tight.

She smiled and kicked the sandals off her feet. She unfastened her skirt at the waist, pulled off her panties, set one knee down on the bed and slung the other leg over him, pulled the fabric off of him and steered her moist crotch toward what she was looking for. She moaned. She took his face in both of her hands and kissed him mightily on the mouth, stroked his shaven head, then rose back up and unfastened her bra, lifted his hands to her breasts and kept moving the whole time, her fleshy embrace flooding him now, and it horrified him to think he was going to come like some underaged junior civil servant, there was no helping it. I'm coming, he whispered. Hold on just a little, she said, but it was too late, he had already come, everything was already wet in her and on him, in and on their crotch, on the bed—the young civil servant had been alone for so long, had been dreaming of something like this for so long that it couldn't have been otherwise.

She lay down next to him.

"Oh, you impatient boy," she said. "You didn't wait for me."

She got up, fetched a towel, and wiped both of them off. She tossed the towel on a chair and slowly undressed. Then she lay down next to him naked and covered them both with a cool sheet. He could feel Zala moving beside him. He touched her thighs and the muscles in them twitched. He ran his fingers down her arm as it moved and looked at her closed eyes. Now, she said breathing fast, we're going to do … something … for me … and this excited him so much, he had never experienced anything like it, a woman masturbating beside him, that he could feel his strength coming back. He lay on top of her and shoved into her, past her fingers, and now they moved slowly, although Zala's fingers kept moving faster and her thighs twitched more forcefully … now, she whispered, I'm getting close, too …

Then we rested and ate apples.

"Tell me something," he said. "If I hadn't been at lunch today, would you have gone with that dark-haired wop, the 'tenente?"

"You mean Guido?"

"Yes."

She laughed.

"What are you saying, you silly."

Then she thought about it.

"It's true, though," she said, "he sings beautifully. Last time he sang this terribly sad song. La preghiera … la preghiera del legionario. The prayer of the legionnaire. About war. About death."

He asked her to sing it. She stared at him a long time. Why should she sing him an army song? And she didn't really know the words. She did know the melody. Like this: lala—lalala. In her clear voice she tried to reproduce the melody that he, Guido, had sung, the prayer of the legionnaire.

"What's wrong?" she said. "Don't tell me you're jealous."

He was jealous. Extremely. He said he didn't care, but she knew he did care. He was in love and jealous of that wop. He felt he could easily put a bullet in his head. That's how things get resolved in wartime. And it would strike a blow for his homeland.

He left in the morning when the roosters had already been crowing for a long time. His eyes bloodshot and unrested, he carefully carried the bicycle out of the entryway, then went back inside where he embraced and kissed her in the twilight. He headed down the road leading out of the village. At the edge of the forest he turned and, clinging to the base of the hillside, began to describe a wide arc around the village. He saw mowers in the distance, with their steady strokes leaning into the earth, into its rich, soft, green surface. He cycled through morning mists, past fields and through damp forests in the dark, lush green of summer.

26.

At the start of the path that led the young civil servant through his vast history of female hearts and genitalia, there was love. At the point when he met Zala the schoolteacher he wasn't yet the Conqueror, at most he was the Needy One. He wasn't the cold-blooded collector and describer, he was a hot-blooded, lonesome young man who had suddenly, amidst the war around him, been displaced to the countryside. True, the young civil servant later became the greatest breaker of women's hearts in Slovene history. At least based on such evidence as the scholarship that deals with this history has available to it. He left behind abundant documentation, including photographs of nearly all the women with whom he'd been involved, with whom he'd lain, slept, had intercourse, or however we're supposed to refer to the prodigious number of couplings described in the bulging folder that before his death he left to his friend from the cultural society in Melbourne. But he wrote beautifully of Zala, and though through all the exhaustive and detailed descriptions he later wrote he never used vulgar words, we can say that his most beautifully written pages are devoted to Zala. The unblushing details of their lovemaking belong at the beginning of his development from minor official to Great Lover. His numerous later entries are more superficial, and in the 1960s they almost turn into statistics. Before Zala he had had a few youthful sexual experiences which he also describes: the housemaid who entered the bathroom while he was bathing, noticed his swollen member and took it skillfully in hand; the girl at the Illyria swimming pool in Ljubljana who wound up with him in one of the changing cabins—or in their case disrobing cabins; the classmate from college days who used to pore over lecture notes with him until they wound up in bed, and the disappointment that followed when he discovered his classmate in another bed, with his friend. But all these episodes are put in the shade by the one that followed that meal with the Italian officers in the hotel in Lower Carniolan Springs. Their breathless encounters during the summer and fall of 1942, which dragged on into the fall of 1943, so overwhelmed and delighted him that he remembered them for the rest of his life. Regardless of all the women that followed, his thoughts and sensual longings kept returning to her. Although he refers to her in his memoirs somewhat ironically as his bed instructor, although at one point he forgets himself and calls her a nymphomaniac, in the process forgetting to ask himself what the relentless sexual drive was supposed to be called that drove him to Zala and so many subsequent women, we can say that she was the one who changed his life.

Otherwise it would be hard to understand how the young jurist and officer of the Yugoslav army reserves advanced to director of the Auersperg forest administration, because this wasn't a time for bureaucratic advancement, much less for forest administration or even

Auerspergs. The war kept unfolding with greater and greater speed, and soon the only ones left administering the forests were the partisans, against whom the Italians launched a fearsome offensive throughout the Auersperg forest in 1942, causing Count Auersperg himself to evacuate his castle just before the village guards took refuge there and were subsequently trapped in a fierce partisan siege supported by Italian artillery, leaving no time for the things people think about in peacetime. There was no time, because the world as Zala and the civil servant had known it was going to the devil, and at great speed, at that. Blood flowed and mortal wounds gaped. It was a time of death. But it was also a time of lovemaking, which in his notes he refuses to refer to as love—it is a word we don't find there. And yet the young civil servant was clearly in love. Every Saturday he rode his bicycle to Dobrava, taking long detours more and more often, often having to drag his bicycle over muddy paths through the forests and fields to avoid the army patrols on the roads, and every Saturday evening Zala opened the schoolhouse door, set his bicycle in the entryway and took him up to her apartment, which smelled of sauerkraut and blood sausage. Every Sunday evening he went back to Soteska, each time encountering greater obstacles than the last, for by the end of 1942 the Italians had a personnel truck or armored vehicle at every major crossroads to stop anyone who appeared. The Italians were getting nervous and were no longer content to examine papers, you had to take everything out of your backpack or bag, down to the last shirt and pair of underpants.

27.

But the civil servant didn't give up. Something that he himself didn't dare call love drew him to her relentlessly. If it was snowing, he got himself a pair of skis and made his way down the broad hillside clearings toward Dobrava, waded through snow drifts with the skis on his shoulder and made his way through the forests with heavy-laden pine branches overhead, which often dumped avalanches of cold wetness in under his shirt collar. The way there kept getting longer and more arduous. One evening in January when it was already starting to get dark and he was far from home, but still just as far from Dobrava, he was trying to find his way to his nearest and dearest through the thickly-set trees of a forested hillside. He was heading slowly downhill on his skis when he suddenly heard some Italian soldiers shouting something like 'Fermo! Alto là!' He dropped to the ground and pressed his face into the snow. Right after that he heard someone shouting in Slovene, 'Down there, look ... on the road!' At that instant bullets started whistling over his head. He had stumbled onto a hillside where the partisans, who occupied the ridge, and the carabinieri down on the road were shooting it out. He knew that, if he cried out, all the gunfire would be directed at him, so he dug into the snow, excavating it with his hands until he could feel the frozen earth. Gradually the wild gunfire abated, the Italian vehicle suddenly drove away, and the partisans saw it off with a victorious burst of machine gun fire. Then there was silence. Slowly he dug himself out of the snow, continued downhill along a frozen streambed, hid from the distant rumble of some vehicle in a deserted house, until he was finally, toward morning but still in pitch darkness, outside the schoolhouse in Dobrava. He rapped their agreed-upon signal on the door for a long time until a sleepy Zala finally opened up. When he told her what had happened, she said, 'You really do risk an awful lot for a ...' There is an ellipsis in the typescript. Perhaps Zala used the word that morning that the civil servant never recorded, perhaps she used it in a perfectly matter-of-fact way, the way she might use the word love, although neither is anywhere to be found in the extensive documentation.

28.

Winter passed, the snow melted, and the civil servant began visiting Zala on his bicycle again. One Saturday evening a car drew up to the schoolhouse. A moment later someone began to knock loudly on the door to her apartment. After long hesitation, Zala opened the door. The civil servant could hear her talking to somebody for a long time. He could hear his Italian words and her answers in a mixture of Italian and Slovene. It was as though she were trying to persuade him of something. He felt a jolt when he recognized the voice of that officer from Lower Carniolan Springs. It was the 'tenente from Friuli, and he remembered his name: Guido. Then the door slammed shut and he could hear her locking it. He heard voices calling out in the yard and then the car driving away.

"It's nothing," she said when she came back. "He wanted to know if anybody is visiting the deserted houses."

"How does he know where you live?"

"How should I know how he knows?" she said, annoyed.

"Why didn't you invite him in for some cider?" the civil servant said reproachfully.

"Don't tell me you're jealous of Guido," she said.

He was jealous, she had said. Of Guido. She could have said, don't tell me you're jealous of that wop soldier, that spaghetti eater, anything. But she had said 'of Guido.' He hadn't forgotten that day in Lower Carniolan Springs, when he had made off with her right under the nose of the handsome, dark-haired 'tenente from Friuli. It occurred to him that her spaghetti-eating suitor could just as easily have made off with her. He knew that his coworker from the office, Antonia P. was still seeing the Italian major. The partisans had let her know through their informants that they were aware of the liaison and that she should stop trying their patience. Zala should stop trying it, too, the civil servant told her, those guys out in the underbrush don't have a sense of humor. Zala was offended. What does it matter to any of you?

"So a woman doesn't have any right to be with whoever she wants?" she shouted angrily. "The war has nothing to do with it."

Now he was offended. He said nothing. He knew she was referring to Antonia, her friend from Maribor. But if she was making excuses for a woman who was almost publicly the lover of the Italian major, who didn't care if she had a horse's face and possibly even liked it—if she made excuses for her, perhaps she was making excuses for herself, as well. He could almost be sure of it. How did he know where she lived? Why had he knocked on her door? Why had he left after a brief conversation? Had she told him to come back later, when he would be gone? If he hadn't been present at the hotel that time, if 'tenente Guido, the officer, had accompanied her that day, if she had slept with him, a soldier of the forces of occupation, was that also supposed not to have anything to do with the war? The partisans shaved the heads of women who got involved with the enemy, and if they suspected they were spies, they shot them. And she says it has nothing to do with the war.

Oh, but it does, and how. These days everything has to do with the war, it impinges on every life. Even the life of a young civil servant.

29.

He found out that the Auersperg forestry office in Soteska was about to be dissolved. Forest management made no sense any longer. Foresters were being interrogated, first by the Italians, then by the partisans. One had even been shot behind a stack of logs, because the partisans suspected him of passing along information about their movements to the Italians. His bouts of lovemaking with Zala on Saturday nights and Sunday mornings became ever wilder and more convulsive. The pain of departure that was approaching manifested itself in the infliction of physical pain. One night in March, to the crackle of rifle fire and the rattle of machine guns coming from the hills in the distance, they embraced, grabbed, stroked, and bit each other endlessly and without climax. He shoved into her madly and endlessly, he slapped her, and she bit his neck several times, and when, gasping, they stopped, he saw that his swollen member was bleeding. When Zala tried to get up out of bed, she dropped to the floor. He leaped out to pick her up, but she got up and went for a towel and dried him with it, while he stroked her hair. It hurts so much, she said, but it's so nice. I know you're leaving, she said.

"Take me with you, lover boy," she said.

He couldn't take her with him. Where was he supposed to go with her? He was twenty-three and she was twenty-nine. He would go to Ljubljana—his parents were in Trbovlje—he would find a place to live and try to find a job.

"What would we live on?" he said.

But that wasn't the issue. He was too young to just up and start living with a woman. And on top of that, he was determined just as soon as possible to get out of this insane country, where everybody was at everyone else's throat and there was gunfire on every street corner. He wanted to live, and the chances of surviving in this part of the world were diminishing by the day. He wanted to live free and he couldn't afford to take on this lonely schoolteacher who was six years older than him.

He came to say goodbye one Sunday morning, as he notes in his memoirs. Antonia was there, her eyes red from crying. Most likely the partisans had been threatening her again. Zala said they were going to mass. He said he'd like to have a word with Zala alone. Antonia said she'd wait outside the schoolhouse. The instant they heard the school door close downstairs, she lifted her skirt. Let me have it one more time, she said. He took her from behind. When he finished, she let her skirt back down and smiled.

"That's better than three doctors," she said, laughing.

That's better than three doctors, he recorded later in his book of memoirs.

He noticed that her eyes were tearing up. If you can, she said, come visit me sometime. I don't know where I'll be, he said. Then write to me, she said. He knew he wasn't going to write to her. He couldn't have if he'd wanted to. The mail was no longer being delivered. The partisans had blown up the railroad tracks and the post offices had all been ransacked and now stood empty.

30.

He went back anyway. Although the entries where schoolteacher Zala appears end at this point, and the memoir resumes in Trieste, where Tea, Olga, Adriana, Jozefina, Helga and Dorotea appear, and following them, in numerous cities from Rome to Melbourne, hundreds of others, Janez Lipnik knew that he went back. With the intuition of an archivist and a sensitive, trembling person he knew that her lover came back to her. He found a list of employees of the Auersperg forest holdings in the Turjak collection. It wasn't for nothing that Lipnik was an anobium, a beetle, a borer, a bookworm. A bookworm consumes books or archival material. He'd been consuming archival material for so long, and here at last was the payoff, this list he was holding with the civil servant's name on it.

His name was Aleksij. Janez Lipnik's hands shook as he held the list and looked out at the fluttering petals of the cherry tree in the courtyard, its white blossoms flying through the air. Among the employees of the Auersperg estate administration in Soteska there was one Aleksij Grgurevič, born in 1920, so the years matched up. This was Aleksij, the same Aleksij who had escaped the siege of Turjak. A lieutenant in His Majesty's army who had apparently become a captain — promotions come fast in wartime — and was with the Village Guards at Turjak, was this same Aleksij. Lipnik could feel his heart thump — I'm a borer, a bookworm, he thought, I've found what I was looking for. A borer lays its eggs in the spines of books or among the sheets of documents. When the larvae mature, they spin their cocoons and out of those come the full-grown insects, the beetles and moths that fly off with all the knowledge they've consumed. Lipnik was flying over the cherry tree in the courtyard. Suddenly everything had become clear to him and it was all so simple: Aleksij, a captain in His Majesty's home army. Gambini was on the list of the Italian military detachment assigned to Lower Carniolan Springs. That's where they met: Guido, the civil servant named Aleksij, the major, Antonia, and Zala. Aleksij later shot Guido, the Italian officer, dead. 'Tenente Guido Gambini. He roared past the startled partisans and Italian gunners on his motorcycle. Some people say he flew through the air. In any case they welcomed the shot he fired with tremendous enthusiasm. He shot him straight in the forehead. Lieutenant Guido, from Udine in Friuli, with whom he'd had lunch one year before in the hotel in Lower Carniolan Springs. Antonia, the major's lover, was also there. Everything added up. From Turjak he fled to Ljubljana, and from there to Trieste. But before that he managed several more times to visit Zala the schoolteacher, who was becoming ever more isolated and frightened in that school that she walked around in like a ghost. He no longer rode his bicycle there—now he arrived on his motorcycle each time. He came back changed. Not just because he was wearing a uniform, but also because now suddenly he had a name. It was still just as dangerous. Although in September of 1943 the Italian army had already begun to disintegrate, now the roads were controlled alternately by partisans, Village Guards, or chetniks. Amid all this chaos the officer of His Majesty's home army still visited Zala. It was dangerous, but for Aleksij, Zala D. was the letter C, she had been marked as C, which is to say as a chapter in his life. A chapter like this was worth risking your life for. The priest was horrified. His cook lurked behind the window curtains. The priest's handyman, Franz, went around carrying some club, some axle, some wire. So far Aleksij had been in many battles with partisans. Once when he'd been out on patrol, they stopped at some house and suddenly heard gunfire. The partisans had surrounded them. That time he saved himself by jumping out a window.

Don't you go getting ideas. Are you sure you're not making this up? Marijana would say. She, who for two weeks now had been unable to say if she'd been to Dugi Otok before or not. Either she was lying or she was telling the truth. I don't have an overactive imagination, Marijana, I don't go making stuff up, I'm a borer, I fly, and everything adds up here. This is the labyrinth of history, the history that roars in my head and reverberates off the walls of the archive. You can get dizzy looking into it, into its abyss, which draws you down toward it, into it. Yet in spite of the labyrinth, everything is logically interconnected, so clearly connected—the entries add up, everything adds up. That night, before he was to roar off on his motorcycle the next morning, leaving his sweetheart one last time, he had a surprise waiting for him. In her apartment he found a man she had taken in because she felt sorry for him. He didn't have any papers. Zala thought he was a woodsman, but from the look of his hands he was no woodsman. Then he said he was from Ljubljana. Aleksij thought about tricking him into going outside and then shooting him behind the school building. He would shoot him straight in the forehead, the way he would shoot that 'tenente Guido, who was still chasing after Zala. Or the way he was planning to shoot that handyman of the priest's, who went around with some sort of implement in hand, as though a man carrying a machine gun, sporting a pistol, and wearing gold epaulettes on his shoulders had anything to fear from some muscle-bound flunky with an axle and wire in his hands. He would shoot him out behind the barn. Did I add this bit, Lipnik thought. Didn't I dream something like this? He'd dreamed none of it, it was all too real for it to have been a dream. An officer who escaped from a house under siege by jumping out a window would be capable of doing that. There's no point provoking him by rattling the door. It's no good showing up in Dobrava in the middle of the night, in the apartment of his sweetheart, Miss Zala the schoolteacher.

Something didn't make sense to him. One time the apartment of Zala D. the schoolteacher was on the upper floor of the empty schoolhouse, and the next time it was on the main floor. Maybe she had some spare room upstairs over the classrooms. And though it was archivist Lipnik's habit to investigate every detail, he didn't let this one stop him. The main thing now was that Aleksij had existed, that he had been a junior civil servant, in 1942 still a novice in matters of love but in love up to his ears, in 1943 a brave yet faithless soldier, a captain, and later also a great conqueror. The civil servant was Aleksij, and the apartment might have been upstairs or it could have been on the main floor. The bicycle could be a Presto or it might not exist at all.

Sometimes I dream about that light-blue bicycle, he thought. She sat on it back when she was still young, fresh as the morning, her skirt fluttering around the wheel in the early morning, but not catching in the spokes, because it was that good a bike, with a net over the back wheel and powerful brakes, of course, because it was almost new.

Toward the end of Aleksij's memoirs there's an almost passing reference to the fact that the partisans shaved Zala's head and shot her friend Antonia.

31.

The phone rang. It was Marijana.

Are you planning to sleep at the archive?

Yes, he'd prefer to spend the night in the archive. With people whom he knew better than he knew his wife. He didn't know her anymore. And if he stayed in the archive, would he even sleep? How can she say 'Are you planning to sleep at the archive?' This is where life is, the life of documents, the life of the mind, no sleeping was done here. Or at home, for that matter—staring at the ceiling, listening to his wife's regular breathing. Thinking of the lives waiting for him at the archive, calling him to join them again. He prefers not to think about her lying next to him, breathing regularly in her sleep, occasionally snoring lightly or moaning. Maybe she's dreaming of jumping off a boat. Between the wooden edge of the boat and the stone pier there's the deep, soft sea drawing her in—she flies, she falls. All of us dream now and then of falling. Lipnik flies over the grassy hillside of some mountain, way down below is a tree, he can see the details of its massive crown and he recognizes it, the tree which winter winds cast down to the ground, it's an oak he's falling into. She dreams that she's falling off a boat and is afraid of falling and drowning in the depths, where a person is deprived of air, asphyxiation, the lungs burst, the eardrums, she's afraid she'll fall into the sea, but—how banal—she falls onto a stone pier, where Beno reaches an arm out to catch her. She ought to wake up before she falls and twists her ankle. But Marijana doesn't wake up, she never wakes up at night, she can be having the worst possible dreams, but she never wakes up. Let her fly, let her fall, fall into a choppy sea full of sharks—she won't wake up. If she did wake up, she'd say, 'Can't sleep again? Why can't you sleep?' And he'd feel the warmth of her body, that invisible aura that surrounds a woman's body and that we call warmth. In fact it's something entirely different—a scent, a shudder, accelerated heartbeat, unseen desire. That desire is always around the body, even when it isn't, when you don't feel or think about it. She'd say 'Why can't you sleep?', reach a hand out, draw her fingers through his hair, while he would reach a hand out to touch the silk fabric she sleeps in, he'd reach under her pajamas and his hand would feel her belly, her back, her breasts, her neck, the warmth of her crotch, everything. This had in fact once happened, she didn't always sleep, there was a time when she woke up and the moon was shining on their bed. And her face was covered in silver, bluish silver, light, when she moaned and called out his name. Do it again, please, do it again. Then they got up and walked around the rocky island. The moon is carrying us, she said.

"It's not very comfortable," she said, "if you're planning to sleep in the archive."

He thought of hanging up without answering.

"I'll be there soon," he said. "Just a few more notes to make."

32.

It's not very comfortable, she said when he tied her up. But it had been her idea. It's one of those silly games, she had said. You tie me to the headboard, my hands, my feet, you blindfold me, then you leave the room and come back in sometime later. He was dumbstruck. He tried hard to think of something to say, but nothing clever came to mind. Am I supposed to be a stranger? was all he asked. Oh, how tedious. You're not supposed to explain every detail. Isn't there any imagination in that archivist's head of yours? Sure, he said, but where am I supposed to get the rope? She helped him find a rope, which they bought at a store. Marijana tested it in front of the saleswoman with a meaningful look intended for him, 'Do you think it will be strong enough?' He actually tied her up that same afternoon. It's not very comfortable, she said. But interesting, she

said, when he used a black kerchief to blindfold her. And while he
excitedly smoked a cigarette in the next room, he didn't know what
was going on, whether he was supposed to be agitated, which he in
fact was, or whether he was also supposed to be wondering 'Who
taught her this?' Then he entered the room and his arousal grew, this
business was truly unhinged and also a little funny, because while he
unfastened her bra, she pulled her hand out of the rope and said,
'This knot wasn't tied very well.' They laughed and went on with it.
His poor archivist's head, which in Marijana's opinion lacked any
imagination, was suddenly so full of this incident out of nowhere;
he was so overcome by it that his head spun at the thought of her
lying there, waiting, wet between her legs before he even touched
her—one time so much so that he had to masturbate in his office at
the Regional Archive. He was interrupted only by Mehmet the security guard as he came lumbering down the hall.

They repeated the experience for the last time on Dugi Otok.
One night while they were there, when he had left her tied up in the
bedroom of their rented apartment, he took a knife from the kitch-
en drawer. She flinched when the cold metal touched her skin.
What is that, she whispered. A knife, he said. It slid over her skin,
over her belly, across her breasts and over her neck. No, she suddenly shouted, this is too much. You can trust me, he said, you can trust
me completely. This is a matter of complete trust. She didn't like it.
That's a dangerous game, she said at breakfast. We're not going to do
that again. One of these days I'll give you a shave, he said, I'll shave
every last body hair off of you slowly. No, you're not, she said, this
has stopped being a game, you have a dangerous look in your eyes.
He didn't realize he had a dangerous look in his eyes, he just thought
some slight bit of imagination had finally broken loose in his poor
archivist's head.

She didn't want him to tie her up anymore. It happened just one
more time, on Dugi Otok. That time he considered bringing a
tradesman who was there fixing the garden fence into the room
where she lay tied up.

33.

He went over to the window and opened it. The light from his workroom illuminated a column of rain. It had been raining for several days now, with only brief intervals when it didn't. He could hear the water gurgling through the gutters, and raindrops were falling all over the cherry tree outside his window as though it were at the bottom of a dispersed waterfall. That will knock them off, by morning the petals will be all over the ground. It won't be white. Whenever the wind shook flowers off the tree, it was white everywhere, as though snow had fallen on the courtyard in the middle of late spring. Now it would just be a slushy soup, and when it dried up Mehmet would come along and sweep it all into a big heap. Then when the ripe, rotting cherries fall sometime later, he'll wash down the asphalt courtyard with a stream of water. And with the cherry tree—first its petals, then its fruit—yet another spring will pass. Each person only has one real spring. Zala and the young civil servant, later captain, had theirs during the war. He and Marijana had theirs on Dugi Otok, beginning with spring in Ljubljana, followed by summer on the island. And all of it was gone—Zala and the civil servant, Dobrava and Dugi Otok. Marijana was still here—but what did she have in common with the sweet young lady who had hiked with him all over the rocky island?

He closed the window and started to put away the meticulously inscribed sheets of paper concerning a person he didn't know and couldn't imagine. And yet he knows his life and now he even knows his name. He knows all of his women from descriptions and photos, no less, but there wasn't a single photograph of him. He can see him riding his bicycle to visit Zala, he can also see him in Trieste or at the Illyria swimming pool in Ljubljana. A former life, now vanished. And yet alive, as alive as could be, more alive than his bookworm archivist's life. He is everything he has experienced, experienced with Marijana on an Adriatic island. And that part is gone. What's left is the archive, full of life, voices, images, bodies intertwined in passionate love, infantry columns moving over the hilltops of Lower

Carniola, the explosion at Turjak, and some flunky by the name of Franz, who keeps showing up with a length of wire in one hand.

I can't read this anymore, he thought. I get drawn into the story too much, I sink in it, I drown. Sometimes I don't know what's the story and what's real, what's night and what's day, morning or evening. Maybe I need to change professions. The cherry tree getting drenched in a column of rain was illuminated by some neon light from the street. He put the memoirs away in a drawer and abruptly headed downstairs. In his usual way he skipped some of the steps two at a time, flying down past the damp, neglected Biedermeier columns with their plaster ornaments. When he reached the big main door, he realized it was locked. He went over to the night watchman's window, but it was dark. He thought that Mehmet might be asleep, that perhaps he'd made a bed for himself under his desk. He tapped on the window. Nobody answered. The light went out in the hall. He looked for a light switch, figuring it had to be somewhere near the door; his hand felt over the coarse wall but the smooth plastic square was not to be found. He thought that maybe the switch was on the other wall, but he couldn't remember ever having turned the light on down here. Mehmet was always here, as reliably as the documents in the archive, as the shelves and safes containing the most valuable documents, the medieval Urbarium, the proceedings of the town council and the landed estates. Mehmet was here every evening, every night, just like the archive itself. But now he was gone. He began to feel slightly anxious. He called out several times, called him by name, but got no response. He thought about going upstairs and making a call from his office, or perhaps sitting at his desk and dozing until things got resolved. Then he heard a clatter followed by a squeal, as though someone were opening a door. He followed the sound and his hand ran over a door. He opened it and with his feet made out steps leading downstairs. It occurred to him that he'd never yet been in the basement. Most of the buildings in this part of town didn't have basements, because the old marshlands were nearby, saturated ground that would undulate when you stepped on it. The buildings were floating on swampland, built on special pillars to keep them from tipping. When there's an earthquake, they'll just sway a little. The world underneath us is all stirred up, he thought. The waters that fed the Ljubljana marsh flowed here from underground sources the other side of the mountains, and one day they'll get stuck, either on the far side of the mountains or here underground. He could hear splashing sounds around the cellar and sensed it was swaying and that maybe, one day, the whole archive would get washed away. Together with the cellar, which served no function. It serves no function because wherever they did go ahead and excavate cellars and try to reinforce them, it didn't do any good, the dampness penetrated even the thickest walls. For an archive, where documents had to be stored at a precise temperature, where the air could be neither too humid nor too dry, this hole he was feeling his way through was utterly useless. Where do I think I'm going, chasing after that noise, he thought, what's down here for me? A sort of anxiety, possibly fear, expanded in his chest. He saw himself in the dark pit of this building gently swaying out in a swamp, drenched in night and a torrent of rain.

Suddenly a shaft of light hit him. He shuddered and instinctively jumped back, up toward the door he'd come in through.

Someone was shining a flashlight on him. He heard laughter. The laughter of some man in the dark.

The laughter came from down there, from the dark, from the other side of the light that was making him squint. He wanted to be upstairs, but on his way up he tripped and fell. He picked himself up and kept running, but stopped in the open doorway. There was a ray of light flashing around down there and dancing on the walls of the stairwell. He heard footsteps coming up the stairs. The glare in his eyes kept him from identifying the person who was blinding him with his powerful flashlight.

"Where do you think you're going?" the voice said.

Lipnik breathed in relief. He knew this voice.

"One of these days you're going to break your legs."

It was Mehmet, the receptionist and night watchman.

"I heard you bounding down the steps," he said, laughing and still shining the flashlight in his face.

"I thought, he's going to break a leg on those steps for sure."

34.

While sitting on his bench in the shopping center, Lipnik thinks about the word absence. Some absence from this world, which is so full of light and music and people wandering lost from one display to the next, looking for one more thing to buy. This is a world he no longer inhabits. That perhaps Marijana no longer inhabits. Where there's really nothing to interest him. He had to come here to sense something new, he had to come with Marijana all the way to the edge—of collapse, of obliteration—to the edge of death to sense his complete absence from the life thrumming around him, his expulsion from the tribe he belongs to, from the depths of the evil at home in this tribe, in these innocent shoppers who are prepared to repeat all of it, do it all over again. This is the same rabble, Lipnik thinks, that hurt, injured and destroyed human lives, this life of the surface concealing the sinister instincts of a sinister mob. Bloated with dissatisfaction, with endless, relentless inner dissatisfaction that at one minute it tries to fill by racing from store to store, or that it stuffs into shopping bags and carts, that it shoves into the abyss of its own emptiness, amid this noise, in this over-stimulated, superficial shopping center life, where nothing remains, only the dissatisfaction that's been stuffed into bags, stuffed down gullets and bellies, into closets and drawers. Beneath this surface of light, countless treading feet, racing and shoving, amid the polite greetings and nods to acquaintances and friends, there rules a peacefulness that could any second change into whoops, the whoops into howls, the howls into hellish violence, the likes of which used to rule around here, all through this country, that used to destroy human lives with blows, with gunshots, lives that perished in caves and mental hospitals, an old invisible evil that's buried very deeply here, beneath the cumulus clouds in the sky, under the glass roof with the rain sliding down it, it's raining and in the presence of all this innocent shoving, squeaking of shopping carts, rhythmically beating music, and beneath the invisible sound of the rain on the roof Lipnik feels a helplessness, a fragility, a wish no longer to be here, to be somewhere else, in the place where it all began, where dissatisfaction and anxiousness aren't shoved and spilt all over brightly lit promenades. Ah, Lipnik thinks, history is more powerful than the present, the archive contains the secret of the evil that's hidden and disguised here with glossy colors and bright lights. Underground there are cellars that serve no function. The archive has a cellar that you get to via a twisting stairway. In the old days these damp cellars that were useless for archival purposes were used for people. Just not for archives, and not even for storing potatoes. For beatings. The Gestapo's torture chambers. His father had been pummeled in the face. Zala's brother had been beaten on the soles of his feet. Later the Udba, the communist secret police, used these cellars. There is a rich subterranean world under our cities, he thought, with caves and cellars, torture chambers and jails. On the other side of the country, in the place where he used to live, near the river, a man who had hanged himself was discovered in a cellar. He had left his shoes on the floor and they were said to have discovered him in his stocking feet. It would be better to hang yourself from some tree and leave your shoes underneath it—why had that fellow hanged himself from a bar near the ceiling in a cellar that smelled of potatoes and dampness? Absence in a forest was different from absence in a cellar, where you were surrounded by walls on all sides. He felt that kind of absence now, here in the shopping center, in its bright promenade. It was almost as though he wasn't here at all. He was submerging in the records of those people who were now completely gone. Along with his helplessness in the gawdy, noisy world around him grows his absence from it and his presence somewhere else that has both passed and perished. That's where his home is, in some lost, perished recollections.

His attention is drawn back to the naked woman that the man with the hairpins sticking out of his mouth has leaned up against the display window. Before that, though, he pulled the hair off her head. It's still there—her hair, that pile of blond hair that he tossed on the floor. Her hollow, empty eyes stare at him. Where is my hair, my beautiful hair, she asks him. She says nothing about the dress they've taken off her. Dresses change, in spring you wear one in the display case, in autumn you wear another, and in the summer they give you a bathing suit. But my hair, they can't just pull your hair off your head, isn't that right, Lipnik?

35.

Just a few days before Janez Lipnik had thought for the first time, 'The cherry blossoms are gone. Spring is gone. Time has lost its momentum. I'm submerging in those memoirs and the others, the ones from the mental hospital.' For the first time it struck him that he had already long been absent from this world. A moth flies out of some archival documents and collides with the window until it finds its way out and then flies through the cherry blossoms—he sees all of this. Wasn't I at Turjak, the borer, the bookworm wonders, and before that in Dobrava? Didn't Aleksij tell me to look after her if anything happened to him? Did anything happen to him? Did he get blown up by a land mine? Or did he really fly on his motorcycle over the forests of Turjak, over Mount Krim, then low over the marshlands south of Ljubljana? For the first time he thought, it's not June, it isn't spring, the cherry blossoms are gone. The asphalt of the courtyard is not covered with white petals, there's a big tree out there, maybe a pine. This isn't the spring of 2000, it's autumn, early autumn of 1943, I can see the leaves that the trees have shed, the beeches, the maples, they haven't started to rot yet, he slips on them as he walks, as he climbs up the steep hillside. In the distance he can hear isolated gunshots, they're killing the last of the wounded. Go on—who would kill wounded men? Outside Turjak Castle and down in Velike Lašče—everywhere they're shooting the disarmed Village Guards who surrendered at Turjak, and not far from there the chetniks that the partisans routed at Grčarice. Right before his eyes is the face of a young boy that a partisan secret policeman shot while he was waiting in line with the other disarmed Village Guards to have his hands tied. He recognized him, this Slovene brother who had attended the same seminar at the technical institute, he turned him around so he wouldn't have to look him in the eye, ordered him to lie down on his stomach, and he shot him in the back of the neck. But his aim was bad and the bullet struck the skull, it left a gaping, bloody hole, crushed bits of bone and gristle, blood spraying onto the soldier standing beside him. This can't be a dream, Janez Lipnik thought, the dream was when I was sitting in the archive and looking at the cherry blossoms falling onto the courtyard pavement. But why can't I get to the end of this hillside? Every time he makes it through the thick undergrowth, he slips on the fat surface of a fallen leaf and off he goes, with all his weight—the greater the weight, the greater the velocity—back down, all the way down to the stream below.

He knew where he was being drawn—to the place where he climbed down out of the tree. But now he needed to hide. There were columns of partisans on the roads. Here and there among them were bound prisoners.

The clouds pressed down over the crowns of the trees. It started to rain.

That afternoon he was just within range of Dobrava. Now he knew all too well what that word meant, range: as far as a rifle can shoot. He saw the belltower and the roof of the rectory. He decided to wait a little longer and knock on her window once it got dark. Zala would put the light out and ask in the darkness who was there. Then she would open the door as she'd opened it for Aleksij and was now opening it for him. He would wash up and then lie down in bed with her. He didn't want to think of Aleksij, whose resting place was up there, over the pines, even farther, over the stars, hovering in the expanses of the heavenly Jerusalem. Maybe he sees him now, maybe he knows what he's thinking—what do we know about what comes after? And hadn't he told him, ordered him, in fact, to look after her if anything happened to him? He didn't know what had happened to him, but he was gone now, Aleksij was, he didn't exist.

He didn't want to think of him, he was thinking of her, how she would lie down next to him in her nightgown, possibly a silken two-piece. He sat down in the moss and leaned his back up against the rough trunk of a huge pine that had the autumn wind whistling through its crown, for now it's still warm, but soon will come winter. He was warm, fatigue coursed all through his body and he fell asleep.

36.

He was woken up by the roar of car engines. Three trucks were slowly crawling through the gorge on the road down below. He could see little bright mushrooms, metal caps, the helmets of German soldiers who held their rifles down at their hips and were making their way over the same bumpy road as the vehicles in front of them. The Italians had left and here were the Germans arriving. He pushed deeper into the forest and waited for the engine roar to subside. Then he went down to the forest's edge and set out down the long, gently sloped clearing toward the roofs of Dobrava. When he came out of the forest, he noticed that the school door was open on the side where her apartment was. A ray of light stretched across the yard. Outside the door he noticed her bicycle leaned up against the wall. A light blue bicycle, a nice, modern bike, a Presto. Suddenly there was a man with a rifle standing next to her bicycle, apparently he'd come out of her apartment. Zala came staggering out right behind him, as though somebody had shoved her out of the entryway. As indeed someone had—two more armed men followed behind her. Immediately Janez Lipnik retreated into the forest and lay down among some ferns. He could see Zala looking over toward the rectory, as if she expected help from there. Then she walked between them along the woodsmen's trail that led uphill and into the forest. Along the trail that Aleksij usually arrived on and that the two of them had sped off on by motorcycle one morning not so long ago, with Aleksij driving and him in the sidecar.

They stopped at the edge, among some short pines.

"Well, out with it," one of them said. "Where's your officer?"

Janez Lipnik could just hear their voices, his face was pressed to the ground and it seemed like they were very close, so he didn't dare look up. He didn't see her face or hear her answer. Zala kept quiet.

"Shoot her, the white whore," another voice said. "Why are you bothering with this?"

"I'll shoot her when the time comes," the first one said.

He's not going to shoot her, Janez Lipnik thought. He's not going to shoot her. There's a German column close by, and if he did, they'd hear the gunshot. If I raise my head, he thought, then he'll shoot me for sure—because he won't have time to think about it. He'll shoot me like they shot that student, in the back of the head, leaving a bloody gaping hole.

He heard a loud slap, a blow hitting her face, the impact of a heavy masculine hand against her cheek. He heard Zala as she moaned, whimpered in startled disbelief, 'Why are you beating me?' Then she began to repeat it out loud, as if hoping that someone would hear her, 'Why are you beating me? Why?'

"Where's your officer?" the first one asked again.

"Bitch," the other added.

Then they were quiet for a while.

"You rutting bitch," the other one said, as if what he'd said before hadn't been enough. "Whoring around night and day instead of teaching our children."

"But I did teach them," Zala said softly. Nobody had heard her before when she called out, there was no one anywhere to hear her when she exclaimed, 'Why are you beating me?' So she tried a different way to get free of these people, who apparently had time— perhaps they were leaning against a tree, or perhaps they were even sitting with Zala between them. Janez Lipnik couldn't picture what was happening over there, because he had burrowed his head in the ground, he was inhaling the damp soil and breathing quietly, even more quietly than Zala was speaking. I taught the children every day, she said.

"And went whoring around at night," said a third who hadn't

spoken till now.

"Where's your officer," the first asked patiently.

"He may be in Ljubljana," she said.

"So he may be in Ljubljana? Or maybe he's out butchering our people."

"I honestly don't know, sir, I honestly don't know where he is."

"Shoot her, the white whore," the meanest one said.

"Maybe you're right," said the first.

He wasn't quite convincing. His voice wasn't so firm. He was trying to scare her.

"If you tell us," he said, "what unit he's in, when he comes to visit you, and when he leaves—if you tell us everything, then nothing will happen to you."

"Shall I tie her up?" asked the third, the one who didn't say much.

"First we could maybe ... At least I could," the mean one said. "Look what a pretty blouse she's wearing."

It sounded like there was some shoving, then the sound of her moaning.

"Leave her alone," the first one said. And a short while later, more emphatically, "Leave her alone, I said."

The mean one was in a foul mood.

"So you really think," he said, "that I'd want to get the clap from this whore?"

"You tore my blouse," Zala said softly.

"All right, tie her up," the first one said. "Do you have scissors?"

He didn't have scissors, so he took out a knife.

"Stop," said the second one. "I've got scissors. They're hers. I picked them up on the way out." Then he laughed, "It's time to clip your hair."

He could hear her moaning, then there was more shoving, and he held his hands over his ears and buried his head in the forest soil. Then he heard them leave along the cart trail. You know, the mean one said, you know, I practically got a hard-on? I should have shot her, the white bitch, a bullet in the head, but not this.

/ 149

37.

When he entered the house, she was sitting on a bench and staring ahead at the table, with leftovers of food on it. So they ate before they were going to take her to the forest. She didn't look up. There were traces of blood between the patches of hair that remained on her shaven head. There was also dried blood on her face, under her nose and over her upper lip, which had been split. He went into the bathroom and drew some water.

"There was nobody anywhere," she said, "nobody anywhere."

That night she sat up and shook him by the shoulder.

"You've got to get going," she said. "They're going to come back."

"They won't come now," he said.

"They will," she said. "And they'll kill us both."

Her vacant eyes roamed about the room.

"Aleksij," she said.

"I'm not Aleksij," Janez Lipnik said.

"Aleksij," she said. "In the morning I'm going to get Antonia. There's such chaos everywhere."

It rained all day. He paced through her apartment, slept, ate, and slept. Then he kept going to the window, looking out into the autumn rain that the wind carried in huge sheets and flung against the windows.

She didn't get back from Lower Carniolan Springs until that evening. She was soaked through.

"Are you still here?" she said, but not in a way that made it sound like he should be somewhere else.

"Where else should I be?" he said. Should I be out in the rain, in the war, he thought, in the forest, up in a tree, or where?

"Have you eaten?" she said as she took off her muddy boots. Then she dried her head and what was left of her hair with a towel, went to her bedroom and closed the door behind her. He heard the bed springs squeak. He went over to the door and listened.

"Are you going to bed?"

He opened the door. The room had once been white with plaster.

Somebody had shot up the ceiling in here.

"Don't open the door," she said. "I'm changing."

But the door was already open. She was sitting on the bed, pulling a sodden stocking off one foot. Her skin was wet, too. The bright, smooth skin of her thighs, now ruddy from the cold.

"Don't look at me," she said, through her moist red lips, looking at him past a fugitive strand of still damp hair. Don't you look at me, either, he could have said, because she was looking him straight in the eyes and her look pierced right through, down into his chest, where his heart was beating hollowly, but faster and faster. Don't you look at me, either, because if you look at me like that, my heart goes out of control, and if you don't look away, I'll never close this door through which I once heard the bed squeaking, through which I once heard you moaning and sighing. But now it no longer matters at all, now you're sitting alone on the bed with that wet stocking in hand, your skin is white and wet and red from the cold, you're looking at me past that strand of hair, and only if you look away, if you tell me one more time not to open the door, but to close it, then maybe I really will close it and maybe I really will leave, so don't say that. And keep looking at me, wet and moist, your lips apart, sitting on your nicely made, squeaky bed, keep looking at me, don't look away and don't cover your white legs, don't do anything, don't say anything.

He went over to her and touched her wet hair. She didn't pull away. She just lowered her head and stared at the wet thing she held in her hand, not knowing what to do with this stocking, so she tossed it over the edge of the bed. He stood before her and slid his hand down her neck. His hands reached toward her other foot, intending to pull off the other stocking, but instead they suddenly reached up and clasped her hips. She leaned her head into his stomach forcefully, and he could feel her shaking, she was shaking for some reason, as though she were on the verge of tears. She didn't start crying, there were just isolated sobs of some sorrow or other, and possibly happiness that she wasn't alone, because despite everything that had happened and was going to happen in this horrible, senseless age, she wasn't alone. In a few jerky motions she pulled his shirt out of his trousers and they lay down. He reached a hand between her wet thighs, while she still had the one stocking on. She was breathing erratically and simultaneously sobbing, only now did she take his face in her hands, his head, and start kissing and pulling him toward her. When she let go of his head, he saw that her eyes had teared up, that something was happening to her that might be unstoppable. He couldn't stop either, and when he closed his eyes he heard the echo of far-off explosions and watched the castle wall collapse, behind which he lay. I can't close my eyes, he thought. He looked at her, at her naked breasts, her wet face, her open mouth that was now emitting some sort of grunts as her eyes stared at the ceiling. Then he looked at the ceiling, too, while he lay on his back and listened to the sound of the rain that the wind lashed onto the roof and the windowpanes. He looked at those holes in the ceiling, the plaster drilled into or ripped off by machine gun bursts, the shattered sky above him.

38.

"I shouldn't be doing this," she had said. "But I don't know how much longer I have to live."

Antonia knew what could happen to her.

For a while she had moved into the hotel in Lower Carniolan Springs. She watched from her window as the Italian army retreated. She and her major had spent the last night together. He had given her a picture of himself.

There was a knock at the door of the hotel room. She looked in horror at the door handle as it moved. The moment she had feared was here.

Two partisans with machine guns came into the room.

"I know why you're here."

"Let's go," one of them said.

The partisan officer scrutinized her for a long time.

"What information did you give him?"

"None."

"You reported to him on our troop movements."

"I did no such thing."

"Do you know why we've come for you?"

"I know why you're here. You're going to shave my head."

"No, in that case, you don't know," the officer said.

She was prepared to have them shave her head. She was prepared to ask them to shave it. She was also ready to kneel. These people are convinced that I supplied the major with information. But what information? She didn't know anything. She had slept with him. She could tell them everything. Fucked. Screwed. Taken a wop dick in her mouth. But kill her? Let her live with her horse face. Everyone said she had a horse face. Except for him, the major. She loved him. She wouldn't tell them that, only Zala knew. Let them shave it. All of it. It will grow back, she had said.

"We're not going to shave your head," the officer said. "Because you're not just a wop whore. If you were just some Italian slut, which of course you are, a slut that gives herself to our country's occupiers ... If it were just that, some rutting bitch that climbs into bed with a man who had our people shot, then we'd shave your head."

"What are you going to do with me?" She could feel the sweat of desperation streaming down her body.

Through the window she could see the tops of the trees moving inaudibly in the warm September wind.

"That remains to be seen. If there's time, you'll go before a court."

But there was no time for a trial. They led her off into the woods and shot her. The hand of the young partisan assigned to carry out the execution shook. He couldn't look her in the face—nobody could. The partisans typically shot their victims in the back of the head, and so he shot her from behind as they were walking down a forest path. Because his hand was shaking, the first bullet only grazed her ear and she was covered in blood in an instant. She grabbed her head and then looked at her bloody hands. She fell to her knees and immediately started to crawl through the brush. The second shot hit her between the ribs and caused her to land flat on her back, and now once again she saw the tops of the trees noise-lessly moving. The faintly rustling leaves. Poplars? Prekmurje has poplars. Around Maribor there are beeches, with pines higher up, firs.

The last words she heard were *goddamn clod*. They were spoken by an officer who came running down the path and tore the gun out of the young partisan's hands. Then he walked up to her and shot her in the forehead with his pistol.

He used some leaves to wipe his hands, which had been spat-tered with blood. His hands were as wide as shovels and although they looked clumsy, they were well-practiced. "What are you look-ing at me for?" he said to the shaking young boy. "Can't take the sight of blood?"

"That's those Ljubljana students for you," he told the others, who were standing awkwardly amid some trees. "When things re-ally start popping they'll run like jackrabbits."

39.

"Aleksij," Zala said. "Don't leave me alone. They're going to shoot me."

"I'm not Aleksij," Janez Lipnik said. Aleksij was twenty-three years old and had escaped from Turjak. He might even now be in Trieste.

"Look at the cuts I have on my head, Aleksij," Zala said.

"Those are from the scissors," Janez Lipnik said. You stabbed at your head on that balcony in Maribor. Did I dream that? Or am I dreaming now? The Germans shot your brother. The partisans shaved your hair off. They cut your head in several places. Am I dreaming if I say I saw you on the balcony? It was raining. I was just eight years old. Now I'm almost sixty. I couldn't help you. And I can't help you now.

"What's going to happen to me?" she said. How can I get back to Maribor?

"Take that handsome light-blue bicycle of yours, the Presto, and ride it to Ljubljana. You can make it from there," he said.

"Ljubljana's a long way off," she said.

"It's not that afar," he said. "I'm going to take Aleksij's bike. The motorcycle would be best, but he's already made off with that. If I'm lucky, I'll be strolling over the Triple Bridge by tomorrow evening.

"My brother?" she said. "Zoran?"

"Yes," he said.

"He's been shot?"

"Yes. In the courtyard of the jail in Maribor."

40.

Several days before he turned up vacant-eyed in the shopping center's dazzling promenade, Marijana had told him that he'd been sleep-walking. It wasn't true that he couldn't sleep, as she always insisted, it wasn't true that he had insomnia while she slept straight through from dusk to dawn and even snored, it wasn't true. The previous night she had heard him talking in his sleep. He was sitting on the bed, speaking incoherent sentences. The top part of his body kept bowing like some Jewish rabbi talking to his God.

For supper she brought out a big bowl full of vibrantly colored salad and said there was no way she could know what was going on in his head.

"What should be going on in it?"

"At night you go through these long ravings. The rest of the time you're silent," she said. "You don't talk to me."

"What should I be talking to you about?"

"About what's going on in your head. You used to at least tell me about your work. Did you find that bicycle?"

"What bicycle?"

"The one they hauled up out of the Ljubljanica. You said it might be the same as the bicycle in that pornographer's notes. Speaking of which, what's happening there? Did you discover who wrote it?"

"You've already asked me that. I told you, he's not a pornographer."

"Well, then, so much the worse—the pervert."

She laughed out loud. Her laughter bothered him. There's nothing funny about this, he thought, what's funny about it?

Suddenly she became serious.

"I know you're not going to like this," she said, "but there's something I have to tell you."

He looked at her. Here it comes. I know what's been bothering you, she'll say. You've been tormented by the thought that I may have been on Dugi Otok sometime before we went, with somebody else. That I may have twisted my ankle when I jumped off the boat. Go ahead, he thought, say it.

"There's some lettuce stuck to your teeth," she said.

She burst out laughing. Every evening he has lettuce stuck to his teeth, because every evening they have a salad that Marijana fixes.

"You've got a green bit stuck between your incisor and canine on the right."

"Does it bother you? It doesn't bother me."

"No, it doesn't bother me," she said. "It's just funny. As though you had a green crown between your incisor and canine."

He set his fork down.

"Maybe it's parsley," he said.

"I didn't use any parsley," she said.

"Or garlic," he said. "Garlic makes you belch at night."

A green bit, either lettuce or parsley. In everyday life the flaws of others bother us. Even if they're our nearest and dearest. When we're overcome with desire, nothing bothers us anymore—more smell, more perspiration, that's what we want. But when we wake up in the morning, we're back at a bit of lettuce stuck between the incisor and canine. Even though we don't normally eat salad in the morning. And we carefully brush our teeth, to be sure. But there's something else in the morning that bothers us. In the morning even more than in the evening. That's right, they hadn't slept together for a long time. How long? I'd like for us to wind up lying next to each other, out of breath. Like that writer, Aleksij? In his eternally repeating story. That's what Lipnik wants. But first, certain words are needed, and he can't manage them. He can't bring himself to ask if she was on Dugi Otok before their vacation. When? Whenever. She can't bring herself to ask what's bothering him—does it have anything to do with her? All she says is, there's no way I can tell what's going on in your head. What's going on in my head? Am I supposed to know what's going on in my head? But if only she would say, does it have anything to do with us? Is that what's bothering you? Then he would say quite a bit, there's quite a bit bothering me, and then they'd be getting somewhere, because when someone says that, they're revealing their jealousy. But Lipnik refuses to reveal it. Ever. Why doesn't she make the first move, why does she talk about lettuce stuck between his incisor and canine—everybody knows that looks silly and repulsive, so why does she have to add that it looks silly and repulsive? All she said was silly, but she was thinking repulsive, of course it's repulsive to have parsley in your teeth, parsley looking like some green crown. She doesn't want to talk—can crowns even be green, who's ever seen a green crown? Gold maybe, but lately even those are getting crowded out by porcelain ones, supposedly because it's not healthy to have that all metal in your mouth. But parsley is okay, and so is garlic. If that's how it is, then it's better to keep quiet. Otherwise she'll say that he has that jet skier racing through his head again. She liked to return to that theme whenever they had a misunderstanding. They'd been together a long time now, and it wasn't possible for them not to have misunderstandings now and then. They understood each other best on Dugi Otok. But now there's this sailboat down there, with two couples sleeping in its hot belly. Two men, two women. One of the men has the ludicrous name of Pepo. The other one's name is Beno and he's an idiot. The same sort of idiot as Guido. Although that Guido was at least sad, he sang that sad song about the death of the legionnaire. And would knock on Zala's door at night. Did she ever open up for him? He doesn't know, because even Captain Aleksij doesn't know that. If he knew, he would have recorded it. That idiot Beno is never sad, he plays basketball on Wednesday evenings and goes sailing in the summers. And Marijana was supposed to have some secret with an idiot like that, a secret involving Dugi Otok? With someone who out of sheer boredom stops by his office, and doesn't just stop by, but each time—and that is to say every, single, last time, besides stopping by to visit, parks one buttock on his desk. It's sheer, freak coincidence that Beno is doing the same kind of work as he is. He ought to be in the stock market. Every day he talks about something falling. Just as a person begins to think that it's raining or snowing, it turns out he's talking about stock prices. Besides, he's a scumbag. He talks about how he can seduce any woman he wants. The old scumbag can't help salivating at every turn, at every opportunity. He goes into a bakery and tells the young salesgirl, 'Do you know why I come to this bakery every day?' And he looks at her with his bright eyes as an invisible trickle of lustful saliva creeps down his chin. The salesgirl smiles, because there can only be one answer, but he surprises her, he lets her wait just a bit, just long enough for any woman to want to ask why, but before she asks, he says, 'Because of the poppy pastries, they're excellent.' And he's made contact, the sly, slimy slug, there's a bond between them, and not just on account of bread and poppy pastries, the next time he'll say that he comes there because of the excellent service, and on and on, until one evening he says, 'You've run out of bread. Would you care to stop by my place for some coffee?' Or some such ridiculous thing, which will work, it will work because he's built a whole edifice of subtle hints, and it still worked.

Beno says that women fall so easily because they have no will power. He's read that somewhere.

Why does a sensitive person like Janez Lipnik, who at least thinks he's sensitive, as does Marijana, not to mention the fact that Zala has thought this way for a long time, why does he have to deal with a couple of idiots like Beno and Pepo, Pepo and Beno, why does he have to wonder if they used some ropes on the sailboat—sailboats are always full of all kinds of lines for tying up wrists and ankles, why does he have to think about some Jana or other who was also on that sailboat and, on top of everything else, took a trip in some bus full of drunken Hungarian soldiers? Did they sing? Did they sing some song on the boat in the moonlight, did Beno sing?—perhaps he has some soul, simple as it may be, and likes to carry a tune. Like Guido. La preghiera ... la preghiera del legionario.

That's the kind they fall in love with. While he has parsley stuck between his teeth. Or lettuce. Whatever.

He'll ask her if she thinks his colleague Beno is handsome.

"Handsome in what way?"

"You know. As a man. As a shark. He could have a role in some movie."

At first she would give him a startled look, as though she were trying to figure out what he meant by that. Then she'd burst out laughing. Bits of food and drops of wine landed on the table.

She said, "There's nothing more unattractive than a beautiful man."

41.

He went out and came back home a little drunk. He'd seen a light on in some suburban tavern, where several men were clustered around the bar. He went inside and knocked back three or four vile-smelling whiskeys. He wasn't used to it and it almost made him throw up. When he got home, Marijana was asleep or at least pretending to be. He envied her calm. He hated her previous life. He thought about waking her up and saying something nasty, like bitch, whore, or maybe hitting her. Then she would tell him everything and perhaps they would make love. The way Zala and Aleksij did. He couldn't wake her up. Maybe I don't love her anymore, he thought, maybe I'm in love with Zala. He was envious, jealous, nasty and drunk. Drunk, jealous and nasty. He slept on the couch in the living room.

"What's wrong?" she asked in the morning. "You're getting strange. You don't talk. You don't sleep. You hide out in that archive, immersing yourself in some stories. And now you're drinking. You never used to drink. I don't understand you anymore," she said in the morning.

Her words kept buzzing in his ears.

"Last time you said that sometimes you feel kind of dizzy. Shouldn't we talk about that?"

She said she'd done some reading about this phenomenon. Among other things, vertigo could be a sign of psychological problems, conflict situations at work, burdensome problems that disrupted an individual's mental balance. The individual's psychological anguish expressed itself physically in the form of vertigo.

He began laughing out loud. That was even funnier than last night's lettuce between the incisor and canine, the green crown. Psychological anguish expressing itself physically? Who ever heard of such a thing? Was she trying to tell him he needed to go see a shrink?

Even though he was tired and disheveled and a little amazed at himself for what had happened—becoming a suburban barfly for a night—and even if his eyes were a bit bloodshot, his mind was functioning perfectly.

"People always prefer to believe what they can't understand," he said, "than what they can understand or could understand if they just tried a little harder. Do you see what I'm saying?"

She could have said, 'Is that jet skier racing through your head again? Did he break in on your dreams?'

That's what she said whenever she started talking about how he was acting strangely and not sleeping. But she didn't mention the jet skier. Instead she said:

"What's wrong? You're not telling me anything. You know I care about your work."

"That's not work," he said. "Nobody assigned me to do it."

Then they were silent.

"Whatever," she said.

Whatever, he thought. Whatever, whateverwhatever. If she's not going to answer, then neither am I, so whatever.

And anyway, what was he supposed to say, when she knew full well that it was a labor of love? Love for the truth. A labor of anxiety that comes to us from out of the past. She knew full well that his job, the one they assigned him, involved searching for evidence of inheritance rights. For denationalization proceedings. For war reparations. He could care less about reparations, he could do that blindfolded. He was immersing himself in some memoirs. Some events in the distant past. So why did she ask him such nonsense? Doesn't she understand that things are mounting up in his head?

42.

"Is it Monday or Tuesday today?"

Janez Lipnik is still sitting on a bench in the promenade of the big shopping center. An older woman almost stepped on the bags at his feet without even noticing that Janez Lipnik was grudgingly trying to move them out of the way. The woman casts greedy glances around, trying to figure out where to go next. Where could she be going, Lipnik thinks, if she doesn't even know which day it is?

"Tuesday," says a gray-haired gentleman, her fellow warrior, fatigued from shopping. So it's Tuesday.

So it's Tuesday, Janez Lipnik thinks. How can they even talk about such trivialities. Parsley or lettuce, gold crowns or green, incisor or canine.

"I always get confused on holidays," the lady says, charging into his bags once again as she keeps looking around, trying to figure out where to go next. "If a holiday falls on a Monday, then I think that Tuesday is Monday, because a Monday holiday feels like a Sunday."

Janez Lipnik grows furious.

So then does she think that Wednesday is Tuesday and Sunday is Saturday?

People have to say something, anything, as Marijana would say.

Then why don't they say that the mountain is green?

Because they can't say 'Look how green the mountain is' when there are no mountains in shopping centers.

Marijana is so damned rational. She has an answer to every question. But there isn't an answer to every question, there just isn't. I know one question she doesn't have an answer to. Whether she'd ever been to Dugi Otok before. That's the one question she couldn't answer, the one thing she couldn't explain if I asked her about it. But she ought to, she ought to explain it, because if she doesn't, he'll think that he's lived so many years of his life with someone he doesn't know. But he won't, he won't ask her. She ought to explain it without his having to ask. Because she's not some archival material you have to sift through to get at the truth. She can answer on her own. Now Lipnik starts hearing some sort of buzzing sound in his head, but he's not sure if it's from the loud music in this brightly lit space or from that jet skier who shredded his nerves once years ago, and who's been shredding them ever since. Now the buzzing and the lady who keeps plowing into his bags are on the verge of shredding them again any instant. She doesn't even notice when she's kicking his bags. The bags contain milk and bread. There's also French cheese, a bottle of Bordeaux and Marijana's silk stockings, there are pillow covers, oranges and a knife. The knife is for slicing bread, but it's still a sharp knife. A knife that could shred his nerves.

At last the lady decides which way to go, toward the shoe store—where else. But before she does, she stumbles into one of his bags (the one with the cheese? or the milk?), and the gray-haired gentleman goes tottering off after her.

It's Tuesday. The Tuesday after the holiday which he and Marijana have remained silent through.

He spent all day Saturday at the archive. On Sunday they were silent. On Monday morning she headed out. But what lingered in his head was not the memory of her leaving or the taxi that she rode off in. What lingered was the memory of their silence. The silence of their Sunday afternoon, the silence of the long night that followed, the silence of the telephone that should have rung on Monday. This is Tuesday now, it's Tuesday, even though the lady kicking his bags is unsure if it might not be Monday, she always gets confused after a holiday. As if one day were like any other. They're not. Monday was the day of Marijana's departure and of the silent telephone. How am I supposed to know what's going on in that head of yours, she said. My head, he wanted to say, is getting plowed up by that damn jet skier from Dugi Otok. That's why I can't say what's going on in my head. Things are building up in there—they don't 'go on', they build up like a vast body of water behind a dam. But he said nothing. Like that mannequin leaning against the window pane—she didn't say anything, either.

43.

Where is your soul wandering? Marijana said. Away from me, she said, someplace else. Doesn't Marijana understand that things are mounting up in his head? Mounting up like some huge body of water behind a dam. The way they mounted up in Zala D.'s head? Among the letters of hostages shot in the jails of Maribor he found the name of her brother. It could have been her brother, they had the same surname. The Germans allowed each hostage who was going to be shot to write one last letter. Zoran D. said goodbye to his mother and father. He's sorry for the suffering they'll endure when they find out he's gone. *Tell Zala how much I missed her. I'll see you beyond the stars, where we'll all be together again. I hug and kiss you all in my thoughts. Zoran.* If that was her brother—and it almost certainly was, and Lipnik the expert archivist, will almost certainly find it out—then the question remains, did Zala receive the letter? Where? She can't have stayed in Lower Carniola—in the autumn of '43 the province was in chaos, with partisans, village guards, chetniks, retreating Italians and advancing Germans. It would have been an impossibility for the young schoolteacher to stay in an abandoned schoolhouse that no one attended anymore, alone and defenseless, vulnerable to suspicious locals, to covert partisan spies, to the rectory across the way, where her reputation was bad, and to some hired hand named Franz, who couldn't forget the way her boyfriend Aleksij, the officer, had humiliated him. That was not possible. She almost certainly wanted to get to Maribor, where her parents and friends were, but that would have been harder than staying in Lower Carniola. She had left, and the only place she could go was Ljubljana. She rode her bicycle toward Ljubljana past columns of retreating Italians, past overturned trucks and dying mules that had been shot at roadside. She threw her bicycle up onto the back of some truck and endured the stares of the black-haired soldiers. But none of them had the will to bother her. She hopped off outside of Ljubljana, as though she were getting off of a train, and they waved goodbye to her. Is that how it was? The city was full of refugees from Styria and Lower Carniola. It was still the best place to lie low, or at least live somewhat unnoticed, despite all the refugees and the frequent transfers of power there was at least a semblance of order there. Did she go to Ljubljana?

44.

The most likely solution was close at hand, much closer than he could have imagined, even in his wildest dreams. It was roughly three feet away. But if you can't see it, it doesn't matter if it's three feet away or three thousand, if it's right under your nose or lost deep in some archive cellar, misclassified perhaps, or possibly in the wrong folder.

He kept going back to the memoirs of The Great Lover in hopes of finding some clue there. At one point Zala talks about her childhood and about another officer, her father. About the evenings when her father's army friends would gather and drink in their living room, while she listened from under her blankets as they recounted their experiences with the artillery or their feats in the cavalry and toasted the young king and the glory of Yugoslavia. Or their stories about the battle for Carinthia. How German patriots bayoneted some Slovene officer named Puncer in the chest. They knocked him down in some peasant house and pinned him to the floor with a bayonet right through his chest. That's the kind of story she heard. Oh, but Lipnik was also familiar with stories like that. Stories about knives. His father's stories from the concentration camp. Then sometimes they sang, *We're marching, we're marching, King Petar's grenadiers.* Oh, Janez Lipnik knew those evenings well. He knew those voices, except that it wasn't the living room they came from — they didn't have one where he grew up — the voices he heard came from their little kitchen. He knew those deep male voices in the night, the way they boomed and the way they sang: freedom's key, freedom's key, our glee. But she heard her mother crying after the men left, as well as Zoran's recriminations. Her brother, who was older than her, often argued with their father.

45.

The solution came from none other than Beno. The most incompetent and indifferent archivist on the face of the earth. He came by his office in the afternoon and perched on his desk. He was chewing gum. He said that he had to get rid of the garlic smell from the salad. The chewing gum didn't bother him, what bothered him was the constant chatter about sailing and the women he took sailing with him. Even more, that he kept sitting on his desk. Lipnik detested his banal, unguarded bumptiousness. Most of all he detested the fact that Beno didn't seem to think that perching on his desk was bumptious at all, but a kind of friendly gesture. Now he's going to say, 'You still working?'

"You still working?" Beno said.

"As you can see," Lipnik said without looking up from his desk.

"It's a nice day out."

It is a nice spring day out, and soon it will be summer, and he so wanted Beno not to talk about sailing.

He asked him to lend him the notes of that pervert guy who screwed his way through the war and emigration and mowed down everything female that didn't run up a tree or jump in a ditch. It would help him liven up his afternoon. Lipnik said he was still studying the case. He so wanted Beno not to say anything about sailing. And he didn't. He said it was raining, really pouring out there, buckets. Lipnik distractedly looked toward the window. Of course it's raining. Drops were sliding down the windowpanes and a fine rain was misting the cherry tree outside, it was drizzling. It's a safe bet Beno isn't thinking about the cherry blossoms—he doesn't even notice them. He's thinking about where he can snag some young thing to go sailing with him. It occurred to him that that stud who had Zala and a few thousand other women may have been like this. No, he couldn't have been as dumb as Beno. Impossible. Nor as unguardedly bumptious as Beno, who on top of everything else doesn't know that it's bumptious and even a shade aggressive for him to park his rear end—or half of it—on the edge of his desk, just a few feet from his files.

"Stock market's falling," Beno said, chewing loudly on his gum. "Did you see today's numbers?"

He knew perfectly well that Lipnik hadn't seen that day's numbers. Why should an archivist spend his time chasing stock market numbers? So that you won't have to rot in this archive, Beno explained to him long ago. Take out a loan and invest it in bonds or stocks, then keep an eye on the numbers in the paper. Sometimes you can practically hear the rustle of the money fluttering down, other times, if it's change, it just clinks. He's not going to let himself rot in this archive. He's going to buy a house on an island in the Adriatic. Maybe he'll open a gym for the tourists. Evenings he'll sit in a pub by the seashore and drink dry red wine—plavac. Lipnik so wanted Beno to go away. He hated him. He hated sailing and Beno and the stock market. And Marijana too, a bit, if it was true. If it was really true?

"You'll rot in this archive," Beno said. He reached across his desk and took a folder with some handwritten sheets off the top of a stack. He opened the folder and leafed through its contents. He read a few lines.

"Oh, what is this now?" he said. "Don't tell me you're dealing with crazy people, too?"

Lipnik knew what Beno was holding. The notes of Ivanka K. During the war she had been a nurse orderly at Studenec. She writes that at that time there were more crazy people outside the mental hospital than in it.

"You're gonna lose it completely," Beno said, tossing the folder down and removing his buttock from the desk.

Lipnik looked at him almost gratefully. A light had gone on in his head. He even smiled at him as he left. Beno looked at him, chewed, and shook his head. When he went out, he left the door open behind him. Lipnik greedily grabbed the folder that Beno had tossed on the desk. It came to him in a flash: Wasn't there some young schoolteacher mentioned in these notes? She'd been brought there on a rainy day. Ivanka K. mentions her somewhere. She describes many of the women who were in her care. But she includes no names. She does name the home guards who in '44 had killed her husband, the mental hospital's blacksmith and stableman. They had completely disfigured his face, apparently in the course of torturing him. Up until now Lipnik had just glanced at her notes. Now he sensed that Zala was in there somewhere—somewhere in the terrible nightmares that nurse orderly Ivanka K. describes midway through the war.

46.

That evening he thought: Ah, these evenings of ours, these salads, this TV news, these legs stretched out on the couch. Halfway through the evening news he suddenly turned the television off. He said he'd rather watch ads for depilatory lotion than those empty heads. He couldn't stand to look at them anymore. Marijana said that she'd still like to see the rest of the news. He can't just turn the TV off on her like that. What would she like to see: The political bullshitters, the intellectual poseurs, or the financial frauds, which would she prefer to watch? She said at least it was a shade more interesting than depilatory creams.

"Do you tweeze, yank, shave?" he shouted. "That's a hell of a lot more interesting."

"Maybe," she said, turning the TV back on. "But right now I'm more interested in seeing what's going on in the world."

"Nothing," he said. "There's nothing happening. Everything has already happened, a long time ago." He pointed at his head. "And it's all in here."

"It's all in here," he said, turning the TV off. "It's all here inside my head. Don't you see?"

She didn't see. She said that what he was doing right then was violent.

"Violence?" he shouted. "This is violence?"

"Yes," she said. "It's tyranny."

"You don't have the first idea what violence is," he shouted.

"Am I going to have to find that out, too?" she said furiously.

He left and slammed the door.

47.

He was trying to figure out where Zala D. was between the time of her last mention in the book of The Great Lover and showing up after the war as a teacher in some elementary school in Maribor. The final entry in their erotic chapter states that unidentified partisans shaved Zala's head and that they liquidated Antonia. That's not the word that the civil servant uses. He writes that they killed her. The accounting term *liquidate* surprised Lipnik again and again every time he came across it in archival documents. It was so arithmetically clean—*7 traitors liq. on the spot*—so simple that he always shuddered at the sight of it. No blood, no wailing, pain, or terror— nothing. One person here, seven people there removed, liquidated, case closed—you'd hardly think that human lives were being ended. He thought that perhaps it was easier for the liquidator to pull the trigger if he thought of his act as a liquidation—not even an execution, just a closure, an erasure, a crossing out, period, the end. Not only was Zala's friend Antonia liquidated, but also her brother. He was liquidated by the Nazis in the courtyard of the central jail in Maribor. As Viktor Klemperer, the Jewish Romance languages scholar, who survived the war under house arrest in Germany, points out, the Nazis used the term, too: seventeen enemies of the people liquidated.

The night before Zoran was shot he wrote a farewell letter. Where was it delivered? To Ljubljana. Zala was in Lower Carniola for part of September 1943, then she left for Ljubljana.

48.

In the morning Marijana called him at the archive. She said she was going to tell him over the phone because she couldn't do it at home. Why can't she? Why? Because he keeps slamming doors. And turning the television off. Because he's always either silent or shouting. She's leaving. What is this about? Why the big hurry, all of a sudden? he said. Everything was going so slowly for so long, and now it's all speeding up. She told him to listen to her for God's sake. I'm listening, he said. He doesn't know what's happening ... in his head anymore, he said. We've been there already.

"Well, listen again, dammit."

He wanted to hang up. Ever since he discovered the notes of that sex maniac, she said, he's been a different person. At first he'd talked vaguely about tracking down some person who appeared in that extraordinary document. Now he didn't talk at all. She can't understand why somebody's notes about adventures in bed should be an extraordinary document. Because it was wartime and in wartime everybody writes about battles, but he wrote about his women. Is that why? She'd spoken with Beno. Aha, Beno, what about? About him, they'd talked about him. Beno also thinks he's been acting strange lately. So does his boss, the director of the archive. Aha, Lipnik exclaimed, aha, my boss! What do those two know! When he mentioned to Beno what extraordinary material he'd come across in the box from Australia, he'd just laughed. You're kidding, Beno had said, so you mean to say this guy fucked his way through the war. Did you hear that? he said. That's all that genius had to say about my discovery, about my research, for God's sake.

"Please listen to me. Please."

There's a person who appears in the memoir, a woman, who has a connection to him, Lipnik. This was the most precise piece of information to come out of him, and even it was murky. And what sort of connection does this probably long since dead or, if she's still living, very, very old woman have to him, to his life? She had tried several times to get him to tell more, not out of curiosity, but because she thought that the man she lived with, her husband, her nearest and dearest, was suddenly experiencing some difficulties. And those difficulties appeared to stem from his discovery, the papers lying on his desk at work or in a locked drawer in the Regional Archive. If she knew what it was about, then maybe she could help him somehow. She could encourage him to get to the bottom of it or completely give it up. Lipnik had never been a particularly talkative person, often he read for hours on end without looking up from his book, and sometimes he just wordlessly looked out the window, enjoying the chance, as he'd told her long ago, to 'think his own thoughts.' But in the past few weeks he'd been 'thinking his own thoughts' so often that it had gotten downright unbearable. The slightest thing would cause him to raise his voice, he'd say things that for the life of her she couldn't understand, and then he'd walk out. He asked if that was everything she had to say. He thought she might have something else to tell him.

"About what?"

"The migration of souls. Didn't you say, 'Where is your soul wandering?'"

He could hear her breathing. She said she didn't understand what he meant.

Then she said she couldn't take it anymore.

<h2 style="text-align:center">49.</h2>

But in fact she could. She was a persistent woman. She tried to rescue the peaceful life that had suddenly vanished somewhere in that head of this ever more troubled man, with whom she'd lived for so many years and whom day after day she knew less well. She invited him out to lunch at a Chinese restaurant.

"It would be good if you could take at least one afternoon off. We'll go out for lunch, like we used to."

"All right, if we're going to do it like we used to."

Once they were in the restaurant he didn't argue with her, but with the waiter, instead, who was unable to explain to him why one of the dishes was called 'ants climb the tree.'

"If you're Chinese, don't you think you ought to know that?" In his clumsy Slovene the Chinese waiter said that some dishes just had peculiar names, names that probably dated back very far. He asked the Chinese waiter why these thin noodles mixed with tiny bits of meat were called that. The waiter shrugged, he didn't know. Maybe he didn't know enough Slovene.

"That's just what it's called," he said.

Lipnik said he couldn't figure out where the tree was. These little bits of meat, these could be the symbolic ants—but where was the tree?

Marijana asked him please not to make a big deal out of this for a change.

"Who's making a big deal out of anything?" Lipnik said, raising his voice. "Am I making a big deal out of this? There's no way the noodles can be the tree, not even symbolically, though the ants could be the—but why would a person eat ants, even symbolic ones?"

The confused waiter looked at him and shrugged.

Of course, Lipnik said, it probably means that in the old days in China your people ate ants. You still eat worms. And fireflies. The waiter frowned. He went to the back of the restaurant and Marijana could see him explaining something to someone. Then the two of them came back to their table. How can I help you, sir? the other man said, also Chinese. The check, Lipnik said, bring me the check for the ants.

Marijana smiled at both waiters. It's nothing, she said, there's no problem, we'd just like to pay. That's all.

She nodded reassuringly. The waiters nodded, too, and smiled. Just the check? the first one said. That's all, Marijana said.

While she paid the check, Lipnik got up and left.

For a while she walked furiously past the stores and cafes of the nearby shopping center, ready to tell him a thing or two one more— one last time. That this couldn't go on. That his getting up and walking away over every tiniest thing had become a habit. Sometimes he would turn the television off and bang the door behind him on his way. She felt sure she would see him any instant somewhere in the shopping center's main promenade, where he usually wandered around aimlessly—actually, with the sole aim of killing time until she emerged from some store or other. Sometimes, while minding the bags that she would hand over to him so she could keep working the shopping center with minimal drag, he would sit on a bench in the huge, brightly lit mall and read.

But this time he was nowhere to be found. She thought maybe he'd gone out to the car. But out in the lot the car was empty, so she took out her spare keys and drove off. She thought that one of these days he would just up and leave.

Hadn't she seen a photo of some missing man in the newspaper a week or so ago?

"Did you know," she had said, "that little Slovenia has almost a hundred missing persons at any given time? Most of them are never found. They disappear."

"All this guy has to do," he said, looking at the photo, "is shave off his mustache and nobody will recognize him."

"Most of them," he said, "just get swallowed up. Maybe one or two go hang themselves on some tree deep in the forest."

"What sort of bizarre thoughts are those?" she said. "There are plenty of unstable people walking around. We can't be responsible for them, too."

"They could move to other countries," Lipnik continued to grind through the possibilities. "They could get lost in the forest— Slovenia has huge, dense forests. They could fall into some cave in the Karst. Or they could deliberately go there, with the intention of living underground for a while and then coming back. But sometimes those people can't come back."

She took the newspaper back out of his hands and looked at the photo of the missing man.

"Slovenia," he said, "is like a sea sponge. Underground it's shot through with holes. With underground rivers flowing this way and that. You follow a river where it goes underground in some nice, flat field and you come back out on some other river at the bottom of a deep sub-Alpine valley."

This evening he again spent wandering the suburbs.

He came back home late, smelling of alcohol, if the stench of brandy can be called that. He lay down next to her and fell instantly asleep. Around four in the morning she saw him sitting beside the window. His face was pale, bathed in neon light. He turned to face her with his red, sleepless eyes and said something strange. Something has wandered into my life. Out of the dark, out of a veil of rain, out of the night, the past. The past is flooding us, he said, it's going to drown us like this rain, there'll be no air.

What did he mean by that? That everything is interconnected, that's what he thinks, or rather senses, interconnected by slender threads. Which can break.

50.

Lipnik read this:

Now, as I write this, I'm on ward number two, the night shift, and I can describe some of my life. My friends laugh at me, they say I've probably caught something from the inmates since I've been working here. But that doesn't daunt me one bit, since the things people have been doing to each other outside these walls with the war on is no more normal than what goes on in our asylum. I recall the incident a few years ago on Three Kings' Day when one of the women grabbed me with such force that she had me on the floor in no time, trying to strangle me with all of a madwoman's terrifying might. I was fighting for my life. I'm not a coward and I'm not frail, having worked on a farm since I was a child. But suddenly I was powerless and I still shake when I remember it. And that's not because of the cold, because I'm wrapped in a blanket as I sit here and write. When the other inmates saw what was happening, they rushed to help me and suddenly there was a whole bunch of us on the floor and even with their help I was barely able to fight myself free of the woman's furious grip. Anyone who hasn't seen how these people live and what they do can't imagine what it's like. But our ward is pleasant, we have about eighty patients here, sometimes more, sometimes less, depending on how many recover and how many new ones are brought in. They can move around freely here—indoors in winter, and in the summer we have a fenced-in garden where they can walk. They get up at seven and go to bed at six. It would be nicer if they didn't bring in people who are sick with something other than mental illness. The tubercular cases are kept in separate wooden barracks to keep them isolated. Just now there's an outbreak of dropsy, with one of the women close to the end, her whole body cracked open in a single wound and the only thing that keeps her alive are injections. I asked the doctor to let her go, to let her die in peace, she's suffering so much. Other than that, most of our patients are either epileptics, paralytics or religious maniacs, and these are the hardest to cure. The saddest to see are the patients who have been cured but have nobody to come get them. And so they wait, at the mercy of their next of kin. Some relatives are reluctant to take them home, out of fear of a relapse, which unfortunately does happen. These patients are condemned to a life sentence here, since where else can they go if their relatives don't want them? One of the patients under my care is a Marija R., destitute, forsaken and spurned by the whole world. She was an illegitimate child, her mother was a maid who worked days, and so the child lived in her uncle's household without any upbringing at all. At fifteen she was sent out on her own and immediately lost her way and had her own child—at that age. She strangled it and threw it into a river. Then she moved to another town, where she had a second child, which she dealt with the same way as the first. She came into the hands of the law and was sentenced to many years, but had a nervous breakdown in prison, so they transferred her to Studenec. She's been here for nine years. She seems perfectly normal and she often complains to me that she'd rather serve out her sentence in prison than deal with the insane people here. She's a great help to me in keeping the others under control, because the women are afraid of her. When she enters a room, she's like a lion, all the others make way, her big eyes flash with a strange fire, and she instills fear in you. Still, I would miss her if she were gone.

51.

When they were having ants climbing a tree for lunch at the Chinese restaurant, the jet skier started roaring through his head again. That jet skier from Dugi Otok was a *furore brevis*. A brief derangement. This happened when they were fleeing the Storm, not some meteorological phenomenon, but a military operation by that name, *Oluja* in Croatian. Fleeing? Janez couldn't stand that word, they weren't fleeing at all, they were retreating, cutting their vacation short, because the radio kept reporting on a vast operation that the Croatian army had launched against insurgent Serbian units in the vicinity of Knin. And playing Croatian military marches. But the radio alone would not have dislodged them from their peaceful—and at that time it seemed—most peaceful of all islands in the Adriatic or any other sea. The war in Bosnia raged on, with the news reporting the bombardment of this city or that, the sirens sounding up and down throughout the interior, and people running for bomb shelters. As one Bosnian refugee said on television, people were rampaging and killing each other like wild beasts through the forests. Afterwards Marijana often asked how it was possible for them to hear those reports—Janez listened to them every morning and evening—and still keep on sunbathing, hiking around the deserted island, swimming, and now and then making love in the moonlight. But they were in love—what else should they be doing?—they were newly married and in love, alone on the island, far from the war. But not far from the jet skier. Onto their perfectly empty, perfectly quiet beach, with the fragrant pines above them and the splash of the water against the rocks below, the jet ski seemed to drop practically out of the sky. Better yet, out of hell, he came roaring straight out of hell. A young man was hunched over on it, wildly pumping the gas, with streams of water flying out behind. He began riding it in a circle around the inlet, then in ellipses, in short spurts when he'd gun the thing, and finally in long serpentines, after he obviously grew tired.

The first time he came roaring in, Janez was asleep.

When he opened his eyes is when he made the odd statement that Marijana repeated many times after that: He broke my dream.

52.

Is it possible that Zala D. was committed to the psychiatric hospital in Studenec for the next to last year of the war? In her memoirs of her wartime service in that institution, Ivanka K. writes about a young schoolteacher who was brought there from Ljubljana. At one point she says that she was from Maribor, that her father had been a Yugoslav army officer, and that her brother had been shot by the Germans in the courtyard of the Maribor jail. Very early on Janez Lipnik suspected this could be her. But why was she there? Had that vicious incident with the partisans caused her to lose her mind? The memoir's author at no point mentions her name, just as she gives no full names anywhere in her text. Most of all, no one expects insane asylums to have functioned during the war. At that time the world was full of insane people and all of them were on the outside.

The author of this memoir—or diary, rather, because part of the text came into existence during the war—wonders the same thing. She writes that she can no longer tell where the concentration of lunatics is greatest, inside or outside, and that the things people are doing to each other beyond the asylum's walls are scarcely more normal than what's happening within them. All kinds of wretches are dying here without being aware of their pitiful state, nurse orderly Ivanka K. writes in her diary. In the most secure ward, the patients squat stark naked on heaps of straw. They can't stand to wear any clothes and immediately tear them off. These are the most seriously deranged ones, Ivanka K. writes. Some of them think that the heaps of straw are easy chairs and that they're sitting in the most beautifully appointed, luxurious drawing rooms. You have to be brave with them, she says, when you bring them morning coffee, you have to lock the door from inside so they don't escape, and you mustn't show you're afraid of them, or they'll attack you. The lives of these people are terribly sad. They squat or sit, eat like animals, and sometimes scream horrifically. You can scarcely believe that they once lived among other people, healthy, handsome and young. The sight of them shakes you to the core and you think, God save me from such a horrible affliction—these people are living corpses. Some of them refuse to eat for weeks on end and you have to feed them like infants. Or by a tube which gets inserted through the nose, since otherwise the patient will clamp it shut with his teeth or bite through it. Fortunately, though, there's always a doctor present. That's one type of patient. Another type just sits for days on end, staring out the window from morning to night or standing motionless in a doorway, so that sometimes you have to push them aside just to get out. These patients get slightly better rooms, each with four iron bedframes with straw ticks on them. The worst ward of all is the one we call the madhouse. That's where we lock up the most uncontrollable, dangerous ones in a kind of coop. Some of them lie on the floor, bound up like children in swaddling clothes, some in straitjackets, while others are even tied down with leather straps. Altogether there are three wards. The first is the madhouse, the second we call the agitated, because the patients there are still agitated, but lucid enough to talk. The third is the calm ward. Nobody screams or shouts there and some of them are practically well and waiting to go home.

53.

The next day he came back. The jet skier. He circled wildly around the placid inlet. Janez said he was going to find the son of a bitch in the harbor and wreck his engine. He said he'd been jet skiing through his head all night long, that it was buzzing in there and when he woke up he was amazed at how still it was all through their house. They changed beaches. But the rattling devil in the shape of a young man wearing a red swimsuit and hunched over his vehicle, clattering wildly and churning up waves all around him, spinning around in tight circles and coming right up next to the shore showed up there, too. That was in August, and Janez said that he couldn't sleep anymore, because that devil kept buzzing all night long in his head. He kept getting up and going back to bed, and in the dead of night he would walk down to the water and then come back into the room on tiptoe, but he still woke her up every time. The buzzing jet ski which threw Janez Lipnik off balance for several days and nights was just a harbinger of something worse, of the war that was now approaching the island. One August morning, when Janez had come back from one of his sleepless strolls, they decided to wait for the sunrise with open eyes and ears and nostrils. They were going to inhale it, take it into their lungs, Marijana said, they would experience it in the freshness of morning on top of the hill overlooking the town. Without the jet skier. As they stood there, up on the hill, she said, 'When you think about how the sun has been coming up like this for a thousand years—for more than a thousand, but it's hard to imagine more than that—when you think about how the sun has been …' But that morning was not like a thousand other August mornings. The roar of hundreds of engines was drifting up from the road down below—these were not jet skis, these were columns of trucks heading toward the harbor, where several ferries were waiting to take them on board. That's the army, Janez said. Something is happening. They drove the car down into town, which was full of young men in uniform who had apparently assembled there overnight from every corner of the island. Despite the early hour, the little café where they usually stopped was full of people and yet oddly quiet, without the usual loud Mediterranean morning greetings and exchanges. Some soldiers ran down the street toward the harbor. The sunrise was like a thousand other August mornings, yet different. Suddenly there was an anxious atmosphere in the town. The blond lady, the owner, who brought them their coffee, had red, tearful eyes. What's going on? They're heading for the mainland, their acquaintance told them. That's my son over there, she said and nodded her head toward a table where several boys in uniform were sitting. They're being mobilized, Janez said.

They really did flee the island.

It's all one and the same war, he said as they drove through villages that had been burned to the ground. That jet ski keeps buzzing in my head and the thing keeps repeating, making my head spin, making me dizzy, the same story over and over, always the same.

54.

The new patient, a young schoolteacher whom they brought in from Ljubljana, spent a short time in the agitated ward but was soon transferred to the calm ward. They brought her by car on a rainy day. She got out of the car calmly and looked around as if at some totally unfamiliar place, which indeed it was, for she had never been here before. She was so self-controlled and alert that the doctor on duty held an umbrella over her head so she wouldn't get wet. Only her eyes gave away that not everything was all right with her. She glanced back and forth, just as everyone does who is admitted here, no doubt she was a little afraid, but her eyes ... They were the only thing suggesting that strange agitation that is a dead giveaway of a person whose head is not functioning quite right.

At the time, just a month had passed, Ivanka K. writes, since another schoolteacher had taken her own life. She had hanged herself on my ward. She was already dead when I entered her room. It practically gave me a heart attack, since I was responsible for her. The agony of taking her down and giving her artificial respiration will never leave me. It was no use. The nurses came running to help, we called for the doctor, but it was too late. She was free of her earthly torment. She had been delusional, always claiming she was doomed and that the devil was waiting at the gate for her soul. While everything was over for her, a difficult time was beginning for me. I had to answer to three doctors and the director, who questioned me about every last detail—where I'd been, what I'd done, and how many paces away from the patient I'd been.

A friend told me, 'See, you've been given another schoolteacher.' But because of what had happened, I was extremely cautious and mistrustful when the new patient arrived. She seemed to be calm— except that her eyes darted around. I sat next to her on the bed and asked her what had happened to her, but didn't find out anything significant. One of the doctors said—I overheard this in the corridor—that her brother had been shot in Maribor. She had been very attached to him. She had found out about it somewhere in Lower Carniola. And since the escalation of the war prevented her from getting back home so she could at least comfort their mother, this started to weigh on her, as it did on so many unfortunate people in those difficult times. She began to do strange, even bizarre things. A doctor told one of the nurses, who then told me, that she had taken her clothes off outside a hotel in Lower Carniolan Springs. For a long time she herself said nothing, but she was calm and everyone was relieved, because they remembered the one who had hanged herself. It looked like we were going to be able to work with her. They moved her to the calm ward. Most of the people there had experienced something terrible since the war had started. The doctors said that time will heal their psychological wounds and that we just need to wait.

But that's not how it was.

During the doctor's first visit she grabbed his long, gray beard and wrapped it around her hand, and we all jumped up and pulled her away from him with great difficulty. We wrapped her up in wet bed sheets to calm her nerves. We stretched six wet bed sheets over a mattress and laid her on them naked, wrapping her up tight in the sheets and tying her down with two long straps that were attached to the mattress. Then we covered her with six dry blankets and two down comforters on top of that. We left her like that for two hours so she could perspire and let her nerves calm down.

Within two weeks the schoolteacher was transferred to the calm ward. For a while longer they heard nothing about her. But, as the doctors say, time itself heals psychological wounds, and they only had to wait. And indeed that is what happened. She gradually calmed down and even began to talk with the nurses and orderlies. Soon after that they released her.

55.

He relaxes.

But then it seems that he hears it again for a second, the jet ski. It buzzes inside his head. At times it whistles. That's Lojze's scythe, he thinks quite clearly: when it flashes through the grass and the fellows take another pass. It hasn't been that long at all since history was a flowing river, when crowds of people pushed through the streets, converging on the main squares of old towns that had such magical names then, each with its own mysterious aura.

Gdańsk, Leipzig, Timişoara, Vilnius—what names!

There was no fatigue back then. He went against the current, against the current of the old regime, as it kept trying to shift back into its old, fetid channel, he had stood up against its threatening power. He went to rallies. To Congress Square, the place where governments fell, and now here another one had fallen. He was thrilled. And the square looked different, too. Like a river gorge that history was about to come thundering through, and he was going to feel it. Time would come roaring through him, wild rapids. Now he was here, in this absent, motionless time, with his eyes fixed on the flickering numbers of that digital clock in the shopping center. Waiting for Marijana to come back from the hairdresser's. Or from the cosmetician's. Something in time had broken. He could sense distinctly that something had happened, but he didn't know what. Images kept taking shape in his head. Mowers! Explosions! Tunnels! A bloody hand loading a pistol. Crowds on the main squares of old towns. Snow that keeps falling off the boughs of pines onto people who have fallen asleep underneath them. Pictures, images, faces, the sound of the rain running down the roof. The moment frozen, the images fleeting.

56.

They stopped for several days in Zadar, which was full of military. Unshaven men in dirty uniforms going and coming from somewhere, sirens at night, and hotels full of refugees. They almost didn't find a place to stay. The roar of the jet ski in his head kept getting worse. He told Marijana what was happening to him. There's a war going on here, she had said, people are killing each other. We don't even know how we're going to get home, and you're worried about some silly jet ski? Always wrapped up in some detail, always some damned petty detail. She's right, he thought. And now I'm wrapped up in that bicycle. On Sunday she'd asked him if he'd found where the bicycle *comes* up in those wartime documents. He didn't tell her. Because again she'd say, 'Always some detail, always some petty detail.' Had she jumped off the sailboat? What would she have to say about that detail: had she jumped off the boat, had she twisted her ankle? What would she say if she knew that he knows, that he knows full well that Jana was on that boat, the same Jana who rode on a bus full of drunken Hungarian soldiers. He knows that they had two muscular idiots with them, Beno and Pepo—if only they could at least be Benjamin and Jože, not Beno and Pepo. But those were details, those were details.

But he doesn't know. He doesn't know until he asks her. And the way she answers will say it all. But until then he doesn't know. He knows what happened half a century ago, but he doesn't know what happened a few years ago. That television flickering in the display window on the other side of the shopping center promenade, it's like an aperture with the beyond shining through it. Not everyone has this gift, but I can look through it and see, Lipnik thinks. I can see my life and I can see their lives. Marijana has known for a long time—he told her long ago that he's able to visualize things very vividly. As vividly as though he were there. So vividly, he can physically sense them. A teacup, the dampness of dew on the morning grass, the blade of a scythe—he can feel these things, he can also hear them: a gunshot at night, bedsprings squeaking, banging on the door. He can see the old trees swaying on Pohorje in the cold winter wind. The snow falling off their boughs onto the men who are freezing down below, pistols in hand. Shooting. Shooting at figures lying at their feet. Those are half-dead or half-alive partisans.

They're lying in the snow under the Pohorje pines. They're killing them, shooting the ones that still move. Lipnik knows their names and faces. They had pictures of themselves taken alongside the bodies, and he knows the names of the murderers, they etched themselves in his memory long ago. He can't erase them.

57.

He can't erase anything. Including Ivanka K., who may have met Zala the schoolteacher in the mental hospital at Studenec. Nor her rounded handwriting, which with its big loops describes the bloody, broken face of her husband. He walked around the big building which is still standing today. He thought about going inside and asking if they knew of an Ivanka K. Perhaps they had some record of her in their archives. He wanted to ask her if the young schoolteacher who came to the hospital in 1944 was Zala D. But now Ivanka K. was joining the shattered images in his head that it was no longer possible to reassemble. Because Ivanka K., who had left behind a record of events in the Studenec asylum, is standing before him and saying that in 1944 the madness that she thought only ruled on the outside finally entered the asylum. She says she doesn't know what happened to the schoolteacher. She'd been released. She had suffered terrible things in the war and undergone a terrible shock. But she had recovered. She had probably gone back to teaching, what else could she do? She, Ivanka K., experienced some terrible things at that time, she had thought there was more madness outside than inside the asylum's walls, but then that madness came inside. Up until then she and her husband, who worked in the hospital's foundry, had hoped to make it through those hard times. But that year the Germans came for the director and took him away on charges that he had hidden wounded partisans and members of the Liberation Front among the patients. Soon after that they arrested another doctor, a clerk, a nurse, and a locksmith. The threat of danger also hung over them and their children. It was perhaps the most dangerous year of the war. The home guards and the partisans were clashing everywhere, and people were disappearing.

In late March of that terrible year, she says, two strangers knocked on the front door of our house at 9:30 at night. One of them was wearing a uniform of the home guard and the other was wearing civilian clothes. They sat with my husband in the kitchen. The children were asleep.

The one in civilian dress said they were going to take Mr. K. to the airport for half an hour to question him. They needed some information. They just needed him for half an hour and would drive him back home. Ivanka K. objected. It's been a long day, she said, what are you thinking of, questioning people at night. What? said the younger man in civilian dress. Do you think we work just eight hours a day? We don't have set hours, he said. We work until midnight, sometimes all through the night if we have to. Don't go, Jožko, Ivanka said. If you go now, you'll never come back.

He never came back, she says.

She looked for him day after day for a full month. She went to the police, to the home guard at the airport, to the high command in Ljubljana, where somebody said, 'Your husband, madame, paid membership dues in the Liberation Front. If that's all it was, he'll be sent to Germany for forced labor. If it was more than that, we can't say what will happen to him. Go home, ma'am, go to your children.' She went home. But in early May she began to hear rumors, started by men who worked with the railway, that the Sava was washing up dead bodies. Three of them were in Laze. She went there, but the German guards told her that they'd already been buried. She showed them Jožko's picture, but nobody recognized him. One of them said that he didn't get a good look at the bodies, but even if he had, they had been in the water for so long that it would be hard to make any identification. There were no names on the graves. She stood in front of them for a long time and waited for some sign to tell her if one of them was her husband.

She would walk through these meadows alongside the Sava whenever they left the hospital to work in the fields. Her husband had been one of the mowers, he did such a good job of it, his scythe would whistle through the grass, and he would also mow around their house first thing in the morning. Now she was sitting here, waiting for the waves to wash his body up on shore. She still had a glimmer of hope that he hadn't been killed. She asked the Sava ferryman how long drowned people usually stayed in the water. They can stay under for up to three months. When the water rises, you'll see how many bodies it brings up. One morning in the middle of May, Ivanka K. says, a neighbor whose husband had also been taken away stopped by to say that some more bodies had washed up.

And indeed, the neighbor found her own husband in the Laze morgue. The two of them looked at him as he lay there, swollen from the water. He'd been stabbed and had a gunshot wound in his head. She examined all of the male corpses. Now she felt she knew what madness was. In this delirium she understood the madness that the patients she tended must experience. What followed was a long, dark dream. She walked among corpses. She took the train to Litija, because the railway men had told her there were some more lying there. From the train between Jevnica and Kresnice she caught sight of a body floating in the water, by the shore, caught in some branches. She felt her heart being squeezed: That's him. She got off at Kresnice and ran upstream alongside the Sava to where that pool was, and while still a ways off, she noticed that some people had gathered. Some peasants had dug out a ditch, and the body was lying in the grass. Her heart was bursting and she didn't dare to go near. 'Is he yours?' asked a peasant. She went up to look. It wasn't hers. It was Janko, the locksmith from the mental hospital, the one they'd taken away sometime before. He had been a tall man, ramrod straight, a fine figure, but now his forehead had been blown away by a bullet to the temple, and the fish had eaten away at his legs.

She stood by the water and waited for it to bring up her Jože. One of the peasants came over to her and said, 'Go up the Sava. I think the gendarmes have discovered another one up there.' They had already buried him, so she showed them his picture. That's not him, said the gendarme, who spoke Slovene. When she came home, she told Janko's relatives where they could find his body.

Lipnik reads:

At noon, after lunch, a gendarme comes by and tells me to show him my husband's picture. When I give it to him, he looks at it and says that's the one, Did you find him, Yes, Where is he? In the Polje morgue is the answer. How I got there, I don't know, I took the children with me, I was shaking all the way, thinking, how will I find him, but then, what a horror people can make of a handsome man. When I lift up the coffin lid, my God, are you really our Papa—Franzka, Marija, look what they've done to our Papa. I look and everything goes dark in front of my eyes, even though I was fully conscious and stayed conscious despite the horrible way he looked. Of course if an uninjured person had been five weeks under water he would look horrible, but he had been bound with a rope thick as a finger, he'd had his hands tied behind his back, the fingers of his left hand were gone, his forehead was gone where he'd been hit, he'd been shot in the temple, the bones of his left arm had been broken. I keep looking at him and I can't believe it's him, but the gendarme catches my attention, he asks if it's him or not, of course it is, the physique, the clothing, everything, but the face, that bothers me. Take a good look, look closely, he says, but I am looking, and still it seems strange, only now do I see that his whole forehead is missing, that's why he looks so strange, those monsters in human disguise disfigured him like this on purpose, so no one would recognize him if he was found. The children are crying so much I can barely quiet them, when I lifted them up to look in the coffin they were so frightened I had to put the lid back on fast so they wouldn't be afraid. Now I've drunk the cup of suffering dry, what awaits me in the future I don't know, the horrible past is behind me, why does it bore into my mind, why must I be so unhappy, my whole life nothing but suffering. I have the children and could live just for them, yet I'm on the verge of despair. It's not that I'm shy of work, work strengthens a person, but the human evil that caused so much suffering, that's what drives you to despair, to think that you have to live among such despicable people. I haven't slept all night, I'm out of tears, I feel I have burning coals for eyes, a wound in my heart that hurts worse than any physical pain.

58.

A few days earlier Marijana had asked, 'Do you think what they think?' Yes, he said. Sometimes I even take their places, the people from the documents. I think that they thought what they thought. You know, you're also thinking what I'm thinking now and then. All the time I'm thinking about what they might have thought, and very often what you're thinking. But that's what you're thinking, Marijana says. What? You're thinking about what your pornographic writer was thinking.

Right. And you're thinking what I'm thinking. I often think about what you're thinking.

In other words, all of this is going on in your head. Yeah, well, maybe some of it really is in my head. Like there's somebody who collects all the information and the events and puts them together into logical units. Things from today are linked to things from yesterday, everything is interconnected, Marijana, with tiny threads of reason. You see, it's the logic that says that it doesn't matter if something is today or tomorrow, time doesn't move, it only seems to us that it moves. Marijana said that she didn't understand, she didn't get it. Doesn't matter, Lipnik said. When I've got it all worked out and all the threads are connected, I'll explain it to you. It'll be so simple. The only problem is that you can't erase anything, but you still have to tie it all together, don't you see?

Nothing can be erased and it all keeps mounting up in his head. Now it no longer buzzes like a jet ski or whistles like Lojze's scythe. Now it bangs on the floor of the big, bright mall on the edge of Ljubljana, it bangs, it flashes on the screens, with the legs of shoppers padding softly past him as he sits on his bench, surrounded with bags, just their legs and their bobbing shopping bags, how should they know what the vortex of history is when they don't even know if it's Monday or Tuesday. Things sway a bit, he can feel them swaying, the huge promenade, the display windows, the mannequin leaning up against the glass, that's because, Lipnik says to himself, the world beneath us is hollow. It seems to you shoppers and strollers that you're having a dizzy spell—so it's not just me, it's the whole lot of you. Don't try to tell me you don't know what it is, this dizziness overcoming the lot of us. I beg your pardon, Lipnik mumbled, but I'm familiar with dizziness, and I'm even more familiar with the dizziness you get from the vortex of history. Down below, he says, underneath this shopping center, everything is hollow. There are huge caves down there, some of them linked by subterranean canals. How do I know? The way the people who explored them knew, they released red dye into them, which flowed from one cave to the next. I know what you're thinking, Janez Lipnik mutters. I know what you're thinking: That's down there, the caves are down there, but up here it's bright and we go from one store window to the next, filling our bags, filling our shopping carts, and at home we'll open the bags and be happy. But if they took it all away from you, Lipnik says, would you still be happy? If they took away everything you have to somewhere out there on the flatlands beneath the rugged peaks. If they force-marched you there and gave you nothing but nettle soup to eat. Took your shopping carts away and the hot dogs and all your other sausages, and the rubberized boats that you're planning to take on the sea, the oars too, and threw it all in a big heap. Then your rings and necklaces, bags and pocket books, eyeglasses and wigs, if they took all of it away. I've seen it in Auschwitz, and my father told me about how they took away everything once they were standing out in the open. That's dizziness, the dizziness of history, and I used to hear about it at four in the morning, they take everything away, a siren goes off for roll call and you have to run out into a big yard, and German shepherds on leashes—we called them wolfhounds—are growling everywhere. Now that's dizziness, when that sort of thing happens, and it will happen to you, Lipnik says, if you don't know what was, what once happened down there underneath us and all around here. That's exactly what will happen to you again, you're going to get dizzy, much worse than today, if you don't even know if it's Monday or Tuesday.

The dizziness also comes from everything turning in circles, or maybe a great big ellipse. But not in time, not in time by a long shot. You think what they're thinking and suddenly you're in another story, and from that story you suddenly make your way into the next, and maybe you get shunted around just a bit on the way so that the circle isn't perfect, which is why Lipnik thinks that it may be an ellipse, not a circle, but a circle makes sense if after all those detours and byways it keeps bringing you back to yourself. You travel back toward your childhood and into your father's story, then you travel ahead toward old age and you bump into the story of Zala D., the schoolteacher, who's at home in your childhood, as well. That's why it's not forward and backward, but around, in a circle or an ellipsis. That's where the dizziness comes from and anyone willing enough can understand that. But why things sometimes spin in our heads, I can't say where that comes from. Lipnik understands that he'll have to go all the way back to his birth and even farther back to his embryo and even farther back, until he starts traveling forward, and that's when he'll realize that there is no forward or backward, upward or down, just a circle, and that he, like everyone else—everyone here or those who we think only remain in some papers in archives, with nothing left of them but their handwriting and papers —all of us move in a circle, and that we encounter each other on its circumference and listen to the earth tremble. And we're amazed at how it's all interlinked. And it's not just that we feel dizzy. The only reason we're amazed is because we don't yet know we're moving in a circle. Living or dead, it makes no difference. Oh come on, Lipnik thinks, what is that, living or dead? Get in line there, you with your carts, and all of you standing in line for the cashier, take roll and you'll see that you're already back in the fifteenth century, one of you on a farmstead way up in the mountains, the other a mercenary somewhere up in the German lands. And the whole line of you is out on the circumference of that circle. It's the events that have marked us, not your bodies or your lines to the cash register— it's the events we've imprinted on others that make us dizzy, and that's why we're constantly moving around the same circle.

59.

Marijana went to stay with her parents.

She said it couldn't go on like this. I don't know what's going on in your head, she said. You used to say things I couldn't understand and now you're silent. You say I should be the one talking. But I have no idea what to say. You used to talk about those documents you discovered at the archive, but now you don't talk about them anymore, either. You don't say anything, she said.

What is it about that woman, why are you obsessed with her? You found her in the memoir of some sex maniac—who is that person? Why do you say you know her? Where do you know her from, how can you know some woman whose name you've discovered at the archive? You raced off to the archive when we saw some bicycle being hauled up out of the Ljubljanica—did you find it? You're not just eccentric, you're completely unpredictable, do you know that? But that's not such a new thing, do you realize that? Some jet skier got you all worked up down on Dugi Otok and while the war was raging over on the mainland, you kept talking about that ridiculous jet skier, and if that isn't an escape from reality, what is? We drove through Serbian villages that had been burned to the ground, and you were moaning the whole time about that jet ski buzzing in your head, now is that normal? You said that everything is interconnected, that that war was connected to the one before, and that history doesn't inhabit time, but actions—now what sort of thought is that? That what happened to your father happened to you—now who ever heard of such a thing? You were never in a concentration camp, you weren't even born then, how could that have happened to you? Why do you keep on with those stories at the archive? Those people are dead, anonymous, gone—we're the ones who are alive, you and me, don't you understand? And now suddenly you keep assaulting me day after day with your silence, how have I wronged you, can you tell me that? How am I supposed to live with a man who's silent, who wanders around all night, then comes back silent again? Every morning, too—silent. How am I supposed to know what's happening in your head now? Life doesn't take place in our heads, or in archives, or memoirs, or diaries—don't you understand that life is here, today, now—does that make no sense to you anymore? I'm going to leave now, and you'll just keep being silent, won't you? You lost your mind on Dugi Otok when that jet ski bothered you. You said then that it had broken your dream. What dream, where were you? You used to toss and turn while you dreamed, like your father, like your drunken, ever more demented father.

Don't tell me you're going crazy like your father did?

You yourself told stories about how he would jump out of bed and go on a rampage out in the yard. Doesn't that make you pause to think?

She threw some books and files into her suitcase.

She oughtn't to have said that, he thought.

He looked at the knife on the table. This knife is dull, he thought, we ought to buy a new one. That Pole shoved a knife into an SS man's chest and when he pulled it out, blood spurted all over him, and the others standing nearby.

Her hands were shaking as she pushed the numbers on the phone. She ordered a taxi. She really did mean to go.

"I can come back anytime," she said. "Just call me and say that we're going to live like we used to. Don't batter me with your silence which I don't understand."

She stood in the doorway and looked at him. All he needed to do was to say a few words. He should ask if she'd ever been on Dugi Otok before the two of them, Marijana and Janez, were alone together on that sumptuous island in wartime. Don't be jealous and don't be crazy, Marijana would say. Let me explain something. But he didn't want any explanations. If he couldn't get to the bottom of what happened with her on Dugi Otok—if she ever was on Dugi Otok before the two of them went there—then how was he supposed to get to the bottom of the truth of those manuscripts lying on his desk? Everything has to be reconstructed—the past in the present, the present in the past. Aren't they the same thing? he thought. No, they're not. The past is dark, our souls grow out of a dark past, out of events we don't know, out of things that happened long before our births, even before each of us was just a bundle of mucous and fibers that wasn't yet a body, though there was already a head, and there was already an ear to listen to the man muttering, the man telling the woman in bed the same story over and over, about the last moments before his departure from a scene of suffering and human death, the same story over and over.

He looked out the window as she was getting into the taxi.

Why hadn't she taken the car?

He opened the window to call out to her, to say at least this, 'Why don't you take the car?'

60.

My father? My father lost his mind? Was my father insane? Was he drunk or was he insane when he jumped out of bed at night, shouted 'Roll call!' to wake up his neighbors, grabbed his blanket and ran through the yard, shouting 'Roll call! Roll call!' and stood in the yard shaking and then ran with that blanket into the garden where the lettuce was growing and started kicking the lettuce, then sometimes threw himself down on one of the garden beds and fell asleep. Marijana knew about all of this, he had told her about it, he was ashamed of his father and ashamed of himself for having to get up so often in the dead of night when his father would come and roust him. Get dressed, boy, he would say. And then there he was in the smoky kitchen, full of dark men from the league of veterans who were already singing 'We Builders With Our Strength.' Go get the accordion, his father said. He got the accordion and his tired, awkward child's fingers looked for the right combination of buttons to play 'We Builders,' a song he already knew the way he already knew 'East and West Come Awake' and 'I'll Buy Me a Hilltop.' His father's powerful hands—now they were powerful, but when he had come from the camp they had been as weak as the hands of a child, though now they were developed again and strong—his father's hands lifting him up with the accordion and setting him down on the table, among the bottles and ashtrays full of cigarette butts, among the plates of bacon and bread, under the kitchen light that dangled by a cord from the ceiling and shone in his eyes. Now play, he said. 'Freedom's Key?' he asked. That's right, his father said, play that. So he played and they, the league of veterans, sang. How about 'Stouthearted Slovenes?' he asked. Yes, he said, play us 'Stouthearted Slovenes.' Marijana knew about all of this. Your crazy father tormented you, she said, he made you play for his drunken friends. And now you're going crazy, too. With jealousy and history and who knows what else. That was a knife. Her words were a knife. Like the knife stuck in the chest of that SS officer. The story his crazy father told. Night after night. When the Russians liberated them, they lined up the SS henchmen on the assembly grounds and let the camp inmates strike them with their feeble fists. Some Pole, his father recounted, some Pole took a bayonet and buried it in an SS man's chest. When he pulled the bayonet back, the blood started spurting. That knife, the Pole's knife, was stuck in Janez Lipnik's head.

The last explosions continued to echo. Although the whole world should have been blown to bits long ago and the last brick flown apart, distant echoes kept reverberating. This was after the big bang, the beginning of the world when it awoke in a quiet morning. It wasn't morning yet, it was still night, because he could also hear his father grumbling out in the kitchen, but it was warm here under the blankets, with the final explosions of the great war echoing in the distance, his father grumbling in the kitchen, along with the voices of the other men who had survived the end of the world.

But perhaps this is before he was born. Maybe he's under his warm blankets, clutching his knees, or perhaps he's in this fetal position inside his mother's belly, with everything gurgling around him, her warm innards fluttering like some big, warm ocean. If this is before he was born, then he's not yet Janez, or even Lipnik, the big guy grumbling out in the kitchen is Lipnik, Anton's his first name, and he's his father, at that. And the one who gets up and walks around carrying him in her belly is his mother, Rosalia, in a pleading voice trying to explain to the neighbor why Anton, his father, has trampled the lettuce out in the garden again.

Excuse me, Lipnik says to the people walking by in the shopping center, this is no archive, this is my personal history, my embryonic history. Nobody turns to look at the man sitting surrounded with bags and muttering to himself, into the abyss of his memory. The tiniest embryonic cell has more data and more history than that whole big building packed full of documents, than all those folders reaching from cellar to attic, more than is kept behind those thick metal doors that take a password to open, protecting the files and documents from fire. There's more history in the tiniest cell than his and all his colleagues' research could ever uncover.

Why would he grab the blanket off their bed in his sleep, run out the door and fling himself on their lettuce? Because in his sleep he heard the words 'roll call', a phrase that always summoned him out to a vast open space in the middle of the concentration camp. He heard the crackling loudspeaker pronounce the phrase 'roll call,' so he ran through the garden and jumped on the lettuce. He heard that the neighbor had said he would tell the police if it happened again and that the people's militia would straighten things out. He can't afford to keep putting out new lettuce on account of roll call. Seedlings are expensive and it's hard to get them in these difficult times.

His big, childish ear listened to everything. His big, childish heart wanted to forget the knife sticking in that German man's chest, it wanted to forget his father's embarrassing nocturnal rampages through the yard and his trampling of the neighbor's lettuce. When he was eighteen, Janez Lipnik wrote a piece for the school newspaper in which he tried to get the knife, the shouts late at night and Freedom's Key, which he played under a swaying streetlight, out of his head. His father was out of the picture, all that was left was the mood, the waiting for the nightmare to end, some great hope.

But when he thinks back on that, his head goes tick tock. That's all that's left, the tick tock of a clock. Once you took away his mother's subdued reading aloud, his father's shouts, Janez's accordion playing, whenever you took away the drunken league of veterans singing, then you had the clock going tick tock. Like his father's story when he was sober, one of the few pleasant stories about how they left the camp. The Russians were coming, their cannon thundering in the distance, and the great army was approaching through the springtime mud over the vast plain, the tracks of their tanks churning up a muddy froth as some city burned in the distance.

61.

I beg your pardon, this is no archive, this is an embryonic memory, ladies and gentlemen. And suddenly he sees them moving toward the exit, actually toward the huge Benetton display that rises up like a curtain, revealing a vast plain in the distance which they're all marching toward, with the springtime, almost summery, warm rain drizzling down on it. Mr. Tuesday and Mrs. Monday in their striped uniforms are pushing a shopping cart along in front of them, filled to overflowing with all the merchandise they've scooped up. More and more of them head out toward the plain. Daddy and Mommy and Little Boy are dragging a rubberized boat behind them — Daddy and Mommy the boat, and Little Boy the oars, perhaps in an effort to escape the worldwide deluge, or perhaps to reach those mountains in the distance, the bare rocky ones, the great rocky massif in the background, more and more people start moving out of the brightly lit mall out onto the plain, and they're wearing striped trousers and jackets, too, the window designer with the mannequin under his arm, pins gripped in his mouth, and the mannequin's wig poking out of his pocket, the stylist from the nearby salon, who may have been doing his Marijana's hair just now, and Marijana herself has to be somewhere in this crowd spreading out all over the plain, the empty, uninhabited space where a town called Ljubljana ought to be but for the moment isn't — its squares and skyscrapers, bridges, castle and old buildings all gone. Only the vast empty space of the vast stage that has opened up behind the display window, only that is here, only the plain and the distance that the throng of shoppers in their striped suits is traversing. At the end of the plain there are tiny barracks, they look tiny from here, but when they come closer they'll see that they're huge and long, each accommodating up to a thousand people, and in the midst of them is a big open space, the assembly grounds, where his father is jumping around and trampling the neighbor's lettuce. He's lived there a year and is waiting to leave, he'll weigh ninety pounds when he comes home from there, but now he just waits and everyone who's arriving will also wait. They'll herd them in and out of the barracks and time will be motionless, for another century they'll dream of the moment that was as long as infinity, the moment before their departure. And no one will even think of laughing at Anton for trampling lettuce at night, because now they'll all find out what it means to wait, not in a line at the cash register, but on the Appellplatz, while cannon boom in the distance, while cannon boom the huge crowd from the shopping center jostles at the entrance to the concentration camp, and now everything will be taken from them, people in uniform standing at the entrance are already doing that, they're confiscating everything the people had only a short time before scooped up in various niches and pavilions of the glimmering building. The rubberized boats all get thrown onto a heap, they won't be of any use, whether for rowing vacations or to escape the worldwide deluge. They throw them onto one big heap, while another consists of washing machines, this one is much heavier, washing machines are heavy, they get wedged so tightly into your elevator that Lipnik can hardly fit in when he tries to go back to his Marijana who is lovingly, eagerly waiting for him in bed. And a third heap is for mannequins, their arms and legs hanging down. One of them gets flung up there with such force that a limb or the head goes flying off, but the heavers of mannequins pay this no heed, they look around to see if there are more mannequins, then they grab one and throw it up top, even if they're left holding an arm. Perfumes and bottles each get their own heap, baby strollers and wheelchairs each get their own, hair and wigs and eyeglasses—separate heaps for each of these, the same as for rings and watches—rings, that's what his father had thrown on a heap, then when Dresden was bombed, before the moment when they were waiting to leave and time had stood still, that was when they herded them out of the camp to help dig out the corpses, harvest the gold, the rings which were hard to pry off the swollen fingers, so they took them, fingers and all, they cut them off and then removed the rings from the fingers, it had been that simple, and perhaps the shoppers should do something similar. Lipnik goes with them, he looks through all of the barracks for the face of his father, but all of a sudden no one has a face, just as nobody in the shopping center has one. Mrs. Monday and Mr. Tuesday have white surfaces instead of faces, which they never really had anyway, even when they kept kicking his bags in the shopping center they didn't have any. Even Beno is here somewhere and he doesn't have a face either, and Mehmet and Marijana, all of them still have their names, but no faces, so he thinks of trying to call one of them, Marijana for instance, he could call her, and his father, too, Anton is his name, but there's no lettuce out on the Appellplatz and there's no Anton, either. There's just a big tree growing there that looks like a cherry tree, but isn't, it has no blossoms, no fruit and no leaves, either, it's a tree that reaches way up in the sky, just like the old Pohorje Slovenes used to believe, a tree that reaches up into the sky like a column of smoke, like the smoke of a burning land, like a sheaf, like a stream of smoke rising up to the clouds that are the source of this steady, warm, springtime drizzle, which is almost like a summer rain.

Now all of them have cast everything off onto the huge heaps that are left standing on the plain, while they are left with nothing but their bodies covered in striped clothing and no longer have any of the things they'd scooped up, nothing at all any more, except for nettle soup, they do have that, but not much of it, that's what they had for breakfast and that's what they'll have for lunch, too, now they're all here and assembled the way they were assembled before. It's quiet and they're waiting to go. There are no names or faces and there is no time. Everything is standing still, motionless, just before their departure. It's morning.

A morning on the circle's circumference.

62.

Maybe it wasn't like that at all that morning. Maybe it was like any other morning. At four in the morning the loudspeakers crackled their daily roll call. First the prisoners assembled in long lines the length of the barracks, then they marched out to a huge camp parade ground with the morning mists creeping past above it. The mists hung gently down to the ground and they were transparent, so you could see through them. From all sides columns of emaciated, exhausted wretches in torn and dirty uniforms, their collars turned up high to frame bulging, hungry, tired eyes, passed through those mists to converge on that space. Tottering legs waded their way through the misty sea, their vacant eyes glistening through the morning darkness. Nobody spoke a word, they proceeded in silence, their lips compressed, as though they hadn't opened in a smile or a kiss for millennia. Columns of prisoners advanced from all sides through the threatening silence toward the place where they would assemble and get their orders. It may not have been visible, but you could sense in the air a kind of relief passing through the seemingly endless rows of emaciated bodies. The building that devoured corpses was no longer emitting smoke. As recently as yesterday a thick, muddy gray column of smoke had risen out of it. When it was humid, the column would come down and mingle with the air among the barracks. The sky would force it to the ground and the prisoners would have to swallow it with their soup. A smoke that stank of corpses and extinction. They would be retching, spitting and coughing the whole time they lifted the miserable portions of food to their mouths. This morning the sinister building was silent. Perhaps some equipment had broken down, but something unnatural had happened to the ovens—nothing was coming out of the chimneys, there was no dirty gray smoke to be seen, no stench, nothing. Silence. The central kitchen must not have been functioning, either, because the cabbage and potato soup was now being cooked in a new barrack hurriedly built for that purpose, while the kitchen was being used as a warehouse. This encouraged a number of the hungriest and most courageous prisoners—and it's not clear whether hunger was driving them, or courage, or both at the same time—to sneak over to the warehouse at night and make off with a half-crate of potatoes. The next night a new group was getting ready to repeat the heroic deed of their comrades. As soon as the first of them stepped out of the barracks he was blinded by a spotlight from one of the guard towers, followed by a burst of machine gun fire. Two soldiers, obviously following standard procedure, first dragged the body off to the crematorium, but because the dark building was no longer consuming corpses, they heaved it onto the barbed wire fence. There the body was left hanging inertly, and the prisoners who walked past it in the morning didn't dare take it down, even though it was their sacred duty, their comradely obligation, their secret commitment to give their fellow sufferer a Christian burial. It wasn't until lunchtime, when they could move around a bit more freely, that they did so. They buried him in one of the barracks, they prayed over him and crossed themselves, and the thing was done. Not long before, a gesture like that would have incurred a beating or maybe even a death sentence, but now everything was different. They wandered around lost in thought, the hangmen and torturers, they strolled across the assembly grounds and past the barracks, looking around distractedly. That day something completely unexpected happened. The commandant approved a double ration of food for them. As though something had stung him, he stood with his feet planted widely apart, his hands on his hips, and suddenly called out, 'Double rations.' At first they couldn't believe it, but then they practically dashed toward the kettle and crowded around it, until they were driven away with kicks and truncheon blows. But he did one other thing, something that contained the promise of change and certain events in the near future. He beat one of the cooks, showering him with verbal abuse as he did so, for hitting one of the wretches in the head with his ladle, simply because he had paused for too long to stare into the kettle of water with bits of cabbage.

Murmurs, subdued exchanges, quiet chatter spread across the

central camp assembly ground which they called the Appellplatz. This meant that the thought of imminent rescue from this hell was spreading among the prisoners. This brave, bold, enticing thought spread like fire, jumping or creeping into everyone. While they rubbed themselves for warmth in the morning frost, their teeth chattering, they inspired courage in each other with modest, apparently insignificant words and gestures. Yet significant enough to cause a stir in their ranks, which their overseers had to work hard to tame. Even so, the murmuring didn't stop. The prisoners stood at attention, their eyes fixed ahead, but nobody in the world could have prevented the barely audible, barely perceptible movement of their lips. It was safest to talk at morning assembly during one of the noisy, pulsating marches that spewed from the loudspeakers on the commandant's walkway. This was when they could say the most to each other, even though normally no one felt like talking in the morning. The broad, forceful beat of the marches merged with the quiet thrum of their murmuring voices, which grew gradually stronger, getting louder and louder, until they seemed on the verge of shouting a single, victorious cry: Freedom. Still, business proceeded as before. After the usual warnings and the announcement of the order of the day, now they would herd them over to the kettles so they could refresh themselves and get ready for the day's hard labor. As they swallowed the hot water containing bits of some strange plant, most likely nettles, that was referred to as breakfast, the mists cleared and the sun appeared between the forbidding chimneys of the now silent crematorium. Those were fine moments, moments of sun and hope. Something had been happening for the past few days, there were no more beatings and they didn't have to watch as some officer shot some starving, emaciated body or remnant of a body and then scornfully used one booted foot to turn the corpse over, or as German shepherds, those werewolves, tore into some exhausted, beaten prisoner who couldn't keep up during a fast march. Those moments weren't fine just because they could sit in peace and sip their hot slop, but also because they could look at the sun. This same sun that had so tormented them and sent many of them to the next world was intoxicating, and the only thing from the other side of the fences that they could observe, the only thing that was free and untainted, now for the third or fourth or who knew how many mornings was rising peacefully, quietly, elegantly, the way a real sunrise should, not the one they knew from prison and the camps. They even thought that the face of the guard, perhaps the same guard who mowed down their comrade the night before with his machine gun and then heaved him up onto the barbed wire, was now drenched in sunlight and strangely illuminated, and showed a trace of good will and kindly courtesy toward the prisoners. Once they had eaten their fill and felt revived, their faces amazingly lost the signs of hardness, of covert resistance and defiance that even their tormentors secretly feared. They were a mass, a nameless crowd that anyone could subjugate and lead. And indeed, their overseers found it much easier to get them into line, kick them, or spit on them now that they were refreshed and stronger—much easier than in the morning, when they had to drive them out of the barracks when they were hungry and freezing, weak and helpless. It fell in on the assembly grounds calmly, this obedient herd, and waited for further instructions. Everything had to pass, would have to pass soon.

63.

When, around nine o'clock, they were still standing on the assembly grounds in their long but now rather wavering rows, ready to head out for their daily toil and suffering in the quarry, they began to exchange significant looks and send puzzled glances toward the low building of the company headquarters, where the officers had retreated as soon as breakfast was over. A sense of anticipation, of some joyful or sorrowful development, whether liberation or death, hung in the air. It was so palpable, so totally present, that once again they felt themselves gripped by the anxiousness they had already felt once before that same day. Whatever tension was inhabiting them gradually began to appear on their agonized faces. Their eyes anxiously darted from face to face of the guards and overseers standing all around them, seeking some sign of disquiet, anything at all, that might reveal and explain to them what was happening. But a herd is just a herd, and it never recognizes when an ideal or fateful moment has come, it never knows when to act. They were a herd, only a herd.

As the hour hand drew close to ten, even the SS men were overcome with a strange restlessness, which at first, given their overwhelming strength and invincibility, they couldn't comprehend, so they tried to conceal it by appearing even more relaxed and self-contained. Without even realizing how and when it happened, they were suddenly all bunched together, quietly talking to each other. Of course the camp inmates, who carefully followed their every movement, could see first one of them start shifting his weight, as though his feet had grown tired from standing for several hours, then another bend over, as though the small of his back were aching, then a few more adjust their caps, scratch under their arms, wipe the sweat off their foreheads, unsling a rifle and then sling it over the other shoulder, or start shifting a truncheon from one hand to the other. At no particular extra effort or risk, they were able to follow their movements, their foot-shifting and scratching, and their motion away from the prisoners, toward the center of the camp's space. As though driven by some invisible force, whether fear or something else, they suddenly reassembled in a heap and began speculating this way and that and waving their arms. This was of course all too clear and eloquent a sign—something was coming, something big had happened or was about to, quite soon. Now the herd finally moved. The restlessness exploded at its center. Howling and flinging their arms, they threw themselves onto a heap, one lighting on top of the other, tearing at each other's clothes, slugging, biting, stomping, roaring, and jumping. They were animals, they were a herd. The overseers instantly came down on them, at first trying to drive them apart with their truncheons, kicks and curses, so they could then get them back into nice, neat rows, where they could keep an eye on each one individually, thus reasserting control. But, as though this time the crowd were being led by some extraterrestrial, invisible force, cunning, or some other influence, they solidified in a dense cluster and refused to let themselves be driven apart. No matter how furiously the cordons of guards and, behind them, SS men with revolvers, tried to force their way into their midst, no matter how inhumanly they raged, the mob stood like a fortress, indomitable, unconquerable, firm. It rearranged and reinforced itself and was silent, the herd was so determinedly and aggressively silent that the guards, armed to the teeth and as stout and powerful as wild boars, sweated from fear and rage. They attacked and withdrew, forcing their way into the silent mass, striking blows wherever they could and roaring. Then the door of the headquarters quietly opened and a lone, tiny little man came walking out toward the battleground. The overseers stepped aside and the prisoners began to waver in mute silence. All by himself the SS commandant marched deliberately across the enormous yard, approaching them with utmost calm. As he got closer, with no warning and without breathing a single word he raised his arm and fired a shot into the silent mass. Somebody moaned, then came the reverberation, as though a bomb had landed in their midst. The screams reached to the sky, they scattered in all directions, they fell to the ground, ran behind barracks, up to the fence, climbed into every ditch, their feet seeking the earth and their hands and mouths snatching at air. Without anyone having to make any particular effort, without having to fire another shot, beat anybody, or set the dogs on anyone, they fell in as ordered. The rows, which were rough and disorganized at first, were easy to manage. Soon they stood orderly, peaceably, at attention, upright and utterly defeated.

Toward eleven the sun began to beat down, but nobody dared to complain or give any sign of dissent. By twelve the sweat was streaming down their faces and if they had to go, they went in their trousers, and all around the place began to stink of urine. At around one o'clock the door of the company headquarters opened and the officers poured out into the yard. The crowd grew petrified in mad anticipation. Slowly, keeping his watchful eyes on the prisoners, one of the officers went up to an overseer and whispered a few brief words in his ear. From his gestures it was possible to make out that this was an order, because he was most likely excited himself, so he tried to keep a grip on himself with choppy hand gestures. The overseer straightened up, stomped his heels on the ground and roared, 'Into the barracks, march!' Throughout the expanse followed similar shouts, like echoes, and with a speed that no one could have expected from those emaciated creatures, the columns began to move back inside. Into the barracks. Soon the dark maws of the barrack doors had swallowed them up, and the enormous yard gaped empty and silent.

64.

That afternoon a strange quiet filled the air over the huge complex of buildings and barracks, a tension that had already been released several times that day, and then each time receded. The air was electrified. The overseers strolled across the grounds and between the barracks, tapping their truncheons against their trouser legs, and the soldiers up in the guard towers had rifles at the ready. The prisoners stayed quiet for a long time, but then the sound of murmuring began to emerge from the barracks, precisely the same kind of murmur as that morning, except that this time it was all the more persuasive and threatening for coming from inside the closed barracks, from unknown worlds, like some subterranean rumble whose origins and cause are unknowable. Nowhere were there those pathetic, emaciated creatures that a single pistol shot could send fleeing to all sides and hiding in every corner. Only the huge, squat barracks from which the murmur was coming. Toward evening it died down and they could almost sense them watching through the cracks and possibly even getting ready to break out into the open, at the mercy of their executioners, yet courageous and daring, looking death in the eye.

Late that evening the wind brought the sound of a distant drumming. Those were the cannon, the rumble of the approaching Soviet army. It was approaching slowly but surely. Like an echo of those distant sounds, the murmuring that had previously come in waves became louder or quieter, or dropped off completely and then mounted again, like an echo the hollow murmuring from the buildings started to mount. A steady, persistent banging on the wall suddenly began to emerge from one of the barracks. Somebody was banging on it with a spoon or some other hard object. Suddenly a thousand blows began to echo off the walls of the barracks as the prisoners began to bang on the walls with their fists, their feet and their heads. Soon the whole camp thundered with the sound of forceful banging. All of them were banging steadily, as if in waves, and alongside the banging they rasped or breathlessly called out or roared strange sounds, pronouncing strange, unknown words. The unbearable rhythm that refused to abate, that the emaciated throats and the tiny, frail hands expressed more and more forcefully, turned into a mighty ritual, a storm that it became impossible to stop. The whole huge space was filled with its own, instinctive ritual, with the fear of pagan, primordial, infinite power and will. The guards stopped up their ears and banged on the barrack walls with their truncheons, shouting and repeatedly having to retreat from this monstrous power that was nowhere to be seen, that was intangible and untouchable, as disembodied as nature itself. Somewhere a machine gun rattled. Then from the speakers in the command tower came the crackling shriek, 'Roll call!' The silence that ensued was even worse and more excruciating. A mute, murderous silence.

The doors of the barracks flew open again and out of them, from all sides, multitudes of starving figures poured, helter skelter, their smoldering eyes flashing wildly up at of the guard towers, where rifle and machine gun barrels were aimed down at them. And at the unknown, dark faces behind them. The mass of bodies coalesced in the middle of the open space, just like they had that morning, they pressed together, as if trying to defend themselves from the threatening barrels. Spotlights shone down from all sides on the gigantic anthill and individuals in it fearfully covered their faces with their hands, as though the flashing light betokened danger for them.

With the help of machine gun barrels and endless shouting from the speakers the overseers managed to assemble the inmates in some sort of meandering rows. They handed out blankets to them and arranged them in two lines, as they did when getting them ready to leave for a day's work in the quarry. They were going now. Where to? On a long hike through the night. Somebody shouted, 'They're going to kill us all!' They didn't leave. The clouds began to emit a light drizzle and the drumming they had heard in the distance soon died down, submerged into the sound of the rain. Around eleven o'clock one of the officers came running out onto the assembly grounds and started shouting at the stiff, freezing, half-sleeping prisoners.

Then they herded them back into the barracks to sleep.

65.

My father was there, Marijana. When I was very young, barely seventeen, I wrote about it. Do you know why? Because I was already a borer, a bookworm, even at that age. I could see the things my father told me about. When you come back from that hairstyling salon or wherever you are, I'll tell you why I wrote that. It was because I was there. It's what I heard, what I saw. I spent whole weeks writing the memoir of his evacuation, which it had taken him fifteen minutes to tell me at four o'clock one morning. I wanted to feel that suspension of time, trapped between rescue and doom. When he told me his stories, I wanted to feel I was there. I don't know where that comes from. It never interested you very much. People lived through all kinds of things, you would say. Why should it matter so much what they experienced just before evacuation? That was the title of a story I wrote when I was seventeen: Just Before Evacuation. Because I listened to it over and over, Marijana, over and over again. There was no ambiguity to it. Rain, waiting, smoke, knife. Marijana, Janez Lipnik said, perhaps I wanted to forget about all that. That's why I wrote it. But when I wrote it, I was there, too. I walked through that camp and I dreamed about it. That doesn't mean that I'm crazy. I just get something like vertigo sometimes. If I hear that song. *Will forge our freedom's glee...* I used to play it on the accordion, on the table with the men from the league of partisan veterans all around. Then they'd herd me off to sleep, usually toward daybreak. When that kitchen wasn't full of singing and politics, my mother would read to me. She would read me fairy tales from Pohorje. I remember one of them well, about a tree that a man climbs up, a man from the south, he climbs up the tree and it brings him to some other land. There are lots of trees on Pohorje and all of them have names, but this was a tree with no name.

It was a marvelously tall tree, the likes of which the world had never seen and never will. It rose up into the sky like the smoke of a burning land, so you could only see the trunk and the sun, but no branches or leaves. The people would have liked to give the giant a name, if only they'd known what sort of branches and leaves it had. For years and years they looked for the hero who would dare to climb up to the first branches. But all in vain, for they couldn't find him. One day a simple man appeared among them, a shepherd. He came from far-off southern lands and promised to fulfill their wish of many years. He asked to be paid well if he was able to do the work, but in advance he wanted three axes, a rope as long as the highest mountain, and an eagle to bring him food. He tied the rope around his waist, he buried the first axe in the tree trunk, climbed up onto the axe handle, then planted the second axe in the trunk and then the third over his head, and he pulled out the first. This way he moved far up the tree trunk. He climbed it night and day. When hunger reminded him that a day had passed down on the earth, he pulled on the rope and consumed the food that was tied to it. When he reached such a height that the rope no longer reached to the ground, an eagle brought him his food. He enjoyed an unending day. After the seventh year the eagle no longer came to him.

I never understood why the hero enjoyed an unending day. Does that mean there was an unending day up there? Perpetual sunlight? If the earth revolves, if it turns on its axis and revolves around the sun, then sometime there has to be darkness, night.

But that didn't bother the man who was climbing the tree, nothing, but nothing bothered him at all, that's how you climb in your dreams, you don't feel the cold, you don't feel any sharp branches, the howling wind, nothing. He did hear the howling wind, but the higher up he got, the less there was of it, just like the rain that caused him to slip on the axe handles, suddenly it was gone, too, and there was no rain or wind or cold or pain, and even the clouds remained far below. The clouds that the borer, the bookworm looked up at whenever he lay on the grass and looked up at the brave man vanishing way up above on the tree with no name. The tree had no name because it had no branches or leaves — the branches and leaves were way up high, where the shepherd from lands to the south must have been after seven years passed. When exactly seven years had passed since he began climbing up the trunk, he reached the first branch of the tree. He had to decide whether to chop it off and slide down the smooth trunk back to the earth or keep exploring the top of the tree. Of course he decided to keep exploring. Who wouldn't? And soon he stepped on the last branch and with that he stood once again on solid ground. All around him there was a huge plain. It got dark — now it really got dark, and the shepherd didn't know what to do until a tiny light flickered in the distance. He went in the direction of the flickering light and watched it get bigger. He arrived at a castle that had just a single window illuminated. He approached that window very carefully and looked inside. A beautiful woman was sitting at a table, lost deep in thought, her head propped up on one hand. He gathered his courage and tapped on the window. 'Young man, where do you come from and what are you looking for here?' the beautiful woman said. 'I need a place to sleep and some work to do. I've been climbing that tree with no name for seven years and finally I've come out on land and now I don't know where to go.' The woman let him stay the night and the next morning she offered him work as a hired hand. 'It won't be much work,' she said. 'You'll tend three horses — a bronze, a silver and a golden one. If you look after them well, you'll stay here with me for a long time. You'll do well, the table will always be set and you'll have whatever you want.'

That tree, Marijana, and the thought of that man climbing up it made me forget about the kitchen and the grumbling men, the roll call and the Pole with the knife. I wanted to forget, that was all.

They said that a house of Germans used to stand by the water. The Drava had carried it off. But it didn't just carry the house off, before that it took the whole family, including five kids that I knew and used to play with. My father had been in the camps and their father had been in the German army, on the Russian front, where he was injured and crippled. The family's name was Remer, they left and at first I felt bad, but then I forgot, I wanted to forget. All my life I've wanted to forget. Like the man from southern lands on that tree. You put your foot on the next step, the next axe handle, and you've already forgotten about the one before. All the things I've forgotten! Those Germans from the house on the Drava, the Remers, now I remember them, but back then when they left late one night, to Germany everyone said, a family with five children, I forgot them. I forgot that somebody hanged himself in the cellar, they said it was a black marketeer, apparently they found bales of textiles down there, worsted yarn, and him dangling among them. In his stocking feet. He had taken his shoes off before he hanged himself. And I remember everything else, the voices of drunken men from the kitchen, talking about politics and singing partisan songs until morning, I didn't want to remember that, either, and least of all the fact that my father would sometimes wake me up and make me play the accordion. *We're builders*, they sang, *and our power will shape our freedom's glee, or the bright sparks from our hammers*. His mother used to pull the trousers onto his drunken father, sometimes he was really deranged from the camp. She was petite, but he kept getting bigger and heavier by the month. I got up and helped her pull the trousers onto my dad. You'll grow up to be a good man, sonny, he used to mutter. Sometimes I think that I just dreamed all of that. Dreams always vanish at the instant we begin to understand them. He, my deranged father, came from a place where your teeth chattered from the cold, from the chilly presence of hell. Where you scream out in horror of eternal flames, where smoke rises up out of it like a tree into the sky, smoke and doubt in the existence of everything that is, even in him, the Lord over the waters and the earth, the smoke from the chimney over the crematorium ovens. Where you wait and wait. Just Before Evacuation. But a borer sees all of this. People who heard it burrowing into books at night, who heard it devouring archival material, called this moment the hour of death. When the spirit is torn, shredded to pieces, crucified in space. Leaving a slit with the beyond shining through.

Freedom's key, freedom's key.

66.

She had left for her mother's. He thought that maybe he had hit her and that's why she left. Had he hit her? What had he done to her that she would just vanish? Why wasn't she coming back from that beauty salon? He would have to go look. Or give her mother a call, maybe she was there. Maybe she forgot that they had agreed to meet here, at the bench in the middle of the shopping center, across from Benetton, across from Philips, midway between Benetton and Philips then, down from the shoe store, that's not where they were supposed to meet. Where is Marijana? If he struck her, then evil had struck. So that the good could prevail. It was obvious that evil existed in the world on account of good. How could good be good if evil wasn't evil? We contemplate evil or even do something evil in order to become aware of good. They were good times, Marijana. I didn't want to strike you on account of those Hungarian soldiers. There was a knife on the table. I didn't pick it up. I hit you on your mouth which used to kiss me, but now just lies. You weren't in that bus, you were on Dugi Otok. So what if you bled a little, you didn't have to go running off to your mother because of that. One woman bit that sex maniac on the ear, then she washed it off and applied iodine. I'd do the same thing if you just wouldn't leave, Marijana.

She was gone. On the other hand, Zala kept getting closer. He could sense her approaching.

He left, too. Before winding up in this shopping center promenade, he had been sitting one morning in the front seat of his idling car, watching the rain slide down the windshield. He thought of perhaps driving back to the edge of town, to the neighborhood with those elegant houses, a big neighborhood with gardens and paths, and pulling up in front of one of them, the one he knew best, and waiting for the door to open and Marijana to appear carrying a bag full of folders and books. As she opened her umbrella, he would push the passenger door open and say, 'No need, you don't need the umbrella, I'll take you to the university.' She'll get in beside him and say, 'You really are strange.' Maybe she'll be silent for a while and then say, 'Did we really need to go through all that?' There will of course be a reproach in that sentence, because it will actually mean, 'Did you really need to go through all that?' But Marijana is a sensible woman and she'll say, 'Did we really need to go through all that?' That will mean that she's assuming part of the blame for the misunderstanding. Even if she doesn't really think that way, she'll say it. In fact she'll think he's obsessed with some documents and events from the distant past, that he keeps going back to his childhood and people who exist only in archival files, with whom she has nothing in common and whom she doesn't even know. This obsession, she'll think, comes at a high price for us. He didn't want to hear these thoughts of hers. Even though she'll say, 'Did we really need to go through all that,' she'll be thinking that he is the cause of this great misunderstanding that she can't take anymore. Do you always think, she'll ask, what other people are thinking? He didn't want to hear that question, or her thoughts, for that matter. He stepped on the gas and did not head toward her mother's house, nor to the archive, but drove out onto the beltway and suddenly knew where he was heading, north, or more precisely northeast, on this rainy June morning he went flying to the north of this little homeland, as the poet once called it.

By midmorning he had walked out to the edge of a wide river and was looking into its turbid, rising water. The snow up in the Alps had begun to melt, the water was rising and carrying along chunks of wood and branches, and a big tree trunk had gotten caught up against the shore. High up above, the bell tower of St. Joseph's leaned down toward the water. It's always been like this, he thought, the smell of the water, the shrubby plants that grow on the steep bank, the smell of the silt, even the fish, he thought, even the fish in this water have that smell, he remembers it well. Next to a wooden footbridge he looked into the opening of a tunnel that led somewhere far back. The Germans built it during the war, the tunnel was actually a bomb shelter, and from the Drava it led somewhere into the bowels of the earth, but Lipnik knew where it led: straight to the Carinthian Railroad Station. As a boy he had often wanted inside that tunnel, but he had never dared to go far, after a few yards he was always stopped by the cold, by the stench of human excrement, the darkness, the iron bars that he might have been able to crawl over, but never dared, never dared to go farther. High up on the embankment he stopped in front of the house where they had once lived, he looked at the curtains over the window and knew that on the other side was a bedroom and a little farther on the kitchen, and through that tall door was where the male voices used to growl. When the curtains over one of the two windows moved, he flinched. Somebody had drawn the curtain aside and opened the window, and some woman started shaking a tablecloth out over the ground, maybe crumbs from breakfast. Their eyes met. As though startled and frightened by him, by the stranger who was standing outside the window and looking straight her way, straight in the window of her apartment, as though she were upset, she suddenly closed the window and drew the curtain across. He was sure she was watching, watching to see where the stranger would go next. Without a thought he headed down the long street and went back down toward the river, standing for a while on the bridge before suddenly realizing that he was in the center of town, that people were walking past him on their afternoon errands and that some of them were turning to look at him, because he was without an umbrella and his hair was wet and stuck to his forehead. He stopped in front of a handsome middle-class house with a balcony, and a second later he made his decision and stepped into its spacious, dark entryway. He ran up the steps and came breathlessly to a stop outside the door that he knew—it was still there, with its bronze fittings and thick, translucent glass. He rang the bell.

67.

He rang the bell and waited to hear Marijana's footsteps in the foyer. He waited for her to open the door and say, Where have you been? I'll explain everything to you, he'll say, and you'll explain everything to me. He thought she didn't hear him, maybe she's powdering her face, or doing her eyelashes with that tiny brush, but as soon as she hears the bell he's ringing, she'll come and open the door, and he'll say to her, Oh, the whole thing is just so insignificant—what's some sailing trip down to Kornati and back? You're right. It's nothing, it's last year's snow, or rather last year's sea. After all these years who cares where you went drinking wine or, forgive me, how you would all pee in the Adriatic. There's no trace of that trip, the sea has covered it all. She didn't open the door, she didn't appear, perhaps she'll get home from the hairdresser's soon and she'll say, Did you get bored? He'll say, it's high time for us to go home. He'll say that, even though he knows that he had a minor accident a few days before. He had learned of some detail from his wife's life that had been clouding his vision. A man sitting amid a pile of bags in the middle of a big shopping center mall, who appears to be absent, whose eyes bulge a little, the way the eyes of exhausted shoppers do—but why has he been sitting there for so long and why doesn't he move? People come here to move, to move as much as possible, because if you don't move, you don't see, you don't appreciate, you don't delight, you don't buy, you go home sad and empty, when your reason for coming here was to go home full, rich inside, enthusiastic. So perhaps somebody going past, somebody who notices him—because for the most part people don't notice him, for the most part people are looking elsewhere, at display windows, at the shelves behind them, or into the distance, at other display windows and shelves—perhaps somebody who notices him, if only because they trip over the bags, will possibly think that he's sad and alone, the kind of person who could do something really nasty. Anyone who's here alone, who doesn't have a loved one to pull by the sleeve to the next display case and the shelves behind it, is sad and alone, the kind of person you need to avoid in a wide arc, the kind who serves as a warning that not everybody feels the same joy as you and I feel, Mrs. Monday and Mr. Tuesday, or the three of us, Daddy, Mommy and Little Boy, so it's best to give those types a wide berth.

A terrible jealousy had inhabited his soul. Oh yes, but then it also passed. Now he'll wait for Marijana and they'll go home together. Janez Lipnik was capable of thinking very rationally about himself. Until one sunny spring day in 2000 everything was fine with archivist Janez Lipnik. And not only with him, but with his desk, over which he would cast a look of contentment before he went home—at all the folded documents in their yellow files, the pencils and yellow felt pens assembled with military precision. Everything about his black desk with the yellow rectangles lying on it was fine, as well as the waxed hallway of the Regional Archive, which he would pass through on his way to lunch each day, as well as his soft rubber soles, which muffled the sound of his calm footsteps. This was the building that time passed through, the inaudible torrent of time, of people and events from the distant past. He had never thought that they stopped here, after they'd been studied, numbered and put into files. He always distinctly felt that they traveled on, the events and the people, from the foggy past into an uncertain future. If anywhere, it was in the motionless calm of this building that you could sense the ebb and flow of invisible, inaudible time, rushing time that anniversaries of births and deaths could not stop, and lively eyes that looked out from yellowed photographs, lively eyes that all the evidence said were now dead, but were, for a person who could feel the currents of infinite time, still alive. They were only visiting here, is what he had often thought, we just take a quick look at them and they at us—and, yes—we also inventorize them, number them, then time carries them away again. The way it will carry all of us away into the uncertain distance, including Janez Lipnik and his wife Marijana, and that's also fine, there's no other way it could be.

It suddenly struck him that things might not be so good at the archive.

Beno asked him why he'd been absent from work with no explanation. The director was going to want one, he'd better get ready.

For a moment he imagined that his office in the archive was empty and that his things were packed into cardboard boxes stacked up against the wall. The window was open and the shutters were banging in gusts of wind and rain.

68.

She had said that she'd never before been on Dugi Otok.

Finally he was determined to get to the bottom of this business, to get some clarity once and for all. If he couldn't get to the bottom of that war story, if his head wasn't able to reconcile the story of Zala the schoolteacher from Lower Carniola with that teacher from Maribor, if there was a hole gaping in the body of evidence regarding how the young civil servant from the Auersperg estate transformed himself into Captain Aleksij, who escaped from Turjak and was reportedly seen in Australia, then he would at least clarify this.

On Sunday morning he went to the archive and Mehmet greeted him reluctantly.

"Don't tell me you're going to spend the whole day in the office," he said.

He didn't reply.

He looked out at the cherries on the tree, which was swathed in morning mist. The rain had stopped for a moment and humidity was steaming up from the earth and off the walls.

He called Marijana. Her mother answered. She said that she wasn't there. I know she's there, he said. Please call her to the telephone. I told you she's not here, she said and hung up. For a while he listened to the dial tone. He tried calling again. This time Marijana answered. In the background he could hear her mother hissing, 'Why are you answering that? He'll hurt you yet.' 'Don't you ever give up,' Marijana said. He said he'd like to talk to her, even if it was one last time. He wanted to get to the bottom of something. You always want to get to the bottom of something, she said. Don't you think you're obsessed with getting to the bottom of everything? He said they had lived together for so many years, he had a right to meet with her and talk, even if only for one last time.

She was silent for a moment.

"All right," she said. "I have to pick some things up anyway."

The carefully folded sheets of paper on his desk remained untouched on Sunday. He walked past a surprised Mehmet.

"Aren't you going to work?" he called out.

He thought, how is it possible that this person addresses me every single time? Suddenly he saw a whole series of images and sounds with terrible lucidity—in each of them Mehmet appeared, first in the receptionist's window, then in the hallway, then carrying a flashlight, and in a thousand other little images and grimaces, always with one of the same three or four sentences: Don't tell me you're going back to work, don't tell me you're going to spend the whole day in the office, one of these days you're going to break a leg. It struck him that today, for the first time, he had used a different sentence, which went: Aren't you going to work? Interesting, he thought. It's like some sort of turning point.

69.

With his heart pounding, but still in a matter-of-fact sort of way, he said:

"Do you remember that year during the war when we were on Dugi Otok?"

"Oh, not this again. Don't tell me you've been drinking on a Sunday morning."

"No, I haven't," he said. "You want to smell my breath?"

"No," she said. "That's all right. I want you to tell me whatever it is you still have to say. And then I'm going to pick up a few last things and go."

"I asked you if you remembered the war in Croatia. We were on

Dugi Otok then."

"No," she said. "I don't remember it."

That's not possible, he thought, it's not possible. He'd started this conversation with that question at least a hundred times, maybe a thousand. And then they always proceeded to talk about the Balkan wars, and how they spent their vacation, and then came the details, the lone little churches, sex by the sea, the fish, the lamb, how quiet the nights were, the seagulls, and sometimes that miserable jet ski. He wanted to start a conversation that would finally get to the bottom of something, but she answered no, she didn't remember.

"Marijana!" he gasped. "You don't remember that we were on Dugi Otok? We left because of the Oluja, the Croatian offensive. Then we stopped in Zadar, and we drove through bombed-out villages."

"You probably dreamed it," she said. "I've never been on Dugi Otok. Not once in my life."

"But you were, Marijana, it was in '95."

"No, I wasn't. That's when I was riding a bus full of drunken Hungarian soldiers. Maybe I wanted them to fuck me. All of them, one after the other."

He looked at her for a long time. He wanted to hit her. He had never hit anyone before. Now he wanted to hit her, whom he didn't know anymore. She didn't know him anymore, either. He hit her. The hand that he had lying on the table just rose up and flew toward her mouth. He hit her with the back of his hand, the knuckles colliding with her lips and teeth. Her eyes looked at him stunned, she hadn't expected this. She groaned audibly. She felt her face: Blood, there was blood on his knuckles.

"I'm sorry," he said. "I didn't mean it."

"What did you mean? What did you mean?"

"What did I mean? What did I mean?"

She got up, but he was already next to her, he leaped to his feet, overturning a cup of coffee on the table and pushing Marijana back down on the chair. She screamed and he put his hand over her mouth.

"You don't want me to gag you, do you?" he said.

She shook her head.

He could feel her trying to get back up, but he pushed back down on her shoulders with all his might.

"Oh yes," he said. "That's right, what did I want? I wanted to tie you up. That's what I wanted. It's what you want, too, isn't it?"

She looked at him with wide open eyes, as though she only now understood. She stopped struggling.

"Do you want that?"

She shook her head.

"Not now," she said cautiously. "Later."

Just as it had a while earlier with Mehmet, now a strange lucidity, a flash of light passed through his head again. There wasn't going to be any later. If he let her go, she'd walk through that door and never, ever come back. If he let her go, she'd go to Beno's. He could shoot that guy, just like Aleksij had shot the Italian 'tenente Guido outside Turjak Castle, straight in the forehead. Settling all accounts with a single gunshot.

"Do you remember where we put that rope?"

He saw her eyes move quickly. She was looking for some way out.

"I think it's in the bedroom," she said calmly. "In the wardrobe, under the blankets."

"It's not under the blankets," he said, jerking a pillow off the couch, grabbing the rope that had lain under it, and putting it around her neck.

"Jesus," she whimpered. "What are you doing? You're going to strangle me."

He tugged on the rope to quiet her down.

"I'm not going to strangle you," he whispered. "Just tie you up. To the bed. Like we used to do. And blindfold you."

Tears streamed down her face.

"No crying, Marijana, no crying."

Tears were pouring down his face, too.

"I can't bear to see you cry. I'll tie you up good, go out and then come back. As a stranger—you remember how it was. We enjoyed it. And we will again, Marijana. But first you're going to have start talking differently, you can't keep talking like you've been doing."

His face soaked with tears, he pulled her along into the bedroom. She stopped in the doorway.

"Please," she said. "Don't."

He pulled on the rope, causing her to lose her breath for a second. She stumbled her way to the bed. Lie down, he said. She lay down. Raise your arms. She raised them. He tied her wrists to the headboard, as in the old days, pushed her knees down flat, pulled her legs apart, tied the rope around one ankle and hitched it up to the wooden bed leg, then did the same thing on the other side. He got a muffler of his out of the wardrobe and blindfolded her with it.

"There, see?" he said. "That didn't hurt."

"Janez," she whispered. "You're not going to do anything to me, are you?"

"Don't be silly," he said. "But you have to be a little afraid," he said. "You yourself said it's the uncertainty that makes it exciting."

He sat down beside her.

"The last time we played this game," he said, "or maybe it wasn't the last time, I'm not sure, but in any case when we played it on Dugi Otok. Do you remember?"

She nodded.

"The development where we rented the apartment was completely deserted. There was a war on, so of course it was deserted. Sometimes we could hear the artillery drumming in the interior and sometimes I thought, people are killing each other over there. There were no tourists and the locals had all fled to the towns. There was just that jet ski buzzing in the distance, I can still hear it. You lay all tied up, half undressed, I went out and lit a cigarette. I was about to come back when I saw an older man working on the fence of the building next to ours. He was stocky, probably a quarry worker, and he had these gnarly hands. Do you know what I thought? I thought, what if that man were to caress you with his gnarly hands? Your smooth, white body with its tender skin, still beautiful after all these years. It was like some delicate, fine membrane covering everything you've underneath it, your liver, intestines, bladder and all that. I wanted to go up to him and say, 'Come see what I've got upstairs.' But just then you called to me. You were laughing and said 'This isn't tied very well,' as you waved one free hand at me, do you remember? That's okay, you don't need to say anything, you can just nod."

She nodded.

He took a handkerchief and wiped the blood off her cracked lip.

"Your lips are beautiful," he said.

"Janez ..." she whispered. "I'm glad you've calmed down."

"But you know I'd never give you away," he said, "and certainly not to that stonecutter. Or to Guido Gambini, either. Not to anybody."

"Who's Guido?"

"An Italian officer. He has a face exactly like Beno's. Same forehead."

She was silent.

"You're probably thinking about something now," he said. "Aren't you?"

"Yes," she said. "What are you going to do to me?"

"The same as always," he said. "But this time I might really shave you first, here and here. And your head. I haven't decided yet. Are you afraid?"

She nodded.

"I'm going now," he said. "I have to buy some cheese and a bottle of wine for after lunch. Okay? I'll be back soon."

He closed the door behind him and stood there for a while. She wasn't calling anyone. But no one could have heard her, anyway. There were two more doors to the hallway.

70.

He turned the key twice in the lock and put it in his pocket. He pushed the button to call the elevator and waited. He heard a few voices from one of the upper floors. Somewhere up there somebody was making a racket with the elevator door, probably hauling some furniture or a washing machine into or out of it. He couldn't wait that long. He headed down the stairs and on his way heard various sounds coming through the doors—somebody had some wild music turned up full blast, 'the jet skier' hissed through his brain, there were smells of Sunday meals, somebody had already begun grilling some sort of meat. When he reached the exit, there was a dark, wide curtain of rain pouring down in front of him. He stood there, unable to push forward into the deluge. He lit a cigarette. An umbrella, he decided to go get an umbrella. He tossed the cigarette into a puddle, turned around and again waited for the elevator. Somewhere upstairs they were still loading a washing machine or items of furniture into it. Damn, he thought, this isn't supposed to be a service elevator. He dashed up the stairs, past the Sunday meat smells, past the jet skier's music and reached the front door of their apartment.

He rang the doorbell. He waited to hear her footsteps in the foyer, she'd come holding her compact and he'd say, 'Oh, what's a little sailing trip to Kornati.' But she can't come to the door, he thought, she can't.

He hurriedly unlocked the door and went in. He glanced at the umbrellas in the foyer and saw that Marijana's was still wet. Of course, she came back today, just a short while ago. Then he slowly made his way to the kitchen. Some moans came from the bedroom. He pulled open a drawer and took out a bread knife. He tested its blade with his thumb. It had been dull for ages, how many times had he said they needed to buy a new one. But people always forgot about knives, there was always something else more important. The next time he goes to the shopping center he'll make a list.

He opened the bedroom door.

She was moving her lips.

He went up to her and untied the muffler from over her eyes. He stepped a few paces back.

She was looking at him with wide-open eyes. He thought she

was about to scream. Let her scream if she wants. She doesn't understand what's going on here, anyway. She doesn't understand that he's
looked into the abyss and beyond wakefulness into dreams, and beyond dreams into the past, beyond his birth, and that he's traveling
back somewhere, constantly back. That every event, the whole se-
quence of events of the past few weeks was borne out of that glimpse
of the bottom, the invisible bottom of a deep abyss, where everything in his life already happened long ago and since then has only
kept repeating. She didn't scream. With wide-open eyes she stared at
the knife in his hand, then she fixed her eyes on his forehead, as
though they might be able to restrain him, stop him at some distance from the bed where she lay. Her mouth opened and he saw her
red throat, here she goes with the screaming. But she didn't scream,
she just panted, it was good she wasn't screaming.

He went over to the bed and bent down on one knee. He used
the knife to start sawing through the rope around one of her ankles.
It went slowly. The knife was dull and the rope had been tied into
several gnarly knots. I tied it too tight, he thought, but that was just
to keep her from laughing, so she wouldn't say, 'Look, this isn't tied
very well.' The rope burst and he stroked the red spot that wrapped
around her ankle. He sawed through the rope on the other side, too,
and then freed her hands. He kneeled down next to the bed and
leaned his head against the wooden headboard. His shoulders were
shuddering. Marijana carefully drew her legs up toward herself,
clasped her hands around her knees and sat quietly in that pose for
a while, still breathing heavily. Then she lowered her legs over the
side of the bed and sat. She put on her blouse, which had lost a few
buttons. Slowly her hand moved toward his dark hair with its streaks
of gray, but then suddenly drew back. She got up and picked the
knife up off the floor and on the way to the kitchen picked up several buttons. She tossed the knife in the drawer, quickly put her
shoes on in the foyer and threw her cape over her shoulders. She
took her umbrella and went out the door. For a while she stood in
front of the elevator. It was still occupied. Then she slowly went
down the stairs and out through the dark Sunday veil of rain.

71.

The next night around four o'clock he woke up and noticed that the room was bathed in silvery moonlight. He felt the bed next to him where his wife, Marijana, ought to be sleeping. It flashed through his mind: She's gone, now, once and for all, she's gone. And all at once he felt reconciled to that, it didn't strike him as anything unusual that she wasn't here anymore. The light was unusual. He lay still for a while trying to figure out where it was coming from, since it had been raining for so many nights, with no stars, no moon, no Marijana, nothing. He got up and went to the window. What he saw was so strange that he didn't know if he was dreaming or if it was real: Outside the window, where the street should have been, there was a garden. That's strange, he thought, where did this garden come from all of a sudden? It was a garden that more than anything resembled the courtyard outside his office window at the Regional Archive, with the same flowers growing in the beds alongside the buildings, and suddenly that courtyard was here, not the street with its long rows of parked cars, but this garden drenched in moonlight, some of which was pouring into his room in a silvery cascade. It was exactly the same sort of courtyard—or garden, on account of the flowers—but the tree wasn't an old cherry tree, this he noticed immediately. This wasn't the cherry tree that he used to rest his eyes on when they were tired from reading documents or strained from looking at the computer screen. This was a tree the likes of which he'd never seen. It wasn't a cherry tree, but neither was it a pine or an oak.

That morning he walked along the Ljubljanica. A light rain drizzled warmly as mists hovered over the water. He stopped beside the embankment wall at the spot where the bicycle had been hauled out of the water a few weeks before. It had been a Presta or Presto bicycle, the kind that some schoolteacher from Lower Carniola used to ride. A schoolteacher who, he now knew, was the very same Zala D. from his childhood. Who had taught him to recite poetry and given him such a big hug for reciting The Nighttime Traveler so bravely and beautifully and without any mistakes, *I am your companion, my name's pestilence.* He had stopped racking his brain over how that women's bicycle had ended up in the water, or whether Aleksij and the adjutant, or rather the civil servant, were one and the same, and Dugi Otok was so far away and off by itself that it was a matter of complete indifference if he—Lipnik—had ever hiked over it, and whether Marijana, his later wife, had only just then hiked over it or if she had sailed there some years before, sometime in prehistory. He looked at the water flowing away toward another body of water called the Sava, which flowed toward yet another called the Black Sea. Water is calming and indifferent to the events caused around it by people, events that collect in impossible knots. When he was little they had lived by the water—that water, called the Drava, flows toward the Black Sea, too. Water takes no heed of time, it covers events and some old bicycle that somebody throws in it. When they haul it out, all covered in algae, they don't haul out the events, the events are trapped inside heads, only in heads. He thought he might stop by the archive, then go to the shopping center, where he might meet Marijana.

72.

Today is Tuesday. The day after the holiday. After holidays he and Marijana go shopping. This is Tuesday, which some woman said might be Monday. Out in the big promenade everything shines and time stands still in the rhythmic beats of the booming music. Around noon he was at the archive. Mehmet had told him to check in with the director. If he's any judge, he'll ask him why he didn't show up at work the week before. He didn't check in with him. He went straight to his office. The door was open and when he went in he was struck by its emptiness. His things had been stacked along the wall in cardboard boxes. He thought he might after all go ask somebody what this was about. If not the director, then Mehmet. Or Nedeljka, the secretary. Or maybe Beno. No, not him, he would have to shoot him in the forehead, like Aleksij Grgurevič had shot Guido Gambini. But what would his forehead look like after that? Perhaps like the forehead of Jože the blacksmith, Ivanka's husband—in other words, there would be no forehead at all, just a bloody hole. He looked at the cherry tree in the courtyard. There wasn't a single white petal left on it now. The rains had long since knocked off everything white and turned it into a wet slush on the ground. Mehmet was waiting for it to dry out, then he would sweep it all up at once. For now, it was still raining, albeit more and more faintly, but soon it would clear up. Noonday silence reigned in the big building, time had stopped, that decanting of history, those distant events, were all completely gone, the faces of people long ago bent over the documents that were preserved here were gone, his office wasn't a canyon that time rushed through, there was a peacefulness everywhere, there had been no war in ages and certainly no emergencies, the stars kept following their precisely marked paths around the Sun, and he thought that he sensed, hovering here, the same pain that on Sunday, two days ago, had inhabited his soul, at first a strange ache, followed by some sort of brief derangement, a *furor breve*, in his words. Standing in the middle of his empty office he felt it had already started when he began losing himself in that unidentified manuscript, when they hauled the bicycle covered in algae and river silt out of the water, when he sensed he was both here and there, with the mowers going past. The windows were open and one of the shutters was flapping and banging against the window frame. Outside a warm wind was carrying the rain along, and it blew a few drops inside. He looked down at the wet spot on the floor.

Then, suddenly, he was inside the shopping center and he had to admit to himself that he didn't know if Marijana was at the cosmetician's or the hair stylist's, where some man's hands, a young man's hands, would be massaging her soapy head. And here he is, sitting with bags at his feet in the middle of the shopping center, waiting for her to come. Wasn't it just a bit too silly, this waiting? Had she come back from her parents' at all? She had gone to her mother's for several days, saying she couldn't take him any longer. Maybe she was already back, maybe she was waiting for him at home. There's that flow of time, he thought, now its thundering rapids are going to catch me up. Something from the dim past has come after me, he could physically feel it, as though he were standing in the middle of a vast torrent that nothing could stop. The old stories are going to open up again. He's their keeper. The keeper of secrets, of stories that certain writers would just drool over, if only they could graze on those distant human lives, but no, they were locked up in him, Janez Lipnik was a file folder with seven seals.

73.

He was talking with Marijana the way he used to.

I'll tell you what it was like, he said.

What was it like?

When I was little, I used to shine, he said. I would start raving.

You shine now, too, she said. You've got a fever.

Now we're grown up. Now we talk differently.

How differently?

More clearly.

But we're less understood.

A whole century has passed through us.

You're not a hundred years old.

I'm over fifty. It's the same thing.

We lived in a house near the water. It got washed away, the Drava carried it off. Just like it carried the Remers' house off, with all five children, him, a German war invalid, the mother, the dog, the cats. A house, our house, was floating down the Drava, and I could see theirs, too, in the distance, it had come unstuck from the river bank long before ours. Hermann, I called, Hermann, wait. Hermann was their youngest son, he played soccer kicking with his left leg and he always lost, because he kicked with his left leg. Then they sailed off. Our house sailed off, too. I dreamed it over and over. Kuibyshev dreamed that he was walking down the street holding a bloody wire. It's the sort of dreams we had. I used to shine and start raving. Objects would get thin and then expand. Moonlight shone into my room. The Slovene book of dreams. It wasn't true at all. We just dreamed it. For practically a whole century. Kuibyshev, a partisan I was friends with as a child, told me, 'As soon as I stop thinking of them as traitors, I don't understand why we had to kill them.' Who did you kill, Kuibyshev? The whole gang, all of them. Did you hold a bloody wire in your hand, did you carry a bloodied truncheon, do you dream about it, Kuibyshev? I don't dream anything, they were traitors, they have to be, don't you see? There's no excuse, none, not even the slightest. You can't just hate a human being out of thin air. But you can hate a traitor, along with all his suffering and tears. The Khmer Rouge sent people who wore glasses to the killing fields, because they were members of the bourgeoisie, and they especially sent people who had smooth hands. You have to have a sign. I often dream about him, Kuibyshev, with the bloody wire in his hand. Don't be afraid, son, my mother would say whenever I shone. This is a tale, the tale of the man who climbed up a tree. It happened on Pohorje, but it's only a fairy tale. He asked if someday he'd also be able to climb that high. Of course you will, his mother said. One day when you're big, you'll climb all the way up into the clouds. Don't be afraid, there's nothing the matter, that's moonlight shining into the room, nothing more, fall asleep, my sweet little boy.

74.

He shivered. As if here were out in a forest. The wings of ducks flying off into the winter night whoosh over the roofs of the shopping center. But it's not winter. So why am I shivering, if it's not winter? Actually I'm alone, he thought. I have no parents, no children. My coworkers are clods who can only talk about sailing and stocks. But history flows through me like an invisible, noiseless river. Ever since those voices started coming from the kitchen. His father's voice, talking about the camp, talking about politics. He comes to get him, lifting him up out of bed. Janez, he'll say, my Janez will play for us now. He played for the men with red eyes and raspy voices. This was the league of partisan veterans, the winners. He stood on the table among the glasses and bottles and bread and bacon and played partisan songs. Marijana will never understand the anxiousness that comes from the past. Those of us who know this anxiousness live with a terrible weight.

And his mother's voice. She read to him about the tree with no name. He still remembers the first sentence: There was a wondrously tall tree, a tree with no name.

Mother also read to him about Lojze's scythe. From The Illustrated Slovene, Volume Forty-Four. I even remember the illustration. It had a young man with a flower in his cap, sharpening a scythe, with the rocky Slovene mountains in the background. Beneath the picture was printed *Alojzij Hočevar Hardware, Ljubljana*.

> Always sharp and always steady,
> like a young girl at the ready,
> buy a scythe that always fells,
> buy the scythes that Lojze sells.

The poem had about ten stanzas, each of which praised the handsomeness and acuity of Lojze's scythes and the efficiency of his whetstones for sharpening them. Why do these details stick in a person's head? To this day I remember two of the verses by heart, because mother had had to reread the poem to me many times—at least as many times as the tale about the man from lands to the south who climbed up a tree, a tree with no name.

> When the dew glints on our blade,
> that's when mowers' luck is made.
> Mowers glide across a field
> Once a Lojze scythe they wield.

His childish eyes could easily picture this scene. Back then you still came across mowers in the countryside. Even in the city, in the parks or the soccer stadium. A lone mower—the one with the flower tucked in his cap—moving across a wide field, as wide as a soccer stadium. There was a soccer stadium on the far side of the river and that's where Lojze's scythe found a lot of work. There were also mowers in that Pohorje fairy tale—the man from southern lands saw them when, in the space of an instant, he came down out of the tree once he had climbed somewhere way up high. And that skeleton called death always carried a scythe. The plague in that song The Nighttime Traveler, hiding with a scythe under its cloak, the blade darting out every which way: I am your companion, my name's pestilence!

He shivered. Back then he was alone and powerless. And now he still was. And he will be to the end. Like a cold, extinguished candle on a future grave.

Suddenly he didn't know if he was sitting in his workroom at the archive, in the middle of the shiny shopping center or in the mental hospital at Studenec, where some woman was telling him the story that she's going to write down. He's sitting where he wouldn't like to be even in his dreams—in reality. In the reality of the mental hospital, in the reality of the document lying on his desk. Here he sits on his bed and listens to the babble of words spoken by women, words that are buoyant and rise up toward the barred windows and then drop back down heavy as stones, onto his head fall the stones of real words from real life. And here is Zala. She's gotten much closer to him in recent weeks, she's come right up close. But Marijana has left and gone far away. Zala approached him from out of his childhood, and he traveled back into a vortex of air, through the thin membrane of wobbly reason, through the space of a chilly forest. He heard an accordion, some familiar melody, and he knew: the two of them, Zala and he, were each approaching from his or her own direction.

75.

"Who said key?"

It's silent in the classroom and the teacher stays sitting at the piano for another instant, then gets up, pushing the bench away, the rough parquet floor squeaking beneath its legs. Childish faces follow her as she walks to the window, stops and looks into the emptiness of a dusky morning. She stands there for a while, as though she's seen something, but there's nothing to see: Chestnut trees, autumn puddles beneath them, dew collecting on the window pane.

"Somebody keeps singing 'key,'" she says into the window, "freedom's key." She turns around to face them. She walks up to the first bench, while in the silence the parquet squeaks loudly beneath her rubber soles. "The right word is 'glee,' not 'key,' not 'freedom's key.'" She walks across the sagging floor to the passage between the benches and stops next to Janez. The edge of the bench digs into her thighs right in front of Janez's eyes, into the taut skirt of the suit that the teacher is wearing, and her round face way up under the lights says in the silence, "Janez, stand up and recite the text."

Janez says nothing as his ink-stained fingers play with the penholder. All faces are now turned toward him.

"Or you can sing it."

Janez gets up slowly. The teacher raps the time against the bench with her knuckles and starts singing.

"... *and the bright sparks from our hammers* ... how does it go from there?"

"... *will forge our freedom's key*," Janez says softly and looks around startled when the entire class bursts out laughing, all of them looking at him and laughing.

"Quiet," the teacher says and the children fall silent. "I knew it was you," she says. "I could hear you. Majda, get up and tell Janez how it goes."

Majda in the first bench gets up, turns to Janez and sings in a clarion voice:

... and the bright sparks of our hammers
will shape our freedom's glee.

"Did you hear, Janez? 'Will shape our freedom's glee'. What will it forge, Janez? What will it forge?"

Janez says nothing. Majda pushes a strand of blond hair back over her ear, looks at him and can't understand how he couldn't know what it will forge, then she can't hold herself back anymore and says, "Fortune's key, will forge our fortune's key."

"That's right," the teacher says and squeaks her way back to the piano. " 'Fortune's key', 'freedom's glee'—is that so hard to remember? It didn't forge our freedom's key, it forged our fortune's key, I mean glee, it's not the sparks that forged it, but our strength, our strength. The sparks don't forge anything, they shape, the light shapes." She sits back down at the piano, strikes the keys and calls out, "Three, four!" and the children begin singing:

We builders with our strength
Will forge our fortune's key
And the bright sparks from our hammers
Will shape our freedom's glee.

Fortune's key, comrade Zala had said. He was in love with her. She had a resonant voice when she sang. She played the piano. She gave him an orange for doing such a good job of reciting at the Pioneers ceremony. About comrade Tito who loves Pioneers. He, Janez, didn't love Pioneers. He didn't love his father who would rampage through their courtyard at night and trample the neighbor's lettuce. And he didn't even love his mother too much, because she was afraid of father yet tried to help him at the same time. He didn't love the league of partisan veterans, whom he had to play the accordion for under the dangling kitchen light bulb. In fact, he hated them all, except for his mother, but definitely including his father, with all his heart. He was in love with Zala. She had given him an orange and a big hug and she had kissed him. She had red lipstick on her mouth. She smelled good. She was soft and warm. And sad. She was often lost in thought. For long stretches she would look out at the suburban Maribor street scene, then turn around and look at the class as though she weren't sure where she was. He thought she was always looking at him. He loved her. Once she had said to him, 'Your father suffered a great deal. You need to understand him.' Janez didn't understand what there could be to understand. He understood—everybody had suffered a lot. Zala's brother had been shot in front of a wall in the Maribor jail, that's what his father had told him. He had known her brother. He had met him in jail before he was sent to Celje, to the prison they called the Old Whistler. Zala's brother, Zoran, had been shot, but beforehand he had been allowed to write a letter. Anton Lipnik, his father, had been sent to a camp, but beforehand they beat him and hung a brick from his balls. After that his balls were as big as pumpkins. He heard this from the men, from the league of partisans in the kitchen, who laughed. Then they went on singing. He understood everything, except for the fact that he had to play the accordion, and except freedom's key, or rather glee, and fortune's key. Bravo, said schoolteacher Zala, how nicely you played it, and she squeezed him tightly to herself, to her soft, supple breasts, and she smelled of makeup. She was sad and she liked him. She lived in the center of town and sometimes rode her bicycle to school. Back then people rode bicycles. Later the only person he liked that much was Irena, but that was much later, in the twelfth grade—she was in the eleventh—on some meadow on Pohorje, during a school outing when she was bathed in moonlight. They could hear the noise of their schoolmates in the mountain cabin while she lay in the meadow, bathed in silvery moonlight. He lay down next to her. Beneath her blue sweater with the white stripe there were two rounded hillocks. He kissed them and reached under her sweater. Her heart was pounding wildly and so was his. But that was much later.

76.

Comrade Zala was often absent from school. Her substitute was an older teacher who was never lost in thought and who always smiled. But even so, Janez Lipnik didn't like her. Her laughter was loud and forced, like the laughter of the league of veterans coming from their kitchen late at night. He liked Zala, who was quiet and lost in thought. Whenever she was absent from school, his teachers would say she was seriously ill and they would cast glances at each other. Sometimes she has to get treated, one of his schoolmates said, because of the war. For Janez Lipnik that was nothing unusual. His father also had to get treated because of the war. Mr. Remer, too, the German soldier who had lost a leg, he should probably also get treated, because he had wounds that kept opening and oozing pus, as Hermann, his son, told him. Lots of people had to get treated. And lots of people would have liked to get treated, but couldn't. So it was no surprise if Zala did, too. Whenever she was gone, he missed her. He would have liked to tell her that he missed her and that there's nothing wrong if she has to get treated, because his father, who was a comrade, ought to, and Remer, who was just Mister—which meant he was from a lower social class, a German soldier who only deserved scorn—he ought to, too. He knew where she lived in town, in one of those handsome buildings with a balcony. Once, when she was still healthy, he walked with her and helped her carry her bag of school notebooks. They parted outside her building, and she told him to go straight home, or else his mother would get angry. But he waited there a while longer, then he went inside the spacious, dark entryway, went up the stairs and stopped outside her door with its brass fittings and thick glass pane that light glimmered through. He knew where she stayed when she was sick and had often stopped outside that door. He wanted to ask when she would be well again and when she was coming back.

In autumn of 1954 his beloved Comrade Zala was missing from school for several days. The teacher who substituted for her said that Comrade Zala was ill. If she's ill, Janez thought, then she should stay in bed. But she didn't stay in bed. He knew that she didn't, because he would go walking past the windows of her apartment. He stood on the empty sidewalk in the afternoon and watched her standing on the balcony. When she saw him, she retreated inside. Her behavior struck him as odd. He was familiar with his father's odd behavior. But he would shout at people, bang his fist on the table and sing partisan songs. She just swept back inside like a shadow.

On the third or fourth day of her absence he saw a big bunch of people on the sidewalk in front of her house. They were murmuring and looking up at the balcony of her apartment. Somebody said the police were at her front door. Somebody knowingly related that the school principal had sent a courier to her house. Even after knocking and ringing the bell for a long time, the door didn't open. He seemed to hear somebody moving around inside, and he even heard some metal sound, like a bowl falling on the floor. The principal called the police. Now they were here, outside her door. Janez Lipnik's childish heart was racing as it did every night his father got him out of bed and told him to get dressed. What was happening with her? How he would have liked to help, whatever it was that was happening. Somebody said if it came to it they would make a forced entry, or in other words, break in. If she didn't open the door, they were going to break it in.

Then Zala appeared on the balcony. She was wearing her nightshirt, which was covered with stains. She was disheveled and she was looking strangely, absently upward, past the walls and roofs toward the Pohorje uplands. A total silence fell over the crowd. Through the open balcony door they could hear the pounding on her front door. It was raining. Drops of water were sliding down her face. Janez thought they were tears. But she didn't seem to be crying, her face wasn't distorted at all, just her eyes, just those eyes which kept staring motionlessly at some point on the roofs of the buildings across the street, or perhaps at Pohorje. Some of the onlookers tried to see what she was seeing—what is she looking at, what does she see? Somebody said she turned strange whenever it rained. It's the sudden changes in air pressure, said somebody else. Somebody said that she'd been wandering around her apartment for the past three days and kept her lights on all night. Janez knew it was true that she was wandering around her apartment and that she wasn't sick in bed. Lord Jesus, said some woman standing under a brightly colored umbrella, she's going to jump.

O Zala, my Zala, how lonely you are! Janez thought, his heart racing. He was afraid, he felt sorry for her, there was something here he didn't understand, either, as with his father. He knew he wished he could help her. But how?

The crowd on the street kept getting bigger and some of them were closing their umbrellas to see her better. Bicyclists dismounted from their bikes and asked what was going on. A motorcyclist riding past with a side car couldn't get through the crowd. He turned off his engine and joined the bystanders.

For a moment Zala turned to look back, as if the escalation of fists banging on her front door had bothered her. The police were trying to break in. She didn't even notice the continually growing crowd of people on the street under the balcony. She raised her hand, holding a pair of scissors, and without looking away from that unidentified point on a wall or a roof or on Pohorje, she cut into her thick, dark hair. Patches of hair fell onto the sidewalk. Bits of hair stuck to her soaked forehead. As she bent her head forward, she kept cutting and jabbing at her hair ever more furiously, until white spots of skin began to appear at her temples and crown, immediately followed by bloody spots. She hacked mercilessly into her hair and even the skin on her head. People were starting to get upset and shout, 'She's going to kill herself!'

At that point Janez felt the sidewalk slide out from under his feet. His head started spinning. The faces in the dark crowd where he was standing, wet faces with caps on their heads, and faces under umbrellas all started spinning. The walls of buildings started dancing around him, and he thought he was going to fall, but he didn't—he managed to lean up against the coarse wall of a house.

Then he broke through the legs of the ever more densely packed, ever noisier crowd, through the bicycles and bodies, and ran and didn't dare to look back, not wanting to see if she'd jumped or stabbed herself with the scissors. O, Zala, how I wish I could have helped you. But I couldn't. I was just a boy, almost sixty years old. And to this day I couldn't help you. I'll be an old man soon, barely eight years old.

77.

On a rainy morning a few days before he suddenly turned up in the brightly lit promenade of the shopping center, he had been in Maribor, ringing the bell at the front door of her downtown apartment. At first there was no sound coming from the other side, no sign that anyone lived there. Then he heard something slide through the foyer, a light went on, and he saw a fuzzy shadow approach through the thick glass pane. The door opened slightly and he saw part of a wrinkled face looking out through the crack. The small eyes observed him for a while, then the mouth underneath them said, "I thought you were the mailman."

He said he wasn't the mailman. He wondered if Zala D., the schoolteacher, still lived here.

"Not for a long time," the old woman said and opened the door. She was wearing some sort of colorful smock and had slippers on her feet, the kind for polishing parquet floors as you slide over them. They glistened and smelled of fresh floor wax.

He said that he had been Zala D.'s pupil. Sometimes he helped her carry notebooks.

"And how can I help you?"

He felt awkward. If he had known how she could help him, he would have told her right away.

"I'd like to visit her," he said. "If you know where she's living now."

The tiny eyes amid the wrinkled face took their time sizing him up. She couldn't decide whether to close the door in his face or let her curiosity get the better of her. Curiosity won out.

"She was your teacher?" she asked.

"Yes," he said. "We all have fond memories of her. I'd like to tell her that."

She opened the door. So he wouldn't have to stand in the hallway.

Then he was in the foyer, which smelled of floor wax and an elderly woman.

"So you don't know?" she said. "She died."

She looked at him with an old person's solicitude, as though he were her relative or otherwise connected to her. Which he was, so how could she do otherwise. They were both silent for a long time.

She told him to wait there—clearly she had no intention of inviting him any farther into her apartment. She slid away and he could hear her shuffling through some boxes, and through the half-closed door he could see her looking through some papers on a table. Then she slid back with a yellowed newspaper clipping.

"Ten years ago," she said. "Also in June."

His hands trembled slightly as he read the headline:

BICYCLIST KILLED

Ljubljana, June 30. Shortly before 5:00pm last night 70-year-old Zala D. was riding her bicycle on Trieste Road heading downtown. Near a tank trap members of the Territorial Defense Force called out to her to stop. The bicyclist did not respond to their warnings and rode into the rear wheels of a truck that was making a turn on the road. Troops of the Territorial Defense gave the injured bicyclist first aid and drove her to the Clinical Center, where she died from severe head and chest injuries at 4:00 in the morning.

"She couldn't hear very well," the old woman said. "That was because of her medications, you know. She took very strong medications."

"I knew she was sick," Lipnik said.

"She had something wrong inside her head," the old lady explained. "Sometimes she'd take scissors and start cutting her hair."

"I know," Lipnik said.

"That kept happening to her," the old lady said. "So she moved in with her nephew in Ljubljana. She was close to a doctor there who helped her a lot. The nephew was Zoran's son, you know, the one the Germans shot. I can give you his address."

"No need," Lipnik said. He asked if she knew what kind of bicycle she'd had, what color it was."

"Oh yes," the woman said. "I don't know what color, but it was an old bicycle that she loved riding, even though she shouldn't have. Everyone told her not to ride it. But you know, during the war in June of '91 our soldiers were so nervous, they didn't pay any attention to where cars were going. All of us were afraid, but the soldiers' nerves were completely shot. They could have shot her for not stopping. I don't know what became of the bicycle—you know, there wasn't much left of it. Maybe some homeless person took it."

"Do you think," he asked, "that same homeless person might have thrown it in the Ljubljanica?"

"I don't understand," the old lady said.

"Neither do I," Lipnik said.

As he walked down the wet street back to his car, which he had parked somewhere along the Drava, he noticed that the houses seemed to spread apart, with the space toward the front broader and more open, while the space at the back narrowed into a kind of passageway. When he reached the water the horizon became flat, inexplicably open at both the back and the front. From the corners of his eyes he sensed that the world at the horizon was slightly rounded. Perhaps this was how some giant animal eye saw it, one that was oblivious to time, but had an acute sense of the landscape—a big, fat, stubborn donkey's eye. His eye.

78.

His geographical position is clear: between the Benetton store with the mannequins in the display window and the Philips store with the electric razors. It was precisely here that he had been stuck when the lightning started and the wind began blowing the clouds toward Krim and Turjak. When the rain started scratching on the transparent roof and the rivulets of water slipping down the glass surface turned into a timeless creeping. Am I stuck here forever, Lipnik wondered, forever in my worn-out shoes in this purgatory, above the inferno that may be down there in the cellar?

Perhaps, Lipnik thinks, perhaps at least beneath my feet, in the cellar and farther down, there's something that's not quite so flat, smooth, bright and carefree in its eternal noonday, perhaps this big, flat surface has its underground. Perhaps that underground is open and rounded like the landscape alongside the river that he'd seen a few days before. This is hard for him to imagine when he knows that the entire country has a network of waterways, holes, caves and passages, that down below Slovenia is riddled with holes like some sea sponge. For centuries the local inhabitants weren't aware of their caves, they didn't know where their rivers suddenly went or why miles away huge springs appeared, streams that flowed out of the rocky foothills of other mountains. Then they poured that red dye, the color of blood, into a river, and saw that it vanishes underground and reappears red, blood-red, miles away at the far end of the country, after flowing through multiple caves and subterranean passageways it merges with still other waters and seeks out new passages through this cavernous underground world riddled with holes. He thinks that this dye, this blood from underground, will flood us one day, the flood will be red, it will surge up from below, flood the banks of the rivers that are fed from below, from out of deep caves it will race across the Ljubljana marshlands, first flooding the cellars that are all useless anyway, burst into apartment house foyers and factory work floors, crash through the windows of theaters and pool up over the brightly lit promenades of the shopping center.

Nobody who walks over this bright flat surface knows of this country's underground world, empty and riddled with holes, but ready to fill up with water anytime. For now it's still hollow, so much so that quite a few people feel what Lipnik now feels, a kind of dizziness. As if his foot had hit the ground in a place that's hollow underneath, as if this hollowness and emptiness, over which the thin flat surface, almost the membrane of the shopping center, has been stretched, sometimes caused everything to sway.

For a second he thinks of getting out of here. Not by going home, but into the forest. The ground there is damp and warm, the tops of the pines and firs, the beeches and maples, sway high above, it smells of moss, in the evening the trees cast long shadows over the clearings, evening itself is nothing more than a long shadow, and morning the sun shining through eyelids. If you wake up in the morning in the forest, Lipnik thinks, a red light shines through your eyelids, and when you open your eyes, you see that it's a ray of sun shining through the tree branches overhead. He thinks of going into the forest. The trees there have their roots planted into the ground, the ground is solid, stretched as taut as can be over the hole-ridden underground, the forest and its roots holding everything together so it doesn't fly apart. This thin membrane here couldn't hold anything together and that's why it sways a little, that's why his head is spinning slightly.

Up above, over his head, the water creeps soundlessly. From the glass ceiling, it runs off somewhere else, down through gutters, alongside walls and into the ground, into the underground torrents that appear on the far side of the country. And if he looks through the wall, he sees the veil of rain enshrouding the landscape. It has been raining mercilessly for three weeks, not all the time, but at intervals, but still it seems that the sky's sluices have been opened and it will never stop pouring. Now is the time to move to the world that's outside. He distinctly feels the darkness drawing him to it, somewhere at its other end is morning, morning on a forested hillside, morning beside a stream. The morning light that's waiting for him somewhere is something different from the light here. This is a light of absence, an unreal light, like the unreal drums, and the other percussion instruments, that bang on his head with their wild rhythm. There is no divine or historical presence here, there is no memory, there is nothing. What there is here is unreality, pure and simple. Wherever only the present exists, no matter how tangible, no matter how material, how full of shopping carts and car trunks it may be, wherever there is no past, and the people and events that have passed are gone, the world is fundamentally unreal, truly and definitively unreal. Outside is the veil of rain, the twilight, and only beyond that is the curtain of darkness where the city lights don't reach. Where, toward morning, when the rain stops, stars will be shining. On one side the sun will go up, and the moon will still be hanging on the other. But first he has to go through the twilight that surrounds the city, because it is in the twilight, the precursor of darkness, its antechamber, that a different world begins. There is a hint of the curtain of darkness, the homeland of memory, there are the events that have passed, the people who are gone. Lipnik clearly senses that when morning, when daybreak, comes, they'll be here. All the ones who are gone and all the ones he has thought about, the ones from his childhood and the ones from before his birth. They aren't just in books and they aren't just in archival documents, they aren't just in diaries and they aren't just in photographs. If their hearts beat, if sexual desire drove them to be with the persons they loved, if longing or friendship drove them there, if they sacrificed, if they endured pain, if they were wounded, if they wept, if they laughed, if their thoughts wandered anxiously through time and through space and they weren't able to understand it—neither time nor space—in short, if they lived, then it couldn't just all go away, disappear. He knows they're not here, they can't be here, because out there, up above and down below there are lots of them, he senses their presence, but doesn't want to see all of the ones who have left, he wants to see those he encountered, in his childhood memories or his embryonic recollections, he knows distinctly that they're every-where out there, wherever the circle of darkness is, in the forests and in the caverns below, in the currents flowing underground, in the caves of the Karst, in the clouds reached by tall trees, trees with no name, in the air, in the light of dawn.

I really ought to go to the forest, Lipnik thinks. Either to Pohorje or all the way to Lower Carniola.

79.

But before then, before he heads into the forest, he needs to go get Marijana. At the beauty salon or the hair stylist's—where on earth is she? These bags, he thinks, I'll have to leave these here for a minute. This cheese, milk, bread, more precisely French cheese, camembert, a bottle of Bordeaux, also Marijana's silk stockings, pillow covers, oranges and a knife. Why does he need a knife—the knife is for slicing bread, but it's still sharp. A sharp knife. He can't drag all of this with him into beauty or hair salons. The bright displays at his temples keep moving faster and faster, from the corners of his eyes, both the right and the left, he sees the left and the right sides simultaneously, kaleidoscopic light from the colorful display cases with the colorful mannequins and their white faces blends together, merges in tiny whirlpools at his temples, the tiny whirlpools spinning like clouds of multicolored smoke, while that jet ski is skimming the sea, the motionless, oil-slicked, incandescent sea, and in the background the sound of an accordion distinctly breaks loose from the undifferentiated musical noise. A woman with red hair stands in the doorway of the hair stylist's, her shoulders blocking his view into the premises. I beg your pardon, Lipnik says politely, may I get past? Sir, says the redhead, bright bands of light penetrating through her red hair like bands of sunlight seeking the floor of the sea, sir, this is a women's hair stylist, if you want a haircut, you'll have to go elsewhere. That's strange, Lipnik says, I thought they didn't separate those things anymore. Here they're separate, says the redhead with the light in her hair. I don't want a haircut, Lipnik says and gets up on tiptoe to see if Marijana is sitting under one of the dryer hoods, he'd recognize her by her skirt, by her hands, by everything, even if he couldn't see her head, he'd recognize her. And he does, there's a young man massaging her scalp. In the place where her hair should be there's a white cloud. That's shampoo, he thinks, that can't be a white cloud. Marijana, he calls out, Marijana. She makes no reply at all, and now that man pushes her head down under the water, causing her to bend forward, then comes another man and starts thumping her on the back. What's going on here, Lipnik nearly shouts. What is your problem? says the redhead with the light in her hair. There's no Marijana here. The first man looks up at him, he'd also like to know what's going on here, and now Lipnik sees that it's Beno. Beno's face is bewhiskered as fashion dictates these days—half-shaven, half-shaggy, leaving a short bristle on your face like a shorthaired terrier. Damned terrier, Lipnik says. That other guy must be Pepo, what a moronic name, but perfect for a cop. The redhead starts shoving him back out into the promenade of the shopping mall as people turn to look at the commotion, the two men come out to the doorway and the woman lifts her head up from the sink, maybe it isn't Marijana after all—in which case if she's not here, where is she?

Where is Marijana?

Where is Zala?

Everything starts happening so fast that the archivist, used to slowly turning over sheets of paper and poring over the anthills of writing on them, can hardly keep up with the speed that they're going in his head—his hurried footsteps follow behind. Now he walks past the bags lying on the floor beside the bench—the lady is there, the one who doesn't know if it's Monday or Tuesday—along with her grayhaired gentleman, the one who knows that today is Tuesday, not Monday, he's there, too, both of them craning their necks to see where the owner of those bags, who was sitting here just a moment ago, has gone. He could stop and say to them, it's Tuesday, don't worry. But he doesn't, he keeps going, and at the intersection of the huge promenade, where more and more people are gathering, he stops for a moment, then turns to the right, perhaps to go look at the beauty salon, but suddenly he realizes that the beauty salon is of no interest to him anymore, who's painting Marijana's fingernails, who's trimming her toenails, who's ripping her toenails out, none of that is of any interest to him at this moment. His attention is being drawn to the stairway that has arrows pointing to it from the shopping center's exit. There is a picture of a green stairway with an arrow beneath it, and his lucid mind tells him that the arrow is pointing to the stairway that he needs to go down. He loses no time following the arrows, which lead him all the way around the building, to the back, where trucks are unloading furniture and upholstered chairs. He yields to a truck and almost gets hit by a car whose mustachioed driver honks wildly at him and growls, he can see him right there growling behind the wheel. He goes a little farther on and there's the stairway, here's where I need to go down, down. As soon as he reaches the very bottom of the stairway and opens the door of a huge auditorium, he hears an accordion, from somewhere far off, through a door on the far side. Now he knows that he really is on the right path. But there are metal objects piled up against the walls of the auditorium and it will be hard to find that door. He walks alongside the shelves where all that hardware has been stacked up. At first glance it appears that all this metal junk serves no purpose. But his ever more lucid mind now grasps that all of this is just an illusion, this disarray, he distinctly grasps the whole problem: chaos is always just an illusion, when in fact it is ruled by order and laws, the mind of the universe governs everything. Consequently, what's lying here on the shelves in broad daylight is not hardware strewn around higgledy-piggledy, but U-profiles and L-profiles. U-profiles and L-profiles fit together. He didn't have time now to test just how, even though he was tempted to assemble a U-profile and an L-profile, but he knows they fit together like a research project at the archive, in the end they always fit together in an ellipse or even a circle, but mostly an ellipse. His fit together in an ellipse, he can see that now, but he has to move on and just a bit farther down, farther down. Just like his mother had read to him in bed: The ancient Slovenes believed that you could go down into a deep cave, and if you dropped down far enough, you would reach the other world—actually heaven, because heaven is not just up above, it's down below. There you behold a radiant landscape, beautiful green pastures, with willows growing alongside water that flows in a smooth, meandering stream, and that's what it's like, a little version of heaven. Handsome young mowers mow the hay there, and you can help them and cut down a few rows yourself, if you like. Lojze is there, mowing with his scythe: When the dew is on the blade, and young fellows wield their scythes, singing, yodeling in the grass. The very best scythes, Alojz Hočevar scythes, May 3rd Square, Ljubljana. At the far end of the auditorium there is an illuminated lectern with someone standing behind it, that's the warehouse manager, he must know if you can still buy a Lojze scythe. Lipnik goes toward him and the closer he gets, the more familiar the man's face becomes. When he gets up close, his suspicion is confirmed: it's Mehmet, the doorman from the archive. Mehmet, Lipnik says, since when have you been working here? Mehmet looks at him for a while, as though he's having trouble recognizing him. Then it comes to him. Oh yeah, it's you, Mr. Lipnik. How did you even recognize me? At the archive you hardly ever glanced my way. You bounded up and down the stairs like a grasshopper. It's been ages since you were at the archive, I remember you used to even spend Saturday mornings there, even Sundays now and then, but it's been ages since you were there. That's why you don't know that I've changed jobs. This is an interesting place, Lipnik says, who would ever have imagined all the things that are hidden under our shopping mall? Oh, Mehmet says. This auditorium here is nothing. Go open that door and you'll see. What door? The metal one over there on the right. Don't be afraid, it squeaks a little, I've forgotten to oil it. Lipnik hesitates, he doesn't want to take a step too far, because if you take a step too far, you can fall into an abyss. So he awkwardly shuffles his feet in front of the long lectern and thinks hard: They say I have two voices, one of them lucid, the other insane. Now I'm speaking in the first voice, and that's because the first voice knows the difference between the first and second voices. The second voice doesn't know the difference. What does the first voice say? The first voice, Lipnik says to himself, the first voice says, 'Go on, at least you'll be able to tell the difference.'

All right then, let's go.

80.

Mehmet nods encouragingly to him, puts on his glasses and bends down over his notes about U- and L-profiles. And probably others, as well, concerning some other, to all appearances chaotically jumbled, but in fact quite compatible profiles.

Before Lipnik can determine if the door really does squeak and really hasn't been oiled in a long time, he hears Mehmet's voice clearly speaking behind him. Thus spake Mehmet: The angel speaking to me turned around and woke me, the way a person wakes up from sleeping. Even though I wasn't asleep. Wakefulness was sleep, sleep was wakefulness, seeing. He said to me: What do you see? I said, 'I see a scroll flying, and the length of the scroll is twenty ells and its width is twenty ells.' It should have told me, This is the curse that will come over the entire land. But it told me something different. This scroll is the Slovene book of dreams. It flies over the land and everything in it will be in your dreams for a full hundred years.

Lipnik can't help laughing. Oh go on, Mehmet, you read that in the archive on the night shift. Out of sheer boredom you read it and memorized it. And what difference does that make? Mehmet asks. You're right, says Lipnik, it doesn't make any difference. But before I go, he says, could I ask you for a favor. Sure, name it, Mehmet says.

"Could I ask you to go upstairs after a while? I've left some bags up there between Benetton and Philips, you'll see them right away. There's an elderly lady and gentleman standing beside them trying to figure out if today is Monday or Tuesday. Could you look after them for a while? And if my wife happens to be there—you've met her, her name's Marijana—ask her to take the bags home with her."

"Fine," Mehmet says. "But you be careful. I think there are steps on the other side. Don't go bounding down them, or you'll get hurt."

Then Lipnik opens the metal door, which squeaks nastily.

81.

But there was nothing there. It was the sort of darkness of which Lipnik might have said: It was nothing, there was something there that didn't exist, it was exactly nothing, a darkness that was nothing. It was the darkness in which he sometimes wished that he didn't exist—not that he didn't exist *anymore*, but had never existed in the first place. It would happen when his tired, childish ear filled up with the shouts of the men's voices coming from upstairs, when he heard a woman's shriek and footsteps running down the stairs, an ear that knew everything about camps and knives planted in chests, about shaping freedom's glee and forging freedom's keys, it took in everything, this childish ear, but it couldn't get full, because it was already exhausted, because it couldn't understand what Lipnik's grown-up ear so many years later still couldn't make connect, even if his eye had clearly read it: All things are exhausting, man cannot make sense of them. The eye is not satisfied with seeing, nor the ear filled with hearing. It was dark because the door behind him had shut just as he expected. When he stepped through it, he didn't expect ever to be able to open it again. He opened it and noticed, high up above, the dazzling neon lights of a warehouse containing U- and L-profiles, and he thought of calling Mehmet the warehouse manager, and if he didn't hear him, then knocking, banging, pounding on the metal door until Mehmet, who had once been the night watchman at the archive but now was a warehouse manager deep under the shopping center, finally heard him. But he didn't really intend to do that. As soon as he left those bags in the vast, brightly lit mall and began his descent, he knew that from here on it was downward for him all the way, as some poet once wrote, for whom it really did then become down all the way, down down down, to find something there, something amid the stars, something amid the vast expanses of space, where his soul soared now, the soul of a poet, and where one day or perhaps very soon there will also be soaring the soul of Janez Lipnik, the archivist, whose ear could not fill and whose eye could not see enough and whose soul did not grasp what had once happened, was happening today and would keep happening tomorrow. He did at least know that he had to go down, to get to the bottom of memory, into the dark that is nothing, and not just any sort of nothing, but the kind that his racing childish heart had first sensed in the dark of the stairway that led to the cellar at 12 Leningrad Street in the city known as Maribor. This now was that stairway, with its cellar smell of coal and apples, he went down the steps with their unforgettable smell of mold, of rotting apples and occasionally of sauerkraut, which the residents of the big red house stored down here in those days, in those years when the sounds of far-off explosions still echoed around here. It was a cool smell, and yet it was also the smell of refuge, because at that time the boy wanted the same thing that Lipnik the archivist wants now—a refuge in the dark, in nothingness, and although he knew perfectly well that somewhere on the coarse, damp wall, somewhere amid the crumbling stucco, there was a switch that his mother had pointed out to him once when they were going downstairs for potatoes, although he knew that all he had to do was turn that black switch and the humming light would go on, he didn't turn the switch, because he didn't want light. He didn't want his father, who would dash downstairs late at night and out into the yard, shouting 'Roll call, roll call!', to notice the sliver of light under the door in the hallway, he didn't want him to pause here and, instead of going out into the yard and to the neighbor's lettuce, clamber down into the cellar, because he knew that then his father would crawl into a corner, huddle up around his big, white belly and moan like he did when he lay on the neighbor's trampled lettuce. He didn't want his great, big body to lean down and say, what are you doing here, why did you run off, why don't you want to play the accordion, what are you afraid of, son? It won't be so bad, the men who were here to visit only ripped out some hair, I have a bloody patch on my scalp, but no worse than when that Gestapo man Schwager beat me with the butt of his pistol in the corridor of the Old Whistler, but I've told you about that, son, I've told you many times, I've showed you the scar that it made. This is why he didn't turn on the light, but felt his way along the wall as he headed down the steps. He knew, just as he'd known as a child crouching in the dark, that an underground tunnel led from the house all the way down to the river, to the Studenci footbridge, and that at that small metal bridge it linked up with another tunnel that had a broad passage, that ran from that bridge on the Drava all the way down deep into the earth, leading under the bank of the Drava as far as the railroad yard and, if you wanted, you could come out at the Carinthian Station. But nobody wanted to come out, because there were bombs going off on the surface and everyone who went there before he was born said that that nobody wanted to leave, because of the explosions from the American bombers that battered the railroad lines and the station, and occasionally a nearby house or two. His bedroom ceiling had a patched-over hole that his father would show all his buddies who came visiting late at night, it was where an American bomb weighing many kilograms came flying through, it pierced through the roof and the attic and then each successive ceiling of the big house all the way to the cellar, where it dug in but didn't explode, because if it had exploded, then the big red house wouldn't be here anymore. Then German soldiers came to defuse the bomb, and if they hadn't, the bomb would have gone off, destroying the cellar, and now Janez Lipnik wouldn't be able to look for that underground tunnel that took you even farther down, to the river, to the bridge, and from there to the bowels of the earth with the trains running on top. That's the rumbling sound of the trains full of bodies, full of livestock, which they're taking to slaughter, livestock that suspects, but doesn't yet know, that strongly suspects and starts stomping and thrashing on the wooden floors of the cattle cars, mucking through its own filth, but doesn't yet know what awaits it. A human being hopes that is not what's going to happen, while cattle hope for a pasture at the end of the trip, even if they suspect, even if they know that the end of this trip is the slaughterhouse, a slaughterhouse for people and for livestock, for those who hope and those who suspect. Now when he reached the bottom, now that he's at the very bottom of the stairway in the long cellar corridor, he knows there are wooden doors on either side of the passageway, and behind the doors there are coal, potatoes and sauerkraut, with a hanged man only behind one of them. That was the merchant who hid English yarn, he hid it in this cellar and he hanged himself here when the authorities of the people's republic were hot on his trail, while the police were looking for him upstairs in his flat, he was already hanging down here, he'd tied the rope to the bars over the window and hanged himself once and for all and everyone talked about it. Lipnik never found out which room the man hanged himself in, his mother didn't want him to know, she didn't want him to shiver whenever she sent him down for potatoes, but still whenever he went to the cellar his heart would start thumping because some day he expected to see the hanged man hanging in one of those rooms that were separated from each other by rough-hewn wooden doors, and yet he knew he could run, when he was down there he often thought he could run from the hanged man, or from his father, who ran past the door of the room where he was hiding, looking for him to play freedom's key. Once you got all the way to the bottom it was no longer as dark as it was higher up on the steps, because down here there was a tiny bit of light that shone through the cellar's barred windows looking out on the street, which were the chutes that they dumped coal into and that he could also just as easily use to escape, because his body was so small he could crawl through them, and if it was too tight, he would strip to his underwear and crawl out through the bars, but he knew he didn't want to crawl through bars that somebody had hanged himself from. So he thought there must be some tunnel leading out of the cellar, one that leads to the Drava, the kind of tunnel that even small castles had in the stories his mother read to him, so why shouldn't the red house have one, just some long trench, it didn't need to be big enough for him to ride his bicycle through or walk upright, it could just be a trench he could use to crawl to the river, just to the river, that's all.

He stopped and listened. He felt a humid draft passing through the cellar, a draft that smelled of river silt, of water, that very peculiar smell the big river had. If he really made it to the river through that passageway, which clearly had to exist—would he get to the end?

82.

Had he reached the end? Or by reaching the tunnel that led to the river had he reached the circumference of the circle—or more precisely, the ellipse—that links all invisible earthly and human things, that passes through the countryside, through the bowels of the earth and the human soul, that churns hot and cold, dark and sunny, through the plains, over the green hilltops and past Alpine passes, through wells and oceans, that intersects rivers, streets bathed in neon, lone villages perching on hillsides—the circle—or perhaps the ellipse—that cares nothing for time that gives rise to images, for the past, for the present or for the future, that knows how pitiful human beings behave on the ellipse, on the circle's circumference—their thin skin, cerebral cortices, delicate genitalia, spongelike lungs, the slime of their brains—from the time they were nothing more than slime, an embryonic bud, to the time when their bones and muscles go slack—what senselessness, what pain all this chaos with its terrible order was, Janez Lipnik was only now coming to understand, only now does he realize why he had to enter this story, enter all of these stories, which have no end or beginning, why he had to be aware of each moment of happiness, each moment of joy, because in an instant they could vanish in the cosmic vortex, the way great love vanishes, or the way the ink on the letters to the Corinthians vanishes—for if I have not love, you must take pains that some letter remains, some word that all this exists—the joy, the love—before they fade, vanish, and spin off into the jolting, sucking, draining vortex of the unknown. For fear is not a word, and the word describing pain is not just a word, but pain itself, which requires no image or explanation, and a brick hanging from somebody's testicles isn't a joke laughed at by drunken men—both by the ones who did it and the ones who listen to a story about it in the drunken hours of early morning and laugh, even if the face of the storyteller is contorted as he tells the story—it isn't possible, it simply isn't possible to relive someone else's pain, there's only your own, only your own—so why talk about it at all, your own or others', if all that's left is a word and if only the person who experienced the pain can later have it in mind? And why does some fellow named Schwager not feel any pain when he uses a wire to tie that brick to your father's balls?—fastens it by wrapping the wire around the skin that connects the testicles to the body and also protects them—is it possible that the only pain that fellow could feel is precisely the same pain, and that all the men who listened to this story and then made jokes about it and laughed all agreed that only that, only the horrible pain that comes from swollen balls, balls as big as pumpkins growing out in some field, that only that sort of pain could make some fellow named Schwager realize that he had inflicted precisely this sort of pain on some other? Also a blow to the head with the butt of a pistol, leaving a scar like the one his father is fond of showing to company, a blow to the head with the butt of a pistol purely and simply because he had said, 'Help me, you're Slovene, too'—only then, the men laugh, would he realize what it meant to get a pistol butt slammed into his head, bursting the skin and causing blood to gush out, that's the only way to know pain, the men agree. But while walking along the circle's—or, rather, the ellipse's—circumference Janez Lipnik grows more and more certain that submerged in the memories that have so obsessed him is not just a word, not even just an image, but reality, a useless reality, but still reality, even if he does wonder who's to benefit from the painful reality of these past people, their passion that gets transformed into death, their arrogance that ends in some miserable humiliation, the bodily violence that ends in hands and knees shaking—for what, for whom? Perhaps it's so we can more easily overcome fear, if we relive it, if we immerse ourselves in it, in that same human soul that's both the soul of endless joy and the soul of pain and the endless fear of nothingness that comes from nothingness, that is nothingness itself, the darkness of memory, the darkness of past actions, of patients crawling in a mental hospital, of the screams of prisoners beaten in the Gestapo's cellars, of kneeling before the rifles of Italian blackshirts, who shoot, wound and kill, beyond the horrible outer limit of terror of villagers lined up before a firing squad, of the naked or half-naked people shot in the back of the head by Communist soldiers, soldiers of the revolution, who then fall into pits, onto heaps of moving, bloody, oozing bodies, of the bayonet in the SS man's chest, which then squirts out blood, of the brick hung from the balls, or the terror of a woman being raped on a forested hillside, on the damp ground, in the cellar of an interrogation chamber.

Does all this fear come from the terrestrial world, out of the bowels of the earth, out of the dense, black soil and the caves of the Karst, from the earth's interior, full of crushed bones and crushed dreams, gouged eyes, skulls with bullet holes in them? He walked and felt that the dizziness had him completely in its grip now, that he was caught up in its vortex, whose earthly and cosmic origins and center were unknown to him. All he knows is that he comes from a past that grows out of a dark soul, the kind of soul that darkness inhabits before it is born, where there's a huge ear sticking out of the slimy embryo in its mother's belly, listening to the story as it's murmured over and over. The story from the book of dreams, the scroll that floats over the land.

83.

Walking through the tunnel, which is high enough for a child to walk through standing up, Lipnik has to crouch over slightly as he heads down toward the river. Even though it's dark, he finds it easy to walk, feeling his way along the damp walls, smelling the river silt, the unforgettable and unmistakable smell of the river called the Drava, which could just as easily be some other river, but for him this smell is something he once picked up here—somewhere close to here it entered his nostrils and has never since left them, somewhere nearby the sound of the water flowing entered his ears, splashing against the banks, the mighty roar and drumming of the layers of water colliding with the bridge piers, carrying of logs and branches, a boat torn away from the shore and the body of a dead dog. The descent to the river goes on and on, the stony chill that the damp walls exude starts giving him shivers. So what if I'm fated, he thinks, so what if I'm fated to pass through the dark tunnel in the earth's bowels to the end of my days—to the end of which days? What if a journey begins here that never brings him to the edge of the river, what if he's going to have to recognize the shapes of the lives that he's sought, and the connections between them, the shapes of the stories he's impinged on with his insatiable curiosity? What if he's going to have to walk through this tunnel for an interminably long time in search of his stories? Perhaps this tunnel doesn't lead to the river as he's always assumed, as his childish memory dictated to him, perhaps he's just going in a circle and this heady wind is just the illusion of a smell, maybe the gurgling of the eddies is just an illusion for his ears, which are exhausted and no longer capable of recognizing anything, anyway, perhaps this light that keeps taking on different shades, first appearing as a slight darkening, then turning into a real shadow, and finally into darkness, is just an illusion for the eye, which thinks for a moment that all of this isn't darkness, isn't a labyrinth, isn't some delirium, but is real, is an image, a likeness, something that the fingers of your hand and the ever more thirsty tongue in your mouth, a tongue that could just about lap up a river by now, a river that ought to be somewhere pretty close, can understand. The stony earthly weight tires him, it has to end soon. And indeed, suddenly a real shaft of light appears, moments later overwhelming the eyes—flooding and overwhelming them so much that for a while they can see nothing. At that instant he hears somebody bang on the door—they must really be banging hard for the sound to carry all the way down here, to the river, which is really close now, right where that mighty flood of daylight is coming from. Someone is banging on the door, but Lipnik can't tell if it's the door that leads to the red house's cellar, or if they're banging on that metal door he went through from the U- and L-profile warehouse. But those are the same door, he thinks, the door he went through to get downstairs, the damp, dark stairway that leads to the cellar, which in turn has a long trench leading to the river, and somebody's fists are banging on it now, and he thinks he can hear voices, too, men's voices. He came down here, calls out Mehmet the warehouse keeper, the former doorman at the Regional Archive. Mehmet is standing on the uppermost step and calling back to some people who are in the brightly lit hall of the warehouse, he has to be down here. The ones still upstairs answer him that they're going to bring flashlights to hack through the darkness with their sharp, long shafts of light and make out the steps that lead down, as the shafts of light dance on the walls and aim down the long trench all the way to the river, where they meet up with the daylight that now illuminates a very big, much wider part of the trench he's come down. Ha ha ha, Lipnik thinks, you're up there, but I'm already way down here. Here's the exit, go ahead, stomp and wave your flashlights, but I'm already out. In the following instant his eyes, ears and nostrils know that he's right next to the river. Now he has to run another hundred meters and at the bridge enter a wide tunnel that leads straight to the railroad station. When he gets there, that will be the end of the story. There you can get on a train and take off. Wherever you want to go. Even though he knows that he has to go through another tunnel, the one they call the bomb shelter, because that wide tunnel will take him straight to the train yard, the Carinthian Railroad Station, where every spring soldiers of the Yugoslav Army load or unload their tanks and artillery. They used to call them the tovarišes, because they were always calling each other tovariš, which meant comrade, the *tovarišes* bustled around their rumbling tanks and trucks and waved little flags and shouted 'left, left,' or 'more, more,' and when they weren't shouting or waving, they would lie or sit all around and ask the boys if they had any sisters—where's your sister?—Janez didn't have one, but he did have Zala his schoolteacher whom the tovarišes would whistle at when she walked past, they whistled and called after all of them in a language he didn't understand. Once he lent them a ball, and for that they let the *momci* climb up on their truck—boys were *momci*, the soldiers were *tovarišes*—the momci were allowed up on the truck while the tovarišes banged away at his poor red ball with their heavy boots, and one of the momci released the emergency brake, and suddenly the gigantic vehicle that had a tank loaded on it began to slide down the gradual slope of the ramp—that's what they called the funny hills that they used to drive tanks and trucks onto the train cars—it began to slide faster and faster down the muddy, rutted hillside, and the momci jumped off of the accelerating, almost speeding monster, which refused to stop in front of the barrack-like brick building, and it didn't even stop in it, but split it in two. Lipnik had to smile now when he thought about the cloud of smoke it produced, and when it abated, that steel beast was looking out through the other side of the building, and all around there were scattered bricks and jutting antennae, because the steel beast with the tank on its back had ploughed through some amateur radio workshop. Antennae jutted everywhere, and the tovarišes, who had dropped the ball, came running from all sides to look at the ruin, it was hilarious, and he'd saved that ball all this time. That's where he had to get. The train station was at the end of the long bomb shelter that had been excavated under the hill—well he knew that no bomb could demolish that hill, no tank, no military vehicle.

84.

When he came out onto the railway station platform, he saw a lone woman sitting on a bench. She seemed to be tired, as though she'd been sitting there for a long time, possibly all day, or perhaps several weeks or even years. He walked toward her to ask when the next train was leaving. He could also have looked at the timetable, but he was meant to approach her, just as she was meant to look up at him, and then he was meant to flinch on recognizing her. He flinched. This was a young woman who wasn't exhausted by years, but from looking for her husband, from wandering up and down the Sava all the way to Kresnice. He recognized her immediately. It was Ivanka K. He wanted to ask her what she was doing in the train station here, far from home, since her home was way on the other side of the country, but she said it before he could even open his mouth. I'm waiting for my husband's murderers, she said. She nodded her head in the direction they would be coming from. Lipnik knew it was Carinthia. Every night trains rumbled off to or in from Carinthia. They put him to sleep in his childhood, they never woke him up. Their sound was as pleasant and comforting as the sound of the village bell, of the Ave Maria and the Indulgences of the Angelus is for children. That's where they'll come from. So they'll be arriving by train, her husband's murderers will be coming by train. Only now did Lipnik notice that Ivanka K. wasn't the only one at the station. On the platform yes, she sat alone on the platform bench, but on the other side he saw men in uniforms, and he didn't know if they were already here before or if they had just now come from somewhere. They had machine guns hanging from straps around their necks, and some of them had heavy pistols in big holsters attached to their belts, perhaps they were Lugers, but he knew immediately that these were officers. Their uniforms were similar to the ones that the tovariši̇̌es wore, and they had red stars on their caps, just like the tovariši̇̌es. They were shuffling around and looking in the direction that the train would be coming from, but despite this everything seemed somehow motionless. Motionless and quiet and even Ivanka K. no longer said anything, and he suddenly felt an agonizing sympathy for this woman who had come so far to await the arrival of her husband's murderers. The motionlessness of that long instant was interrupted only in the distance, far beyond the tovariši̇̌es' heads, as the warm spring breeze caused the leaves of the poplars and some pathetic fruit tree to shiver gently, then moved the flag with the star that flew at the train station barely at all, inaudibly, and caused the tops of the trees to rustle for a brief moment and then fall silent again. In the silence he looked up at the windows of the red building. Both bedroom windows of the Lipniks' apartment on the second floor were open. His father and mother were each standing at one of the windows. She had recently had a perm—that's what they called the hairdo that women came home with from the hairdresser's on some Saturdays and holidays—she'd had it done in honor of his father's return from the camp. She was still young and she wore glasses with thick lenses and her hair was in a perm. She was pregnant, although not yet visibly so. Perhaps the perm was in honor of father's return, but she couldn't yet know she was pregnant, that she would have a son, and that several years later he would play the accordion at four in the morning when his father and his friends woke him up, he would play freedom's key, freedom's key. Father was thin—tall but thin, and he almost looked frail in the other window. His cheekbones jutted from his broad, Pannonian face, and his eyes were sunken. He had arrived from the camp a few days before, and just weeks before, as he was waiting for their departure from the camp, those sunken, deathly afraid eyes had witnessed a Pole plant a knife into the chest of an SS guard. He waved to them, but they didn't notice him. They were also looking in the direction of Carinthia, from where the train was supposed to arrive. How is it possible, Lipnik said loudly enough that Ivanka K., sitting on her bench, could hear him, that I never thought of this? Outside the windows where I slept for so many years, beneath those windows, several years before, a whole army had detrained on its way to its death. Father and mother must have seen it—why had they never told him? It didn't matter if they never told him, because here he was witnessing the whole thing himself, and even the two of them were watching in anticipation to see who would be loaded onto the trucks that had meanwhile appeared on the ramp, that grassy, gentle incline, rutted by car wheels, that he and his friends and sometimes also the tovariše used to play soccer on—no, soccer they played farther down, where the terrain was even, or farther up, where the trucks were parked now and soldiers with rifles were standing, and officers in riding breeches, with big pistols holstered to their belts, possibly Lugers, with stars on their caps and gold epaulettes on their shoulders. The day is crystal pure, pellucidly pure, everything is suddenly so clear and simple. Now he is here.

The train is here, too, from Limbuš it passes through Studenci to arrive at the Carinthian Railroad Station, the smoke stretching back and up behind the locomotive the length of the whole valley, it puffs, it chugs, pulling the heavy load of its long serpent of cars behind it. When it stops and puffs heavily a few more times, the soldiers with rifles suddenly line up and surround the whole length of cars. A second group comes running and forms a gauntlet leading down to the trucks. It's still quiet, a few loud orders slice through the air, and the doors of the cattle cars slide open with a bang. A few uniformed men jump out the open doors onto the tracks, glance around, and use their caps to beat the dust off their tunics and trousers, as though getting ready for morning assembly, for the raising of the flag, the onward flag of Glory, but before they realize where they are, a hail of blows starts to fall—of rifle butts, boot kicks, truncheons and fists, all pushing them toward the gauntlet that leads to the trucks. Ivanka gets up and shouts: Serves you right, home guards, you bloody bastards. Only now does Lipnik notice that he's on the platform, on the street, on the ramp, with crowds of people gathered all around, shouting, spitting, waving, cursing. A dark crowd in broad daylight, a dark crowd of indistinguishable faces, a jumble of bodies jostling at the edge of the gauntlet that surrounds another jumble of bodies, these with the frightened faces of young boys, most of them looking like peasants. How do I know that? Lipnik wonders. I know, these are the faces you see at country fairs. The huge space around the railway station has been trampled by thousands of legs impatiently waiting to kick, mouths waiting to spit, arms waiting to slug, the whole huge area seething with violent limbs intertwined in a single dangerous, threatening beast that can't wait for blood, for the pain of those impotent bodies in their violent, agonizing, victorious, lustful embrace, the embrace of the approaching end. Kill them, the crowd roars. Janez Lipnik looks up toward the window. What are you going to do, Father, he says, what are you going to do, are you just going to watch, Father? You're the league of partisan veterans, tell those commanders of yours, the ones you serve wine to each night from government supplies, the ones your son Janez has to play freedom's key for, tell them to make this stop. His father doesn't hear him, but his mother does and says, he's just back from the camp, you don't understand, climb up the tree, she says, pull the blankets up over your head. But there is no tree here anywhere, nor is there any bed where he could pull the blankets up over himself. He's standing at the Carinthian Station in Studenci and holding his hands over his ears against the shouts, the smacking sound of the blows. His wide-open eyes see the blood spurting from skin split open. Kill them, kill them, howls, roars and shrieks the dark beast with the hundreds, the thousands of throats, its thousands of limbs darting around, the soldiers landing the measured blows of their rifle butts onto heads, onto bloody crowns, into bellies, inciting the dark beast of the Slovene people, now swollen with a desire for violence, for blood, for hair ripped out by the roots, for kicks to the bodies that writhe on the ground, that are crushed by the wheels of trucks, that writhe in the dust and among bunches of trampled grass. The rabble of soldiers and the rabble of the crowd is drunk on itself, on its swollen desire to punish evil, which it intends to punish with evil, an even greater, even worse, even more unbridled and blind evil, an unspeakably harsher violence from out of the deepest impulses of its Christian souls, home to the dark regions of hell, of retribution, of torture and suffering, at last releasing an evil kept suppressed at the bottom and hidden till now, raging in its most untrammeled, unstoppable form. Are they going to kill them right here? No, not before they use blows and kicks and howls to get them onto the trucks, battering them with sticks so fiercely that the wooden ends of their bludgeons splinter, and get bloody and broken, then they bind their hands with wire—they've brought along big spools of it—then they cut it with shears and expertly wrap it around their wrists in figures of eight as they hold them at the smalls of their backs, the sharp metal cutting into the skin till they bleed, cinching them tighter with pliers till the metal cuts through the flesh right to the bone. Lipnik sees Ivanka's face and her rounded handwriting appears before his eyes, the loops that she learned to write in the people's school: Bloody bastards, Hun guards, now you'll pay for your treasonous deeds, for your pieces of silver, for drinking our blood, where is that bloody Reichmanov, they need to kill his family, too, I see them every morning when I go to work at the mental hospital, you've destroyed our family's happiness, you bloodthirsty bastards, you hyenas in human disguise, a thousand-fold curses, you'll find no peace, not even your souls or your relatives, now comes the time we've longed for, when the people judge their murderers the same way you did us, and your bloody spiritual pastors, who offered the people communion that we Communists honored, you have to be punished, too, it's you who are guilty of allowing us to lose the faith that you inculcated in us, you bloody monsters. Lipnik thinks that her unhappiness is so great that she wants a bigger, even worse unhappiness, the unhappiness that the dark creature seeks, the sinister crowd, some of whom have not experienced anything bad, but Ivanka doesn't care, it wasn't enough for her to say bloodthirsty bastards, traitors, Hun guards, monsters—she wants worse and far more momentous words. We Communists, she said, even though she didn't exactly know what the word meant, just as she didn't know the word revolution, having heard it from the priest for the first time, but now she wanted to hurt them good, the bloodthirsty bastards, she wanted them to shake in fear of the terrible unknown, so she said, 'We Communists are going to punish you. The Slavic brotherhood'—now there was a mighty and momentous phrase, even greater than Communists and the people—the Slavic brotherhood will take its revenge on you and punish you. She saw hordes of Slavs riding in from the Steppes, from Moscow and the Dnieper, they would punish them. She caught her breath, picked up another stone and went from momentous to more familiar vocabulary: You goddamn bastards, double-goddamn bastards. And now, at last, the goddamn bastards are on the trucks, the crowd calms down, here and there somebody shouts: Kill them. But the beast is tired, it's catching its breath, and now all it wants to do is watch while they finally drive off, the goddamn bastards looking quite pathetic now, deserving of pity and compassion, beaten, bloodied, tattered and terrified. Somebody heard what he was thinking, somebody heard. Somebody saw that he was the only one who didn't howl and roar, kick and throw stones—just him. Lipnik shuddered as though sensing some sort of shadow engulf him. It wasn't a shadow. Wasn't that guy at Turjak? somebody said. His voice was familiar. He noticed that everyone on the platform had turned to look at him. An empty space formed around him. The person who had said it walked up to him and now Lipnik recognized him. It was Franz. The handyman of the good father from Dobrava, the fellow that Aleksij Grgurevič, captain of His Majesty's Home Army had wanted to take outside and shoot behind the barn. He was dressed in riding breeches, he had a pistol holstered to his belt and gold stitching on his shoulders. But his face was still pimply. He had big pustules on his nose and cheeks that looked like they were ready to pop any second. His cap was tucked into his belt so that it wouldn't slip off his head in the course of the tasks he'd just completed. You still wanna shoot me behind the barn? Franz said. You're confusing me with someone else, Lipnik said. I'm not confusing you with anyone, Franz said. He was holding some sort of rod, a bludgeon, with a clump of bloody hair stuck to it. That was Aleksij who said that, he rushed to explain. I never said anything like that. Aleksij was a lieutenant in His Majesty's army, and at night he'd shoot at the ceiling. It's true, Franz said, and then he was going to shoot me out behind the barn. Lipnik was overcome with terror. So there, you see? he said. It wasn't me. He looked up toward the windows where his father and mother should have been standing, but both windows were vacant. Now they're sitting in the kitchen, he thought. Why don't they come back to the window so I can wave to them, Father could come down and explain that he's a member of the liberation movement. He saved a couple of English pilots and drove them through the occupied city, and that's why they tortured him in Old Whistler and hung a brick from his balls, so that they swelled up big as pumpkins. Maybe it really wasn't you, but then the two of you left for Turjak together. It's true, I was there, Lipnik said in a shaking voice, but I didn't shoot. Franz called to some officer named Kostya. Come over here, he said, and have a good laugh with me. This guy was at Turjak, he said, and he says he didn't shoot. He wouldn't have been able to, Kostya said, if he was praying the whole time. The two of them had a good laugh. Not a long laugh, because there was very little time left. Come on, come on, Kostya said, move back, people, it's time for us to get them out of here. Throw this one in the back, too, he said. Turn around, Franz said, put your hands behind your back. He bound them with the wire he'd been holding. He had powerful hands. He had worked a lot in his life, Franz had, and that's why his hands were so powerful. Lipnik could feel the wire cutting into his skin and through it.

85.

Then he fell the way people fall in dreams. At first they fly, then they start to fall, and sometimes they wake up before they hit the ground, but other times they never do. In his childhood Lipnik had flown many times over a long, grassy hillside. It was beautiful when he flew, sometimes down close to the lush green growth, at other times high above it, over the river, over the forest, over the town where he saw the number 4 bus—always that one and no other. Now he was falling into a story that he had chosen for himself, because he had wanted to understand something, but this time he'd taken one step too far. He took one step too far when he walked through that door of the U- and L-profile warehouse, where he left everything behind and headed into the lower reaches of his consciousness, into the nether reaches of the world, on a dizzying downward path, falling. Something became clear to him for an instant, as though it came from some former life or possibly some former dream: The ancient Slovenes had believed that you could descend on a rope into a deep cave, and if you went down far enough, you would reach the other world—heaven, in fact, because heaven is both up above and down below. There you see a radiant countryside, beautiful green meadows, willows growing beside a body of water that flows in a smooth, meandering current, and it's like being in a miniature version of heaven. Handsome young mowers do the mowing there, and you can help them and mow a few swaths yourself, if you want. But something else became clear to him while he was falling, something his mother had long ago told him about mowers who have a pretty feather tucked into their hat band, or maybe a flower, a sprig of rosemary, any green growing thing: When the dew is on the blade, that's when mowers' luck is made.

Now he was falling into an abyss, somewhere in the forest around Kočevje, he suspected. Not far from the place, he thought, where he first stood beneath Zala the schoolteacher's window. Where a short time ago he had climbed up the tree, the way ants do. She is correcting her students' notebooks now, he thought, while I'm falling into an abyss—isn't that ridiculous? This has to be some cosmic misunderstanding, he thought. We'll clear it up any minute. But they didn't. He landed on a heap of bodies. A heap of naked bodies. Some of them were wearing undershorts, while others had nothing on at all. They were warm bodies, bloody, shot through, battered. Bodies covered with bruises and wounds inflicted before they were thrown into this abyss. They weren't all dead. Some of them were moaning. Up at the edge of the abyss they were being shot in the nape of the neck, each one separately. In the head or the nape of the neck. Some were just machine-gunned. It didn't matter, since there was no getting out of the abyss alive, and it was about to be filled in with the help of explosives. Before they were thrown into the abyss, they were beaten, and some had the gold teeth pried out of their mouths, so as not to waste them. What about the glasses, Lipnik thought. What did they do with the ones who wore glasses? For the most part they were young boys with good eyesight, but a number of them wore glasses. The mountain of glasses I saw at Auschwitz. I see them in my dreams. Among them I look for his, my father's. When I wake up, I realize that he didn't wear glasses back then, he was young, he could see well, he was as healthy as an ox. When he came home he weighed just ninety pounds. When he came home his wife Rosalia got a permanent, when he came home, he saw a transport of home guards being driven off to the killing forests. Then he began eating endlessly, monstrously, and for a long time he refused to talk about what he'd experienced—he just ate and drank and a few years later, when he was still drinking, he trampled the neighbor's lettuce and shouted Roll call! Roll call! And then when he started drinking with his friends from the league of veterans, he began to speak about what had happened to him. He ate a lot, too, and within a few years he was a fat man. I remember his white belly, he'd throw off the blanket because he was hot and that belly was like a mountain of shifting flesh on the bed. Later I saw bigger bellies, but his was the only one I wished would explode. Because that wasn't the same person whose glasses were taken away at Auschwitz and thrown on a heap. That is a landscape from hell. Winter, with the poisonous Russian wind blowing in from the steppes. Where your teeth chatter from the cold of a chilly presence. Where the existence of everything is in doubt—including His, the Lord's, and mine—and the existence of everyone who no longer is, is smoke, has literally gone up in smoke. The smoke of a burning land and of all living things that it bears. Where did they put the glasses? *Veni Spiritus Sanctus*, come. I don't want to experience this to the end, all the way to the end. Moans could be heard from all corners of the pit. Lots of them were still alive. Somebody who managed to hide a pocket knife in his undershorts will slice the flesh off his buddy and put thin strips of it in his mouth. He'll survive. Up at the edge of the pit things fell silent for some time. They've stopped shooting, no more bodies fall onto the moaning, slippery, bloody human heap. A while later there are several powerful explosions. They are using dynamite to fill the pit in. When the smoke cleared, there was far less moaning, because there were far fewer still alive. And when the smoke cleared and it was already evening up top and all the guards had gone for the night, Lipnik noticed that a tree was leaning into the abyss. A perfectly clear, archivally lucid thought, the thought of a borer, a bookworm, who knows his own Latin name—*Blatta germanica, Periplanetta Americana, Anobium*—a borer or bookworm in everyday parlance, a thought as clear as this occurred to him: In the accounts of the men who escaped from the pits, from the caves of the Karst where the bodies of slain home guards were thrown in June 1945, there is no mention of the name of the tree they climbed to get out of that moaning hell, full of murdered or half-murdered and severely wounded naked bodies. What sort of tree was it? During the explosions a tree fell into the pit. A tree with no name. He knew immediately that this was the tree he would use to get out of the pit. It was the tree with no name that the survivors climbed up to tell what had happened there. At the same time he knew with equal lucidity that this was the tree he would climb to get to the other world. It's the tree the ants climb, the ants climbing the tree. And it's the tree that the man from the south climbs, and he is that person. He, Lipnik, named for a tree, will climb a tree whose name he doesn't know. Mother, he said when she would read him the fairy tale from Pohorje, will I some day climb up the tree? Of course you will, son, she said, of course you'll climb it. I have a trench, too, he said, that goes from the cellar to the Drava. I can hide in it whenever I want. And come out by the river. Ah yes, she said, but why would you want to hide? She knew why he wanted to hide. On account of his father, who had been tortured in the Gestapo's dungeons and who kept telling the same story about how they had waited to leave the camp—on account of him. Each time she would put away her glasses with their thick lenses and say, you can climb it and get off wherever you want. On some green meadow, for instance, where young mowers are mowing. These days they'd be making a racket with gas mowers, like that jet ski on Dugi Otok, he thought. But in his story it was three mowers advancing like a star across the sky. He was happy, because he had that tree, and he would often fall asleep thinking about it. Whenever the men from the league of partisan veterans raged on in the kitchen about politics and whenever they started singing freedom's key, he wished that that tree were here. So his father couldn't come and order him to bring the accordion. So his father couldn't run through the neighbor's lettuce shouting 'Roll call, Roll call!' He often climbed up that tree, even past the meadow being mown. When the dew glints on the blade, that's when mowers' luck is made. But he had decided to get out of the tree where the young schoolteacher, Miss Zala, taught school in Dobrava near Lower Carniolan Springs.

86.

He thought he could hear a sort of drumming sound up above that wasn't gunfire and wasn't explosives going off. Perhaps a storm was building, or perhaps they were still banging on the metal door. He climbed up until he saw light, a sort of aperture that he pulled himself through. He crawled through the window of the warehouse cellar, he heard somebody say, here's where he crawled through. He didn't care if he'd crawled out of a cellar or a pit, through a window or an opening left behind by an explosion. Voices, gunshots, the jet ski buzzing, the thousands of stories of words that kept getting jumbled, a whole century in his head, the sound of his accordion—all of this remained far behind. Now he was in the forest and he knew they were going to say, 'He walked out of the mall and left these bags on the floor.' That's what they'd say, the lady and gentleman who don't know if it's Monday or Tuesday, they'd say that he'd gone to the hair stylist's, and there they'd say that he headed off toward the warehouse. Perhaps they'd discover that he'd bought a bus ticket to Kočevje. Perhaps they'll think that he headed to those vast forested territories where the Serbs used to live. Now the houses are empty or have been burned down. He had seen that when they drove back from Dugi Otok. Perhaps they'll think that he occupied one of those houses. If anybody thinks about him at all. No matter, now he was in the forest and he knew that now he finally understood something. This: The trembling of a living being, the flutter of cherry blossoms in the spring breeze beneath his window, the heaving shoulders of a young woman crying as she explains the previous night's betrayal to her beloved, the trembling thighs of a dancer performing her first dance, and the amorous voices of singers fading in and out on a winter night. And this: Everything that lives trembles in an effort of love and joy, but a frightened puppy also trembles, its wet skin twitching, the knees of a calf buckle with the fear of death as it's led off to slaughter, the hand of a killer trembles signing a confession after interrogation, a bird flutters in a cat's claws—it is the flutter of fate, the trembling of a life's story, of oncoming waters that flood and buffet you through the straits and rapids and calm you in the still waters of hidden pools. All of this is love and all of it is death, which is why everything is constantly trembling.

Before he sets out for that house that has lights in the windows, where Zala the schoolteacher is correcting her students' notebooks, he'll sit for a while under the tree. Maybe he'll stretch out and fall asleep. It had rained for three weeks and now the stars were out, and soon the horizon would begin to brighten. In any case, at daybreak he'll continue his journey barefoot, because he wants to feel the morning dew of the forest meadows. When mowers come out to the meadow at the foot of the forested hillside first thing that morning, under a tree on the hillside they'll discover the shoes of a person seen earlier walking down the road that leads out of Lower Carniolan Springs. Just his shoes. He'll be long gone by the time they arrive and their scythes start to whistle through the morning grass glistening in the sun.

Translator's Afterword
A Madness That Heals

In May 1945, as the Allies were declaring victory across Europe, in the far northwestern corner of Yugoslavia Marshal Josip Broz Tito's Partisans were at last driving the German forces of occupation out of the country and secretly preparing to settle accounts with their most hated opponent of all—fellow Yugoslavs, whether Serbs, Bosnians, Croats or Slovenes, who had lent their support to the Axis occupiers during the previous four years.

Although the Partisans purported to be a broad coalition of anti-Fascist forces, their leadership was in fact dominated and discreetly manipulated by the Yugoslav Communist Party, so that from the war's outset, few on devoutly Catholic Slovenia's social and political right could see any place for themselves or their Church in such vehemently anti-clerical, anti-religious company. Because the tragedy of the war confronted each individual with a single stark either/or choice, Slovene society's polarization became absolute and the scene was set for a civil war that took place alongside the more visible World War engulfing all of Europe.

During the final weeks of the war, with Germany's doom writ large, hundreds of thousands of German soldiers, right-wing Yugoslav combatants, sympathizers and camp followers streamed northwestward, out of Yugoslavia to what they presumed would be safety. In one of Winston Churchill's more ignominious wartime decisions, the British forces then occupying southern Austria detained the Yugoslav refugees, eventually boarding them onto trains with the promise that they would be sent to safety in Italy. But as, one by one, the cattle car doors were locked and the trains sent off in the opposite direction, back into Yugoslavia, the refugees' fate darkened.

Tito had ordered his wartime secret police to await the arrival of the trains at stations throughout Slovenia. Having been, during his long years of exile in the Soviet Union, one of Stalin's most diligent pupils, Tito now resolved to work through the problem of his captive antagonists by applying his teacher's notorious maxim: "No person, no problem." The arrival of these trains, their human cargo headed for mass execution, stands at the very heart of *The Tree With No Name*.

The novel's protagonist, mild-mannered Janez Lipnik—whose name alone serves up a double dose of the essence of Sloveneness, almost as if a character in some American novel were named "Average Joe Appleseed"—is the demographic equivalent of an American baby boomer, the child of a World War II survivor heavily scarred by his wartime experience. During the German occupation Lipnik senior's support for the Partisans earned him torture and deportation to Auschwitz, and after the war his stress-induced eccentricities haunted Janez's childhood, leaving an indelible mark on him even as an adult. It was the legacy of this and similar violence widely inflicted by the Germans, Italians and their local confederates, on the one hand, and, on the other, of the courageous Partisan exploits that ultimately led to victory, that formed the unyielding core of popular mythology and official history all through the following forty-five years of Yugoslavia's existence.

Victors write one-sided history. But it's one thing when that history exalts our group and tramples some remote, foreign foe in the dust, and quite another when the trampled foe turns out to be our neighbor, our schoolteacher, or our best friend. While Tito's secret police may have physically eliminated some 12,000 Slovenes among the approximate total of 100,000 war captives summarily shot throughout Slovenia in late spring and summer 1945, they never succeeded in making them disappear. At first there were the rumors, the eyewitness accounts of the large groups of disarmed, uniformed *domobranci* (Home Guards) being detrained and then force-marched to hastily rigged holding pens on Ljubljana's outskirts or trucked to remote rural locations throughout Slovenia, most often to forests. Then, in the 1950s, came a few first-hand accounts, published by Slovenes in emigration, of survivors who, only lightly wounded, managed by dark of night to drag themselves out of the mass graves, sinkholes and mineshafts where the bodies were dumped by the hundreds and thousands, and find their way across country to refuge in the family home or over the border to safety and freedom. It was, in fact, the possession and private circulation of one of these memoirs, bearing the title *We Lie Murdered in Kočevje Forest*, that led to Drago Jančar's arrest, trial and sentence to one year in prison on sedition charges in 1974, when he was a young journalist. After some brief glimmers in the press in 1975—again swiftly suppressed—the forbidden subject suddenly emerged with unprecedented force in the 1980s, as a number of Slovene intellectuals and dissidents began to write openly about the post-war massacres as the nation's gravest unhealed wound. Since Slovenia won its independence in 1991, the most recent resurgence of public attention has surrounded the discovery and forensic investigation of the mass grave sites themselves, a painstaking, prolonged process that has been underway since about 2000 and has yielded up incontrovertible proof of the crime and its extent.

Yet the contemporary Slovene society that Jančar depicts in *The Tree with No Name* remains unmoved by these shocking discoveries. More than two decades into its transition to democracy, Slovenes remain largely polarized into hereditary, unquestioning camps of Partisan and Home Guard, Communist and Catholic, red and white, victimizer and victim. In the words of the unknown author of one of the wartime diaries Janez Lipnik discovers in the course of his work, they are *"walking listlessly, lifelessly. Treacherous. Conniving. Bent on revenge."* For their listless, lifeless, vengeful descendants roaming the shopping malls more than sixty years later, the consumer culture of post-communism is a welcome opiate to avoid reflecting overly much on reality, past and present—which, as Janez Lipnik demonstrates, is a painful process and runs the risk of insanity or worse. Janez Lipnik, archetypal Slovene, distinguishes himself from the crowd with his relentless questioning. And while his inquiries may sometimes focus obsessively on seemingly trivial, banal or tangential things, when they do succeed in breaking out of their orbit they pierce through the wall of myth and denial that his parents' generation set up long ago to maintain a now-defunct authoritarian political regime and avoid madness themselves.

One would think that, after more than thirty years of documentation and open discussion, this national tragedy would at last have been settled. But one has only to think of the 150 years that have passed since our own Civil War and the abolition of slavery to know that national traumas and schisms take a perversely long time to heal. The greatest perversity of all would be if it turned out that human society has some inherent need for strife and polarization. This possibility—that history is by its nature a tragedy repeating over and over—is one that Jančar has explored in his earlier novels and short stories, although in his role as a public intellectual he is anything but fatalistic. He has, in fact, been an acute diagnostician of social dysfunction, striving for nothing less than his subject's full recovery. In which case, what better outcome than if he can use those premonitions of tragedy to shock his countrymen awake? And what better offering to give them than Janez Lipnik, one of their own, in his determination to convert history from two dimensions into three, discovering first-hand the shape of the tragedy as experienced by the vilified other—his neighbor, his schoolteacher, his best friend and himself.

Michael Biggins

SLOVENIAN LITERATURE SERIES

ANDREJ BLATNIK
LAW OF DESIRE
Translated by Tamara M. Soban

*"We go to the movies. We read books. We listen to music. No harm in
that, but it's not real."*

Following his short story collection, *You Do Understand*, is this
expansive collection of sixteen tales about "urban nomads" lost in
a labyrinth of pop culture. A best-seller in Eastern Europe, *Law of
Desire* is Andrej Blatnik at the height of his powers.

Law of Desire is published by Dalkey Archive Press.

Visit **www.dalkeyarchive.com**

MICHAL AJVAZ, *The Golden Age.*
The Other City.

PIERRE ALBERT-BIROT, *Grabinoulor.*

YUZ ALESHKOVSKY, *Kangaroo.*

FELIPE ALFAU, *Chromos. Locos.*

IVAN ÂNGELO, *The Celebration.*
The Tower of Glass.

ANTÓNIO LOBO ANTUNES, *Knowledge of Hell.*
The Splendor of Portugal.

ALAIN ARIAS-MISSON, *Theatre of Incest.*

JOHN ASHBERY & JAMES SCHUYLER,
A Nest of Ninnies.

ROBERT ASHLEY, *Perfect Lives.*

GABRIELA AVIGUR-ROTEM, *Heatwave and Crazy Birds.*

DJUNA BARNES, *Ladies Almanack.*
Ryder.

JOHN BARTH, *Letters. Sabbatical.*

DONALD BARTHELME, *The King.*
Paradise.

SVETISLAV BASARA, *Chinese Letter.*

MIQUEL BAUÇÀ, *The Siege in the Room.*

RENÉ BELLETTO, *Dying.*

MAREK BIENCZYK, *Transparency.*

ANDREI BITOV, *Pushkin House.*

ANDREJ BLATNIK, *You Do Understand.*

LOUIS PAUL BOON, *Chapel Road.*
My Little War.
Summer in Termuren.

ROGER BOYLAN, *Killoyle.*

IGNÁCIO DE LOYOLA BRANDÃO, *Zero.*
Anonymous Celebrity.

BONNIE BREMSER, *Troia: Mexican Memoirs.*

CHRISTINE BROOKE-ROSE,
Amalgamemnon.

BRIGID BROPHY, *In Transit.*

GERALD L. BRUNS, *Modern Poetry and the Idea of Language.*

GABRIELLE BURTON, *Heartbreak Hotel.*

MICHEL BUTOR, *Degrees. Mobile.*

G. CABRERA INFANTE, *Infante's Inferno.*
Three Trapped Tigers.

ARNO CAMENISCH, *The Alp*

JULIETA CAMPOS, *The Fear of Losing Eurydice.*

ANNE CARSON, *Eros the Bittersweet.*

ORLY CASTEL-BLOOM, *Dolly City.*

LOUIS-FERDINAND CÉLINE, *North.*
Rigadoon.
Castle to Castle.
Conversations with Professor Y.
London Bridge.
Normance.

MARIE CHAIX, *The Laurels of Lake Constance.*

HUGO CHARTERIS, *The Tide Is Right.*

ERIC CHEVILLARD, *Demolishing Nisard.*

MARC CHOLODENKO, *Mordechai Schamz.*

JOSHUA COHEN, *Witz.*

EMILY HOLMES COLEMAN, *The Shutter of Snow.*

ROBERT COOVER, *A Night at the Movies.*

STANLEY CRAWFORD, *Log of the S.S.*
The Mrs Unguentine.
Some Instructions to My Wife.

S.D. CHROSTOWSKA, *Permission*

RENÉ CREVEL, *Putting My Foot in It.*

RALPH CUSACK, *Cadenza.*

NICHOLAS DELBANCO, *Sherbrookes.*
The Count of Concord.

NIGEL DENNIS, *Cards of Identity.*

PETER DIMOCK, *A Short Rhetoric for Leaving the Family.*

ARIEL DORFMAN, *Konfidenz.*

COLEMAN DOWELL, *Island People.*
Too Much Flesh and Jabez.

ARKADII DRAGOMOSHCHENKO,
Dust.

RIKKI DUCORNET, *Phosphor in Dreamland.*
The Complete Butcher's Tales.
The Jade Cabinet.
The Fountains of Neptune.

WILLIAM EASTLAKE, *The Bamboo Bed*.
Castle Keep.
Lyric of the Circle Heart.
JEAN ECHENOZ, *Chopin's Move*.
STANLEY ELKIN, *A Bad Man*.
Criers and Kibitzers, Kibitzers and Criers.
The Dick Gibson Show.
The Franchiser.
The Living End.
Mrs. Ted Bliss.
FRANÇOIS EMMANUEL, *Invitation to a Voyage*.
SALVADOR ESPRIU, *Ariadne in the Grotesque Labyrinth*.
LESLIE A. FIEDLER, *Love and Death in the American Novel*.
JUAN FILLOY, *Op Oloop*.
ANDY FITCH, *Pop Poetics*.
GUSTAVE FLAUBERT, *Bouvard and Pécuchet*.
KASS FLEISHER, *Talking out of School*.
JON FOSSE, *Aliss at the Fire*.
Melancholy.
FORD MADOX FORD, *The March of Literature*.
MAX FRISCH, *I'm Not Stiller*.
Man in the Holocene.
CARLOS FUENTES, *Adam in Eden*.
Christopher Unborn.
Distant Relations.
Terra Nostra.
Where the Air Is Clear.
TAKEHIKO FUKUNAGA, *Flowers of Grass*.
WILLIAM GADDIS, JR., *The Recognitions*.
JANICE GALLOWAY, *Foreign Parts*.
The Trick Is to Keep Breathing.
WILLIAM H. GASS, *Cartesian Sonata and Other Novellas*.
The Tunnel. *Willie Masters' Lonesome Wife*.
GÉRARD GAVARRY, *Hoppla! 1 2 3*.
ETIENNE GILSON, *The Arts of the Beautiful*.
Forms and Substances in the Arts.

C. S. GISCOMBE, *Giscome Road*.
Here.
DOUGLAS GLOVER, *Bad News of the Heart*.
WITOLD GOMBROWICZ, *A Kind of Testament*.
PAULO EMÍLIO SALES GOMES, *P's Three Women*.
GEORGI GOSPODINOV, *Natural Novel*.
JUAN GOYTISOLO, *Count Julian*.
Juan the Landless.
Makbara.
Marks of Identity.
HENRY GREEN, *Back*.
Blindness.
Concluding.
Doting.
Nothing.
JACK GREEN, *Fire the Bastards!*
JIŘÍ GRUŠA, *The Questionnaire*.
MELA HARTWIG, *Am I a Redundant Human Being?*
JOHN HAWKES, *The Passion Artist*.
Whistlejacket.
ELIZABETH HEIGHWAY, ED., *Contemporary Georgian Fiction*.
ALEKSANDAR HEMON, ED., *Best European Fiction*.
AIDAN HIGGINS, *Balcony of Europe*.
Blind Man's Bluff.
Bornholm Night-Ferry.
Flotsam and Jetsam.
Langrishe, Go Down.
Scenes from a Receding Past.
KEIZO HINO, *Isle of Dreams*.
KAZUSHI HOSAKA, *Plainsong*.
ALDOUS HUXLEY, *Antic Hay*.
Crome Yellow.
Point Counter Point.
Those Barren Leaves.
Time Must Have a Stop.
NAOYUKI II, *The Shadow of a Blue Cat*.
GERT JONKE, *Awakening to the Great Sleep War*
The Distant Sound.

GERT JONKE (cont.), *Geometric Regional Novel.*
Homage to Czerny.
The System of Vienna.
JACQUES JOUET, *Mountain R. Savage.*
Upstaged.
MIEKO KANAI, *The Word Book.*
YORAM KANIUK, *Life on Sandpaper.*
HUGH KENNER, *Flaubert.*
Joyce and Beckett: The Stoic Comedians.
Joyce's Voices.
DANILO KIŠ, *The Attic.*
Garden, Ashes.
The Lute and the Scars.
Psalm 44.
A Tomb for Boris Davidovich.
ANITA KONKKA, *A Fool's Paradise.*
GEORGE KONRÁD, *The City Builder.*
TADEUSZ KONWICKI, *A Minor Apocalypse.*
The Polish Complex.
MENIS KOUMANDAREAS, *Koula.*
ELAINE KRAF, *The Princess of 72nd Street.*
JIM KRUSOE, *Iceland.*
AYSE KULIN, *Farewell: A Mansion in Occupied Istanbul.*
EMILIO LASCANO TEGUI, *On Elegance While Sleeping.*
ERIC LAURRENT, *Do Not Touch.*
VIOLETTE LEDUC, *La Bâtarde.*
EDOUARD LEVÉ, *Autoportrait.*
Suicide.
Works.
MARIO LEVI, *Istanbul Was a Fairy Tale.*
DEBORAH LEVY, *Billy and Girl.*
JOSÉ LEZAMA LIMA, *Paradiso.*
ROSA LIKSOM, *Dark Paradise.*
OSMAN LINS, *Avalovara.*
The Queen of the Prisons of Greece.
ALF MAC LOCHLAINN, *Out of Focus.*
The Corpus in the Library.
RON LOEWINSOHN, *Magnetic Field(s).*
MINA LOY, *Stories and Essays of Mina Loy.*
J.M. MACHADO DE ASSIS, *Stories*

MELISSA MALOUF, *More Than You Know*
D. KEITH MANO, *Take Five.*
MICHELINE AHARONIAN MARCOM, *The Mirror in the Well.*
A Brief History of Yes.
BEN MARCUS, *The Age of Wire and String.*
WALLACE MARKFIELD, *Teitlebaum's Window.*
To an Early Grave.
DAVID MARKSON, *Reader's Block.*
Wittgenstein's Mistress.
CAROLE MASO, *AVA.*
LADISLAV MATEJKA & KRYSTYNA POMORSKA, EDS., *Readings in Russian Poetics: Formalist and Structuralist Views.*
HARRY MATHEWS, *Cigarettes.*
The Conversions.
The Human Country: New and Collected Stories.
The Journalist.
My Life in CIA.
Singular Pleasures.
The Sinking of the Odradek Stadium.
Tlooth.
JOSEPH MCELROY, *Night Soul and Other Stories.*
DONAL MCLAUGHLIN, *beheading the virgin mary*
ABDELWAHAB MEDDEB, *Talismano.*
GERHARD MEIER, *Isle of the Dead*
HERMAN MELVILLE, *The Confidence-Man.*
AMANDA MICHALOPOULOU, *I'd Like.*
STEVEN MILLHAUSER, *The Barnum Museum.*
In the Penny Arcade.
RALPH J. MILLS, JR., *Essays on Poetry.*
MOMUS, *The Book of Jokes.*
CHRISTINE MONTALBETTI, *The Origin of Man.*
Western.
OLIVE MOORE, *Spleen.*

NICHOLAS MOSLEY, *Accident.*
Assassins.
Catastrophe Practice.
Experience and Religion.
A Garden of Trees.
Hopeful Monsters.
Imago Bird.
Impossible Object.
Inventing God.
Judith.
Look at the Dark.
Natalie Natalia.
Serpent.
Time at War.

WARREN MOTTE, *Fables of the Novel: French Fiction since 1990.*
Fiction Now: The French Novel in the 21st Century.
Oulipo: A Primer of Potential Literature.

GERALD MURNANE, *Barley Patch.*
Inland.

YVES NAVARRE, *Our Share of Time.*
Sweet Tooth.

DOROTHY NELSON, *In Night's City.*
Tar and Feathers.

ESHKOL NEVO, *Homesick.*

WILFRIDO D. NOLLEDO, *But for the Lovers.*

FLANN O'BRIEN, *At Swim-Two-Birds.*
The Best of Myles.
The Dalkey Archive.
The Hard Life.
The Poor Mouth.
The Third Policeman.

CLAUDE OLLIER, *The Mise-en-Scène.*
Wert and the Life Without End.

GIOVANNI ORELLI, *Walaschek's Dream.*

PATRIK OUŘEDNÍK, *Europeana.*
The Opportune Moment, 1855.

BORIS PAHOR, *Necropolis.*

FERNANDO DEL PASO, *News from the Empire.*
Palinuro of Mexico.

ROBERT PINGET, *The Inquisitory.*
Mahu or The Material.
Trio.

MANUEL PUIG, *Betrayed by Rita Hayworth.*
The Buenos Aires Affair.
Heartbreak Tango.

RAYMOND QUENEAU, T*he Last Days.*
Odile.
Pierrot Mon Ami.
Saint Glinglin.

ANN QUIN, *Berg.*
Passages.
Three.
Tripticks.

ISHMAEL REED, *The Free-Lance Pallbearers.*
The Last Days of Louisiana Red.
Ishmael Reed: The Plays.
Juice!
Reckless Eyeballing.
The Terrible Threes.
The Terrible Twos.
Yellow Back Radio Broke-Down.

JASIA REICHARDT, *15 Journeys Warsaw to London.*

NOËLLE REVAZ, *With the Animals.*

JOÃO UBALDO RIBEIRO, *House of the Fortunate Buddhas.*

JEAN RICARDOU, *Place Names.*

RAINER MARIA RILKE, *The Notebooks of Malte Laurids Brigge.*

JULIÁN RÍOS, The House of Ulysses.
Larva: A Midsummer Night's Babel.
Poundemonium.
Procession of Shadows.

AUGUSTO ROA BASTOS, *I the Supreme.*

DANIËL ROBBERECHTS, *Arriving in Avignon.*

JEAN ROLIN, *The Explosion of the Radiator Hose.*

OLIVIER ROLIN, *Hotel Crystal.*

ALIX CLEO ROUBAUD, *Alix's Journal.*

JACQUES ROUBAUD, *The Form of a City Changes Faster, Alas, Than the Human Heart.*
The Great Fire of London.
Hortense in Exile.
Hortense is Abducted.

JACQUES ROUBAUD (cont.), *The Loop.*
  Mathematics: The Plurality of Worlds of Lewis.
  The Princess Hoppy.
  Some Thing Black.
RAYMOND ROUSSEL,
  Impressions of Africa.
VEDRANA RUDAN, *Night.*
STIG SÆTERBAKKEN, *Siamese.*
  Self Control.
  Through the Night.
LYDIE SALVAYRE, *The Company of Ghosts.*
  The Lecture.
  The Power of Flies.
LUIS RAFAEL SÁNCHEZ, *Macho Camacho's Beat.*
SEVERO SARDUY, *Cobra & Maitreya.*
NATHALIE SARRAUTE, *Do You Hear Them?*
  Martereau.
  The Planetarium.
ARNO SCHMIDT, *Collected Novellas.*
  Collected Stories.
  Nobodaddy's Children.
  Two Novels.
ASAF SCHURR, *Motti.*
GAIL SCOTT, *My Paris.*
DAMION SEARLS,
  What We Were Doing and Where We Were Going.
JUNE AKERS SEESE, *Is This What Other Women Feel Too?*
  What Waiting Really Means.
BERNARD SHARE, *Inish. Transit.*
VIKTOR SHKLOVSKY, *Bowstring.*
  Knight's Move.
  A Sentimental Journey: Memoirs 1917–1922.
  Energy of Delusion: A Book on Plot.
  Literature and Cinematography.
  Theory of Prose.
  Third Factory.
  Zoo, or Letters Not about Love.
PIERRE SINIAC, *The Collaborators.*
KJERSTI A. SKOMSVOLD, *The Faster I Walk, the Smaller I am.*

JOSEF ŠKVORECKÝ,
  The Engineer of Human Souls.
GILBERT SORRENTINO, *Aberration of Starlight.*
  Blue Pastoral.
  Crystal Vision.
  Imaginative Qualities of Actual Things.
  Mulligan Stew.
  Pack of Lies.
  Red the Fiend.
  The Sky Changes.
  Something Said.
  Splendide-Hôtel.
  Steelwork.
  Under the Shadow.
W. M. SPACKMAN, *The Complete Fiction.*
ANDRZEJ STASIUK, *Dukla.*
  Fado.
GERTRUDE STEIN, *The Making of Americans.*
  A Novel of Thank You.
GWEN LI SUI (ED.), *Telltale: 11 Stories*
LARS SVENDSEN, *A Philosophy of Evil.*
PIOTR SZEWC, *Annihilation.*
GONÇALO M. TAVARES, *Jerusalem.*
  Joseph Walser's Machine.
  Learning to Pray in the Age of Technique.
LUCIAN DAN TEODOROVICI, *Our Circus Presents . . .*
NIKANOR TERATOLOGEN, *Assisted Living.*
STEFAN THEMERSON, *Hobson's Island.*
  The Mystery of the Sardine.
  Tom Harris.
TAEKO TOMIOKA, *Building Waves.*
JOHN TOOMEY, *Sleepwalker.*
JEAN-PHILIPPE TOUSSAINT,
  The Bathroom.
  Camera.
  Monsieur.
  Reticence.
  Running Away.
  Self-Portrait Abroad.
  Television.
  The Truth about Marie.

FOR A FULL LIST OF PUBLICATIONS, VISIT: www.dalkeyarchive.com

DUMITRU TSEPENEAG, *Hotel Europa.*
The Necessary Marriage.
Pigeon Post.
Vain Art of the Fugue.

ESTHER TUSQUETS, *Stranded.*

DUBRAVKA UGRESIC,
Lend Me Your Character.
Thank You for Not Reading.

TOR ULVEN, *Replacement.*

MATI UNT, *Brecht at Night.*
Diary of a Blood Donor.
Things in the Night.

ÁLVARO URIBE & OLIVIA SEARS, EDS.,
Best of Contemporary Mexican Fiction.

ELOY URROZ, *Friction.*
The Obstacles.

BUKET UZUNER, *I am Istanbul*

LUISA VALENZUELA, *Dark Desires and*
the Others.
He Who Searches.

PAUL VERHAEGHEN, *Omega Minor.*

AGLAJA VETERANYI, *Why the Child is*
Cooking in the Polenta.

BORIS VIAN, *Heartsnatcher.*

LLORENÇ VILLALONGA, *The Dolls'*
Room.

TOOMAS VINT, *An Unending Landscape.*

IGOR VISHNEVETSKY, *Leningrad*

ORNELA VORPSI, *The Country Where No*
One Ever Dies.

AUSTRYN WAINHOUSE, *Hedyphagetica.*

CURTIS WHITE, *America's Magic*
Mountain.
The Idea of Home.
Memories of My Father Watching TV.
Requiem.

DIANE WILLIAMS, *Excitability:*
Selected Stories.
Romancer Erector.

DOUGLAS WOOLF, *Wall to Wall.*
Ya! & John-Juan.

JAY WRIGHT, *Polynomials and Pollen.*
The Presentable Art of Reading Absence.

PHILIP WYLIE, *Generation of Vipers.*

MARGUERITE YOUNG, *Angel in*
the Forest.
Miss MacIntosh, My Darling.

REYOUNG, *Unbabbling.*

VLADO ŽABOT, *The Succubus.*

ZORAN ŽIVKOVIĆ , *Hidden Camera.*

LOUIS ZUKOFSKY, *Collected Fiction.*

VITOMIL ZUPAN, *Minuet for Guitar.*

SCOTT ZWIREN, *God Head.*